I0818295

What Readers Are Saying

Based on factual crime stories with dynamic characters, Michael Vecchione's Fallen Angel, Book #3 is a chilling study in the struggle between good and evil. You travel with Michael Gioca to the scenes of the crimes. The setting is New York, the murders stack up. You'll be enthralled by the unknown work that goes on without the public's knowledge to bring perpetrators to justice. There are failures, setbacks, and the fears keep building. The unanswered question lurks in the background: Does good ever really overcome evil?

--Donna Keel Armer, author - Solo in Salento: A Memoir (Italian Translation: Un'Americana in Salento); The Cat Gabbiano Mystery Series: The Red Starfish and Moringa~Tree of Life

BOOK III

FALLEN ANGEL

A TRUE CRIME FANTASY

ANARCHY, CHAOS ... PEACE?

MICHAEL VECCHIONE

Red Penguin
BOOKS

Fallen Angel - A True Crime Fantasy - Book 3

Copyright © 2024 by Michael Vecchione

All rights reserved.

Published by Red Penguin Books

Bellerose Village, New York

ISBN

Print 978-1-63777-650-6

Digital 978-1-63777-648-3

No part of this book may be reproduced in any form or by any electronic or mechanical means, including information storage and retrieval systems, without written permission from the author, except for the use of brief quotations in a book review.

To the boys.... Charlie and Leo, Pop-Pop loves you!

CONTENTS

Prologue 1

PART ONE

Chapter 1 9
Chapter 2 14
Chapter 3 21
Chapter 4 27
Chapter 5 32
Chapter 6 37
Chapter 7 43
Chapter 8 48
Chapter 9 54
Chapter 10 61
Chapter 11 67
Chapter 12 72
Chapter 13 79
Chapter 14 86
Chapter 15 91
Chapter 16 97
Chapter 17 102
Chapter 18 108
Chapter 19 115
Chapter 20 120
Chapter 21 126
Chapter 22 131
Chapter 23 138
Chapter 24 144
Chapter 25 150
Chapter 26 157

PART TWO

Chapter 27 167
Chapter 28 172
Chapter 29 177

Chapter 30 185
Chapter 31 189
Chapter 32 197
Chapter 33 203
Chapter 34 209
Chapter 35 218
Chapter 36 225
Chapter 37 229
Chapter 38 235
Chapter 39 243
Chapter 40 251
Chapter 41 257
Chapter 42 265
Chapter 43 273
Chapter 44 281

PART THREE

Chapter 45 289
Chapter 46 294
Chapter 47 300
Chapter 48 306
Chapter 49 312
Chapter 50 314
Chapter 51 319
Chapter 52 324

PART FOUR

Chapter 53 331
Chapter 54 336
Chapter 55 341
Chapter 56 347
Chapter 57 355
Chapter 58 358
Chapter 59 365
Chapter 60 371
Chapter 61 375
Chapter 62 380
Chapter 63 386

Acknowledgments 395
About the Author 397
Also by Michael Vecchione 399

Be careful who you trust, the devil was once an angel.

~Anonymous

PROLOGUE

When the delivery truck from Samson Industrial Appliances cleared the last gate of Attica Correctional Facility in upstate New York, Ricky Sabar and Jax Chase were free.

The cell mates, who were among the most dangerous prisoners in what was the state's most secure prison, successfully carried out their escape- planned and orchestrated by Sabar's guardian angel, his buddy Jiz... otherwise known to all mankind as Satan.

Their ultimate destination, chosen by the EVIL ONE, was Brooklyn.

As he had done for decades in cities around the world, Satan had chosen Brooklyn for *HIS* most recent campaign of anarchy, chaos and evil.

HIS plan: instigate horrific crimes committed by unwitting pawns of *HIS* choosing; then do whatever necessary to see that they avoid capture and arrest. If caught, and put on trial, *HE* used *HIS* wiles to ensure they would not be convicted and punished.

Satan's ultimate aim was to wreak havoc across the borough by shattering the public's confidence in their justice system. And once the peace and tranquility enjoyed by Brooklynites was severely damaged, if not destroyed entirely, life in the Borough of Churches would never be the same.

When a priest in the Vatican's Office of Exorcism in New York noticed the upheaval that was occurring in American cities following the acquittal of perpetrators of heinous crimes that struck at the very fabric of society, something about the dates of those crimes left him perturbed left him perturbed. All the crimes preceded satanic exorcisms he either witnessed or performed. After doing additional research the priest uncovered similar instances in cities around the world.

In America,, the Devil was successful because crimes like those studied by the priest that resulted in trials, were lost by the prosecution because the Devil used his wiles to adversely affect the investigations and the verdicts, thereby ensuring the outcomes he desired.

To combat the EVIL ONE's presence and foil *HIS* plan, a secret organization was formed under the auspices of the US government and the Vatican to ensure the arrest and conviction of those who committed the crimes instigated by *HIM*. It was made up of clerics from the Vatican's Office of Exorcisms, and law enforcement officials from the US Department of Justice. Its leader was a former United States Attorney General, John Caldwell.

The organization's mission was to identify, recruit, and give support to local prosecutors in jurisdictions where the EVIL ONE was operating without anyone being aware of its unspoken goal.

When Brooklyn became ground zero, the organization, at the recommendation of one of its clerical members, Monsignor Salvatore Romano, chose Michael Gioca, Chief of the Brooklyn District Attorney's Rackets Division, to be its soldier in the war against Satan.

Gioca and Romano grew up together in Brooklyn, and, though separated for several years because of their careers, remained lifelong friends.

Romano followed his friend's career for years. The overwhelming success Michael enjoyed was proof to the monsignor that he possessed the knowledge, skills, and guts to take on, and beat the

EVIL ONE. To Romano there was no other choice. Gioca was simply the best and most successful prosecutor in New York City.

From the moment Michael accepted the assignment, he handled every crime instigated by the EVIL ONE. And except for one, Gioca defeated his adversary every time.

That one failure involved Ricky Sabar.

His acquittal for the murder of a former Catholic nun on the Coney Island boardwalk, instigated by Satan, was the EVIL ONE's finest moment.

Months before the Coney Island murder, Satan, calling himself Jiz, befriended Sabar, a known arsonist. He needed Sabar to set fire to a prominent Manhattan hotel, *The Calla*, as part of a revenge plot.

Fire Marshals Kathy Baer and her supervisor Alex Gazis had worked on and were instrumental in uncovering the crucial evidence that led to Gioca winning an earlier case involving the murder of a New York City firefighter that was instigated by the EVIL ONE. It was for their work in that case that *HE* wanted revenge.

The EVIL ONE knew that a fire in a luxury New York City hotel, where arson was suspected, would be big news and would necessitate fire marshals being called to the scene to investigate. *HE* also counted on two of the city's best marshals being assigned to the investigation. *HE* was right.

Because of the skill and determination they demonstrated in solving the firefighter murder case, Baer and Gazis were assigned to investigate *The Calla Hotel* fire.

When they entered the hotel room where the fire started, the floor suddenly collapsed and Gazis and Baer fell to the floor below. The fall killed Gazis and paralyzed Baer.

Fortunately, after months of rehabilitation and physical therapy, Baer recovered from her injuries, and more than a year after the tragedy, would testify at the trial of Ricky Sabar for the arson murder of Alex Gazis, and the attempt to murder her.

Initially, Sabar and Jiz, who were the unknown suspects because they were only seen walking around inside the hotel before the fire began, and not seen igniting it, Sabar was not arrested and Jiz was never identified.

It was months later that Sabar, with Jiz spurring him on, raped and killed the former Catholic nun in Coney Island. Later, with Satan's help and interference, he was found not guilty.

However, during the Coney Island murder trial Sabar's photo appeared on TV and was identified by two witnesses. They came forward and told authorities that they saw him and another person start the fire.

When Sabar was released from custody after his acquittal in the Coney Island murder trial, there was a band of fire marshals who were waiting for him outside and placed him under arrest for the arson at the *Calla*.

Jiz was never identified or captured.

Although the arson/murder took place in Manhattan, the case couldn't be tried in that borough due to a conflict of interest. A relative of the Manhattan District Attorney's wife died in the fire, thereby precluding his office from handling the prosecution.

At a high-level meeting of law enforcement and judicial officials, including John Caldwell, the case was transferred to Brooklyn. Michael, who knew Sabar, and his puppet master, very well, was assigned to prosecute it.

To his disappointment, he lost the former nun's murder case and Sabar walked free because Satan, in the guise of Jiz, interfered with his main witness. And when the witness refused to testify the case crumbled.

Michael made a valiant effort to salvage it, but in the end the jury was firm. There would be no conviction.

Now he would be getting another crack at Sabar. And he wasn't going to miss this time.

And he didn't.

To avoid a repeat of what happened in the Coney Island case, Michael employed a strategy that kept the witnesses safe and free from Satan's influence.

Ricky Sabar was convicted in *The Calla Hotel* murder.

Sabar and Jackson "Jax" Chase became cell mates after Sabar was sentenced to 25-years-to-life and sent to Attica to serve his time.

This displeased the EVIL ONE because *HE* was not done with *HIS* mission in Brooklyn.

HE had a lot more to do, and to accomplish that, *HE* needed *HIS* most valuable and successful pawn, Ricky Sabar.

PART ONE

CHAPTER ONE

An hour outside of Attica, the driver of a Samson Appliance truck pulled into a truck stop rest area to use the bathroom and to get coffee. He had a long road ahead of him and this stop would be his last chance for several hours to relieve himself and recharge for the drive ahead.

He had no idea that the two men hidden in his cargo compartment were anticipating this stop and had crawled out of the washing machines the truck was carrying. They waited a few minutes to allow the driver to walk to the bathroom, then opened the cargo area door and slid out. After closing it they made their way to a plain, unremarkable, blue Chevy sedan waiting for them in an out of the way area of the parking lot.

So they wouldn't call attention to themselves, they slipped off their orange prison jumpsuits before leaving the truck. Since it was summer, two men dressed in tee shirts and gym shorts would seem perfectly normal to anyone who happened to see them approaching their car.

Pretending to check the pressure in the front left tire, Ricky Sabar bent down and reached into the wheel well and found the car keys taped inside, just as he expected. When both Jax and he got into the car a gym bag with fresh clothes and an envelope containing five hundred dollars was sitting on the floor in front of the rear bench seat. They quickly dressed but before driving out of the rest area, Sabar, holding the now empty gym bag, went to the car's trunk and opened it.

He put the bag inside and then quickly lifted the carpet covering the floor of the trunk exposing the spare tire compartment. He reached in and removed a black plastic bag that Jiz told him would be there. He closed the trunk, got back into the car and handed the bag to Jax.

The quality of the two guns it contained surprised Jax. "Holy shit, no motherfucker better mess with us," he said, as Sabar drove out of the rest area just as the driver was returning to the truck with his coffee.

"We did it!" Sabar yelled, pounding the Chevy's steering wheel as he entered the highway. "Fuck, yeah!" Jax whopped as he slapped the dashboard in front of him. "Now, let's get the fuck out of New York. I can smell the ocean and feel the sand waiting for us down the Jersey Shore."

The escape plan worked perfectly, which was no surprise to Sabar. He had come to trust and depend on his good friend Jiz, who set up everything. Down to the smallest detail, Jiz left nothing to chance. Of course, Sabar had no clue as to who Jiz really was and that *HE* had an ulterior motive beyond helping a "friend" escape from prison. The EVIL ONE wanted Sabar out on the street because *HE* had plans for him.

Of all the pawns Satan used to spread *HIS* evil in Brooklyn, Sabar had been the only one to escape capture and punishment, that is, until his arrest for *The Calla Hote*l fire. And he would have gotten away with that as well, if two inconspicuous hotel workers, who remained silent for over a year, hadn't seen Sabar on TV during news reports of his murder trial in Brooklyn and gone to the police to identify him as the arsonist.

From the moment the jury, after hearing a near flawless case for the prosecution, sided with Michael and found Sabar guilty of the *Calla* murder, Satan began to plot his escape. But it wasn't until after Sabar was sentenced and sent to Attica to serve his time, that the EVIL ONE put the finishing touches to *HIS* plan.

HE first ensured that Sabar would be sharing a cell with Jax Chase, because *HE* knew that Jax was the perfect partner for Sabar in what *HE* was planning in Brooklyn.

Next, *HE* caused the Director of Purchasing for the prison to suffer a career-ending heart attack. *HE* then enlisted one of his minions, a nerdy dude named Tully, to apply for and secure that position. Once that was done, *HE* identified the correction officer, Jack Daley, who was assigned to oversee the inmates who worked in the purchasing department on the day shift. *HE* immediately set about corrupting Daley with a temptation that he couldn't resist.

One evening after Daley's shift, a beautiful young lady just happened to be having a drink in the pub frequented by officers assigned to Attica prison. When Daley walked in, he immediately noticed her at the bar and took the seat next to her. The woman was sitting to his left so he was unable to see the strange looking mark *SHE* had on the other side of *HER* face.

SHE smiled at Daley and introduced *HERSELF* as *SHE* extended *HER* hand. "Hi, I'm Lena,"*SHE* said as *SHE* held onto Daley's hand just long enough for him to get the message that *SHE* was up for some fun. Daley had a reputation for being a ladies' man, even though he was married. He loved *HER* aggressiveness and immediately bought *HER* a drink.

One drink led to many, and when their conversation turned to sex, Daley asked the woman where *SHE* was staying. *SHE* told him *SHE* was visiting an old college roommate and had taken a room in a nearby motel. Daley wasted no time and offered to drive *HER* to *HER* room.

During the short drive the woman began to massage Daley's inner thigh and just as they pulled into the motel parking lot, *SHE* grabbed and began to stroke his now erect dick. Not wanting to wait even the short time it would take to get to the room, Daley opened his pants, and Lena took him into *HER* mouth. He would later find out *SHE* was recording the entire liaison in the car and that *SHE* also snapped a photo of Daley's car and the license plate when they left the pub.

For the next hour, Lena and Daley had sex in *HER* room, all of which was captured on a video camera *SHE* had set up earlier that day.

Daley left the room with a big smile on his face. A smile that would soon be wiped off.

As Daley approached his car, he was confronted by Jiz who needed Daley's cooperation if the most important part of his escape plan was to succeed.

Daley initially balked when Jiz told him what *HE* needed, but the officer quickly agreed to take part in the escape plan when Jiz pulled out *HIS* phone and showed Daley the recordings and the email address *HE* had for Daley's wife.

With Daley secured and Tully ensconced in the prison purchasing department, Jiz met with both of them to explain their roles in *HIS* plan.

Several of the industrial sized washing machines in the prison laundry were scheduled to be replaced. Jiz was aware of this because he had inside information from another of his minions who worked at Samson Industrial Appliances, the company that had a contract with the prison to sell, service and replace all types of appliances used by the institution.

When new washing machines were to be delivered to the prison, Jiz was alerted by Tully. On that day two of the inmates assigned by Tully to work in his department, Sabar and Jax Chase, under the supervision of Correction Officer Daley, were ordered to move the old machines out of the laundry and onto the loading dock of the prison. The machines were loaded onto the Samson Appliance truck so they could be hauled away once the new machines were off-loaded.

Once this was accomplished, Tully called Daley on his radio and asked if the truck was ready to leave. When he answered the call, Daley turned away from the truck as Sabar and Jax scrambled into the cargo area. Each got into one of the old washing machines that were now waiting for the truck driver to haul them away.

After telling Tully that everything was loaded and ready to go, Daley turned back to the truck, and quickly closed the rear cargo door. Moments later the driver, with several delivery documents in hand, came onto the loading dock, checked to make sure the rear door was closed properly, then got into the truck's cab and drove off. Exactly ten minutes later, the truck was driven through the outermost gate of the prison with Sabar and Jax.

Soon, Satan would have his man back, and a bonus: a new pawn, Jax Chase.

CHAPTER TWO

It was another beautiful, sundrenched morning in Zihuatanejo, on Mexico's southern Pacific coast. Michael and Kathy Baer spent it relaxing at the pool of the five-star *Playa de Zihuatanejo* resort where they enjoyed the first five idyllic days and nights of their ten-day vacation.

It was the first time the couple had been away together since they began dating after the *Calla Hotel* trial. Michael secretly booked the trip and surprised Kathy when they were celebrating her birthday, a month before, at *Sala*, the restaurant in Astoria, Queens where they first acknowledged their feelings for one another.

Michael chose Zihuatanejo because he always wanted to visit the beach where the final scene of one of his favorite movies, *The Shawshank Redemption,* was filmed. No film could beat the *Godfather* in Michael's eyes, but Morgan Freeman and Tim Robbins' masterpiece came pretty damn close. And the last scene where parolee Ellis Boyd Reddit, played by Freeman, sauntered up the beach to reunite with his good friend and former fellow prisoner, Robbins', Andy Dufresne, as he worked on his small fishing boat, touched Michael as few movie scenes ever had. The reaction when the two unlikely friends, strangers who bonded over the horror of prison life, saw each other, showed the audience how much friendship meant to them. And now they were free! It was pure movie magic and moved even the hard-bitten Gioca.

In the six months since the end of the *Calla* trial Michael and Kathy grew close. But because of their respective jobs, they decided against moving in together and kept their own apartments.

Kathy's work as a fire marshal required that she be away from home quite often. And when she was involved with an investigation, she usually worked late into the night.

As for Michael, because of his ongoing war with the EVIL ONE, it was essential that he keep his own place. He worked from home a great deal, and because of the secrecy he was sworn to, he couldn't expose Kathy to it. If they moved in together, he would have to lie to her if she became curious or inquisitive about what he was up to, and that was something he didn't want to do. Living together, Michael felt, would also put Kathy in more danger than their dating already had. He wouldn't be able to live with himself if the EVIL ONE harmed her to extract revenge or to punish him.

However, they did not hide their relationship from their bosses, families, and friends. Everyone was happy with it, especially Kathy's parents who got to know Michael when he visited her while she was recovering from the devastating injuries she suffered when she fell through the hotel room floor while investigating the fire at the *Calla*. He took them out to dinner several times to give them a break from the vigil they were keeping for Kathy and told them all about himself and his family.

As for Michael's father, sister and sons, although they knew who Kathy was because Michael was trying the case against the animal who caused her injuries, he "formally" introduced her to his crew one Sunday afternoon at his sister's home.

Pam hosted a get-to-know-you dinner in Kathy's honor, and she outdid herself. She prepared a traditional Italian Sunday meal, featuring her red sauce, pasta, meatballs, and sausage.

Artie, Pam's husband, who fancied himself a wine connoisseur, was in charge of the *vino,* and he did not disappoint. They started with a dry prosecco from the Veneto region of Italy and moved on to Michael's favorite *Nero d'Avola* for dinner.

For dessert, it was cannoli, which Michael bought at *Court Street Pastry* near his apartment, and espresso with sambuca.

By the time they were ready to leave the table, everyone was full and happy. And Kathy was a hit. When Michael later walked his sons to their car both Michael Jr. and Kevin told him how much they liked her and were excited that they were together.

"You deserve to be happy Dad," they said when they reached the car.

Michael hugged and kissed them and, before they could see his emotional reaction to their words, he shooed them into the car and told them to drive carefully. As he walked back to Pam's house, he wiped tears from his cheeks and dried his eyes.

The next day Michael heard from his father and sister. Both raved about Kathy.

While Pam immediately began to talk about planning a wedding, his father was a bit more cautious. He didn't want Michael to go through the pain and misery he suffered during the divorce from another Kathy in his life, his first wife.

"Son, she's great, and I can see how much you like her and how much she cares about you," he said. "But I remember how crazy you and your wife were about each other at one time, and that didn't prevent the two of you from destroying your lives with that awful divorce. I just want you to go slowly and make sure you know what you're doing."

Michael understood what his father was saying and although he wouldn't admit it, he had no intention of speeding up the relationship only to have it crumble like his marriage. He couldn't go through that pain again.

"Dad, I hear ya'. Thanks for the advice and for looking out for me.

I learned a lot from my past and I'm going to take it slow, just as you suggest."

As it turned out Michael had no way of knowing that Kathy Baer felt the same way.

The day after Pam's dinner, Kathy spoke to her parents and was excited about meeting Michael's family, telling them how warm and welcoming they were. But before her mother, who fancied herself as Kathy's relationship advisor, could offer her unsolicited advice, Kathy told her parents that she too had learned a difficult lesson from her past.

Kathy, like Michael, had a personal reason for not wanting to move in together. A secret she kept from him, as he had about his war with Satan.

Before she met Michael, Kathy worked on a case in Queens with a very personable, handsome, and talented assistant district attorney. After the investigation and trial, they began dating. It quickly got serious. Both were young and couldn't wait to be together, so they took an apartment in a luxury building in the high-end Queens neighborhood of Forest Hills.

Unfortunately, the prosecutor, who worked in the Queens DA's homicide bureau, was constantly busy with investigations and trials. And Kathy, being a newly minted fire marshal, was low person on the totem pole, so she was sent on assignment to fires all over New York City. Although they lived together, they were rarely home at the same time, and their relationship suffered. After a few months the two agreed to separate and Kathy moved in with a friend until she found another apartment.

Not wanting to suffer the same fate with Michael, it was easy to agree to their plan to keep separate apartments for now; moving in together would wait until both were ready, willing, and able.

The casual, yet serious relationship Kathy and Michael enjoyed worked well. They saw each other as much as their work permitted and spent nights in the other's apartment when they could.

And now they were on their first vacation together.

The morning in Mexico was wonderful, and since it was time for lunch, Kathy and Michael gathered their things together and headed to their room to freshen up and change out of their swimsuits. When they walked in the message light on their phone was blinking.

Both saw it and both were struck with the same thought, '*our stay in paradise is about to come to an end.*'

Each hoped that the message was not related to a family illness, or accident, since both had elderly parents back home, and Michael had two sons.

The other possibility was that one of their respective jobs had called to summon them home for an important investigation. However, because there were many fire marshals in the fire department who did her job, that was less of a worry for Kathy than Michael.

For him there was only one warrior in the war against Satan.

Michael called the resort's telephone operator who told him in her Mexican accented English, "The call is for you *Senor* Gioca, from a *Monsenor* Romano."

Before Michael returned the monsignor's call, he took a few deep breaths to calm himself. He wasn't angry about hearing from Romano, he knew his job and understood that the war with the EVIL ONE took precedence over most of his life. Michael was pissed that the call could mean that his unspoiled, peaceful time with Kathy might be in jeopardy. They had half of their vacation left and he wanted to make the most of it. But he knew that if duty called, he couldn't ignore Romano.

After telling Kathy it was "work" calling, and he needed to find out what they wanted, he excused himself and took his cell phone out onto the room's balcony and punched in the monsignor's number.

Romano answered on the first ring. "Michael, I'm so sorry to disturb you," he said. "I wouldn't have done it if this wasn't important."

"And hello to you too, *Monsenor. Como estas?"* he asked playfully using a few of the approximately ten Spanish words he had picked up during his five days in Zihuatanejo.

"I'm well Michael," Romano hurriedly answered, "but what I'm calling about is not a joking matter."

Picking up on the tension and urgency in Romano's voice, Michael told him he was sorry. "Sal, you really sound serious. Has *HE* struck again after all these months?"

"Michael, *HE* may be involved in what I'm about to tell you, but it's too early to know for sure. Sabar has escaped from Attica. He and another inmate got out by somehow hiding in a delivery truck. The prison warden is certain that he had help from someone on the inside... and Caldwell believes on the outside as well."

"Mike, we know you're in Mexico and probably safe, for now. But we wanted to alert you to the escape, so you and Kathy would be warned and on your guard for the rest of your stay."

"Sal, I understand, and thank you. But we're thousands of miles away from New York. Couldn't you have waited until our last day? Sabar has no idea where we are."

"Michael, you must have been in the sun too long and your brain may be fried a bit. Have you forgotten who you've been battling for the last couple of years? If *HE's* behind the escape, as I'm sure we'll soon learn, being thousands of miles away in another country will not stop the EVIL ONE if *HE's* looking to extract revenge."

Just then Kathy came out onto the balcony and told Michael that the hotel manager was at their door and needed to speak to them immediately.

Michael told Romano what was going on. The monsignor's reaction was "Wow! That was fast. Go talk to him and call me back."

After speaking to the hotel manager for about 10 minutes and quickly explaining to Kathy what happened in Attica, Michael called Romano back.

"Sal..." Michael started but before he could finish the sentence, Romano jumped in. "Yes, Michael, that's all Caldwell's doing."

What the monsignor was referring to was what the hotel

manager had told him and Kathy. A contingent from the Mexican federal police was down in the lobby. The sergeant in charge informed the manager that he and his men would be patrolling the hotel grounds, the lobby, the restaurants, and the floor on which Michael and Kathy were staying, "Until the two Americans check out in five days."

The manager had no clue as to why the *federales* were there, and certainly no idea who ordered it. All he knew, as he told Michael and Kathy, was that the order had come from *"El jefe a cargo,"* the boss in charge.

"Caldwell is taking no chances," Romano continued. "He didn't want to order you home, because as he said, you've earned this time away. To protect you for the remainder of your stay he leaned on someone in DC to get things done."

"Sal, I know it's necessary, but don't you think this is a bit of overkill?"

"No," Romano answered emphatically. "In fact, if Sabar and his cohort have not been captured by the time you get home, you'll both need protection here as well. Caldwell wants your return flight information so he can have agents pick you guys up at JFK when you arrive."

"Okay, I understand. I need to get off now so I can fill in Kathy, and "Don't worry I haven't forgotten the rules. I'll simply tell her that this is being done out of an abundance of caution because of the escape. Brooklyn DA Price and the Manhattan DA used their contacts at the State Department to get this protection put in place. And if Caldwell's agents pick us up at JFK, I'll tell her they're NYPD Intelligence Division detectives."

Romano wished Michael a peaceful vacation and promised not to disturb him again unless it was absolutely necessary.

Two days later, the necessity became a reality.

CHAPTER
THREE

With Sabar driving, the Chevy pulled out of the rest stop parking lot and headed for the southbound New York State Thruway. The thruway was always busy so they were not likely to stand out as they would on rural back roads. They'd take the thruway down into New York City where they'd then travel through one of the tunnels connecting Manhattan to New Jersey. Once in Jersey it was the New Jersey Turnpike that would bring them to where they needed to get to.

As Sabar explained to Jax in their cell one night before the escape, his friend Jiz, "The guy who put this whole plan together," had a place on the Jersey shore for them to hide until things cooled down.

Jax knew nothing about the shore, and he wanted some idea of where they were heading. "Tell me about it," he said to Sabar.

However, he was asking the wrong guy. Sabar had never been to the Jersey Shore either.

He was born and raised in New York City and never left the five boroughs. And of those, he had only been to four...*ish*. Staten Island may as well have been a foreign country to him. And as far as

Queens, he only stepped foot in the borough once to continue talking to a girl that he met on the subway who lived there.

So Sabar could only tell Jax what he learned from Jiz about the area where they would be hiding out.

"Jax, I know it's a beach area, but I ain't ever been to the Jersey Shore. And since you ain't been there either, Jiz told me that's why he picked it for us to lay low. No one down there will know us. And since neither of us is connected to the place in any way, Jiz says the cops won't even think of looking for us there."

"Jiz also told me that because it's summer, the shore will be packed with people from all over the east coast who rented houses and apartments for the season. We'll be lost in the crowds. And when the weather gets colder, the place is deserted, so there's very few to be raised up. And since we'll be there all summer, we won't be strangers."

Nevertheless, Jiz ordered Sabar to play it safe and change their appearance to minimize the chance that they would be recognized in the event the Attica escape became bigger news.

"What are we gonna' do for cash?" Jax asked. "The five hundred in that envelope is only good for now."

"Don't worry, man. My boy told me he has that covered."

Jiz told Sabar during his last prison visit before the escape, that he hid "About ten grand," in the apartment that he rented for them.

"Ten grand! That's all? That ain't gonna' last very long with two of us needin' to eat, buy clothes and stuff at the drugstore," Jax answered.

"Jax, chill," Sabar told him. "My man says he's working on a score that will get us enough cash to get away from the east coast and into Mexico. We just got to be patient."

"I hope you're right, 'cause if this Jiz guy fucks us, and we get caught, we going back to Attica, and our time there ain't gonna' be pretty. They gonna' put you and me in the hole, and we ain't ever gonna' get out of solitary."

Sabar knew that Jax was right, but he had no choice other than to believe that Jiz would take care of them.

"Listen man, we ain't got no alternatives. We got to count on Jiz to do what he said he'd do. We are where we are because of him, right? We're free, and we gonna' stay like this if we follow his lead. Trust me, he ain't gonna' fuck us."

Just then a phone began ringing in the car. Sabar knew who was calling because Jiz told him he hid a cell phone in the car, so he'd be able to reach them. However, Sabar didn't know where the phone was. Luckily, they were coming up on another highway rest stop. Sabar pulled in and parked as far away as possible from the main building.

The phone kept ringing as the two searched for it. Sabar found it taped to the underside of the dashboard behind the steering column. He answered it, and as expected, it was Jiz.

After Sabar told Jiz where he and Jax were on the thruway, Jiz told him, "There's been a change of plans. You need to find a place to hold up for a few hours until dark." Jiz said that once it was dark, he'd call him back with further instructions.

In actuality there was no change in *HIS* plan. *HE* lied to Sabar when *HE* told him about the Jersey shore hideout and the cash that was stashed there to ensure that he would go along with the prison escape and not worry about being captured. That phone call and what would happen in two days were the next steps in *HIS* actual plan.

Instead of going to the Jersey shore, *HE* was setting up Sabar and Jax to rob a jewelry store in Brooklyn. To entice them he would tell them the store was expecting a large shipment of diamonds from Europe in two days. And the diamonds were worth millions.

However, there were no diamonds. It was all a ruse. The EVIL ONE had no need for material objects like diamonds.

What *HE* wanted...no, what he craved was the outrage, chaos, and heartbreak that would result when Sabar and Jax, to avoid being sent back to Attica, killed the police officers the EVIL ONE knew were on special undercover assignment on the street where the jewelry store was located. Those officers would be a surprise because *HE* had no intention of alerting them to cops being there.

After nightfall, Sabar and Jax were sitting among a throng of summer travelers in the very large dining area of a thruway rest stop somewhere in the Hudson River valley well north of New York City.

When they were on their fourth or fifth cup of coffee and their second hamburger and fries dinner, Jax began to lose his patience.

"Ricky, what the fuck is up with your man Jiz. We been sittin' here for hours and them counter people are gonna' be gettin' curious. Some state trooper walks in; they may point us out thinkin' we here to rob the place. Can't you call him?"

"Jax, he don't like me to do anything he ain't told me to do. He said he'd call, and he will. And besides, it seems like a long time, but we only been here a few hours. Patience, brother. And, where you got to be, anyway?"

"Man, I ain't got much patience. That's how I wound up in Attica."

"What you mean?" Sabar asked.

"I grew up in a small town in northern New York, way up near the Canadian border. When I was ten, my old man, a trucker, took off with some bitch he met at a truck stop up in Canada. From then on it was just me and my mom, who worked as a nurse's aide at the local hospital on the night shift."

"When I was in high school, I was always getting in trouble with my buddies. No big things, just shoplifting for money to buy weed, and pills."

"We had someone who always sold to us, until one day he wasn't around anymore. We went over to the next town to hit up a dealer someone told us about and it turned out to be an undercover state trooper. We got busted and because we were over seventeen they offered us a deal. We could enlist in the Army or go to prison for a few years. For me it was a simple choice, I chose the Army."

As for the other guys, Jax said that he thought they'd do the same, but when he got out of the service three years later and went home, he found out that the two guys arrested with him chose to fight the charge and it didn't go well. They were convicted at trial, received thirty-six months in prison, and were on parole.

He said that he met them one afternoon to have a few drinks and catch up. That's when he found out that his two friends learned nothing from their prior experience with the law. They were now the drug dealers for the many users and junkies in the town and county where they lived, and they offered him a piece of the business.

"And like an asshole I took it. But, Ricky, I was just out of the Army, I had no job, and I couldn't live off my ma."

Things were going well, Jax told him . He was making enough money to get his own apartment and take care of his mother who, because of painful arthritis in her knees, had cut down on her hours at the hospital.

"I even bought my own wheels."

Then one day everything changed.

"Me and my guys was in this bar just outside of our town havin' a great time, when these biker dudes came in." He said they were customers of his until a few months before when they accused him and his partners of selling them bad dope.

"For those months I had seen them around and mostly they was cool. But for some reason that day they wasn't. They clearly was lookin' for trouble."

Jax said that one of his friends was talking to a woman at the bar and when he went to the restroom one of the bikers grabbed the woman's ass. When his friend returned the woman told him what happened.

"All fucking hell broke loose," Jax said. "Me and my other buddy went to help our friend, who was getting' the shit kicked out of him by two or three of the bikers."

He told Sabar that he was trying to stop the beating when he saw the biker he was struggling with go for something in his pocket or in his belt.

Jax said, “I thought gun or knife.”

“It was dark and hard to see. But I wasn’t gonna’ wait. So I picked up an empty beer bottle and hit him over his head before he could do me.”

The guy went down like he was shot. He was dead. And the ‘weapon’ Jax feared turned out to be a skeleton key the guy carried on his key chain.

“It was the key to his grandpa’s store. His father, a retired state trooper, testified at my trial that his grandpa gave him the key for good luck just before he died.”

When Sabar reacted to his last statement with a strange look, Jax said, “I know what you’re thinking. Don’t ask me how a key is a good luck charm. It sure as shit wasn’t for him, and it certainly wasn’t me. At trial, the jury didn’t buy my self-defense claim. I got convicted.”

“Ricky, man, I was so pissed at that verdict that I threatened the jury. And at my sentencing I threatened the judge, who then gave me twenty-five to life. And before they took me back to the cell behind the courtroom, I turned to my lawyer and broke his nose when I headbutted him.”

“And since the guy who died was the son of a cop, I got treated like shit in the joint. So, I ain’t ever been a good or obedient prisoner. And I hate cops, correction officers, and anyone who carries a badge. Fuck THE MAN.”

“Holy shit,” Sabar said “No wonder you’re so antsy to get the hell outta town. I don’t blame you. But when we finally get to Mexico, you can forget all that shit and live.”

Just then Sabar’s phone rang. It was Jiz.

CHAPTER FOUR

After a quick conversation, Sabar told Jax that Jiz wanted them go to a motel a half-mile off the thruway, just south of Albany, about ninety miles away.

"I got the address and name of the place and Jiz wants us to rent a room for two nights. When we get to the room, I'm supposed to call him," Sabar said.

Jax wasted no time. "Let's get the fuck out of this place," he said, as he got up from the table and headed to the car.

Two hours later they checked into the *Motel New Yorker*, located in the middle of nowhere, NY. As instructed, Sabar made the call, and was told to put it on speaker so both he and Jax could hear what Jiz had to say.

"Like I told Sabar, there's been a change in the plan," Jiz began.

"You guys ain't goin' to New Jersey right away. There's a quick detour I want you to make, and when you hear what it is you're gonna' be very happy. It's an easy job, and the score of a lifetime."

Jiz said that right after their escape he received information from a trusted source about a jewelry store in Brooklyn that was expecting a delivery of diamonds worth millions.

Leiser's Fine Jewels had been a fixture in the predominantly Jewish, Midwood section of Brooklyn, for decades. The store was owned by eighty-four-year-old Mordecai Leiser, who inherited the business from his father, Aaron, who had been a Belgian diamond merchant.

In January 1939, the year before the Nazis invaded Belgium, Aaron and his pregnant wife Sophie, left the country and emigrated to the United States to escape what they feared was coming. They settled into a small apartment in the East New York section of Brooklyn, where later that year Mordecai was born.

When the boy was three years old, the Leisers, now with a newborn daughter, Elsa, bought a home in Midwood to accommodate their growing family. Three blocks away they opened the jewelry store.

Over the years the store became a neighborhood institution. It was the place to go for engagement and wedding rings and for birthday and anniversary gifts. Aaron Leiser was always good to his customers, a practice he passed on to Mordecai, who took over the business after his parents died.

Another of Aaron's lessons to Mordecai was to make sure he donated to the campaigns of all the local politicians, and more importantly, always donate to the campaign of whoever was running for mayor and then to the mayor's reelection. Mordecai listened to his father and learned well. He became one of the present mayor's largest donors.

His closeness to City Hall gave the Midwood Merchants Association,, a very powerful voice in Brooklyn. Mordecai had served as president for the last twenty years.

"The jewelry store is the place you're gonna' hit," Jiz said. "Once you've done the job, you can head to the shore apartment and lay low. I got a guy to fence the rocks, and with that money we can all get the fuck down to Mexico and live like kings."

Sabar could barely contain his excitement. He started whooping and stomping around their small room until Jax told him to shut up.

"Before I agree," Jax said, " I want to know what your man told you about this jewelry store. I don't want to hit some place where the security is tight, which it has to be if millions in diamonds is getting' delivered there, only to get our asses arrested. Brother, let me tell you somethin', I ain't goin' back to the joint. I'll kill to make sure that don't happen."

That is exactly what the EVIL ONE was counting on.

Jiz told him not to worry, because only Mordecai, and his eighty-year-old wife, Esther, would be working. "And the one security guard in the store is their long-time friend Morty, who's the same age as the wife."

"You're shittin' us," Jax said in disbelief. He could not believe that a store like *Leiser's* could survive without more security.

"I ain't lyin'," Jiz answered. "That neighborhood is a very low crime area, and because everyone in that neighborhood knows that the local cops often buy there, and because they also got customers from the Colombo and Gambino families, they never have any trouble. No one would ever try to rob the place if they wanted to live to enjoy what they stole."

"So then why the fuck are we doin' it?" Sabar and Jax cried in unison.

"Because I got it all planned. We'll be in and out and gone before any pigs or bent noses know the place was even hit," Jiz answered. *HE* then went on to calm them by revealing how it was going to go down.

Jiz said, "Like clockwork, every other Thursday, the store gets a shipment of diamonds from a dealer who comes from Manhattan. The next delivery is two days from now."

"And, because they're so confident that no one will hit them, my man told me that the dealer always shows up at 3 p.m."

Jiz said that the best time to hit the store was 4 p.m. because that's when the security guard goes home, "And them two old people ain't gonna' put up no fight."

Sabar asked, "What about the cops? I'm sure they got patrol cars around that neighborhood."

"You right," Jiz answered. "That's another reason why four o'clock is the best time. It's when the local cops are changing shifts. So there'll be little, if any, danger of gettin' caught. 'Cause, before them cops get into their cars, you two will be outta the store and on your way to Jersey with a bag of those shiny rocks."

"Wait a minute," Jax said, "Whatcha mean, 'you two'? Where the fuck are you gonna' be. Why ain't you there with us?"

Jiz lied and told him that *HE* couldn't be with them when the robbery took place because it was too risky.

"I been scoping out the place since my contact told me about the diamonds. I even went into the store pretending I wanted to buy a ring for my girlfriend. So they seen me, and others on the block may have too. I don't want anyone giving my description to the cops after the robbery, and them connecting me to Sabar because of the other things we done together. That wouldn't be good for any of us, including you. I'll see you down the shore."

Jax, of course, had no clue that the EVIL ONE was using them the way *HE'd* used all his minions and pawns since he began to haunt Brooklyn. *HE's* the instigator, the watcher, but never the doer.

And when *HE* told Jax and Sabar not to worry because there would be no police in the area, that too was a lie. *HE* knew there would be cops there. In fact *HE* was counting on them being there. Because it was not a robbery *HE* was setting up, it was an execution.

The EVIL ONE had no interest in diamonds. What *HE* wanted was for Sabar and Jax to kill cops.

HE knew about an agreement between the Midwood Merchants Association and the NYPD to have an undercover, plainclothes, police team on *Leiser's* block every other Thursday, to coincide with the diamond delivery. However, *HE* kept that from Sabar and Jax.

HE also knew that the police undercover team would be tipped off that the two Attica escapees were spotted in and around the vicinity of *Leiser's* on the day of, and around the time of the 'robbery,' because *HE* would place the call to 911 *HIMSELF*.

And of course, *HE* kept that from Sabar and Jax as well.

And because *HE* was aware that Sabar, and especially Jax, dreaded going back to prison, *HE* was confident that when they approached the store and were surprised by the cops, the two would open fire with the guns *HE* left for them under the spare tire in the trunk of the Chevy. Guns which were far superior and powerful than those carried by the NYPD. *HE* was certain, Sabar and Jax would walk away, and the cops would not.

As it turned out, *HE* was only partly correct.

CHAPTER FIVE

Thursday night was party night at the *Playa de Zihuantanejo,* and since Michael and Kathy were going home on Saturday, they decided to make the most of what the hotel was offering, notwithstanding the overprotective *federales* who followed their every move.

The evening began with an all you can drink cocktail hour on the pool deck, with entertainment provided by a terrific mariachi band. Next was an enormous barbeque and pig roast on the beach, featuring the hotel's special margaritas made with local tequila. Dessert was enormous bowls of fruit from all over Mexico, ice cream, and Mexican coffee spiked with *Kaluha.* After dinner it was tequila shots and dancing to the hotel's resident DJ, who spun tunes until well after midnight.

By the time Michael and Kathy got back to their room, they could barely stand, let alone call the hotel operator to find out why the message light on their phone was blinking.

"Michael look," Kathy said, pointing to the light. Michael saw it but ignored it.

"I see it," he said.

"Whatever it is can wait until we wake up. If it was really urgent someone would have alerted those *federales,* who are all over us, to let us know."

"I'm going to sleep, now. And I'm never touching another shot of tequila for the rest of my life," Michael slurred as he fell onto the bed fully clothed.

Kathy didn't react because she didn't hear him. She was fast asleep, also fully clothed, even before Michael made his vow about future drinking.

The phone ringing in the morning did not awaken them, but the pounding on their door did the trick. Both Michael and Kathy jumped up and were out of bed in a shot.

"What the fuck is that?" Michael said, as an equally bewildered Kathy shook her head. It took a few seconds for them to realize they were still in their clothes from the night before, and when they did, they began to laugh so hard they nearly didn't hear the pounding on their door that had resumed.

Michael opened the door to find two *federales* and the hotel manager standing there.

"Mr. Gioca," said the hotel manager, "I'm sorry to have disturbed you but you didn't check your messages from last night and you haven't answered the phone this morning. Your people back home are worried. The *Monsenor,* Romano, I believe, asked us to make sure you and the senorita were all right, and to tell you that he needs you to call him. *Es urgente,* it's urgent."

Fortunately, Kathy was in the bathroom when the manager mentioned Romano, so Michael didn't have to make up a story about who Romano was, and why a monsignor was asking him to call. He stumbled out onto the balcony and called him.

"Thank God," were the monsignor's first words when he

answered. "Michael, you had us worried when we couldn't contact you last night and this morning," he continued.

"Sal, what's going on? Why were you so concerned? You know we have these *federales* up our asses because you put them there."

"Mike you're right, but with the EVIL ONE you can never be certain of anything. I need to tell you what's happened. Then you'll understand. Can you talk?"

When Michael said that he could, Romano began by telling him that the day before, two cops were brutally murdered in Brooklyn.

"The police have a guy named Jackson Chase under arrest for the murders."

Michael heard but didn't understand. Perhaps it was the hangover, or the rude wake-up that he had just suffered through, but Michael couldn't suppress his annoyance and interrupted Romano.

"Sal, with due respect, that's what you needed to tell me? That's why you had the hotel roust us out of bed the way they did? What you've told me is tragic, but what's that got with me, or us?"

"You didn't let me finish. It was *HIM.*" Romano answered.

"Caldwell's initial instincts were right. The escape and now this shootout in Brooklyn, has the EVIL ONE's imprint all over them."

Just as Michael was about to react, Romano continued, "There's one more thing I need to tell you. In addition to the two cops, there was another fatality at the scene. Your old friend Ricky Sabar was with Jackson Chase, and now he's in the city morgue. Sabar was shot and killed during the shootout with those two cops."

"Holy shit! Is Chase the guy Sabar escaped with?"

"Yes. Chase, whose nickname is 'Jax,' and Sabar were cellmates."

Hearing all this from Romano, Michael no longer needed the usual two cups of the strong Mexican coffee he had been enjoying with breakfast for the past nine days to start his engine. He was now fully awake, and both curious and anxious to hear the details of what happened in Brooklyn.

"What's with the shootout?" he asked.

"Mike, there's a lot to tell you. But not on the phone. We'll talk when you get back. Caldwell has already spoken to DA Price. The case is yours."

"Sal, I'll be home tomorrow in the late afternoon, your time. I'll call you when I'm settled. If it's not too late, I'll meet you at your office and you can get me up to speed."

"No matter what time I hear from you it won't be too late."

Romano then added, "Enjoy your last day in paradise. And you and Kathy stay safe...what was I thinking, of course you will. I forgot, you have *federales* 'up your asses,'" Romano added sarcastically.

"Okay Sal, you've made your point. I'll see you tomorrow."

"Have a safe trip back, Mike. And as always, I'll be praying for you."

When Michael walked back into his room, Kathy was sitting up in bed scrolling through her phone. She looked up and saw the troubled look on Michael's face.

"Bad news from home?" she asked.

As much as he hated not being totally honest with Kathy, Michael nodded and proceeded to tell her a half-truth. "Really bad news. Two police officers were shot and killed yesterday. The detectives assigned are speculating that it's related to the prison escape we were warned about two days ago."

"Wow!" she said. "But why do they think that?"

Michael told her about Jax being captured and that he was identified as the guy who escaped from Attica with Sabar.

"They also told me that Sabar was with him, but he's now dead."

Stunned, Kathy began to say something when Michael jumped in, "Kathy that's all I know. Apparently, there's a lot more. When I get back, I have a meeting set up and I'll know more after it. We have one more day here and I didn't want to spoil it by spending any more time on the phone."

"I see you took a shower while I was talking to Brooklyn. I'll do the same and then let's hit the breakfast buffet before they close . I'm starving."

The next morning a taxi idled at the resort entrance right on time waiting for Michael and Kathy. With the death of Sabar and the capture of Jax the federales were called off their protection detail. So as a courtesy, the resort's concierge arranged the ride to the local airport for his departing guests.

The trip home would take most of the day. Their first stop would be in Mexico City. From there they would catch a connecting flight to JFK in New York.

While waiting for the New York flight, Michael called Romano to let him know where he was on his return trip before asking him if there were any more updates. The monsignor again told him that he'd have to wait for an update until they met.

"Michael, you know that these cell phones are not secure so I can't risk talking about *you know who*. Be satisfied with what I told you. It's status quo for now, but there is a lot to talk about."

"Okay Sal, but it's going to be late when I get back to Brooklyn. Are you sure you can stay up that long to talk?"

"Worry about yourself, my friend," Romano answered. "I'm not the one who'll likely have jet lag. So, if *you're* too tired to talk when you get home, we can wait until morning to meet."

"Monsignor, I see you haven't lost any of that sarcastic wit in the ten days I've been gone," Michael replied with a laugh.

Now laughing himself, Romano said, "Mike, call me when you're on your way to me and I'll make sure I have a couple of strong espressos waiting for the both of us. Stay safe and God speed."

When they arrived at JFK airport in New York, Michael kissed Kathy and put her in a taxi. Then he caught another one to his apartment. On the way from the airport he called his family to tell them that he was back from Mexico. When he got to his apartment, he dropped off his luggage and called Romano.

"Sal, have those espressos hot and ready, I'm on my way."

At 11 p.m. Michael walked into Romano's office in Red Hook ready to resume his war with the Evil ONE.

CHAPTER SIX

It was 12:30 a.m. when the monsignor finished filling Michael in on the limited knowledge he had about what happened at *Leiser's Jewelry.*

Romano, awake since dawn, was ready to call it a night. Michael, still on Pacific Time, had many more questions which unfortunately the monsignor could not answer. But when he saw that Romano could barely stay awake and was yawning incessantly, he concluded that it was time to wrap things up.

"Sal, clearly, you're tired, and you don't have all the info yet. I know you're going to mass later this morning, so let's pick this up after you get back from church and have spoken to Caldwell. You're likely to know a lot more when we meet again."

"Mike, you have to be tired as well. You're operating on adrenaline so go home, get some sleep and when we see each other again, I'm sure I'll have plenty more to tell you. And I'll make it a point to get the names of all the cops and the lead detective for you."

"Good because I have questions for the first responders to the shooting, especially the cop who put out over the air the erroneous description of the shooter who got away. I have to find out where he got it from. And I need to speak to and meet with the lead detective, whose name I need to know."

When Michael got back to his apartment, just as Romano had predicted, he began to feel the effects of the jet lag. He climbed into his bed hoping for immediate sleep but instead, what Romano had told him about the incident kept intruding.

The monsignor told him that the press reported the incident as an attempted robbery gone wrong, but he agreed with Caldwell's assessment. Even with his limited knowledge of the facts, Michael knew it was the opening salvo of another battle with the EVIL ONE.

The sun was high in the sky when the phone woke him. He quickly answered thinking it was Romano, and that he had overslept. But it was Kathy checking up on him. Michael filled her in as best he could and told her he was expecting to work all day.

"Well, I'd like to be sympathetic," she said chuckling, "But guess what? There was a suspicious fire in north Brooklyn, Williamsburg I believe, and I've been called in to work on it. So it's back to the grind for both of us."

Michael offered his condolences before adding, "I'll be thinking about those ten days in Mexico all day, maybe all month, no...all year. The hardest part of my day will be trying not to smile while I'm in the midst of this grizzly murder. Thank you for being there with me."

It was unlike Kathy to be at a loss for words, but that's the situation she found herself in. She had no response, just tears of joy.

Sensing them, Michael told her, "I'll call you tonight."

After a shower, Michael dialed Romano. "Mike, I was just about to call you. I hope you slept well. You're going to need to be sharp today."

"Monsignor, I'm good to go. Do you have anything for me?"

"I've been on the phone talking to Caldwell all morning, so I have just about everything we know to this point. When can you get here?"

Thirty minutes later, Michael walked into Romano's office with two cappuccinos and a bag of donuts.

Over the next ninety minutes the monsignor told Michael everything he had learned.

"Unlike *The Calla Hotel* fire," Romano began, "The EVIL ONE was nowhere to be seen when Ricky Sabar, who was driving, and Jax Chase parked their Chevy down the street from *Leiser's Fine Jewels,* around 4 p.m. last Thursday."

Michael interrupted, "Sal, how are you so sure *HE* was not somewhere in the vicinity?"

"Caldwell was able to get a copy of the footage the police obtained from a security camera mounted on the building on the corner of the street where the jewelry store is located. As Sabar and Jax begin to walk toward the store they go out of camera view," he explained.

"We watched it looking for Jiz or anyone we thought looked suspicious. The only person we saw on the street was a guy who the police have spoken to. And before you ask, it's not *HIM.*"

"The witness, Guy Raimondi, was rounding the corner onto *Leiser's* block and saw two men get out of the Chevy. He said the driver tapped his wristwatch before both men headed in the direction of the jewelry store. According to his statement he assumed that something was wrong with the man's watch and they were going to *Leiser's* to have it repaired. The witness said he continued on his way."

"Raimondi told a detective that moments later, when he was inside his apartment which is down the street from the jewelry store, he heard shots. When it ended, he said he was curious, so he went down to the store, and it was chaotic. He said he hesitated saying anything because he didn't want to get involved. But when a cop went up to him and started to ask him questions in a very arrogant manner, and started hassling him for information, 'You know how you cops can be' were his words to the detective, and he told the cop what he saw."

"Sal, do the cops have anyone who witnessed the actual shooting?"

"Mike, I'm getting to that."

Romano went on to tell Michael about two sisters who live in a second-floor apartment in a building directly across from *Leiser's.*

Eva and Joanie Snow had just returned home from grocery shopping and were unloading the items from a shopping cart right outside the front door of their building.

Eva told the police that she carried several bags of groceries to her apartment, and while her sister Joanie was putting the items away, she went back down to her cart on the street to retrieve the last two bags. As she stepped out onto the sidewalk, she noticed two men, one tall, and the other average height, walking toward *Leiser's.*

"We now know the tall guy to be Jax Chase, and of course the other was Sabar," Romano said.

Eva told the police that she thought it was her imagination, but as she looked closer, she saw that both were carrying big guns. As the two approached the front door of *Leiser's,* two other men dressed in jeans and t-shirts, with badges hanging around their necks, seemingly came out of nowhere and yelled, "Stop! Police!" The two men with the big guns turned and started shooting at the cops.

"Those two police officers were Norm Tenuta and Chris Massey, both of the 70th precinct and assigned to special undercover protection duty in an arrangement *Leiser's* had with the NYPD."

Eva scrambled back inside the vestibule of her building and ducked down. Through the glass front door she saw what happened next.

"She said, 'The cops were hit and immediately went down. But they must have gotten off some shots, because the shorter man fell to the ground and didn't move, and the bigger of the two grabbed his leg, which was covered in blood.'"

"Eva saw him limp up the block, get into a car and drive away."

About two minutes later, uniformed police responded to the

scene, and put one of the wounded cops into a patrol car and drove off.

"The second wounded cop, according to Eva, was loaded into a private car that drove away with someone in the back seat doing what appeared to be CPR on him."

"Eva said neither of the men in the private car had on police uniforms."

"One other thing before I tell you about that private car. Immediately after Chase limped away, Eva got to her feet and for the first time saw that Joanie, her sister, was in the vestibule cowering in a corner."

"Joanie was interviewed by detectives later that night. And although what she saw was limited, it could be useful, Michael."

Joanie told the detectives that after the shooting stopped, she saw a "tall guy" limp away from where the shooting happened and disappear "Up the block" and out of her view. Then seconds later she saw a car race past the front of her building.

"You're right Sal, she does corroborate some of what her sister saw, which could be helpful with a jury," Michael said.

"Now tell me about that private car. And do we know who was driving and who was administering the CPR?"

"The car belongs to Paul Sira, a police officer assigned to the 70th precinct. He was the driver. The person administering CPR was another cop from the 7-0, Dennis "Denny" James."

Romano said that they had just gone off duty but were still in the station house when the shooting occurred and heard the report of it come over the desk sergeant's radio.

Denny grabbed a portable radio, and both jumped into Sira's car. They got to the shooting scene just as the uniformed cops were putting Norm Tenuta into their patrol car to take him to the hospital.

Because there were no other police vehicles there to take Chris Massey, Sira and James loaded him into the back seat of Sira's car. James administered CPR while Sira sped away enroute to Kings County Hospital.

"Despite the actions of their fellow police officers and the hospital's medical staff, Tenuta and Massey both died in the emergency room."

"Now," Romano continued, "You might think that this was the end of Denny James' and Paul Sira's day, but it wasn't. Nor was it the end of their connection to the case."

"Sal, what are you saying?"

"Michael, Denny and Paul were the arresting officers of our killer, Jax Chase."

CHAPTER SEVEN

"As Sira and James were racing to the hospital with Massey," Romano continued, "Sira momentarily slowed to navigate around an automobile accident several blocks from the scene of the shooting."

The monsignor told Michael that Denny James looked away from Massey for a moment and saw several people attending to the driver of a car that had mounted the sidewalk and hit a streetlamp. He was able to get a quick look at the injured driver and noticed he had blood on his face and what appeared to be blood on his pant leg.

He thought nothing of it until after Massey was taken into the emergency room.

"Something told PO James that he and Sira needed to go back to that car accident and check out the driver," Romano said.

When they arrived at the accident a large crowd had gathered. The driver of the car was lying on a gurney and being attended to by emergency medical personnel when Denny and Sira walked up to him. One of the paramedics was about to wrap a bandage around the driver's leg when Denny told him to stop.

"Apparently that displeased people in the crowd," Romano said, "because they began to yell at the EMS technician to get the injured man into the ambulance, and not 'listen to that fuckin' pig,' referring to Denny."

"Sal, didn't you say that Denny James was off duty?"

'Yes," Romano answered.

"So how did anyone know he was a cop,?" Michael asked.

"Beats me," Romano answered. "According to Denny, he didn't identify himself as a cop investigating a shooting that the driver may be involved in until the medic asked who he was. And that was *after* he heard someone in the crowd refer to him as 'that fuckin' pig.'"

When he heard that, Michael thought, '*Sal might not know the answer, but now I think I do.*' He made a mental note to ask both Denny James and Paul Sira more about it.

Romano continued. "Denny asked the medic if he had gotten the driver's name. He answered, 'Yeah, eventually.' When Denny James asked what he meant by 'eventually,' the medic said that the driver told him that his name was 'Rod Cushley.' But after the driver was out of the car the medic noticed something on the front seat. It was an ID card from Attica prison with the name Jackson Chase and the driver's photo."

Denny told the medic to hold off attending to Chase so he could take a look at the wound on his leg. Once again someone in the crowd yelled, "The medics need to get the injured man to a hospital." Others chimed in, "We got your ambulance number and we gonna' report you if you don't move right now."

When the medic heard that he became concerned. He said to Denny that he needed to quickly bandage Chase's leg and, "Get the fuck outta' here before there's a riot."

"Denny wouldn't back down," Romano said. He asked for a few seconds to look at the wound before the medic bandaged it. As soon as he and Sira saw it, both recognized that it was a gunshot wound.

Denny immediately called over the police radio to a colleague who was at the shooting scene. He asked if Eva Snow was still there. When he was told that she was, he gave the location of the accident and said, "Bring her here now." Denny then told the medics they needed to wait before taking Chase away.

The medics, anxious because the crowd was getting bigger and louder, were prepared to ignore Denny's request, and load Chase into their ambulance when a patrol car pulled up. Eva Snow was escorted out of the car and brought to the gurney where Chase was now sitting in an upright position. Eva looked straight at him and said, "That's him. That's the guy who shot the cops in front of the jewelry store."

"Once the identification was made," Romano continued, "Sira arrested Chase and advised him of his Miranda rights. When the crowd heard that some of them began to charge toward the gurney that Chase was laying on. The police believe they were trying to get him away from the arresting officers."

After Chase was loaded into the ambulance, Sira and Denny James jumped in to ride with their prisoner to the hospital.

"Mike, here is where it got very serious and may complicate things later," Romano said.

While enroute to the hospital Denny James began to question Chase who claimed that he couldn't hear what Denny was asking him, so Denny moved right next to Chase and leaned over him.

"When Denny did that, Chase grabbed the cop's off-duty gun from the small holster clipped to his belt and pointed it at Sira who was sitting at Chase's feet. As Chase pulled the trigger on the revolver, Denny grabbed for it and managed to wedge the webbing between his thumb and forefinger into the spot where the hammer would strike the firing pin and prevented it from going off."

Now with adrenaline fueling his rage, Denny pummeled Chase about the face with his free hand as Chase struggled with Sira who was attempting to disarm him.

"When they arrived at the hospital Chase was rushed into the emergency room where he was treated for the injury to his forehead that he suffered in the car accident, the gunshot wound to his leg, which still contained the bullet, and what was diagnosed as a fracture of the orbital bone of his right eye."

The action Denny took in defense of Sira, although necessary and lifesaving, would later haunt the prosecution of Jax Chase much to Michael's frustration.

"Sal, I assume that after Chase was treated in the emergency room the cops followed through in completing the arrest process."

"Yes Michael. Chase's wounds were tended to, after which he was admitted to the hospital. His room is under twenty-four hour guard."

"Later that day a bedside arraignment was conducted with an ADA from Price's office standing in because you were not around."

"Wait a second! Later that day?" Michael asked.

"If Chase was operated on for the removal of the cop's bullet in his leg, how could he be ready for arraignment so soon after surgery? Didn't his attorney argue for a delay until his head was clear of the effects of anesthesia so he would understand what was happening?"

From the moment that he began to fill in Michael on the facts, Romano dreaded getting to this part of his recitation because he knew how his friend would react.

"Michael, there was no surgery on Chase's leg."

"What? Why not?" Michael asked in a tone that Romano knew had taken all of his friend's strength and control to suppress his anger.

"Caldwell told me that once Chase was arrested DA Price was ordered by the administrative judge to send an ADA to the hospital so Chase could be arraigned as soon as he was out of the emergency room."

Apparently, the judge conceded to pressure from the mayor and the police commissioner to move the case along because the uniform cops and detectives were threatening a work slowdown if Chase wasn't dealt with quickly. Their unions believe that the deal between the Midwood Merchants Association and the NYPD left Massey and

Tenuta without adequate protection and backup, and the result was their murders."

The ADA that Price assigned to the arraignment, Josh Turner, who Michael knew well, was an experienced ADA from the homicide bureau. He was a veteran homicide prosecutor who tried dozens of murder cases.

According to Romano, Turner's plan was to arraign Chase and ask the presiding judge to order that the bullet in his leg be removed immediately because it was evidence.

"Caldwell told me that when the ADA told Chase's lawyer of his intention, he didn't object, which surprised the ADA. We now know why there was no opposition."

"Just before the proceeding began," Romano continued, "ADA Turner received a call from a doctor who said that he treated Chase in the emergency room and if he intended to ask the judge to order the bullet in Chase's leg to be removed, it could not be done."

"According to the doctor, the surgery was very dangerous and would jeopardize Chase's life because the bullet was too close to his femoral artery to risk going in to remove it."

"Because of that statement, the ADA never asked the judge for an order to remove the bullet. It's still in Chase's leg."

"Sal don't worry," Michael said. "That was the emergency room doctor giving his opinion. I'm going to have the hospital's chief surgeon take a look at the leg and the X-rays and get his opinion."

"Was the arraignment completed?"

"Yes Michael. Chase was held in remand, and has been admitted to the hospital, where he is under twenty-four-hour guard."

Romano added, "I was able to get the name of the assigned detective, Tony Martino, and I think it's time for you to get out to the 70th precinct and meet with him and officers Denny James and Paul Sira. They'll be at the station house when you get there."

Michael thanked Romano for the briefing and got up to leave. As he did the monsignor said, "In case I didn't say it last night, welcome home. Now, go with God, you're gonna' need Him."

CHAPTER EIGHT

As Michael drove to the 70th precinct station house, he called the DA's office security desk. He was grateful that the officer on duty, Gene Jarko, was a veteran of the office and knew Michael well. He told Jarko that he was working on the Massey and Tenuta murders and asked him to call ADA Josh Turner and patch him through to his cell phone when he reached him.

He also asked Jarko to find the chief of surgery for Kings County Hospital. "And Gene, when you get the doctor, apologize for disturbing him on a Sunday. Tell him you're calling for me and that it's extremely urgent. And like with Turner, put him through to my phone. I'm in the car headed to the 70 precinct to interview a detective and a couple of cops, but don't worry about disturbing me. Thanks."

Michael's phone rang five minutes later. It was Josh Turner.

"Josh, sorry to bother you on Sunday. I'm calling about the arraignment of Jax Chase that you handled a few days ago. Tell me about that call you received from the ER doctor at Kings County regarding the bullet in Chase's leg."

Turner told Michael what the doctor said, and also mentioned that before the doctor's call when he told Chase's attorney his intention to ask the judge to order that the bullet be removed, he was surprised that the lawyer didn't object.

"Mike it was like he knew that I'd be getting that call from the ER doctor telling me that it was too risky and dangerous to remove. It was spooky if you ask me."

"Josh, what was the ER doctor's name?"

"John Milton," Turner answered.

"Josh, thanks for the information. And I apologize again for bothering you."

"Mike, it was no bother. Call me anytime if you need anything else."

Michael continued on his way to the 70th precinct troubled by what Turner had said about Chase's lawyer's indifference. He thought to himself, *'Could it be?'*

Michael wouldn't get the answer until he spoke to Kings County Hospital's chief of surgery.

When he walked into the station house Michael was directed by the desk sergeant to the detective squad room on the second floor. There he saw Tony Martino, in conversation with two uniformed cops who he assumed were Denny James and Paul Sira. Michael knew Martino from a cold case homicide the two worked on very early in his career in the DA's homicide bureau.

He walked over to the group and when Martino spotted him he stood and offered his hand. Michael smiled and returned the handshake. Tony Martino had not changed a bit since Michael last saw him. Think Dean Martin with a badge and gun. Tall, handsome, friendly, and as good a singer as Dino was, that's how good a detective Tony Martino is.

"It's been a long time, Mike. What was it ten years ago when we worked that cold case of the elderly woman who was stabbed in her apartment in Midwood. You always thought it was the pizza delivery kid and I admit I was skeptical, but you broke your ass to find the evidence to arrest and convict him."

"Tony the crime was twenty years ago and was a cold case when we solved it ten years ago, but who's counting. In the years since the conviction I found out that the elderly woman was the grandmother of a guy who dated my sister when they were in high school. She ran into him about a year ago and he told her all about how her brother and 'some sharp looking detective' solved the murder of his grandma."

"We made a good team back then, Mike," Tony said. "I'm hoping we got a little magic left in us to bring this tragedy home."

Martino introduced Michael to Denny James and to Paul Sira.

"These are the heroes who collared that mutt Chase. Talk about good police work, these two were sharp enough to recognize that an auto accident they passed on the way to bringing Chris Massey to Kings County Hospital, might have something to do with the shooting. If they hadn't gone back to investigate, who knows when we would have collared Chase. Once he got to the hospital he could have limped out of the ER, jumped in a cab, and vanished."

"Actually that was all Denny," Sira said. "He spotted the accident and insisted we go back to it after we dropped off Chris. I was only the driver. And Denny saved my life in that ambulance. He's the only hero here."

"Stop it Paulie," Denny chimed in. "If not for your quick thinking back at the station house to jump into your own car when we heard the shooting report come over the air, we might still be waiting for a free radio car to bring us to that scene."

Now looking right at Martino and Michael, Denny said, "Neither of us is a hero, we just did what we were trained to do, be good cops." However, after he said that he dropped his head. Martino noticed and asked Denny if something was wrong.

"Tony, I'm just pissed and disappointed that we never found Chase's gun. We were so preoccupied with getting him out of that mob scene we didn't check the car after the medics removed him from it. By the time we got back the car was gone."

Then Sira jumped in, "We went to the precinct parking lot where it was towed to and searched it. No gun. We fucked up. I hope that doesn't cost us a conviction of that bastard."

Michael took this all in before telling them that he appreciated, and admired, everything they did and that he'd figure a way around their not finding the gun.

"Guys, no case is perfect. We have to use what evidence we have and what may come later, to put together a case that will convince a jury to send Jax Chase to prison for the rest of his life."

"And today we start that process," he said. "I'm going to speak to both of you individually and I want to make sure that you tell me everything. No detail is too small. I need to hear everything that you did at the shooting scene, everything that happened at the crash scene, and in the ambulance on the way to the hospital."

Both cops understood.

Tony Martino interrupted. "Mike, before we start the interviews there's something else you need to be aware of. Let's go into the boss' office," he said. When they walked into the squad commander's office, Tony closed the door.

"Let me start by saying I'm sorry. I didn't mention that we haven't found Chase's gun because I figured you knew that. That's my bad. But I had no clue that those guys blamed themselves for it. From what I've been told it was chaos at that accident scene, and anybody could have grabbed the gun and took off with it....I appreciate what you said to them about it."

Michael nodded and the detective continued, "But that's not why I asked to speak to you in private. Before we start the interviews there's something else you might not be aware of that you need to know."

"Does this involve either Denny or Paul?," Michael asked.

"No, but you need to hear it because the defense may bring it up and may use it if there is a trial."

Martino told Michael that when the first cops arrived at the scene of the shooting, minutes after Chase fled, they immediately checked the condition of Massey, Tenuta, and "The perp who we've now identified as Ricky Sabar."

"Then one of them broadcast over the police radio, and I'm repeating word for word: 'Central, one shooter is DOA (Dead On Arrival.) The other shooter, a five foot five-five foot six Hispanic, limped away, got into a car and took off."

"What!" Michael said, trying very hard to control his anger and disappointment.

"I know Mike, it's a bad fuck up. But when you hear what that cop has to say about it how it happened, you'll see it was a perfectly understandable fuck up."

"Tony, let me correct you on something you said before you told me about this. Understandable or not, it's exculpatory evidence that I'll have to turn over to the defense. So it's not a question of whether the defense *may* bring it up or *may* use it, the attorney will *absolutely* bring it up and will *positively* use it."

"The defense attorney will argue to the jury that 'The cops arrested and beat the shit out of the wrong man. And how do we know that? We know it because one of their own officers broadcast the information over the official police radio, the description of the actual shooter who got away: a five foot five, five foot six, Hispanic. Look at Mr. Chase, he's a tall white man.... It's no wonder that they didn't find a gun in my client's car.'"

"Tony, the defense will say that the police settled on the first person they thought did the killing because he had blood all over him, which he did, because he was in an automobile accident. And because two of their own were murdered on a street several blocks away, just for doing their job."

"When I turn that police radio broadcast over to the defense, I'll be handing them reasonable fucking doubt!" Michael fumed.

"Mike, I talked to the cop who put the description out over the air. He told me what happened, and it's weird. You should hear it directly from him. Maybe when you do you'll figure out a way to lessen the blow," Martino said.

"Of course I want to hear what he has to say. Can you get him here?"

"I knew you'd want to talk to him, so I have him on call. He can be here when you're ready."

Michael said he wanted to speak to Denny and Sira first, "So tell him to be here in a couple of hours. What's his name?"

"Everyone at the precinct calls him Gabe," Martino answered. "His full name is Gabriel Angelos."

CHAPTER NINE

For the next two hours Michael listened to Denny James and Paulie Sira. With the exception of not finding Chase's gun, there was little difference from what Romano told him.

However, because of his suspicion about who in the crowd at the scene of the car accident was demanding that Chase be taken away in the ambulance, and who also may have made that gun disappear, Michael grilled both Denny and Sira.

Sira was no help. He told Michael he was too distracted by everything to pay attention to some "Fucking loud mouths" as he called them.

Denny, however, said he saw who was mouthing off.

He told Michael, "The guy with the biggest mouth was a reverend who must have come out of the church that's right on the corner where Chase crashed into the light pole."

"Why do you say he's a reverend," Michael asked.

"He was dressed in black with one of those little white collars they wear. And there was another guy with him who was also screaming at us."

"Was he a reverend as well?" Michael asked.

Denny started laughing before he answered. "Sorry to laugh. I don't think so. Because if he was, then he's the strangest looking cleric I've ever seen."

A very curious and anxious Michael asked why Denny felt that way.

"Mr. DA, the dude wasn't in no collar, and he had red dreadlocks! What reverend is gonna' have red dreads? Who in church is gonna' take that guy seriously?

"Could you ID him if you saw him again?" Michael asked.

"Nah, he had one of those pandemic masks on. But I know they knew each other or were together because he kept turning and saying something to the reverend right before they shouted that shit at us."

Michael took a deep breath to hide his anxiety over what Denny had just told him, then asked about Chase's injuries. "You were with him in the ER when he was examined, so tell me about his injuries," he said.

"From what the doc in the ER told Paulie and me, Chase has a fracture of the orbital bone of his right eye, a broken rib, and a ruptured spleen."

Worried that he and Sira were in trouble, Denny said,"I know the injuries sound bad, but Mr. DA you got to realize that Chase was going to shoot Paulie because he didn't want to go to jail, so we did everything we could to get him to let go of my gun."

The injuries did concern Michael but he didn't want to lose Denny because he feared he would be arrested. So he told him not to worry. "You guys are not in trouble." He then told him what he would likely argue to the jury. "No one would expect two police officers to do anything different. You guys were struggling with a murder suspect who had a gun pointed at one of you and was pulling the trigger. They're gonna' see you and Paulie as heroes."

Many months later at trial he would learn how wrong he was. At this early point in his fact gathering and preparation he neglected to factor in the EVIL ONE, who would exploit the injuries to Chase as evidence of unnecessary police brutality.

When he finished interviewing them, he told the cops that he'd need them to testify in the grand jury in a day or two, and cautioned them not to speak to anyone, including their police colleagues, about their stories.

Michael gave that admonition because of the real possibility that Satan would try to influence them in some way or manipulate the evidence they were prepared to put before the grand jury, to fit *HIS* narrative.

Next up for Michael was to interview Gabriel Angelos.

When Tony Martino brought him into the interview room where Michael was waiting, the cop was literally shaking. *'This poor guy must have taken a verbal beating from his fellow cops because of his fuck up,'* Michael thought as Gabriel sat down.

From the look on his face, Michael also wondered if Angelos was worried that he would recommend to the police brass that he be disciplined because of his blunder. Of course, Michael had no intention of doing anything like that.

"Gabe," Michael began, using the cop's nickname in an attempt to calm his nerves. "I'm Assistant DA Michael Gioca and I'm trying to find out everything that happened on the street in front of *Leiser's* jewelry store last Thursday."

"Tony Martino told me you came onto the scene after the shooting, and you made a radio transmission that I want to ask you some questions about, okay?"

Angelos, clearly shaken to his core, simply nodded. He hadn't said a word yet and Michael was worried that his emotional state was going to prevent him from remembering exactly what happened and speaking freely about it.

To calm him and alleviate his guilt and worry, Michael told him that he understood what he was feeling.

"We can't change the past, Gabe. But with your help I can put together a case that will see to it that Jax Chase never again sees the outside of a prison. I need you to tell me everything you remember about that day, especially what was in your mind when you made that radio call."

"There may very well be a way for us to minimize the damage that I'm sure you believe you caused and are probably taking a lot of shit for. But I can only do that if you're honest and truthful with me."

"I'm not looking to hurt you," Michael continued, "And I give you my word that I'll go to bat for you if anyone tries to fuck with you over this. Because in my heart of hearts I believe there is a good explanation for what you said on the radio. Now tell me what happened."

When Michael was finished speaking, Angelos looked over at Tony Martino who gave him a nod indicating that Gioca was a straight shooter, then he turned to Michael and said, "Thanks I needed to hear that. I'll tell you everything."

Gabriel Angelos told Michael that he had just turned out for the start of his four-to-twelve tour that Thursday. "Me and my partner, Joan Powers, were getting all our gear together, and making sure that the radio and computer in the car was up and running, when we heard the 10-13, (police code for 'officer needs assistance') come over the air. Central said that witnesses are reporting that two cops are down and bleeding on the street in front of *Leiser's* jewelry store."

Angelos said that when he and Powers arrived he saw three men, all bleeding, lying on the street in front of *Leiser's*. He recognized Massey and Tenuta but didn't know who the third guy was. He went over to the third guy and checked his pulse. "He was dead," he said.

"Then I went over to Massey, who was still alive. Powers checked Tenuta and called out that we needed an ambulance. I took out my portable radio and was about to call for help when this woman came over to me. She was real excited and said that she saw 'the guy that got away.'"

Angelos told Michael that he had no idea at that time what happened, “So what the woman just told me didn’t mean much, but I felt it might be important. So I asked her what the ‘got away’ did and what he looked like.”

“She told me she lived across the street and pointed to a building. She said she was at her window and saw him shoot the guys on the ground, pointing to Massey and Tenuta. She described him as a ‘five foot five to five foot six, Hispanic,’ who, after the shooting, limped up the block to a car and drove away.”

Angelos said that radio cars and cops began to converge on the scene. One radio car took Tenuta and a civilian car with Paulie Sira driving took Massey. After the injured cops were taken away he said he called over the police radio with the description of the ‘got away’ shooter.

“Mr. DA, I thought I was doing the right thing. Two of my brothers were shot and looked bad, so I wanted to get the description of a shooter I got from someone who said she was an eyewitness, out over the air as soon as I could. I now know that was a mistake.”

At that point Angelos dropped his head and began to sob. Michael told Tony Martino that he needed a break to give Angelos some time to calm himself.

Outside the interview room, Michael asked Tony if he got a description of the woman and her contact information from Angelos.

“Mike I’m gonna’ wait for an answer. Let’s go back in and let him tell you what he knows about her. Then I will fill you in on what we did.”

After ten minutes, Angelos opened the door to the room and told Michael he was ready to continue. “Thanks for that Mr. DA,” he said.

“Gabe, my name is Michael. ‘Mr. DA’ is Marty Price.”

Angelos smiled, nodded, and continued.

“I know your next question because it was Tony’s next question after I told him what I just told you. I didn’t get her name. When I finished the call to central with the shooter’s description, I turned to where she had been standing and she was gone. I looked all over for her but didn't find her. I asked my partner and the other cops on the scene if they saw the woman I was talking to. Not one of them saw me talking to anyone."

Hearing that, the hair on the back of Michael's neck stood up. He got out of his chair and asked Angelos, "Can you describe her?"

"Yeah," he answered. "She was about forty, average height, about a hundred and twenty pounds. She had on a black jacket and jeans, and her hair was in red dreads. She was mixed race, I think, and her most prominent feature was...." Before Angelos could finish his answer, Michael said, "An ugly black mole on the left side of her face."

"How the fuck do you know that?" Angelos and Tony Martino said in tandem.

Michael realized he had made a mistake and quickly tried to make light of his remark. "Guys, I was only joking. I'm reading a novel right now and one of the main characters is a witch with red dreads who has a mole on her face. But Gabe, did your woman actually have a mole?"

Angelos answered that she did, and Michael moved on to ask if he got her exact address, "Or, is her pointing to a building the best you have?"

Tony Martino answered instead. He told Michael that after Angelos told him what happened, they went back to the scene the next day and went into the building the woman pointed to.

"We went to every apartment in the building, knocked on every door and spoke to anyone who answered. No one knew who we were describing. No one had ever seen a woman in that building who fit that description."

"That night we went back and hit all the apartments we didn't get an answer to during the day. Same result. Mike it's like she was a ghost or maybe that witch from the book you're reading," Tony said with a chuckle. "But don't worry we'll find her."

'No Tony, she's not a ghost or a witch. That SHE is also a HE, some-

times. And we ain't ever gonna' find HER, or HIM, Michael thought to himself.

Just then his cell phone rang. It was the DA's office front desk. "Gene must have reached Dr. Marcus," he muttered under his breath, as he excused himself to talk to the Chief of Surgery for Kings County Hospital.

CHAPTER TEN

Dr. David Marcus was a longtime friend of the Gioca family. Michael's mother and father were patients of his from the time he opened his private office on Eastern Parkway in the Crown Heights section of Brooklyn, where they lived at the time.

It was Dr. Marcus who assisted in the delivery when Michael was born in Crown Heights Hospital, and three years later in the birth of his sister Pamela. Michael's mother placed great trust in the young doctor who played a significant role in caring for her children, for her and her husband.

Years later when the Gioca family decided to leave Brooklyn for a home in the leafy Queens Village section of the city, Dr. Marcus was no longer practicing on Eastern Parkway. He moved to a permanent position in the surgical team at Kings County Hospital. After several years he became Assistant Chief of Surgery, and shortly thereafter was promoted to Chief.

When Michael began his career at the Brooklyn DA's office Dr. Marcus, then in his sixties, was entrenched in the Chief's position. And when Michael became the head of the DA's Homicide Bureau he wasn't shy in calling on the doctor for a second opinion in several important murder cases.

When Michael was unhappy with, or unsure of the validity of a finding by the city medical examiner, he leaned on his long-time family ties and reached out to Dr. Marcus who was only too willing and eager to help the now grown and successful baby boy he helped deliver many years before.

"Doc, thanks for answering my call," Michael began, "I'm sorry to bother you on a Sunday but I really need your help."

"Michael, you never need to apologize for calling me. And before you get to the reason for the call, how's your father doing? I hope he hasn't had any complications from the medicine that quack doctor told him to take a year or so ago?"

The 'quack doctor' Marcus was referring to was actually the EVIL ONE. Over a year before, *HE* went after Gioca's father in an attempt to get Michael to abandon the war against *HIM*. The EVIL ONE counted on Michael recognizing that *HE* was responsible for putting his father's life in jeopardy in the hope that he would abandon the war to spare future harm coming to his family.

Fortunately, Michael's recognition that *HE* was behind the attempt allowed him to get immediate help for his dad, who as a result suffered no permanent injury or serious harm. After a few days in the hospital, during which Dr. Marcus was consulted by his treating physician, Michael's father returned home to resume his normal life. The EVIL ONE's ploy only strengthened Gioca's resolve to continue the battle and win the war.

"Doc, dad's doing well. No repercussions, no complications, and no relapse. Thanks for asking."

"That's good to hear. Give him my best. Now, you called. How can I help?"

Michael told Marcus that he was assigned to the Tenuta and Massey murder case and brought him up to speed on what happened, including the incident with Chase in the ambulance.

"When Chase got to KCH (Kings County Hospital) he was examined in the ER, and it was determined that the wound in his leg was caused by a bullet. He was treated for injuries to his head, eye, ribs, and spleen, but nothing was done for the bullet wound other than applying topical meds and wrapping it in a new bandage. He was then admitted to the hospital."

"Because this was a double cop killing, the mayor appealed to the city administrative judge to order that Chase be arraigned as soon as possible. The judge agreed and the arraignment was scheduled for later that day in Chase's hospital room," Michael said.

He told the chief surgeon what Josh Turner intended to ask of the judge at the arraignment about the removal of the bullet because it was evidence in a murder case.

Michael also told Marcus that before the proceeding began, the ADA received a call from John Milton who said he was the ER doctor who treated Chase. He repeated verbatim what Milton said to ADA Turner.

"Dr. Marcus, do you know this Dr. Milton?" Michael asked.

"Mike, the name is not familiar to me, but I'm in the surgery department not emergency medicine," Marcus answered.

"Doc, that bullet is very important to the success of this case. If I get it tested at the ballistics lab and it's a match for one of the cops' guns, it will seal the deal on this guy's guilt. But to do that I need that bullet out of Chase's leg."

"Michael, I understand. What do you want me to do?"

"I'm asking you to personally examine Chase's leg and give me a surgeon's opinion as to whether it's safe to remove the bullet. And if you say it is, I'll get a court order to allow you or one of your surgeons to do it."

Marcus agreed to examine Chase. "Mike, it'll have to wait until tomorrow. I'm out east in South Hampton at a friend's home but I'll be at the hospital in the morning. I'll examine the patient and call you with my opinion."

Michael thanked him and told the doctor to call him as soon as he could.

"If you say the surgery is a go, I'll prepare a motion and hopefully have a judge's order for the surgery by the afternoon."

"Doc, thanks for all this. Enjoy the rest of your day."

Before he hung up Michael had one more request, "Doc, will you check out this Dr. Milton? I'd like to talk to him no matter what your finding is."

"Mike, I'll take care of that and let you know what I learn."

When Michael was finished with Marcus he returned to Tony Martino and filled him in. "That's great," Tony said, "But even if we get lucky and the doc gives the go ahead for the surgery, you still have to convince a judge. That ain't gonna' be easy."

Michael knew Tony was right, but he felt that with the imprimatur of the Chief of Surgery for KCH, and affidavits from eyewitnesses Eva and Joanie Snow, a judge would grant his motion with no hesitation.

"Tony nothing is a lock, but we do have three people murdered here, two of whom are cops. I think a judge will not want the headlines that a denial would generate. It wouldn't be good for his or her career," Michael answered.

"Now, are the Snow sisters available for an interview?" Michael asked. "If they are, I can wait around and speak to Eva and Joanie today. Thereafter I can prepare affidavits for them to sign so I'll have them if I need them."

Martino said he'd call and find out.

The sisters were available, and Michael interviewed them late that afternoon.

He was impressed by Eva's memory of the shooting, her attention to detail, and the articulate way she re-told what she saw. When she expressed compassion for the dead police officers and their families her sincerity was real. But when she expressed sorrow for "the dead bad guy," being in the wrong place at the wrong time, Michael knew her empathy would impress jurors. Eva wouldn't be seen as just a partisan prosecution witness, but as a witness for all the people, telling just what she saw.

Joanie, however, was very different from her sister. She was a bundle of nerves when she spoke, which indicated to Michael that she was still shaken and frightened by what she witnessed.

And, although she did not see as much of the incident as Eva saw, what she did see was extremely important to Michael's case. So he wasn't prepared to give up on her. He knew she would need a good amount of preparation before she testified in a grand jury and at trial.

But there was another issue with Joanie, her drug use.

For years Michael dealt with crucial witnesses who refused to admit their obvious drug use. Some even denied past addiction despite being in recovery. This called their credibility into question.

Joanie was different. She didn't hide that she was a recovering user. Her candor was refreshing and impressed Michael. She would need a lot of preparation before she took the witness stand, but he was confident that he could mold her into a strong, effective witness who would corroborate the testimony of her sister.

When Michael finished interviewing the sisters, he prepared their affidavits and told them they would be needed in the grand jury in a few days. He also cautioned them about speaking to anyone about the case, before telling them that "Det. Martino will give you his cell phone number so if anyone tries to speak to you, call him immediately."

It had been a long day, and Michael was ready to pack up and head home, when Martino told him that there was one more witness who he was able to reach. "Mike, this guy's outside at my desk, I think you should get his story on paper before he gets amnesia about what he knows."

"Amnesia, what are you talking about?" Michael asked.

"When I bring him in you'll see why I said that. Let's just say that he might be the member of a certain family that usually discourages its members from talkin' to the cops and cooperatin' with your kind."

"Tony, are you saying that the guy's hooked up? He's a wiseguy?"

"I'll leave it for you to draw your own conclusion. You want to talk to him?"

Michael told Tony to bring him in. He couldn't leave the stationhouse without interviewing the last known eyewitness to the events in front of *Leiser's*, Guy Raimondi.

CHAPTER ELEVEN

When Raimondi walked into the interview room Michael thought to himself, *'This guy just walked out of central casting.'*

He was fifty-*ish,* five foot five, maybe. As round as he was tall and dressed in a royal blue *Puma* tracksuit. The zipper on the jacket strained to remain intact due to his large belly. And on his feet, snow-white *Clyde* model *Puma* sneakers. To finish off the outfit Raimondi wore oversized Ray Ban Wayfarer sunglasses and carried an unlit enormous *Romeo y Julieta* Churchill sized cigar.

Michael didn't have to hear a word he had to say. Just looking at the guy he understood why Tony Martino said what he did about him. Michael thought, *'The only mystery with this guy is who was he with, the Colombo or the Gambino family?'*

Not expecting to get much out of him, because these guys aren't known for their cooperation with law enforcement unless there's something in it for them, Michael was surprised by Guy Raimondi.

After getting past the questions about where Michael's family came from in Italy, where he grew up and went to school, Raimondi was a terrific witness.

His recollection was remarkably detailed, and he didn't hesitate when he told Michael what he saw.

He was right on the money with his description of the two men who got out of the Chevy. And he immediately identified them when Martino showed him photo arrays that contained their mug shots.

And as for Sabar tapping his watch, Raimondi took that as an indication that it needed to be repaired. "When I seen him do that to his watch, I didn't think nuthin' was up with them walkin' to the jewelry store," he said.

Raimondi then told Michael how he felt and what he told the police when he returned to the scene after the shooting. After hearing that, Michael thought to himself that he and Martino may have jumped to the wrong conclusion about Mr. Raimondi.

"Mr. G, when I seen those two dead cops laying on the street with bullet holes in them, I made sure to tell one of the detectives who I was, where I lived, and what I seen. I gave him my cell number and told him to call me any time. I feel bad for them cops' families," he said as he made the sign of the cross.

Michael secured Raimondi's assurance that he would testify in the grand jury and at trial. Before letting him leave, as he did with the other witnesses, he advised Raimondi not to speak to anyone about what he told Michael.

"Don't worry Mr. G, I'm like a vault, I ain't gonna' say nuthin'. You call me when you need me, and I swear on my mother's grave, I'll be there."

Tony showed Raimondi out and before Michael could say a word, Martino said, "You know Mike, maybe I was wrong about that guy. He looks like a wiseguy and dresses like one, but he don't sound like one."

"Tony, you took the words out of my mouth. We may have jumped to a conclusion that we should be ashamed of. Here we are two Italian Americans doing to one of our own what we complain that others do to our people. We stereotyped him. We both believed he was a gangster because his last name ends in a vowel, and he dresses like a character from '*Goodfellas.*' However, after hearing him, I don't believe he is. I think the clothes and the way he carried himself were all an act. Having said all that, for the sake of the case, please check him out. I need to know all about Mr. Raimondi."

It had been a long day and Michael finally felt the jet lag kick in. Up to that point he was running on adrenaline, but now he just wanted to drive home and get to sleep.

He thought about calling Kathy but he remembered that she probably worked all day as well. '*She has to be as tired as I am right now,*' he thought. So instead he sent her a text message promising to call her the next day.

When he drove out of the stationhouse parking lot his cell phone rang. It was Romano.

"Sal, I'm on my way home and I'm beat. Can whatever this is wait until the morning?" he asked.

The monsignor could hear the fatigue in his voice. "Mike, I only wanted to find out how things went with the witnesses and with Denny James and Paul Sira. The details can wait until we see each other tomorrow."

Michael gave him a quick synopsis of the day. "For the most part it went well. But I won't know if the most important piece of evidence, the bullet in Chase's leg, will be available to me until sometime tomorrow morning."

He briefly told Romano about the transmission of the bogus identification, his discussions with Josh Turner, and Dr. Marcus, and his strong suspicion that the EVIL ONE had *HIS* hand in all that. He ended with, "A few prayers wouldn't hurt."

Romano told him to consider it done and added, "Drive carefully."

It was noon the next day when the call came in.

Michael was at his desk and saw it was Dr. Marcus. He took a deep breath to calm himself before he answered.

"Michael," Marcus began, "I have news."

Gioca braced himself and asked, "Good or bad?"

"I'm sorry to say that you're not going to like what I'm about to tell you."

The doctor told Michael that he did a thorough examination of Chase's leg, had new X-rays taken, and consulted with his deputy chief surgeon to discuss the results.

"Michael, we cannot do the surgery to remove the bullet," he said.

"The risk of nicking the femoral artery because of where the bullet now sits, is very high. If the artery is compromised in any way during the procedure, Chase will bleed out because we won't have the time to stem the bleeding before he goes into cardiac arrest."

Michael listened carefully and pounced on one word that the doctor seemed to pass over quickly. "Doc, what do you mean by where the bullet *NOW* sits?' Isn't it in the same place as when the ER doctor saw Chase last week?"

Marcus hesitated before answering, "No Michael it isn't. It moved."

"I checked the x-rays from that day and the bullet was nowhere near the femoral artery. If I, or any of my surgeons, were in the ER and saw that x-ray, we would have overruled Dr. Milton, who I looked into, by the way, and we would have advised your ADA accordingly."

'Fuck!', Michael whispered as he tried to hold in his anger and disappointment.

Because of what Marcus just told him, Michael hesitated before asking his next question. He was afraid of the answer.

"Doc, what did you find out about Dr. Milton?"

"I found nothing," he said.

"I checked with our HR department, and they never heard of him. I asked the ER chief and she didn't know who I was talking about. She also told me that the only doctor who attended to Chase when he was brought in was one of her residents, and his name is not Milton."

"To be certain I wasn't leaving any stone unturned, I called the

New York City Health and Hospitals Corporation, the group that runs all city hospitals, the New York State registry of physicians, our licensing board, and finally the American Medical Association. No one had anything on a Dr. John Milton. The closest I came was the New York State registry. They had a Joseph M-i-l-t-i-n, a podiatrist who lives in Plattsburgh near the Canadian border. Mike, are you sure your ADA got the correct name from the guy he spoke to?"

Michael was sure, because he now knew that Josh Turner didn't talk to an actual doctor. He was speaking to the EVIL ONE.

He couldn't tell that to Marcus, so Michael just said that he would check again with the ADA and if he was mistaken about the doctor's name he would get back to him.

"Doc, thanks for everything. It's not the result I hoped for but I'll find a way around it."

"Mike, I'm glad you said that. I forgot to mention that the x-rays taken when Chase was brought into the ER and the new ones I ordered today were shot with new, highly sophisticated equipment. The pictures are as sharp as can be. You can see the bullet clearly. If you showed them to the NYPD or FBI ballistics experts, perhaps they can answer any of your questions about the bullet and you can do something with the pictures?"

"Wow. That's great news, doc. I'll have one of my detectives come over to you to get the x-rays." He then added something to ensure that the films were handed to his person and not to one of Satan's minions.

"Doc, when my detective gets there, have him show you his ID of course, and then ask him for the note that I will give him. It'll have the address of your old office on Eastern Parkway and the name of the hospital where you delivered me and my sister. If he doesn't have it, or the information is incorrect, don't give the x-rays to him, and call me immediately."

Marcus was clearly puzzled but thankfully didn't ask any questions. So Michael didn't have to lie to him. He just said, "Okay, Mike, good luck."

CHAPTER
TWELVE

That night Michael met Romano for dinner at *Emilio's*, the restaurant where the monsignor is treated like the Pope.

Because of its location near both Michael's apartment and Romano's office, it had been their unofficial meeting place since Michael agreed to work for Caldwell and his secret group. The food and wine are superb, and Romano is never presented with a check, although he always left a big tip for the waiter or waitress.

When Michael walked in the monsignor was seated at his special table and Emilio, the owner, was pouring him a glass of *Brunello di Montalcino,* the cleric's favorite Italian red.

Emilio greeted Michael warmly, saying as he poured a glass of the wine for him, "*Michele, come stai,* how are you? I haven't seen you in a long time."

"Emilio, I missed you, your food, and of course, the wine. It's been months since the *monsignore* and I have been here together. But all is well, and I'm very hungry."

"Don't worry," Emilio answered, "I'm going to take good care of my two friends tonight. *Mangerai bene.*"

Nodding in agreement, Romano said, "We will eat well, of that

I'm sure." He raised his glass in a toast, "And here's to beating the EVIL ONE again," he said, as he and Michael clinked glasses.

Michael uncharacteristically gulped down the entire glass.

Romano noticed and said, "What's wrong? This wine is too good to gulp. It's meant to sip and savor. And since you're not doing that, something must be bothering you."

"It's the case," Michael said. "I'm concerned."

"Talk to me."

Michael told the monsignor all about the witnesses he interviewed on Sunday and gave his impression of each.

He began with the two cops. "Denny James and Paul Sira need lots of prep before they'll be ready to testify at trial. It's not *what* they say, it's *how* they re-tell what happened that I'll have to work on."

"If I'm going to be successful with the argument that both were justified in doing what they did to disarm Chase, they've got to convince the jury that they were in mortal danger when he grabbed that gun from Danny's holster."

Then, almost as if he were trying to convince himself, he said, "They're both smart, savvy, street cops so I'm confident they'll be ready when I need them to be."

He told the monsignor about an idea he was kicking around to bolster and corroborate the cops' testimony.

"I'm thinking of calling an instructor from the police academy as a witness to ask about the training police recruits receive for situations like the one they were in. I spoke to one before I came to meet you and he told me that recruits are taught the law of self-defense, and what it permits a police officer to do in defending himself and/or a partner when a suspect has a gun pointed at either of them in close quarters."

"I asked if he was familiar with what occurred in the ambulance with Chase, and when he said he was. I asked him for his assessment of Denny's and Paulie's conduct. His answer was that they followed the law and their training."

Michael continued, "The law of self-defense in New York allows a person who is in reasonable fear for his or her life, to use whatever force is necessary to protect themselves, including deadly force.

"So, if all goes well with the testimony from James, Sira, and the instructor, I'll be able to argue that the cops were actually *restrained* in their actions because they could have shot Chase to protect themselves and didn't."

"What do you think?" he asked Romano.

"I'm not an attorney," the monsignor answered. "However, being as objective as I can be, despite my role in the prosecution, if I were a juror, the police instructor's testimony would lead me to conclude that the two cops did what was necessary to stay alive!"

Michael nodded and continued.

Without going into full detail, he told Romano what Sira, and especially James, said about the crowd at the scene of the car accident. "Sal, that and what I learned from Gabriel Angelos and the radio transmission of that bogus description of the shooter who fled the scene, tells me the EVIL ONE *was* there that day, despite the fact that neither you nor Caldwell saw *HIM* on the street cameras."

Romano, not flustered by what Michael just told him, asked him to continue.

While Michael took a sip of his wine, the monsignor just looked at his friend and thought that Brooklyn was very fortunate to have him at the helm.

Michael next talked about Eva and Joanie Snow.

He said that Eva was by far his best witness. "She saw everything. She's smart, articulate, and had nothing in her background that would cause a juror to question her veracity. She remembered every detail of what happened on that street and had no problem identifying Chase when she was brought to the scene of his car accident."

"Sal, she's a star. If I had to construct a prosecutor's ideal witness, Eva Snow would be my model. As for her sister Joanie, she's good but not nearly as much as Eva."

He told Romano that Joanie described where she was, in a corner of the vestibule of her apartment foyer during the shooting, and what she saw. "However," he said, "She was shaky and obviously frightened. She'll need a lot of preparation."

"Joanie is also a recovering drug addict. But strangely, I believe that part of her life is what will win her over with the jury."

"You're going to have to explain that to me," Romano interrupted, his skepticism obvious from the tone of his voice.

"Sal, she doesn't try to hide her addiction, nor make excuses for becoming a junkie, she owns up to it. She freely admits that she was weak and made a grave mistake which cost her dearly. But she is proud that she recognized her problem and took the necessary steps to enter recovery. So far, she's succeeding."

"Her willingness to tell the hard truth about herself to twelve perfect strangers will impress the jury, and I believe it will go a long way in convincing them that she's telling the truth about everything."

"Mike, I understand and I agree. A redemption story is both powerful and inspiring," Romano said.

Then came Guy Raimondi.

Michael confessed to jumping to conclusions about him that he now knows were unfair. "Tony Martino checked him out, and Raimondi is not a wiseguy. The way he talks and the way he dresses-it's all pretend. He's like an Elvis fan on Halloween who dresses up like the King and talks like him when he knocks on a family's door and announces, 'trick or treat.' I think the jury will be entertained by the guy. He has, to use one of my dad's favorite expressions, 'the gift of gab'. And despite his outward appearance, they'll be impressed by his sincere expression of sorrow for the families of the murdered police officers. Sal, they're gonna' love him."

Having listened to Michael up to this point, Romano was puzzled. He took a sip of wine and said, "Michael I'm confused. From what you've told me, you should be thrilled with your case. Yet you say you're troubled. Why?"

Just then Emilio brought a plate of cold *antipasto*. "Pick on this while I prepare your meals," he said. Michael stabbed an olive and told the monsignor all about Gabriel Angelos, his radio transmission, and the woman with the red dreadlocks and the mole.

"Sal the woman with the red dreadlocks was the EVIL ONE. *HE* took a similar form early in our war. Remember the Robby Thomas and the Susan Hayes murder cases? But I can't tell that to the detectives who are looking for this 'witness' day and night, nor can I stop it, and that really irks me."

"But what bothers me even more is that I'm not sure how I'm going to overcome the real damage the description has done to the case."

"Then there's Dr. John Milton, and the bullet in Chase's leg."

Michael told him everything he learned from his friend Dr. Marcus. Including that Milton doesn't appear on any list of medical professionals anywhere in the country. "It's got to be *HIM*, again, Sal."

"If 'Milton' hadn't spoken to the ADA before the arraignment, I would have the bullet, which I'm certain came from either Massey's or Tenuta's gun. That evidence alone would convict Chase, despite the erroneous radio call. So my other concern is how do I make chicken salad out of chicken shit!"

Romano listened without interrupting. When Michael was finished the monsignor had a smirk on his face.

Taken aback by the reaction, Michael stared right at him, and, in his best Joe Pesci in *Goodfellas* imitation, asked, "Do I amuse you?"

Romano cracked up laughing. He knew that his old friend would understand the smile eventually.

"First let me say that I wasn't smiling because of that crude, but apropos, food reference. Man, it's been a long time since I've heard that expression. But I digress. Let me tell you why I smiled," he said.

"With the red dreads woman, you had *HIM* pegged as soon as Angelos told you she was the source of the description. As for Dr. Milton, it took a bit of work by your friend Dr. Marcus, but you eventually figured out that the doctor was the EVIL ONE. But you missed the significance of the names of the cop and the doctor. That's why I was smirking."

"I'm not following you," Michael said.

"The cop *HE* used to deliver the crucial message that screws up your case, Gabriel Angelos, his name is Greek for 'The Angel Gabriel,' God's messenger. Gabriel delivered the news to Mary that she was pregnant with Jesus; to Zechariah that John the Baptist was born; and in the Hebrew bible, he delivers an important message from God to the prophet Daniel."

Michael sat stunned as Romano continued.

"And the doctor who thwarted the removal of that bullet from Chase's leg, John Milton, the EVIL ONE was doing it to you again. 'John Milton' was the name of Al Pacino's character in the movie, *The Devil's Advocate.* Pacino played the Devil!"

"So Mike, don't you see, *HE's* taunting you! Or as we used to say when we were kids...God forgive me... *HE's* fucking with you. *HE* wants you to know that *HE's* in charge, that *HE* has the upper hand, and is in control of how this case is going to go."

Michael didn't know what to say.

Just then Emilio approached with their pasta, and both the monsignor and Michael were silent while they enjoyed his rigatoni Bolognese.

When they were done and the pasta dishes were cleared away, Romano felt compelled to say something to his friend who he sensed was upset, maybe even somewhat humiliated.

"Michael, don't beat yourself up over this. There's no shame in not recognizing what *HE* was doing to you. *HE's* been doing that to people for centuries. If you roll over and let *HIM* get away with it, then you'd have a reason to hang your head. But I know you and I've seen how well you've handled *HIM* since we began. *HE* should be concerned."

"You've dealt with a lot worse than this and beat *HIM* every time. You'll overcome these problems as well. I have faith in you, as does Caldwell. You'll find a way."

Romano ended with, "And never forget your ally above. Have faith that He'll give you the strength and knowledge to beat our evil adversary once again."

Now it was Michael's turn to smile. He looked at his friend and thought, *'He always seems to know just what to say when I need a boost to my confidence.'*

"Sal, from when we were kids, no matter what kind of trouble we were in, or predicament we got ourselves into, you always knew what needed to be done or said to make things right. And you've just done it again, for me. Thank you."

Michael lifted his glass and toasted the monsignor as a waiter delivered their main course to the table.

Michael's comment triggered memories of their time together in the old neighborhood. And for the rest of the dinner, the two friends reminisced. By the time they finished dessert, both were ready to call it a night. Of course no check was presented, but it was Michael who left the generous tip this time. When they left the restaurant Romano thanked him for dinner and asked if he wanted a lift home.

"Padre, it's me who needs to thank you, for the company, and for the pep talk," Michael replied.

"You made me feel so much better and gave me a lot to think about. I'm gonna' walk home and do just that." Michael then hugged his friend.

"I'll be in the grand jury for the next few days," he said, "I'll call you when I have an indictment.

As Michael walked away Romano said to him, "Please don't forget, because Caldwell will be on me for updates."

CHAPTER THIRTEEN

As Michael walked into his apartment his cell phone rang. When he saw who it was he smiled but knew that *he* should have made the call first.

"Kathy, I'm sorry for being out of touch for so long. How are you?"

Kathy Baer started to laugh. "Michael, you took the words right out of my mouth. That was going to be my opening line."

The two hadn't communicated since they had spoken on Sunday morning. "Kathy, I know I promised to call last night, but after the day I had with all the witness interviews I was wiped out. Again, I'm sorry."

Kathy told him that if he did call on Sunday night she wouldn't have answered. "That fire I was assigned to was more troublesome than I thought. Several cars in the parking lot of the 90th police precinct station house in Williamsburg were set on fire. They lost two squad cars, an unmarked detective vehicle, and the precinct commander's private car. All were totally destroyed."

"Holy shit!" Michael said. "Do you have any witnesses, or suspects?"

"Not really, although a resident who was walking his dog told the cops that he did see a strange looking woman with red dreadlocks and some kind of growth on her face, coming from the entrance to the parking lot around the time we believe the fires broke out. But we have nothing else."

When Michael heard that he nearly dropped his phone. Shocked and lost in thought, he didn't say a word until he heard Kathy ask, "Michael, Michael, did I lose you?"

"No Kathy, I'm still here. The phone must have frozen for a few seconds." Knowing full well what her answer was going to be, he asked, "So have you guys had any luck finding that woman?"

"My guys and I, along with the precinct detectives, and the NYPD Major Case Squad, have combed that neighborhood, knocking on doors, stopping people on the street, even going door to door of the businesses nearby, but we've had no luck. No one that we've spoken to has ever seen anyone fitting that description in the neighborhood. The thinking now is that she's either a complete outsider or a ghost."

'Or Satan,' Michael thought to himself.

Trying not to convey concern about the EVIL ONE drawing Kathy into this battle, Michael simply laughed at Kathy's remark about her witness being a ghost. "You're too good at what you do to fret over a missing witness. I'm sure you'll find her. Patience is a virtue," he said.

Now it was Kathy who laughed. "You must be tired and punch drunk to start throwing clichés at me. It's time to get some sleep. The remainder of the week is going to be very busy for you... and for me."

Michael agreed, but before he hung up they made plans to see each other on the weekend. "Kathy, be careful. To set police cars on fire in the precinct parking lot, tells me that the arsonist is as ballsy as she is dangerous."

"Honey, I'm always careful. I don't know when we'll be able to talk again, so I'll see you on Saturday. I can't wait."

"Neither can I," Michael replied.

After saying a final good night, Michael immediately called

Romano to tell him about the woman with the dreads being involved in Kathy's case.

The monsignor was half asleep when his phone rang. But after he heard what Michael said, he was wide awake.

"Sal what are we going to do about this? *HE's* now really fucking with me! Should we take over Kathy's case?"

"Mike, calm down. I'll speak to Caldwell in the morning, and I'll call you after. For now concentrate on your case; you have the grand jury this week, right?"

"I start the grand jury presentation tomorrow afternoon. Call me as soon as you know what Caldwell wants to do."

Michael hadn't heard from Romano when he walked into the grand jury room the next day to begin the presentation of his case against Jax Chase.

His first witness was Guy Raimondi. And as he predicted, the jurors loved him. When Guy concluded his testimony, he stood up in the witness box and in his best south Brooklyn accent said, "Youse have a nice day. And I'll see yiz, when I see ya." The jury room exploded in laughter.

Next came the Snow sisters. Michael called Eva first and she set the stage for the remainder of what the grand jury would hear in the days to come. Michael's perfect witness was just that. And Joanie, who Michael spent part of the morning preparing, was better than he expected.

It was a good first day but Michael knew that he couldn't take any bows yet. Denny James, Paulie Sira, and Gabriel Angelos were scheduled for the next day. And he had no clue as to how they would be received by the grand jury.

What he did know is that they all needed to be well prepared and reminded that their demeanor on the witness stand was as important as what they had to say. Michael had a long night ahead of him because all three cops were waiting in his office to work his magic with them.

The long night paid off. The three cops were excellent.

Gabriel Angelos was first up. Because his testimony was the most problematic, Michael put him in the leadoff spot. If Angelos' testimony needed a boost, he had Denny James and Paulie Sira to follow. Their heart-breaking story of scooping up their brother officer, Chris Massey, and driving him to the hospital as Denny gave him CPR and mouth to mouth, and their harrowing tale of the confrontation with Chase in the ambulance, he hoped would provide cover for Angelos' erroneous description of Chase.

What he didn't expect was Angelos and later Sira, breaking down in tears in the middle of their testimony. The effect that had on the jury was palpable. When Michael walked out of the grand jury room at the conclusion of the day's testimony, he was certain that his plan worked.

Back in his office Michael flopped into his desk chair. The adrenaline high he was on since the morning began to dissipate and he was exhausted. However, it was worth it, because the day went even better than he hoped it would.

He planned to finish his presentation with an instructor from the police academy to testify to recruit training, and with a ballistics expert from the police lab.

Michael took Dr. Marcus' suggestion and showed the enhanced x-rays of Chase's leg and the bullet to the expert a few days before. It paid off. He was prepared to testify that the bullet was the same caliber, size, and shape of ammunition issued by the NYPD to its officers for use in their on-duty guns. And was identical to the actual bullet the medical examiner removed from the body of Ricky Sabar during his autopsy. It was a bullet that came from Chris Massey's gun, the expert found.

The ballistics testimony wasn't as definitive as Michael would have liked, but it was the best he was going to get.

As he reviewed his notes for the witnesses, his cell phone rang. It was Romano.

The monsignor promised Michael that he would call immediately after he spoke to Caldwell about how he wanted to proceed with the police precinct parking lot fire. But he was so busy and preoccupied with his witnesses that he didn't realize he hadn't heard from Romano until he saw the monsignor's name on his phone.

"I thought priests were not supposed to lie," a half-joking Michael said when he answered the call.

"I haven't lied to anyone. I'm a man of the cloth. How dare you accuse me of deception," Romano responded knowing his friend didn't mean it.

"You told me you'd call me right after talking to Caldwell. That was two days ago! Did I hear from you? NO!.... I would call that deception at the very least."

The two old friends were having a bit of fun with each other, until Romano got serious.

"Mike, since no one was hurt in the fire, Caldwell wants to leave the case to Kathy and her colleagues and not get us involved. He thinks it's cleaner that way. If he were to swoop in and grab it for you, he fears that will raise eyebrows and too many questions. He is very protective of our secret mission and doesn't want to risk it being exposed."

"He also believes the EVIL ONE is trying to distract you from the Chase case. *HE* wants you to split your attention between it and the fire. A divide and conquer strategy."

"Caldwell is confident," the monsignor continued, "that because the EVIL ONE started the fire and not one of *HIS* minions, the authorities will never solve the case, never arrest anyone, and it will eventually be closed."

A prediction that would eventually become fact.

"What about Kathy being in the middle of this?" Michael asked in a tone that conveyed his disagreement with the decision. "Is he aware of the danger she may be in? Has he forgotten the things *HE's* done in the past to get to me?"

"He is aware and he hasn't forgotten. In fact he told me to tell you that, unofficially, you should keep an eye on the fire case through Kathy. By doing that you'll know if she's in danger."

"And, if she does have a problem, what then?" Michael asked.

"He'll do whatever is necessary to get her out of harm's way," Romano answered.

"Mike, I'm sorry but that's the business we're in. Caldwell knows what he's doing and is good at it. And, be assured, I'll be praying for her, as I do for you every day."

Michael told Romano that he wasn't happy with Caldwell's decision but since he had no choice, "I'll have to abide by it."

"Sal, I'm really tired, so I'm going home. I'll call you tomorrow after I charge the grand jury. If they indict Chase *you* fucking tell Caldwell. I'm too pissed to talk to him."

"Mike, I understand. I wish you *buona fortuna.* Although you're so good at what you do, luck doesn't play a role. *Buona notte,* my friend."

The next afternoon, following the testimony of the two expert witnesses, Michael charged the grand jury on the law they were to apply to the facts of the case. After ten minutes of deliberations the grand jury returned an indictment against Jax Chase for the murders of Police Officers Norman Tenuta and Chris Massey.

Michael called Romano as he walked back to his office after the grand jury vote.

"Sal, the jury did the right thing. Chase has been indicted for the murders of the two officers."

"That's good news Mike. And as you made clear to me last night, *I'll* call Caldwell to let him know."

"About last night, padre, I'm sorry to have talked to you the way I did. I was out of line. I know the decision was not yours so I shouldn't have taken my anger out on you."

"My friend, thanks but no apology is necessary. I understand how you feel and if I were in your place I'd feel the same way," Romano said. "Now go home and relax, the tough work on this case is ahead of you. But I, no we, have the utmost confidence that you'll beat *HIS* ass again."

"Thanks Sal and, *buona notte* to you," Michael said with a laugh.

In the days that followed the case was assigned to Brooklyn Supreme Court Judge Eila Cooper. When Michael was notified of the assignment he was thrilled. Judge Cooper was a no-nonsense judge who held attorneys to very high standards. In her courtroom lawyers had to be thoroughly prepared, always on time, and above all else, respectful to the court, the law, and to jurors.

She also had the well-earned reputation of being 'a people's judge.' Defense attorneys hated having to appear before her. Their complaint was that she ruled in favor of the prosecution far more often than she did for the defense, and they were right.

Michael never tried a case in her courtroom, although he appeared before her many times. Those cases all ended with the defendants pleading guilty. Undoubtedly they were following the advice of their attorneys who knew that if the client went to trial and lost, Judge Cooper would not spare the rod in her sentencing. Better to take the prosecution's plea-bargained offer than risk being a victim of the judge's heavy hand.

Two weeks after the grand jury's action, Michael walked into Cooper's courtroom for Chase's supreme court arraignment and met, for the first time, Elton Combes, Jax Chase's attorney.

CHAPTER
FOURTEEN

Elton Combes had a reputation for being one of New York City's finest and most successful criminal defense attorneys. He was also known as a long time champion of left-leaning progressive causes. Defending a cop killer was right in line with his politics. Michael was not surprised to see him.

However, no matter his politics, Combes didn't work for free, and he was expensive. *'Since Chase is the EVIL ONE's boy, did HE trick someone into paying Combes' fee?'* Michael wondered.

"Mr. Gioca, it's a pleasure to meet you," Combes said as he extended his hand and introduced himself. "Although we've never had occasion to oppose each other in the courtroom, your stellar reputation is well known to those of us on the defense side. I look forward to the challenge of doing battle."

Michael thought, '*No wonder this guy is so successful. He's slick, polite, and has a way of endearing himself to those around him, just like a con man. Juries must eat up his bullshit.'*

"It's good to meet you Mr. Combes, and thank you for the kind words," Michael said. He handed a copy of the indictment to Combes and told him that he'd have discovery to him in a week.

Combes nodded and turned to the judge who took the bench. "Mr. Gioca and Mr. Combes, are you ready to begin?" Judge Cooper asked. Both attorneys nodded and the judge told her clerk to have the defendant brought in.

A few moments later Chase was wheeled into the courtroom. Although he was still recovering from the bullet wound to his leg, the court officers were taking no chances with the escaped murderer and cop killer. He was cuffed to a wheelchair, both hand and leg.

When Chase was in place at the defense table, he looked up at Combes and asked, "Who are you? Are you my lawyer?" Combes leaned over and whispered something to Chase, who nodded.

Michael watched the interaction between the two and by Chase's reaction it was clear that he understood and accepted what Combes said to him. Witnessing their interaction triggered something in Michael.

'Did Combes tell Chase who hired him and who was paying his fee? Michael wondered. He needed to learn the answers to both questions because he was certain they would play a role in the trial of *The People of the State of New York v. Jackson "Jax" Chase.*

Michael was right. What he didn't realize was that the answers were in cell block VI, cell F, on the 6th floor of the Brooklyn House of Detention on Atlantic Avenue, just a few blocks from his office.

After his arraignment Chase was brought back to the jail on Atlantic Avenue, and returned to cell F, which he discovered he now had to share with a prisoner who was brought in that morning while he was in court.

Frankie LePage was new to the Brooklyn House, but he was not a prison virgin. He was brought down from Attica State Prison where he was serving time for grand larceny. LePage was in Brooklyn because he was hoping to have his conviction thrown out. He was scheduled to testify on his own behalf at a hearing before the same Brooklyn judge who sent him to Attica for seven years.

LePage had acted as his own attorney and the grounds he cited in his *pro se* motion to set aside the verdict, were ineffective assistance of counsel and prosecutorial misconduct. But now he was receiving legal representation from Elton Combes, who his father was paying for.

LePage refused to accept responsibility for his own actions. In his motion papers he blamed his conviction on, "My dumb ass trial attorney and the corrupt prosecutor." What he chose to ignore was that the prosecution's case was so strong, the jury that heard the evidence returned a verdict against him in fifteen minutes.

But here he was back in Brooklyn because he was able, with his father's help, to have his request for this hearing granted and heard by a judge who was known to favor defendants. All he had to do now was convince the judge that it was all a big mistake. "A travesty of justice," LePage wrote in his papers, using a term some jailhouse lawyer in Attica told him would work miracles.

When Chase saw his new cell mate, he broke into a big smile and grabbed LePage in a bear hug. "Bro, it's you. Holy shit!" Chase said. "They told me I was getting a celly, and I was worried it was gonna' be some asshole who snored and smelled."

Chase and LePage knew each other from Attica. When LePage first got to the prison they were cellmates for about a week until Chase was moved to the more secure section of the prison, where he wound up sharing a cell with Ricky Sabar.

"What are you down here for?" Chase asked.

LePage told him and added that he was confident that he wasn't going back to Attica. "I'm gonna' show that judge some shit that I didn't know was happening when I was on trial. My daddy been working for me whilst I was away and he come up with some good shit."

"Your daddy? Whatchu mean? I thought he was a preacher. What, he now a PI?" Chase asked.

"Nah, he's still a preacher. But he knows lots of big people here in Brooklyn and in the city. His church is over in Midwood near Nostrand Avenue, where I grew up. He and my mom's, who died when I was three years old, been living above that church since they come to Brooklyn way before they had me."

When Chase heard LePage mention Midwood it sounded familiar to him, as did Nostrand Avenue. "Frankie, tell me again where your daddy's church is. Exactly what streets?"

When LePage told him, Chase couldn't believe it. '*That's where I crashed that car,*' he said to himself. He then remembered the reverend who was shouting at the cops while he was on the gurney outside the ambulance. '*Could that be Frankie's father?*.

"Jax, what's up man. Did I say something wrong? You got all quiet."

"No, no, no, I was just thinkin' of something," Chase answered.

Chase then told LePage about the accident scene and the reverend. "He was giving a lot of shit to those pigs. Could that have been you daddy?"

LePage said, "Coulda been. It's right near his church and my daddy hate the cops. He always tell me they be hasslin' him and the nuns in his congregation for years. He think the corrupt mother-fuckers be lookin' to get paid to leave him alone, but he won't do it. Remember I told you that he know a lot of big people in Brooklyn, so when the cops break his balls, he just go and tell 'em. Cops don't like that, but they leave him alone for a while, until the next time."

"Jax, you want me to ask my daddy if it was him doin' the yellin'? Maybe he can help you," LePage volunteered.

"Yeah, thanks." Chase answered.

"No problem. I owes you for takin' care of me when I got to Attica. If you ain't talk to them guys on the cell block that week we was together, I woulda been someone's bitch forever."

"And do me one other favor," Chase asked. "If it was your daddy, ask him who was the guy with the red dreads that was with him. That guy seemed to be feedin' your daddy shit to say to the cops. I'd like to know him too."

LePage told Chase he didn't know anyone with red dreads. "But don't worry, I'll speak to my daddy when he comes on a visit."

Three days later an excited Frankie LePage returned to his cell after a visit from his father. Chase was pacing, anxious to hear what LePage had to say.

"Jax, you ain't gonna' believe what I found out. I talk to my daddy about you and, guess what, he already know all about you. It *was* him at the car crash yellin' at them pigs who was stallin' so the ambulance couldn't take you to the hospital. He said you charged with killin' two cops, who he say probably deserved it. He lookin' to help you beat this rap. And the guy with him with the dreads, daddy say he new to the congregation and he got lots of smarts. He hate cops just like daddy."

LePage went on to tell Chase that "It was the guy with the red dreads who told daddy to ask his rich friends to help him pay for a lawyer for you, 'Because' he say, 'You can't go to trial with no bullshit legal aid lawyer.' So daddy did, and he say that he hired Combes because he is the best."

Chase now understood who Combes was talking about when he told him at the arraignment that Chase had friends on the outside that he didn't even know he had, who paid his fee.

Chase began to thank LePage, when Frankie interrupted. "There's one more thing, Daddy told me to tell you that you need to put him on your visitors list 'cause he need to come talk to you. You ain't know it yet, but you about to become a born again Christian."

CHAPTER
FIFTEEN

One week later on visiting day at the Brooklyn jail, Chase had a visitor.

He didn't recall that he added Frankie LePage's father to his visitors list, so Chase was puzzled when one of the prison guards told him that he had someone waiting for him in the visitors room.

He walked in and scanned the room but didn't recognize anyone. When he saw someone in clerical garb at one of the visitors tables waving and calling his name, he remembered that he put Rev. Vernon LePage's name on his list.

When Chase got to the table the reverend introduced himself, and he and Chase shook hands.

"It's good to meet you Jackson. You did my son a solid up in Attica, and now I want to help you," LePage said.

"Reverend, it's just 'Jax'."

"I appreciate what you did for me, getting that lawyer," Chase continued. "I been reading up on Combes and he seems to be real good." LePage nodded, acknowledging the thanks.

"And I also got to thank you and that guy with the red dreads for speaking up at that car accident. I seen him tellin' you what to say, and you then givin' those cops a lot of shit," Chase said laughing. "Who is that guy?"

LePage hesitated before answering, which made Chase uncomfortable.

"He's a new member of my congregation. But why do you need to know that?"

"Reverend I didn't mean nothin' by it. I just thought I'd put his name on my visit list if he want to come see me sometime."

When LePage didn't react, Chase hurriedly said, "Frankie told me that you need to talk to me. I hope you still want to help me with my case."

"Yes Jax, I'm here to help."

LePage told Chase that he had been around prisoners for a long time and he knew some tricks to make his stay in jail somewhat easier.

"Tell me Jax, were you raised a Christian?" LePage asked.

Chase shook his head. "My mom was a Christian. She dragged me to Sunday school when I was a kid, but I hated it." He said that as soon as his mother dropped him off and went into church, he would cut out the back and play with his some of his friends who cut out too.

"That's good," LePage said. "So when I tell the jail authorities I need to save your soul and that you about to become born again, I got a back story to tell them if they doubt me."

Chase made a face which told LePage that he had no clue as to what the reverend was saying.

"Jax, you thanked me for getting that lawyer for you, so you know I'm trying to help you, right?"

Chase nodded.

"Do you trust me?"

Chase nodded again.

"So listen to me and do what I say."

In a whisper LePage told him, "Starting with today's visit I'm gonna' come see you several times a week. They'll let me in 'cause I'm gonna' tell the warden's office that I'm counseling you."

"When I believe the time is right, I want you to go to your prison counselor and tell him that because of my visits and our talks, you found religion and want me to instruct and baptize you."

"You got to say that you want to be born again. Those are the magic words," LePage added.

"And if they question me and ask if I believe you're for real, I got that story of you runnin' out of Sunday school to hit 'em with."

Chase heard everything LePage said, but he still didn't comprehend what the reverend was telling him.

"I ain't no pussy Rev. And I don't want no one to think I am. I don't want or need no religion," he said.

"Listen Jax," LePage whispered, "It's all bullshit. But trust me, when I'm done, it'll be a lot better in here for you."

"And after I baptize you," LePage continued, "I'm gonna' preach in my church all about how I saved your soul, and here's why. I know lots of big, influential people in this town, some is even in my congregation. They'll be impressed by what we did, and they'll want to tell that to the world! So at your trial, me and them big shots gonna' take the witness stand to let the jury know that you a reformed newly minted Christian, and not who the DA says you are. We gonna' say that the DA got the wrong man."

"Jax, I want you to beat this case."

"I hate cops," the reverend continued, "because they locked up my son for nothin'. My friend with the red dreads say, two less cops on this earth, the better we all are. I agree with that."

"And I really hate the DA's office. They lied and cheated at my son's trial to convict him, and he now gonna' be locked away in a cage for seven years."

"That's why we doin' this. You feel me?"

Chase finally got it. "Reverend LePage," he said raising his voice, "Thank you for your counsel and your guidance. I need you to come see me as much as you can."

LePage, in a voice that others could hear, said “My son, I hear your cry for help. I’ll speak to the warden and I’m sure he’ll allow me the extra visits so I can continue my work with you.”

LePage told Chase to bow his head. He placed his hands on him and pretended to say a silent prayer. “God bless you,” were his last words before he walked out of the visitors room.

Over the next several weeks, with the warden’s permission, LePage visited Chase for ‘counseling,’ every two days. After a month, the time was right for Chase to see his jail counselor to tell him that he was born again and wanted to be baptized by Rev. LePage.

Permission was granted, and several weeks later in the jail’s chapel, Jackson Chase was “Blessed with the water of salvation,” as the reverend said when he baptized him.

To the outside world Chase was born again. To LePage and that member of his congregation with the red dreads, whose idea it was to engage in this charade, it was the first step to ensure that Chase was found not guilty of the murder of Norman Tenuta and Chris Massey.

Michael had no clue that any of this had gone on.

He learned all about it a few months later when Kathy Baer alerted him to a radio interview of Rev. LePage.

Earlier that day she received a call at her office from an anonymous source who told her that she should listen to a particular Brooklyn radio show that afternoon. “Someone is going to be interviewed about a case you have an interest in,” the caller said.

Thinking the case was the police precinct parking lot fire she was working on, but having no luck in solving, Kathy tuned in to hear the host announce that Rev. Vernon LePage would be on to talk all about Jackson Chase, “The alleged killer of police officers Chris Massey and Norman Tenuta.”

Kathy *was* interested in the case because she knew that it was Michael’s. When she called to tell him what she just heard, Michael’s reaction was, “Who the hell is Rev. Vernon LePage?”

He’d soon have the answer. And it was one he didn’t like.

LePage told the interviewer, Julie Pope, that he became involved with Jackson Chase when he received a request from his son, who, he added, was "tragically and unjustly confined" in the Brooklyn House of Detention, "To visit a fellow prisoner, brother Chase."

LePage said his son Frankie was wrongfully convicted a few years back of grand larceny and was serving his sentence in Attica, where Chase was his cellmate for a short time.

He said his son told him that Chase was a fine man, who rescued him from some real trouble during their time together in prison.

"My boy is no tough guy, and when he was set upon in the prison by bigger than him, Chase went to his aid and quashed the trouble. So when Frankie asked me to go see Chase in the Brooklyn House, to give him some help and counsel, I was happy to do it."

LePage said that he found Chase to be, "As fine a man as my son told me he was."

He told the interviewer that Chase was lost and wanted spiritual guidance because he had been a Christian early in his life but had lost his way.

"He asked me to bring him back to Christianity, which I did. I counseled him and taught him, and when he was ready I baptized him. I'm proud to say that Jax Chase has been born again. And knowing him the way I now do; I can say that I find it impossible to believe that he killed two New York City police officers in cold blood. Ms. Pope, the police and the district attorney have arrested the wrong man."

When the interviewer asked how he could be so sure, LePage said there were three reasons.

"The first is a police radio broadcast, from the scene. Minutes after the shooting, a police officer transmitted over the official NYPD radio that a shooter got away and gave his description as a five foot five-five foot six, Hispanic male. Clearly, Ms. Pope, that couldn't be Mr. Chase. Jackson is a tall white man."

LePage said the second reason is that despite having that description, the police arrested Mr. Chase for the murders of Tenuta and Massey. "They did that only after they found out he was in Attica for killing the son of a retired New York State trooper. They then proceeded to extract retribution and beat the man to a pulp."

"Their thinking: 'he killed the son of a cop, *so'*... please excuse my language Ms. Pope, 'who gives a shit if he doesn't fit the description of the shooter who got away. Let him rot in the Brooklyn House of Detention, until someone gets him off.'"

"And last, if Chase shot those two police officers, then fled the scene in the car in which he was later arrested, why was no gun found in that car? Why was no gun found anywhere between the shooting scene and where the car accident occurred? The answer, Ms. Pope, is because Jackson Chase did not shoot those cops."

"That's how I can be so sure."

CHAPTER
SIXTEEN

After listening to the interview, Michael was speechless. He sat at his desk and didn't move until his cell phone rang. It was Kathy.

When he answered he was barely audible. "Michael, are you okay?" she asked.

He didn't respond. So, she asked again, but this time she yelled into the phone. Michael snapped out of his trance and apologized.

"Sorry, I was thinking."

'*Was LePage just a man of the cloth doing a good deed at the request of his son. Or, could he be the reverend from the car accident scene who seemed to be doing the bidding of the guy with the red dreadlocks, that Denny James told me about,*' Michael wondered.

If it was the former, LePage's feelings about Chase and thoughts of his innocence were understandable because of what Chase did for his son. And, if '*he testifies for the defense, I'll handle him on cross-examination,*' Michael thought.

On the other hand, if it was the latter, then LePage was a clear and present danger to the prosecution, and the radio interview would not be the last '*I hear from him,*' Michael told himself.

A man of the cloth corrupted and co-opted by Satan to become *HIS* pawn, something Michael believed was impossible, would insert himself into Chase's defense and would do everything he was told to do to subvert the prosecution's case.

Michael needed to find out quickly which LePage he would be dealing with. With Kathy on the phone he began to put a plan in motion that he hoped would give him the answer.

He asked her to have the Fire Marshal's office trace that phone call she received alerting her to the radio interview.

If the trace revealed that it was made from a phone belonging to Rev. LePage or his church, Michael would send investigators to interview him to determine if the reverend was being truthful when he said on the radio that he was motivated to counsel, baptize, and support Chase to repay him for saving his son in Attica. Michael would then prepare for the potential testimony from LePage as he would any defense witness.

However, if the trace produced no results, or the fire marshals were unable to determine the source of the call, it would confirm what Michael felt in his heart of hearts: it was the EVIL ONE who made it, that *HE* instigated LePage's 'kindness' to Chase, and his likely testimony on Chase's behalf. Michael would then have to prepare for LePage in a very different way.

Kathy told Michael that she would have her tech people get on the trace immediately.

"I know how busy you are but maybe a little break would help you clear your mind and recharge," she said. "How about dinner at my place on Saturday? You can even stay over. Sunday bagels and coffee would be a great way to top off the weekend. What do you say Michael?"

He didn't hesitate, "I'll see you Saturday night. And I know just what wine to bring. But I hope I'll hear from you before I see you."

"Michael, don't worry. As soon as I hear from my tech people I'll call you. Now go home and get some sleep."

When he hung up with Kathy he called Monsignor Romano. He wanted to put part two of his plan in place.

"Sal, I have a request. I need Tim and Dina again."

Tim Clark and Dina Mitchell were investigators who worked for Michael in the rackets division of the district attorney's office. However, when he began his assignment with Caldwell, Michael could no longer use them without first getting the district attorney's permission.

In past cases when he needed their superior investigative and people skills, Michael asked Romano to have Caldwell speak to DA Price. The DA was very happy to accommodate the former Attorney General who chose Price's Chief of Rackets to work on a top secret government assignment. Price considered it a feather in his political cap. So anytime Caldwell asked for the DA's help, the answer was always yes.

As for Tim and Dina, they were unaware of Michael's role in Caldwell's group. Therefore, anytime he gave them an assignment in one of the cases involving the EVIL ONE, the investigators believed it was for a high profile rackets case. They always delivered and never let him down. It was why Michael wanted them assigned to him again.

Before Romano could ask why the investigators were needed, Michael told him that Kathy Baer received a call at her office alerting her to the LePage radio interview.

"Sal, you and Caldwell said I should monitor Kathy and her fire case, and to let you know if there was interference or trouble from Satan. That call to her is not *exactly* on point; however, *HE* did reach her on her office phone to alert her to the interview. A message I'm sure was for me. The caller said the interview was about a case 'she had an interest in,' the Tenuta and Massey murders. Her only interest in that case is ME!"

"*HE's* trying to intimidate me. *HE* wanted to make sure I heard that interview because LePage potentially creates a serious issue for the case, *AND, HE* used my girlfriend to deliver that message."

Romano listened and finally spoke. "Michael before I phone Caldwell I want you to tell me more about the interview, more about the person who was interviewed and what serious issue you believe could be raised, and I'll get to Caldwell as soon as we're done."

Michael did as Romano asked.

"Mike, over the years I've gotten to know many of the Protestant clergy in Brooklyn, but I've never heard of Vernon LePage," Romano said.

"Are you sure he's a legitimate reverend?"

"No I'm not," Michael responded. "That's why I want Tim and Dina. I need them to do a deep dive into this guy. They're good with people so I'm confident they'll find the answer to that question.

"Okay I understand," Romano said

"I'll tell him about LePage and what he said in that interview, and you need the investigators to find everything there is to know about him, because he's a likely defense witness. I'm sure getting Tim and Dina will not be a problem."

"Also be assured that I will alert Caldwell that the EVIL ONE using Kathy to deliver the message about LePage's interview concerns you. He knows how you feel about her, so he'll take your concern very seriously," the monsignor said.

"Great, thank you."

Romano wasn't finished.

"Mike, I wouldn't be your friend if I didn't say this, you can't let this concern with Kathy distract you or throw you off your game. *HE's* done that to prosecutors around the world. It's why *HE*'s been so successful creating chaos and upheaval. But when you came along and began to battle, you've shown *HIM* you're different. *HE* can't beat you. So, knowing how close you are to Kathy, *HE* believes *HE's* found a weakness, your Achilles heel. By reaching her and making sure you know *HE* can get to her, *HE* believes you'll be so troubled, so concerned with her safety and welfare, that *HE'll* finally defeat you. And with defeat *HE* believes you'll quit. I won't let that happen, Caldwell won't let that happen, and you *can't* let that happen."

The next morning when Michael walked into his office, Tim Clark and Dina Mitchell were waiting for him.

Romano woke him up at 6 a.m. to let him know that Caldwell reached DA Price the night before and said, "Tim and Dina are yours for as long as you need them."

"And Michael, Caldwell told me to tell you that he's heard you. More will be done to make sure no harm comes to Kathy. She won't know it, but as he did with your family a while back when you were concerned about them, he's assigned undercover agents to watch over her."

"Sal, please thank him and let him know how much I appreciate it. Also tell him that he need not worry about me being distracted. Each time the EVIL ONE does something in an attempt to weaken my resolve to beat him, the stronger it gets."

"And one more thing, you didn't say it, but you don't have to worry about me doing anything or saying anything to Kathy about her protection. I learned how to cover that when I had to keep it from my dad, sister, and the boys."

Romano laughed, saying, "The thought never entered my mind," but Michael knew his old friend was just being kind.

CHAPTER SEVENTEEN

After he told them the history of the case and what he knew of the players, Michael explained to Tim and Dina what he needed them to do and why. Not being able to reveal who Michael strongly felt was controlling LePage, he merely told them that he expected the reverend to be a character witness for Chase.

"Guys, a man of the cloth attesting to Chase's character, after baptizing him because he found God, will make a very compelling witness. And if there are followers of the reverend who he persuades to testify after he tells them the story of Chase's redemption, that's a formidable defense that I'll need plenty of ammunition to defeat," Michael explained.

"I need to know everything you can find about Rev. LePage. Is he a legit reverend? Does he have a church? And if so, what's the size and composition of his congregation? Are any of them notable, respected, prominent, heavy weights that will impress a jury with their name, occupation, and background before they utter a word of testimony for Jackson Chase?"

He added that time was of the essence because on Monday, when the case was next on Judge Cooper's calendar, he expected her to set a trial date. "From what I was told," Michael said, "She's been directed to start jury selection in a few weeks."

The People of the State of New York v. Jackson Chase was on a fast track. Michael heard from contacts in the courthouse that the administrative judge was pushing Cooper to move the case to trial as soon as possible. Apparently he was feeling the heat from the same sources who pressured him to have Chase arraigned so quickly after his arrest.

A trial that involved the brutal murder of two cops while they were on special assignment because of a deal between the mayor's office, and the Midwood Merchants Association, and approved by the NYPD, was something the powers that be wanted over and done with quickly.

Add to that the alleged murderer was an escapee from New York State's most secure prison, which raised all kinds of questions in the state capital, one could see why the squeeze was on to get Chase to trial.

Tim and Dina were smart, savvy investigators so Michael didn't have to say anything more. They knew what needed to be done and got right to it. "Mike, we'll keep you posted," Dina said as they left the office.

On Monday, Michael was in Judge Cooper's courtroom bright and early. What he thought would happen, did. Judge Cooper set the trial to begin three weeks from that day.

She told Michael and Elton Combes that if any issues which needed her attention arose during those three weeks, they were to call her chambers immediately and she would convene a session of the court to deal with them.

"As for discovery, Mr. Gioca, has it all been provided to the defense?" Cooper asked.

When Michael told her that Combes had all he was entitled to, the judge said, "Good, because I don't want any issue that could delay the start, unresolved."

She adjourned the session, adding, "I'll see you gentlemen in three weeks."

As soon as Michael got back to his office, he called Tony Martino.

"Detective Martino, *come stai?*"

Martino laughed and told Michael that he was well. "Boy you sound like you're in a good mood," he said. "Things must have gone well in court this morning."

"Tony, they did. We're set to start the trial in three weeks. That should make everyone on our side very happy. And I had a great weekend!"

Michael kept his date with Kathy on Saturday night, and it was perfect! Being a great cook, she prepared a terrific dinner, which Michael complemented with a bottle of his favorite *Nero d'Avola*. The wine was the perfect companion to the rigatoni Bolognese Kathy surprised him with.

After a lazy morning of bagels, coffee, and the Sunday newspapers, the two took an afternoon walk and topped off the day with an early dinner at Kathy's favorite neighborhood restaurant.

Although Michael wanted to spend another night with her, he needed to go home to prepare for the next day's court appearance. Before he left they embraced, and while holding her Michael said, "You know I could get used to this." All Kathy could do was nod in agreement, because her tears wouldn't permit her to speak.

Michael kept the details of the weekend to himself but brought Tony up to date on the trial schedule set by Judge Cooper. He told him that he would need to begin contacting the witnesses and setting up dates to prepare them for their testimony.

"No problem Mike. I'll get right on it. When do you want to start talking to them?" Tony asked.

"Tony, if you can get one or more starting tomorrow, that would be great. Some of them are going to need a lot of prep, so the more time I have with them the better."

"I'll start with notifying Denny James and Paul Sira."

"Tony when you do that please notify the training officer from the police academy who testified in the grand jury to call me so I can schedule his prep session."

Michael wanted him because he was certain that Combes would try to convince the jury that James and Sira weren't protecting themselves when they beat Chase, they were punishing him for what they believed was the execution of two fellow officers. He needed the training officer to tell the jury that the cops were following the law and doing what they were taught in the academy.

"No problem Mike. I'll also find out when Gabriel Angelos is working and notify him."

"As for the civilian witnesses, Guy Raimondi doesn't live far from the station house, so I'll go over to him now and see if he's available for this afternoon. If he is, I'll drive him down to your office. And I'll call Eva and Joanie Snow to find out when they're available."

Michael thanked Tony and next called the Medical Examiner's office to schedule the ME who performed the autopsies for a prep session. He also reached out for Dr. Marcus, ADA Justin Turner, and a ballistics expert from the NYPD lab.

Michael decided that he would face the issue of the bullet in Chase's leg and the reason it was not removed, head on. He felt that being up front with the jury and getting this all out during the prosecution's case would serve two purposes.

It would show, and hopefully impress, the jury that although the bullet could be crucial evidence of the defendant's guilt, the prosecution was not so bloodthirsty as to put a man's life in jeopardy to retrieve it.

And, he was certain that if he waited for the defense to put this issue before the jury and argue that the prosecution was hiding something that was damaging to its case, any attempt by him to explain it away later, would not have much impact on the jury. So, bringing the issue before the jury first, and doing it on his terms during the prosecution's case, was essential.

Ten minutes later Turner was in Michael's office being prepped for trial testimony. Josh Turner was a smart, experienced prosecutor, and he knew why Michael was going to use him at trial. Consequently, his preparation didn't take very long. After an hour, he was gone and as Michael was putting away the documents and notes he used to prep Turner, his phone rang.

"Mike, I got Raimondi for this afternoon," Tony Martino said. "We'll be at your office at two. Is that okay?"

"Perfect Tony. Any luck with the others?"

Tony told him that both Denny James and Paul Sira would be there the next morning and Gabriel Angelos would come in on Wednesday morning.

"I haven't reached the Snow sisters yet but I left a message on their apartment answering machine. Do you believe they still got one of those? Their home number is the only one they gave me. I'll stop by their apartment on my way home after my shift. If they're home I'll tell them they need to talk to you and I'll get their cell numbers if they got them."

Michael spent the afternoon with Guy Raimondi. Tony Martino brought him to the office and offered to stay until the prep session was over so he could drive Raimondi back home.

Raimondi was excellent.

When they were done, Michael shook his head and smiled as he watched Raimondi and Tony walk out of his office. The prep session went well and Raimondi was excellent. It was his attire, and something he said to Michael before he left that caused the reaction.

When Michael first met Raimondi he was dressed and sounded like the stereotypical Brooklyn, Bronx, Queens, and Staten Island wiseguy gangster. When he testified in the grand jury, Raimondi was totally different. He wore a gray double breasted suit, a white shirt with a maroon tie, and black Gucci loafers.

"He dressed like John Gotti," Michael said later that night when Kathy called him and asked how Raimondi did in the grand jury. "He answered the questions in his pronounced Brooklyn accent, but he refrained from any Brooklynese street expressions until he said goodbye to the grand jurors. Kathy, they loved him."

When Tony brought him in for his prep session, Michael had all he could do to stop himself from laughing out loud. Raimondi reverted to the way he was dressed when they first met. This time, however, his track suit was bright red. He was wearing a white polo shirt with the collar outside his jacket, and green sneakers. He looked like a walking version of the flag of Italy!

Like his grand jury testimony, his prep session was terrific. He answered Michael's questions completely and without hesitation. However, unlike in the grand jury, he occasionally used the Brooklyn street lingo expressions that were second nature to him, in his answers. Each time he did Michael pointed it out and warned him against using them.

"Guy, the jurors are Brooklynites like you," Michael said, "but they'll probably be people who come from very different ethnic and racial backgrounds than you. They may take offense or think you're stupid and classless if you testify that way. And they may hold it against you and choose to ignore or disbelieve what you've told them."

"Guy, you're neither stupid nor low class. So, remember, you're not in the street or on the corner bullshitting with the guys, when you tell those twelve people what you know. Before you answer, think about what you're going to say and *HOW* you're going to say it. Okay?"

Raimondi stood and offered his hand to Michael. When he took it, in very measured tones and with only the hint of that Brooklyn accent, he said, "Mr. Gioca, I understand all you've said, and I accept all you've said. I swear on my mother's grave that you have nothing to worry about. And just so you know how serious I am about helping you, I'm gonna' practice speaking in front of the bedroom mirror in my apartment."

It was Raimondi's little goodbye speech that brought the smile to Michael's face.

CHAPTER EIGHTEEN

Over the next week Michael prepped Denny James, Paul Sira, and Gabriel Angelos. At the start of their prep sessions, James and Sira were somewhat hesitant and unsure. It was clear to Michael that they blamed themselves for the missing gun but were more troubled and worried about how the judge and jury would react to what happened in the ambulance.

Even though he himself was concerned about the missing gun, to reassure James and Sira, and himself, Michael told them that he believed the missing gun problem would be negated by the testimony of the eyewitnesses.

"Guys, we have three terrific witnesses who put Chase and Sabar on that street, two of whom saw the actual shooting. I won't lie and tell you the missing gun isn't a problem, but it's a problem I can and will handle."

As for their actions in the ambulance he took another tact.

When he finished prepping them Michael asked James and Sira to stay. He was scheduled to prep the training officer from the police academy next, and he wanted James and Sira to hear what he had to say about their actions in that ambulance. He hoped it would relieve them of their anxiety.

He was right. When they left that day, Michael felt that both would do extremely well on the witness stand.

It was much the same with Angelos. When Michael asked him about the radio transmission, he hung his head and said that his error was haunting him. "I'll never forgive myself if Chase is acquitted," he told Michael.

Gioca was ready for Angelos' reaction.

He remembered how he acted in the precinct interview room back when Michael first met him. So, before he sat with Angelos to prep him, he called a psychologist, Dr. Emily Schmetterer, who he got to know from a prior case, to ask for her insight on how he should handle him.

Her advice was on the money.

Tough love, or at least a version of it, was the answer. Holding his hand and commiserating with him would only go so far. Dr. Schmetterer told Michael he needed to make sure Angelos faced his demons, was honest about his feelings, and was prepared to admit that he made a mistake.

What she said next called to mind what Monsignor Romano said to Michael about another witness, Joanie Snow, when they discussed her honesty and candor about her drug addiction and her recovery.

"Mr. Gioca, a redemption story, is both powerful and inspiring. If police officer Angelos does everything I've suggested, he will have the jury eating out of his hand."

So, with the doctor's advice ringing in his head, Michael played amateur psychiatrist, and professional prosecutor, for the many hours he worked with Angelos. And, as with James and Sira, when he left Michael's office he did so with his head held high, and with an unmistakable air of confidence about him.

On Friday, Michael spent a few hours with Dr. Marcus. To accommodate the doctor's schedule, Michael prepped him in his office at Kings County Hospital.

Marcus was a veteran when it came to testifying because he was often called upon to provide expert testimony in both civil and criminal trials over the many years he worked at the hospital. His answers to Michael's questions were crisp, complete, and scholarly. But it was his delivery that pleased Gioca the most.

That evening Michael met Kathy for dinner. He was in an upbeat mood throughout the meal as he told Kathy how well his prep of the cops turned out.

"That's great Michael. How did it go with Dr. Marcus?" she asked.

"His prep went very well," he said. "But Kathy there's more."

Michael began to smile as he continued, "On the witness stand Dr. David Marcus has few peers. But the best part of his testimony is the way he delivers it. He answers in a polished, authoritative, booming, but controlled voice. It sounds like the almighty delivering a sermon from on high. He's going to be great in front of that jury."

Michael spent the next day working with the medical examiner who performed the autopsies, a doctor and nurse who worked on Massey and Tenuta when they arrived at the emergency room, and the doctor who examined and attended to Jax Chase when he was brought into the same ER after the ambulance delivered him to the hospital.

In addition to prepping them about their work on the wounded cops and Chase, Michael prepped them all to answer that they had never heard of Dr. John Milton, in the event the issue of who ADA Turner spoke to before Chase's arraignment became part of the trial.

On Sunday, Michael interviewed and prepared the members of the Massey and Tenuta families who identified the bodies at the New York City morgue. He followed that with the prep of a ballistics expert from the NYPD lab.

The expert would testify that, using the enhanced X-rays of Chase's leg taken at Kings County Hospital, he measured the image of the bullet, and in his opinion it was the same caliber and size as the bullets issued to all NYPD officers for use in their on duty guns.

By Sunday evening, with two weeks to go before jury selection, Michael had prepared all his witnesses with the exception of Eva and Joanie Snow.

Although he was at it for a week, Tony Martino was unable to reach the two most important, and only eyewitnesses to the murders. On Monday morning he called Michael to tell him why.

"Mike, it's Tony. Eva Snow is dead."

Tony said that he was finally able to reach Joanie Snow on her cell phone. "I could barely hear her when she told me about her sister."

"I went over to her apartment right away and when she answered the door she collapsed into my arms. When I got her to calm down she told me the story."

"Joanie said that two weeks ago Eva kept a 9 a.m. appointment she had with her dentist's office to have her teeth cleaned. Like clockwork she did that twice a year," Tony said.

Joanie told him that the dentist's office is a few blocks away from their apartment building and the procedure takes about an hour. After Eva's cleaning, the sisters planned to do some shopping, so Joanie stayed in their apartment to wait for Eva to return. "She said that it was well over an hour, and her sister was still not back. She started to worry, so she called the dentist's office."

"All she was told was that she needed to get to the office right away. So, she ran, and when she arrived she panicked when saw an ambulance parked outside."

When she went in she was met by the receptionist who ushered her into the dentist's private office. That's when the dentist told her that "Eva died in the chair."

When she asked what happened, the dentist said that the hygienist who was scheduled to do the cleaning brought Eva into the procedure room and told her to sit in the chair and relax while she retrieved some supplies she needed for the cleaning procedure. Eva was left alone when she did that.

When the hygienist returned it appeared that Eva had fallen

asleep, so she tried to wake her. When she didn't respond the hygienist checked Eva's pulse and didn't find one. She yelled for help and the dentist responded. He also checked for a pulse and if Eva was breathing. When he found none and no breath sounds, his staff called 911.

"Joanie told me that it was the EMTs who pronounced Eva dead," Tony added.

When Tony first told him the bad news, Michael was shocked into silence. He heard everything Martino said about the circumstances of the death, but he could not utter a single word.

Finally, he asked, "Tony, why didn't Joanie tell you or me about this right after it happened?"

"Mike, she admitted to getting my phone messages, but she was too distraught to talk and too scared to leave her apartment."

Tony continued, "Joanie is not the most stable person, so when her sister died like that she broke down. They have no family, only each other. When I asked her why she didn't call me, she said she was too afraid. Despite what the dentist told her, Joanie believes Eva was murdered and she might be next. She said she thinks it has to do with this case."

When he heard that, Michael thought, '*She might very well be right.*

"Tony, do you think it's a coincidence that just when you began to reach out to Eva and Joanie so I could prep them for the most crucial testimony of this trial, the best witness in my case dies in such an unbelievable way?"

"No, I don't believe in coincidences," Tony replied. "Especially after what I found out from the ME."

"Even though there were no obvious signs of violence on Eva's body, the medical examiner is required to do an autopsy in unexplained deaths like this one. Before I called you I checked and was able to speak to the chief ME. He confirmed that the body *was* brought to the morgue. But Mike, you need to be sitting down when you hear what I'm about to tell you."

Michael braced for the worst, but he knew in his gut that he wouldn't be surprised by what Tony was about to say. "I'm sitting. Let's hear it."

"Mike, the chief himself did the autopsy on Eva and he couldn't determine a cause of death, so he classified it initially as 'undetermined.' This was not unprecedented, so he did what he has done in the past in situations like this, he sent samples of Eva's blood, skin, bodily fluids, and sections of her vital organs to the lab for further analysis.

"He got back the results yesterday," Tony said, "And this is where it gets crazy. The lab found nothing that would explain her death."

Tony said that as a result the ME can't call it death by natural causes, or an accidental death, nor can he classify it as a homicide. "Mike, he said he has no explanation for why this healthy, young woman, in the prime of her life died in that chair. Officially he listed Eva's cause of death as 'undetermined.'"

Michael didn't react immediately. He sat thinking, '*The ME might not have an explanation, but I do. The EVIL ONE murdered the best witness I had against Chase! And HE did it covertly, with no possible explanation, so I would know it was HIM. I can't let that stop me.*'

"Tony, where's the body?" Michael asked.

"Why? How would knowing where the body is help us? I just told you what the ME said."

"I have an idea," Michael answered.

Tony told him, "Joanie said after the autopsy the ME released the body and a few friends arranged for a funeral and burial."

"Tony, please find out where Eva is buried and let me know."

"And Tony, when you talk to Joanie let her know that I need to see her. The trial is scheduled to begin in two weeks, and I'm running short on time. I need to prep her, now more than ever."

"Do you believe you can get through to her? She does seem to like and trust you."

"It's gonna' be tough but I'll try. She's scared out of her mind," Tony said.

"Tell her you'll pick her up and bring her in. That should work. And if it doesn't, I'll go to her. What do you think?"

"Mike, all of that sounds good. But you didn't see how broken she is. To get her to cooperate in a way that's gonna' pay off at trial, I got to tell her something that will put her at ease."

"Okay, I hear you," Michael said. "Tell her we'll protect her until she testifies, and then we'll move her anywhere she wants to go. Do you think that will do it?" Michael asked.

"I'll let you know. I'll go see her right now."

While he waited to hear from Tony, Michael began to work on his idea. The first step required Caldwell to enlist the help of the FBI. So Michael called Monsignor Romano.

CHAPTER NINETEEN

"Sal, are you in your office?" Michael asked when the monsignor answered his call.

"And a very good morning to you too my friend," Romano sarcastically responded.

"I'm sorry," Michael said. "I know that was rude, but something disastrous has happened and we need to talk. Can I come to see you?"

Twenty minutes later Michael walked into Romano's Red Hook office. "Please forgive me for the way I spoke before," he said, as he put two large cappuccinos and a bag of the monsignor's favorite almond croissants on his desk.

"Forgiveness depends on how hot the cappuccino is," Romano responded with a smile. He pointed to the chair in front of his desk and said, "Sit and tell me what's happened."

For the next hour Michael filled in the monsignor on the status of the case and his preparation, and ended with the Eva Snow "disaster," as he called it.

"Sal, Eva was the best and most complete and convincing witness I had. That leaves me with her sister Joanie, if she'll still testify, as my only eyewitness to the shooting. And to call her problematic is an understatement. I'm hoping Tony Martino can persuade her to speak to me and then I'm going to have to work my ass off, first to convince her to testify and then to prep her so she's ready."

"I understand," Romano said. "I assume your idea has something to do with filling in the hole in your case created by Eva's death?"

"Exactly!" Michael said. He jokingly added, "Sal, you're getting good at this. Soon you'll be able to try these cases yourself and you won't need me any longer."

Romano laughed. "As I told you many times when we were kids, stop with the bullshit, and tell me how can I help?"

Michael responded with an explanation of what he needed from Caldwell. It would strengthen his case and help to ensure that justice will be served. It involved significant FBI resources that could turn the jury in his favor.

Romano understood. "I'll speak to Caldwell right away. I know time is of the essence and I'll make sure he knows that. This may be a tough ask for him with the FBI, but my money's on the former Attorney General."

When Michael got back to his office Tim Clark and Dina Mitchell were waiting for him. Michael called the investigators as he drove from Red Hook and asked to see them.

"Guys, how's it going with finding info on Rev. LePage," he asked.

They told him that it's been tough going. "Mike, at first we ran into a lot of opposition," Tim said. "However, when Dina used her contacts a few people agreed to talk to us."

"But they were of little help," Dina offered. "I spoke to my mom and dad who have been faithful church goers since I was a little girl. And they've been doing charity work with black clerics in Brooklyn for decades. Dad put me in touch with a few, but none of the ministers we spoke to knew LePage, although they heard that he had some 'big shots', their words, in his congregation. That surprised me."

When Michael asked why, Dina told him that the African American and Caribbean clerics in Brooklyn were a very close knit group. "They may represent different congregations, and have different constituencies, but they all have similar problems, which makes for lots of cooperation among them. Mike, if they are unfamiliar with LePage, then I'm starting to think he may not be legitimate," she said. "And having heavy hitters in his congregation under those circumstances, is very unusual."

Tim followed with, "But Mike we do have some leads on some people who have been seen going to services in his 'church,' if you can call it that, on Sunday mornings. Dina and I are gonna' stake out the place this weekend and see what we can see."

Curious about Tim's comment about LePage's church, Michael asked him for an explanation.

"Mike, the building is on the corner in Midwood where the car accident occurred, and it's in disrepair. It's brick and mortar with pieces of the mortar missing throughout the exterior. What passes for the church is a storefront on the street level. Its front windows are covered with plywood when open for services, and when it's not, steel gates cover the entire front of the store."

"We checked with the buildings department and found out that LePage and some of his followers live in the apartments over the church. The Cathedral of St. John the Divine on Morningside Heights, it ain't."

"Okay, keep at it and let me know what you see and/or find out on Sunday. And guys, please be careful," Michael said as they left.

When he checked his watch he saw that four hours had passed since Tony Martino left to speak to Joanie Snow, and there was no word from him. And it was two hours since he left Romano, and he hadn't heard from the monsignor either. Michael hoped that no news was good news.

He decided to take a walk to get something to eat. He was lost in thought when he realized that he was right outside *The Queen* pizzeria, so he bought a slice and a Coke and sat in the park outside the Brooklyn Supreme Court building to eat his lunch.

When his cell phone rang Michael said a silent prayer for good news before he looked to see who was calling. When he saw it was Tony his gut and his faith told him it was the news he prayed for. So he started to walk back to his office as he answered.

"Yes!" he yelled when he disconnected the call after Tony told him that he was on his way with Joanie Snow.

Before he walked into his building, Michael looked skyward and said, "Thank you."

Joanie was a mess. She was shivering despite the warmth of Michael's office and she was holding onto Tony's arm so tightly that Michael was sure the circulation was cut off.

Tony told her to sit in one of the chairs in front of Michael's desk and as she did she missed the seat and fell onto the floor. When Tony helped her up she was crying.

"Mr. Gioca, I'm no good to you," she said. "I'm scared outta my mind that they're gonna' kill me like they killed Eva. And I can't remember anything."

Michael let her breathe before asking if she was hungry or thirsty. When she told him she'd like some tea, he called one of his assistants and asked him to get it.

"While we're waiting, let me start by saying how sorry I am for your loss. I know how close you and Eva were and I can't imagine how devastated you are over her death. I will do anything to ease your pain, and to help you, including, as I'm sure Tony told you, moving you out of your apartment to anywhere you want to go."

Just then the tea arrived and Joanie took a big gulp which seemed to calm her a bit.

Michael continued, "Tony told me, and I can see for myself, how frightened you are. Joanie, I can move you to a hotel today. You can live there until the trial is over, and then we'll find a more permanent home for you. And no one, other than me, Tony, and our investigators, will know you're there. How does that sound?"

Joanie finished her tea, looked at Michael and calmly said, "Mr. G, Thank you. That sounds great. I really can't stay in my apartment. Yes, I'm afraid, but more important it's where I lived with my sister since I completed drug rehab. Everything there reminds me of her. It's too painful to be there."

She then dropped her head and said something that surprised and delighted Michael.

"I hate to admit this Mr. G, but I'm a little ashamed of myself. If those bastards killed my sister, then I should be strong and testify, *for her*. But until now, I felt helpless. But you, and Tony, of course, have shown me that I'm not alone in this. I'm ready to help you put that motherfucker in prison forever."

CHAPTER TWENTY

Michael spent the next several hours working with Joanie Snow.

As he expected she was shaky at the start but as they worked she became more confident. By the time they were finished for the day, Joanie was ready for the witness stand. So ready that Michael wished that her testimony would start immediately, because as good as she was *that* day, there was no guarantee that when she took the witness stand, she would hold it together and convince the jury that Chase was a murderer.

'The night before she testifies is going to be a long and busy one,' Michael thought to himself as Joanie and Martino prepared to leave. Tony was taking her home to get what she needed for her hotel stay.

Earlier, right after Joanie agreed to cooperate, Michael called Romano and asked him to approve the expenses to cover her hotel accommodations. And if it became necessary, to approve the cost for agents or investigators to guard her. Romano said it would not be a problem but he needed some time to arrange it. He suggested Michael cover that night and he'd reimburse him.

Michael gave Tony his personal credit card and asked him to

check Joanie into the Brooklyn Marriott Hotel, which shared the building where the DA's office was located. It would only be for the night. Michael would find different lodging for her in the morning once Romano got back to him.

When they left Michael checked his watch. It was 7 p.m. and he was starving. The slice of pizza he had for lunch was a distant memory. He decided to kill two birds with one stone. He called Romano again to ask for any news from Caldwell and to invite him to *Emilio's* for dinner.

When Romano walked into the restaurant he was surprised that Michael was already there. Emilio greeted the monsignor and escorted him to his table.

Michael had a glass of red wine in front of him, and Emilio promptly filled the empty glass at the monsignor's place from the bottle of *Chianti Classico* that Michael ordered.

"*Salute*," Gioca said as he and his friend clinked glasses. Before Romano could put down his glass, Michael asked about Caldwell.

"Please, can I enjoy this first sip before you nag me about him?" a seemingly annoyed Romano said as he placed his glass on the table.

Michael was a bit taken aback by Romano's response. He didn't know what to make of it until the monsignor could no longer hold his look of aggravation and burst out laughing.

"You know what Sal, not Monsignor Sal, just Sal from the old neighborhood, fuck you!" Michael responded, *sotto voce*, as the two continued to laugh. "You had me. I was thinking what did I do to bring that on? Little did I know that it was nothing more than you breaking my chops."

"I'm sorry Mike. I thought you could use a laugh before I gave you the bad news," Romano said in a low and very serious tone.

Once Michael heard the words 'The bad news', he gulped his wine and braced himself for it.

Romano broke into a big smile and said, "Caldwell has gotten the FBI to agree to do what you need."

Michael was stunned. He thought he misheard what Romano said.

Romano saw the look on his face and said, "I got ya'... again," before bursting into laughter louder and heartier than before.

Michael ultimately got the joke, and although he was annoyed at how his friend played it, he was thrilled with the news. *'If Sal breaking my balls is what I had to go through to hear that news, it was worth it,'* he thought as Romano poured him another glass of wine.

"Son of a bitch," Michael finally said, a little too loudly as the white haired elderly woman sitting at the next table shook her head and gave him a disapproving look.

"You almost caused me to have a heart attack with that 'bad news' crack. I already started to think about what else I could do to make up for losing Eva as a witness, and I was drawing a blank. So to hell with grandma over there, you are a son of a bitch.... But you're a good one; you came through for me. Now pray that my idea works."

Romano smiled, the two friends clinked glasses, as Emilio came to the table. "Are you gentlemen ready to order?" he asked.

After dinner, the monsignor drove Michael the short distance to his apartment. Before Michael left the car Romano assured him that the expense issues would be taken care of in the morning, and added, "You'll be hearing from the FBI sometime during the day."

Michael thanked him and began to leave the car. Romano grabbed his arm to stop him, and said, "Mike I'm sorry for all the joking but I thought you could use a few laughs because you've been working so hard."

Michael paused before responding in a very serious tone of voice, "Sal no apology necessary. But if you ever do that to me again, I can't be held responsible for what I might do."

Romano, now concerned that he may have gone too far, said "I hope I wasn't out of line. Sorry."

It was Michael's turn to laugh. "Ahh! Now I got you!" he said as he left the car and walked around to the driver's side. He leaned in the open window and said, "Payback's a bitch. Good night *monsignore*."

All Romano could do was laugh as he drove away.

Two weeks later Michael was in Judge Cooper's courtroom for the first day of jury selection.

During that time, Joanie Snow was settled into a motel in the Sheepshead Bay section of Brooklyn, miles away from the courthouse. There was no reason to assign guards to protect her, so she was alone. She was content but anxious to get her testimony behind her so she could start her new life. Michael would have one final prep session with her once a jury had been selected. Joanie was to be his first witness.

As for Guy Raimondi, POs Massey and Tenuta's family members, the medical witnesses from Kings County Hospital, including Dr. Marcus, the medical examiner, and the ballistics expert from the NYPD lab, Michael spent the previous week fine tuning their testimony. He was very pleased by how they handled themselves.

Denny James, Paul Sira, and Gabriel Angelos were prepped again. In addition to making sure their direct examination was perfect, Michael cross-examined the hell out of them! They were ready to go.

And in the event he needed him, Michael prepped the training officer from the police academy once again.

There were two areas left unsettled, however.

Tim Clark and Dina Mitchell were still working on finding all they could about Rev. LePage, but Michael was not concerned. He wouldn't need their findings unless LePage took the stand during the defense case, which was at least a week or two away.

And, while his plan with the FBI was in play, he was told that it would take some time before a determination of success or failure could be made. If it was the latter, his idea for repairing the damage to his case caused by Eva Snow's death was worthless. On the other hand, if it was the former, Michael was confident he'd be able to use what the FBI found to overcome that damage.

The wild card, however, was the timing. If a successful result came too late for him to use in the prosecution's direct case, it would be of no help. However, if Elton Combes made a mistake, either on cross examination of a prosecution witness, or during the defense case, his error could open the door to a rebuttal. That would allow Michael to present the FBI results to the jury for their consideration when deciding if Chase was guilty or not.

As he stepped up to begin the jury selection process, Michael hadn't yet heard from the FBI. To prepare for a worst case scenario, he posed questions to the potential jurors as if the FBI result was negative, or a positive one that came too late for him to use. And, when he decided which jurors to strike, he employed that same thought process.

Three days after they began, Michael and Elton Combes completed the jury selection process, and for the first time all twelve regular, and four alternate jurors, were assembled in the jury box.

The ethnic, racial, and religious composition of the group reflected a cross-section of Brooklyn's population. And while Michael was never completely happy with the final composition of any jury he selected over the years, he was fairly certain that there were no trouble makers among them.

However, knowing the EVIL ONE as he did, it was important that he stay vigilant for any sign of a problem. If *HE* reared *HIS* ugly head, Michael needed to quickly come up with a way to neutralize *HIM,* as he did in one of his earlier cases.

In that case the EVIL ONE approached two jurors right outside the courthouse while they were on their lunch break and persuaded them to vote for the acquittal of a defendant that *HE* seduced into killing an off-duty police officer.

A case with overwhelming evidence of guilt ended in a mistrial because the two compromised jurors ignored the evidence and refused to go along with their ten colleagues who voted to convict.

To prevent a recurrence in the retrial, Michael persuaded the presiding judge to sequester the new jury. This meant that to ensure the integrity of the process, when the jury was not in the courtroom, they would stay together under the watchful eyes of the court officers assigned to protect and guard them. It took *that* jury thirty minutes to convict the defendant.

Michael was prepared to do whatever was necessary to ensure the integrity of this jury, which was sworn in by Judge Cooper. After her preliminary charge on the law, and her admonishment about discussing, reading about, and watching or listening to any reports of the case, she dismissed them and adjourned for the day.

The first witness they would hear from was Joanie Snow.

CHAPTER TWENTY-ONE

At 9:30 a.m. Judge Cooper took the bench, called the court to order, and saw that Jax Chase was not at the defense table.

"Where's the defendant?" she asked her clerk. The answer was, "He's getting dressed."

She turned to Elton Combes and was about to ask him what was going on, when the court officers ushered Chase into the courtroom. It was immediately apparent to everyone what 'He's getting dressed,' meant.

Unlike his attire during jury selection which consisted of dark slacks, an open collar blue dress shirt, and running shoes, Chase was wearing black dress shoes, a medium gray suit, and a shirt of the same color with a clerical collar.

'What the fuck is this? The born again Christian is a born again minister?' Michael wondered.

Fearful of creating an issue for appeal if the defendant was convicted, neither the judge nor Michael said anything about Chase's sudden 'ordination' into the ministry or the clerical garb that he would likely be wearing throughout the trial.

Michael also wasn't concerned. Since Chase hadn't dressed like that for the three days of jury selection, he felt that the jurors would see through the sham and hold it against him. *'What a mistake. The people one-Jax Chase zero,'* he thought to himself.

When the defendant was settled at his table, Judge Cooper asked that the jury be brought into the courtroom. Michael watched as they walked to their seats and saw the surprise on their faces when they looked over at the defendant. Their reaction to Chase's clerical garb confirmed what Michael thought it would be.

When Michael stood to deliver his opening statement, he felt a surge of confidence which carried him through his address. When he finished he was confident that his outline of the evidence had a positive impact on the jury.

Next it was the defendant's turn, and Elton Combes wasted no time in attacking Michael's case.

"Jackson Chase is innocent! The police arrested the wrong man," he began. He proceeded to hammer home the highlight of his case, the police radio broadcast from Gabriel Angelos.

He told the jurors to listen to the broadcast very carefully, "You will hear a police officer, Gabriel Angelos, broadcast to the entire city the identification of the real killer, a five foot five to five foot six hispanic. Is it that man? Of course not."

He asked the jurors to scrutinize the prosecution's case and the witnesses called to support it. "Among those witnesses will be cops who beat, and left for dead, an innocent man."

"Oh they'll tell you Gabriel Angelos made a mistake," he continued, "and point to a bullet in my client's leg, which they want you to believe he received during the gun fight, as proof of the mistake. However, they can't tie that bullet, with any certainty, to either the gun belonging to Massey, or the gun belonging to Tenuta."

Then taking full advantage of Eva Snow's death, he said, "The prosecution has only one eyewitness from a Brooklyn street teaming with apartment buildings that looked out over the scene of this shooting. And that eye witness will testify that she was a drug addict."

He ended with: "No matter what the prosecution tells you to dirty up my client—that he was an escapee from Attica State Prison, which we don't deny—that he was doing time for murder, a killing that you'll hear was self-defense—I implore you to keep an open mind. There will be a defense case and we will show you who Jackson Chase really is and that he did not kill those police officers in front of *Leiser's* jewelry store."

"With the help of one of Brooklyn's most respected Christian ministers, who you will hear from, Jackson Chase found religion; he was born again. And as you can see from his garb, during the last several months, with Rev. Vernon LePage's instruction and spiritual guidance, Mr. Chase was ordained. Now *Rev. Chase* is a practicing minister tending to his flock...the poor unfortunates imprisoned in the Brooklyn House of Detention."

"Ladies and gentlemen, I am certain that when you have heard all the evidence, you will see through this sham of a case and find Rev. Jackson Chase not guilty."

After listening to Combes, and seeing the jurors hanging on every word, Michael knew that he had his work cut out for him. Despite that, he was confident that he would overcome the theatrics with solid, logical evidence delivered by a lineup of civilian witnesses and law enforcement experts with no motive to lie and especially no motive to hang this double murder on an innocent man. Because if Chase was innocent then the actual cop killer was still out there, ready, willing, and able to kill a cop again.

'And if I get lucky,' Michael thought, *'the FBI will come through, and seal the deal.'*

Joanie Snow was Michael's leadoff hitter.

All the hours they spent together, and all their hard work paid off big time. Joanie was a star.

When she was done, she left the witness stand after three hours of direct and intense cross-examination, full of confidence with her head held high.

And when she passed Michael on her way out of the courtroom, she smiled, and whispered, "Thanks, I'm gonna' be okay."

Later when he told Tony Martino how well Joanie did on the stand, Michael mentioned that smile and her comment.

"Tony, when you've done this as long as I have, you get jaded. You think nothing will phase you. But that smile blew me away and her comment reinforced why I do what I do. And as strange as this may sound, I truly believe we did save Joanie Snow."

Over the next two weeks Michael's case went in as well as he could have expected.

Guy Raimondi followed Joanie.

Dressed in a blue suit, white shirt, and a muted blue and red striped tie, he took the witness stand and entertained the jury with his own brand of Brooklynese. At the same time, he wowed them.

He was strong and precise in his testimony; his identification of Chase was definite and unwavering in the face of strong cross-examination by Combes. And as Michael thought it would, his empathy for the dead police officers impressed the jury.

When he climbed down from the witness stand he nodded goodbye to the jurors, who, to a person, returned the *arrivederci* with nods of their own.

Denny James and Paul Sira were next, and were great on direct, but took their lumps on cross.

However, being upfront about what happened in the ambulance and not minimizing what they did, and why they did it, Michael believed, went over well with the jury and somewhat neutralized Combes' vicious examination of the two cops.

When Gabriel Angelos testified he sat straight in the witness chair, looked right at the jury, admitted to making an error and offered no excuse for making it.

"I got the description of the other shooter from a woman who walked up to me while I was tending to officer Massey. I made a mistake. I should have checked her out, and checked out the information she gave me, before I put it on air."

Although Angelos didn't make an excuse for his mistake, Michael knew that an explanation was necessary so the jury would understand the circumstances under which he made it. They had to hear and 'see' what was going on in front of *Leiser's* when he arrived. To figuratively bring the jury to that street, Michael asked Angelos to paint a word picture of the scene and how he felt when he saw the carnage in front of him.

"Mr. Gioca, I been a cop for a lot of years, and I've seen a lot. But when I seen two of my fellow officers, two of my friends, laying on the street bleeding from gunshot wounds to their bodies, I was shaken to the core. I know their families. I been to parties and ballgames with them...." Angelos didn't finish his answer. Instead he dropped his head so the jury wouldn't see the tears.

After several seconds Michael asked him if he had finished his answer.

"No," Angelos answered emphatically.

Looking directly at the jury, he said, "As hard as it was seein' them like that, I ain't ashamed or embarrassed to say, that when I seen that third guy bleeding from a big neck wound, his face covered with blood... even though he brought it on himself... I felt for him and his family. Nobody should die like that."

On cross-examination Combes used Angelos as if he was a defense witness. He painstakingly took him through the moment the woman gave him the description and emphasized that he believed her to be an eyewitness to the shooting, "Which is why I put the description out over the radio," the cop said.

Combes ended his cross asking, "Where is that woman today?" All Angelos could say was "I don't know. We couldn't find her."

Combes had no additional questions.

CHAPTER TWENTY-TWO

The jury was clearly displeased with Angelos' answer. The looks of utter disbelief while shaking their heads troubled Michael but he didn't hang his head.

'Thank God that's not the end,' he thought, and called his next witness.

During the next two days the jury heard from the medical examiner, the doctors and nurses from the emergency room at Kings County Hospital and Dr. Marcus. Michael used him to set up his final witness, the ballistics expert from the NYPD lab.

At the conclusion of the expert's testimony Michael didn't rest his case. He still hadn't gotten definitive word from the FBI on their work.

From the time Caldwell cleared the way for Michael to enlist their help, Gioca was in regular contact with the lab technicians tracking their progress. It was his hope that the work would be completed in time for him to put the finishing touches on the prosecution's case.

But it was not meant to be.

The morning after the ballistics expert testified, and just before he left his office for the courthouse, Michael received a call from the FBI lab. Their work would not be completed in time for him to use on his direct case.

He was disappointed. However, he told the lab to keep working. If they were successful and came up with a positive result, he would use it if Combes made a mistake and the judge allowed him to put a rebuttal case before the jury.

"It's a long shot," he told the lab tech, "But we've got to take it."

When he arrived at the courthouse prepared to tell the judge that he had no additional witnesses, he was surprised by the large group of people gathered on the front steps kneeling and praying. Leading the prayers was Rev. Vernon LePage and standing several feet behind him was the EVIL ONE in the guise of a strange looking man with red dreadlocks.

As Michael passed *HIM* on his way into the building, *HE* fixed on Michael with an ominous stare. But Michael wasn't shaken. The EVIL ONE was a regular courtroom spectator from the first day of the prosecution's case. That played right into Michael's plan. The stronger the connection between the man with the red dreadlocks and the defense, the better the odds that his plan would be successful.

The EVIL ONE's presence in the courtroom was first brought to Michael's attention by Denny James and Paul Sira earlier in the trial. When they finished testifying the judge gave the jury their regular afternoon break. Michael went into the corridor outside the courtroom to make a phone call, and he saw Denny and Paul waiting for him.

"Mr. Gioca," they said, "There's a guy sitting in the back of the courtroom with red dreads, and he's wearing a black covid mask. He's the guy who was yelling at us with the reverend at the car accident scene when we collared Chase."

That identification would become key for Michael.

From then on, each day the red dreads man was there Michael made a point to bring *HIS* presence to the attention of the court officers. Because, if the FBI lab found what Michael was looking for, it would be important to the success of his plan that *HIS* regular presence was officially recognized and noted.

After Michael announced to the court that he had no additional witnesses, Elton Combes began the defense case. His first witness was Rev. Vernon LePage.

LePage was called to provide the jury with evidence of Chase's good character.

His testimony, which he delivered as if he were in his pulpit preaching on Sunday morning, was essentially the same as his interview with Julie Pope on her radio show. And as part of his plan, Michael didn't object to any of Combes' questions nor to any of the reverend's answers.

The reverend's only addition was his account of Chase's ordination as a minister, and the news that "Reverend Chase has developed his own congregation consisting of poor, unfortunate inmates, in need of spiritual guidance locked away in the Brooklyn House of Detention."

LePage told the jury that it was his regular visits to Chase and the spiritual guidance he provided, which "Jackson soaked up like a sponge," that caused the Lord "To look down on brother Chase, and when He did, He saw a changed man. One with a voice, and story the Lord could use to bring His word to those who needed it most."

LePage continued, "So He summoned me to ordain Brother Chase as a minister of His holy word."

Combes, had one final question, "After getting to know Rev. Chase, and after seeing how he reacted to all your instruction and guidance, in your opinion, could Jackson Chase have committed this horrendous crime?"

When he heard the question, Michael used all of his self-control to refrain from cheering. *'Combes took the bait,'* he said to himself.

Under normal circumstances, Michael would have strenuously objected to this question, but he was playing a long game. He needed the answer he knew was coming if his plan was to have any chance of working. So, although the judge looked at him waiting for the objection, Michael sat silently as LePage answered emphatically, "No, he could not."

When LePage finished his direct testimony, Michael asked the court for some time before he began his cross-examination. Since the jury was due for a break the judge told Michael he had fifteen minutes.

Before he left for court that morning Michael met with Tim Clark and Dina Mitchell. He anticipated that Combes would call LePage as his first witness, and he wanted an update on LePage, if the investigators had one.

They didn't.

Michael was disappointed, but not defeated. A trial attorney with his experience always prepares for the worst case scenario. Unable to use what he hoped Tim and Dina would find to dirty up LePage, he planned a cross-examination around what he expected LePage's direct testimony would be. And after he heard it, he was ready.

He began by asking LePage how and when he got to meet Chase.

Michael asked that question because he knew that the reverend's response would serve several purposes for him.

LePage began his answer by telling the jury that Chase was an inmate in Attica State Prison where he was serving a sentence for murder. "My son was also serving a sentence in Attica when he met Rev. Chase."

Revealing to the jury that Chase was a convicted murderer was crucial to the success of Michael's case.

LePage continued his answer, "One day in Attica my son was set upon by some very bad men, fellow inmates. They had some sort of disagreement with him and were going to hurt him in retribution until Rev. Chase stepped in and stopped it."

LePage turned and looked at the jury and said, pointing to Chase, "That fine young man rescued my boy. So, a few months ago, when I went to visit my son in the Brooklyn House of Detention, where he was imprisoned while he and his lawyer appealed his conviction, he introduced me to Rev. Chase. Mr. Gioca, that's when I first met that fine young man."

Michael couldn't have asked for a better answer. It would allow him to argue during his summation that the value of character testimony from someone who barely knows the individual he's vouching for, is practically worthless. And, it showed that LePage owed Chase a big favor, which was returned when he testified on Chase's behalf.

Michael finished his cross with questions, the answers to which he intended to use as the basis for a motion to the judge if the FBI came through for him.

He walked to the rail separating the well of the courtroom from the spectator section, pointed to the gallery and asked LePage, "Reverend, do you see the man with the red hair and covid mask sitting alone in the last row?"

The question brought an objection from Combes that was overruled after Michael asked the judge to give him some leeway.

LePage made a show of trying to locate the person Michael asked about, then answered, "Oh yes, you're referring to Brother Jiz. Sure I know him. He's a valued assistant to me and a member of my church."

"And, reverend, did he ever accompany you when you visited the defendant in the Brooklyn House of Detention?"

"Yes he did, Mr. Gioca. After my first visit, which was a solo visit, Brother Jiz was with me every time."

"Did Brother Jiz give solace and comfort to the defendant in tandem with you?"

"Absolutely. Brother Jiz is a wonderful, compassionate man who came to know and love Rev. Chase as I have."

Michael asked, "Was he with you when you were providing spiritual guidance to the defendant, and instructing him in, as you say, 'The Lord's way', in preparation for his ordination?"

"Yes sir he was. Brother Jiz, as I have just said, is my valued assistant."

"So, you must know that he's been in this courtroom as an interested observer every day since we began to present the evidence in this trial? In fact, sitting in that same spot."

"Yes, I do," LePage proudly answered. "Because I was going to be a trial witness, our... I mean Chase's lawyer, Mr. Combes, told me I wasn't allowed to be in the courtroom until after I testified. So Brother Jiz was here at my direction, and was an interested observer. I told him to make sure he did not miss a word of what went on during your persecution of Rev. Chase. He was my eyes and ears."

Michael had what he needed, and then some. During his summation he would make good use of LePage's slip of tongue when first referring to Combes as 'our lawyer,' before correcting that to 'Chase's lawyer.'

When LePage finished his last answer, Michael simply thanked him and sat down.

When he glanced over at the defense table he saw a look of bewilderment on Combes' face. *'Don't worry Elton,' he thought, 'soon it'll become very clear... I hope.'*

LePage was followed by other 'so-called' prominent citizens of Brooklyn, who just happened to be followers of the reverend and members of his church. Each testified that they met and got to know Chase through Rev. LePage. They said that they regularly visited the defendant in the Brooklyn House, which was very rewarding, because "Rev. Chase was such an inspiration." And each offered the same opinion as LePage when Combes asked about Chase's character.

Michael employed the same cross-examination for all of LePage's flunkies: "When did you meet the defendant, and how did you get to know him?"

He did it to elicit answers that he knew would be well-rehearsed and virtually identical. When he got them, Michael hoped that it wasn't lost on the jury, to whom he would later argue that the answers were worthless.

'Rev. LePage and brother Jiz sure worked long and hard with this

group,' Michael thought when he sat down after he questioned the last of them.

Judge Cooper looked over to Combes and asked if he had any additional witnesses.

Combes wouldn't risk calling Chase in his own defense knowing Michael had the ammunition to tear his testimony apart, especially the born again/ordained minister charade, the reason Chase was doing time in Attica, and his escape.

Nor could Combes risk Michael asking his client to explain what a guy, born and raised in upstate New York, was doing on a street in Midwood, Brooklyn with a fellow Attica escapee Ricky Sabar, and how he got a bullet in his leg.

Character evidence was all Combes had.

He was banking on LePage and his devotees to convince the jury to acquit Chase because people of their caliber, Brooklyn elites, wouldn't testify for a murderer, or for someone who hadn't proven to them that he was incapable of doing what the prosecution charged him with.

So in response to Judge Cooper, Elton Combes announced that he had no additional witnesses and rested the defense case.

CHAPTER
TWENTY-THREE

After sending the jury back to their room, the judge asked Michael if he intended to call additional witnesses in rebuttal.

At this point Michael needed to buy time. The evidence was set up so if the FBI came through, he was confident that when the judge heard his argument she would allow a rebuttal case. However, he didn't know if the lab technicians were close to an answer. And if not, he had to find out how much more time they would need.

Since it was late Friday afternoon Michael decided to ask the judge to allow him to give her an answer on Monday morning. That would give him the weekend to find out the status of the FBI's work.

Judge Cooper granted his request but told him, "If you decide that you're going to proceed, I order you to tell Mr. Combes, and to leave a message on my chambers' voicemail."

Now addressing both Michael and Combes, Cooper said. "Absent a message from Mr. Gioca, I expect both of you gentlemen to proceed with your summations on Monday."

Judge Cooper had the jury brought back into the courtroom to dismiss them for the weekend. "I'll see you bright and early on Monday morning at 9:30 a.m.," she said.

Michael hurried back to his office and called his FBI contact. The news was not good. Michael was told that the lab would need at least another week or so before they could give him an answer.

On Monday morning, Judge Cooper called the court to order. "Mr. Gioca, since I had no message from you over the weekend, I assume that you will be resting your case. Is that correct?"

Michael answered, "Your Honor, that's correct."

"Okay gentlemen, let's proceed to summations."

The jurors were brought into the courtroom and Elton Combes began his closing argument.

For the next hour and thirty minutes, Combes first harped on the description of what he called 'The actual shooter' that Gabriel Angelos broadcast over the police radio.

Smartly, rather than attack Angelos, Combes embraced him as a witness. He told the jury they "Should believe him, because he was candid and forthright on the witness stand."

He told the jury to ignore the ballistics expert, "Because unless he had the actual bullet to examine, his testimony was simply sophisticated guess work." Of course he offered no explanation as to how a bullet just happened to find its way into the defendant's leg.

As for Denny James and Paul Sira, Combes simply told the jury that they should have been arrested for "The brutal, unprovoked and unnecessary assault on my client. What those storm troopers said should never be given any credence. They arrested the wrong man, attempted to kill him in that ambulance so a trial wouldn't be necessary, *AND,* they never found the gun that the prosecution says my client used to kill those police officers."

And last, he made sure the jury did not forget Rev. LePage and what Combes called the "Impressive array of upstanding citizens of faith," who all testified that "Rev. Jackson Chase" was not the kind of person who would wantonly take the lives of two New York City police officers."

He closed with, "Ladies and gentlemen who are you going to

believe, those fine citizens or that junkie Joanie Snow, the only so-called 'eye witness' they have?"

During Combes' address Michael watched the jury. He was looking for and hoping for some reaction that told him they were not buying what Combes was selling. Much to his disappointment he saw none. To a person the twelve regular jurors and the four alternates, remained stoic. Michael knew he had his work cut out for him if he was going to convict Chase.

Although his case was flawed, Michael was confident that he had proven Chase's guilt beyond a reasonable doubt. He had to make sure that the jury saw it the same way.

He began by countering Combes' phony embrace of Gabriel Angelos.

"Mr. Combes tells you to believe officer Angelos, but he only wants you to believe what Angelos put out over the police radio. He wants you to reject the rest of his testimony when he told you the description he broadcast was a mistake."

"I'm asking you to accept *everything* Angelos told you. And accept it with this in mind: is it so hard to believe that he made an error and acted precipitously while he was helping a fellow officer who was bleeding out right in front of him? Ladies and gentlemen, the stress Gabriel Angelos was under at that moment had to be overwhelming. Who among us can say that we would have acted perfectly under those circumstances? I think the answer, if we're honest with ourselves, is none of us."

Michael then moved onto the testimony of Joanie Snow, "The junkie, as Combes so callously and cruelly called her."

Michael argued that Combes must not have been paying attention to Joanie's testimony when "She honestly and candidly told you about her addiction, but also told you about her battle with recovery. Opening up like that to twelve perfect strangers takes guts. Joanie Snow didn't have to come forward and expose her private life and her battle with addiction, but she did, so you all could hear the truth about what happened to those police officers in front of *Leiser's* jewelry store. For that she should be commended and believed."

Michael asked the jury to recall how clear and certain she was when she testified. "She didn't exaggerate or falsely elaborate when she recounted what she saw. She could have easily told you she saw the entire episode, and none of us would have been the wiser. But she didn't. She told you only what she witnessed from the corner of that vestibule where she was cowering when the shooting began."

"And think about this ladies and gentlemen" Michael continued, "what motive could Joanie Snow possibly have to lie about seeing Chase do what he did that day? The answer is none."

Michael then corrected Combes telling the jury that Joanie Snow was the only eyewitness to place Chase on that street. "Guy Raimondi positively identified Chase as one of the men he saw get out of the Chevy, and walk toward the jewelry store with the driver, who Raimondi said, "Was dead on the street when I went back after the shooting. Ask yourselves, was that a coincidence?"

When he discussed Denny James and Paul Sira, Michael knew he had to walk a fine line. The only witnesses to what happened in that ambulance were them, and Jax Chase. However, because they were excellent when they testified, answering every question directly and without hesitation, Michael was confident that the jury believed that Chase pulled the gun from James and was about to shoot Sira. "And although he tried," Michael said, "Combes was unable to rattle them or shake them out of their story."

After arguing that the expert testimony from Dr. Marcus and the ballistics technician was unimpeachable, Michael took a page out of Combes' summation playbook. As the defense attorney did with the Gabriel Angelos radio transmission to hammer home his point, Michael dwelled on the advances in X-ray technology that both the doctor and the ballistics tech talked about, to ensure that the jury did not ignore the significance of their testimony.

He reminded the jury that the ballistics tech said, "Those extraordinary X-rays gave me pictures of the bullet so sharp and clear that I was able perform the tests and get results that I can swear under oath are precise and accurate."

Michael wound up his summation by pointing out to the jury that they should reject the testimony of Rev. LePage and his followers.

"To begin with, none of them were on the scene in front of *Leiser's* so their opinion that Jackson Chase did not, or could not, shoot and kill Tenuta and Massey is baseless," he said.

"And what makes it *worthless* is that LePage had a motive to lie, and he persuaded his followers to back him up to corroborate that lie. And they did. Not because they truly believe in Chase, but because LePage asked them to. How could they say no to their pastor?"

"LePage lied for Chase because he owed him. The defendant saved his son in Attica, and now he was returning the favor by trying to save Chase here in Brooklyn."

"Ladies and Gentlemen, the defense claims that Jackson Chase did not kill officers Tenuta and Massey. He argued that the NYPD just grabbed the first and most convenient suspect and arrested the wrong man. I urge you to reject that claim. It's absurd to think that the police would arrest *just anyone* for killing two of their own. Why? Because that means a cop killer is still out there. And if he's killed cops once he wouldn't hesitate to do it again."

"We have the right man. We have the person who murdered officers Tenuta and Massey, and he's sitting right over there." Michael then pointed to Chase and said, "Do what the facts and the law demand that you do, find Jackson Chase guilty of murder."

Six days later Judge Cooper declared a mistrial when the jury announced that they were hopelessly deadlocked and could not agree on a verdict.

Jackson Chase was not convicted, but he wasn't free either. Michael told the court he would be ready to try him again on whatever date the judge set.

Judge Cooper said she'd see both attorneys in three weeks, "When we'll do this again."

CHAPTER TWENTY-FOUR

That night Michael and Kathy sat in *Sala*, the restaurant where they had their first date. Over a pitcher of sangria they discussed what happened in Judge Cooper's court that afternoon. Michael was disappointed but not beaten, especially after speaking to the jury when they were discharged by the court. The vote was 9-3 for conviction.

"Kathy, to a person they told me that if I had another eyewitness to the shooting the three holdouts would have voted to convict. Because only Joanie Snow identified Chase as the shooter, the three felt that wasn't enough for them to convict."

"They all thought Guy Raimondi was a good witness but he didn't see the shooting. And since I didn't have the actual bullet from Chase's leg the three holdouts were reluctant to put much weight on the ballistics expert's testimony."

"Another problem for the holdouts was the beating Denny James gave to Chase in the ambulance. They said it was above and beyond what they believed was necessary to disarm him. They felt that before the man was convicted Denny was extracting revenge on him."

As he said it Michael thought, *'Just as Romano thought it might, it certainly did complicate things.'*

"But the clincher for the three holdouts was LePage. They absolutely believed him and were impressed by the testimony of his constituents."

Kathy tried to cheer him up by reminding Michael that he had three weeks to shore up the case. "You'll hear from the FBI well before then, and if it breaks your way, their findings will fill what seems to be the major hole in your case. Have faith."

Just then their food was served and it was as delicious as they remembered from their first visit to the restaurant. Julio, the owner and Michael's longtime friend, did not disappoint. They split a seafood paella and a perfectly cooked branzino, after which their waitress brought dessert, which was Julio's treat. The flan and *crema catalana* was smooth, sweet, and delicious. They declined espresso but did accept 2 glasses of, what Julio said was, "a light *Fino* sherry."

When they left the restaurant they were sated, a bit high, and very horny. He drove to Kathy's apartment where they tore each other's clothes off. After a night, a morning, and an early afternoon of love making, the furthest thing from Michael's mind was the mistrial.

When they finally got out of bed Kathy made them an omelet, toast, and a pot of strong coffee which Michael asked for because after the meal he intended to head to his office.

"I've got the FBI lab tech's number on my desk. I'm going to check in to get an update," he said. Kathy understood and wished him luck.

It was 3 p.m. when Michael kissed Kathy goodbye, and 3:45 when he punched the number for the FBI into his phone. Although it was Sunday, the lab tech told him on Friday that he would be working over the weekend. In fact the technician was somewhat upbeat telling Michael he thought he was close to a resolution.

Michael's call went to voicemail. He left a message and settled in to catch up on some rackets division work. Although his position in the DA's office was a cover, to keep the facade in place, he carried out his duties as Rackets Chief in between cases against the EVIL ONE.

It was 5 p.m. when Michael's cell phone rang. It was the FBI.

When Michael heard the report, he was ecstatic. He immediately called Tony Martino.

"Tony I'm sorry to disturb you on a Sunday but I couldn't wait to tell somebody the good news."

"Mike, it's no problem. You heard back from the FBI, didn't you?"

"Tony I just hung up with the lab technician who has been working on my request. And I believe it has finally paid off. The headline, Eva Snow was murdered!"

From the day he heard that Eva died in her dentist's chair, his gut told him that the EVIL ONE was responsible. He couldn't share the feeling with anyone other than Romano and Caldwell, which he did when he asked for their help to enlist the FBI.

As soon as he received word that Caldwell was successful in getting the FBI lab involved, he met with Tony Martino and Joanie Snow.

At the meeting all Michael told them was that he felt Eva's death needed a closer look. He said that through no fault of the city medical examiner who performed the autopsy on Eva, he thought the ME report was incomplete. "They just don't have the equipment to look for what I believe is evidence that Eva was murdered," he told them.

Michael's statement surprised both Martino and Joanie. Visibly shaken Joanie asked Michael to explain.

This is where he had to be creative. He told her he had been investigating and trying homicide cases for a long time and no matter how strange or unusual the death was, he and the detectives always uncovered how the victim was killed. He said that some took longer than others, but they were always able to solve the puzzle. "Joanie, with Eva's death we just need more time and another set of eyes."

"Someone I know in the federal government owes me a favor and

I asked him to request the FBI's forensics lab take a look at the case. My buddy came through. The FBI has agreed to help us."

"So here is what I need," Michael said. "I want you to give me permission to exhume Eva's body so the scientists and forensic experts at the FBI lab can go over it with a fine tooth comb, using the sophisticated equipment that the medical examiner in New York doesn't have. They'll be looking for evidence that hopefully will prove that Eva was murdered."

Michael had Joanie's answer before he finished his sentence.

"Absolutely! You have my permission. If my sister was murdered by some fucking animal connected to Chase she won't rest in peace until the person or persons who killed her are held responsible."

"Mike, what did the FBI find?" Tony asked.

Michael told Tony that the first significant discovery was the red hairs found very deep in Eva's throat.

"Tony, the FBI says they belong to a male, are curly and they likely came from someone with dreadlocks."

"Holy shit! That scumbag Jiz who hangs with the reverend has exactly that kind of hair, AND, it's red!," Tony shouted into the phone.

"There's more."

"The FBI medical examiner says that Eva's cause of death was asphyxiation. He found evidence of internal trauma, in layman's terms, marks, consistent with something having been shoved deep into her mouth and throat which prevented her from breathing. It's his opinion that she was choked to death by that object. And Tony, those marks were found very close to where the red curly hairs were recovered."

"Mike, your gut was right all along," Tony said. "Now what do we do?"

"The first thing is we go back to the dental office and re-interview everyone who was working the day Eva was killed. I'm going to call in the morning to set it up, because we need to do this as soon as possible. If we get lucky I have a motion to make before Judge

Cooper and I'll need to do that before we begin the re-trial in three weeks."

"Mike, I'm at your disposal. And if we need help, Denny James is more than willing."

Michael told Tony he'd be in touch.

After hanging up with Martino, Michael called Monsignor Romano and gave him the good news. "When you tell Caldwell please thank him for the help. If I'm right, this new evidence will bring about a much different verdict."

"Michael, I'll phone Caldwell as soon as we hang up, but I'm puzzled. Exactly how is this going to make a difference at the retrial? You still don't have that second eyewitness. Eva Snow is not walking into that courtroom to testify."

"Sal, if the judge agrees with the motion I'm prepared to make, I'll have better than a live Eva Snow, I'll have her grand jury testimony."

Romano told Michael he was now totally confused and asked for a detailed explanation. "I'm going to have to tell all of this to Caldwell so I need you to go slow and educate me."

Michael did as the monsignor asked. Before they hung up, Romano told Michael that he'd be praying for him, "Because you're going to need all the help you can get."

On Monday morning Michael called and arranged to have everyone he wanted to speak to in the dentist's office on Tuesday at 8 a.m., one hour before the office was scheduled to open.

That morning Michael met Tony outside the office. He wanted to make sure that Tony was briefed on what he needed to ask the dentist's staff.

"As you know, Tony, everything points to that fucking guy Jiz being responsible for killing Eva. Anything that they may have seen or heard that puts him here the morning Eva came to have her teeth cleaned, is what I'm looking for."

Tony said he understood and he and Michael went into the office in search of something, anything, that Michael could use to corroborate his belief that Jiz murdered Eva. If he found it he'd have the evidence to win the motion he intended to make before Judge Cooper.

As they were winding up the staff interviews, which produced nothing that Michael could use, the first patient of the day walked in. When Michael saw him, he was suddenly struck with a thought.

"Tony, did you or one of your colleagues get the patient list for the day Eva died?" he asked.

Tony hesitated, then sheepishly answered, "Mike we never did."

"So those patients were never questioned?"

"That's right," Tony answered.

When Michael and Tony walked out of the office that morning, Martino had the list. "Mike, I'm on it. I'll let you know what I find out."

CHAPTER
TWENTY-FIVE

It was mid-afternoon three days later when Tony Martino showed up at Michael's office with Denny James, and a young woman who Michael didn't know.

After Tony explained why they were there, and who the young woman was, they all went into a conference room so Michael could interview Jeanette Longo.

When Tony went over the patient list with the dentist's receptionist he learned that one of the patients with an appointment that morning failed to keep it. That patient didn't call to cancel and never rescheduled.

Tony, with Denny James' help, first interviewed all the patients who kept their appointments. None had any information that would help Michael.

They called Ms. Longo and asked to see her. She agreed to meet them at her apartment, but when they sat down to interview her, Longo was reluctant to talk. Reluctant witnesses were a hazard that homicide detectives had to navigate all the time. So Martino employed a tactic that he used in the past when faced with a reticent witness: he talked about the victim to engender empathy.

Jeanette Longo was about the same age as Eva, born and raised in the same Brooklyn neighborhood as Eva, went to a Catholic elementary school, as Eva had, and, like Eva, her parents had passed away.

"So you can see that Eva was much like you. Now we can really use your help. No, let me correct that, her sister Joanie, can use your help. Eva was all the family Joanie had. Her death left Joanie alone. And all she wants is that justice be done for her sister."

It worked. Jeanette told Tony and Denny what she knew and repeated her story for Michael later that day.

The morning Eva was murdered, Jeanette had an appointment with Dr. Aronowitz, the dentist, for her six months check up and cleaning.

"I got to the office around 9:15 for my 9:30 appointment. As I walked up to the front door, I saw a man with red dreadlocks come out of the alley on the right side of the office. He stared right at me with this menacing look on his face. I know the office's fire exit door is in that alley because I once had to use it when there was a false fire alarm while I was in the dentist's chair. So I said to myself that the guy probably came out of that door."

At this point Jeanette began to tremble. Michael calmed her and she continued.

"Mr. Gioca, I was spooked. His look scared the shit out of me. I wanted no part of entering that office after seeing him. I simply ran. I checked behind me as I got close to my apartment building and thank God the guy didn't follow me."

Michael could barely contain his excitement. Jeanette Longo may have saved his case. To not give away his emotions, Michael calmly asked Jeanette to describe the man.

She told him. Except for the clothing he was wearing that day, Michael was sure it was Jiz, the EVIL ONE. To be certain he showed Jeanette a photo array, or photo lineup, he had Tim and Dina prepare.

Hoping that this day would come at some point, Michael asked the two investigators, "During your surveillance of LePage did you ever see a guy with red dreadlocks hanging around the reverend?"

When they told him they had on several occasions, Michael told them to take a photo of the guy and put it into a photo array, "In case I need it someday."

That day was here.

He showed the array to Jeanette and without hesitation, she chose the photo of Jiz. "That's him. He's the guy I saw outside Dr. Aronowitz' office, the one who scared me with that look," she said.

Michael had what he needed. So after a few perfunctory questions he thanked Jeanette for her help and told her, "Tony will take you home. But before you leave I have a big favor to ask. I'm going to need you to tell a judge just what you told me today. The courtroom will be empty except for a guy called Jackson Chase, he's the defendant, his lawyer, and me and Tony. Will you do that for Eva?"

As he expected, Jeanette began to tremble, but then she surprised him. She calmed herself, sat upright in her chair, and told him she'd do it.

"And, Mr. Gioca, if you need me to tell a jury what I know, I'm ready to do whatever is necessary. If I was in Joanie Snow's position I'd want someone like me to be there to help."

"Thanks Jeanette, that's very brave and kind of you. I'll let you know if I need you beyond the hearing."

In actuality Michael wouldn't need Jeanette at trial. She was necessary for the hearing where there was no jury present. If the judge ruled in his favor she wouldn't be permitted to testify implicating Chase in the death of Eva, because he wasn't charged with that murder. So her testimony would be prejudicial and no judge would allow it.

When Tony left with Jeanette, Michael called Judge Cooper's chambers. He asked for a date and time to make a presentation to the court that had a direct impact on Chase's re-trial. He told her he'd be preparing a motion and would have it to her and to Elton Combes first thing in the morning.

The judge said she wanted to read the papers before giving him an answer. "Make sure that Combes knows he'll have one day to respond," Judge Cooper added.

Michael delivered the motion papers to the courthouse himself, but he had Tim and Dina deliver them to Combes' office with the message from the judge about the timing of his response.

Two days later, having received and read Combes' response to Michael's motion, Judge Cooper called both attorneys and set a court date to hear arguments and, if necessary, to take testimony, for Thursday of the following week.

Michael had Tony pick up Jeanette early that Thursday morning so he could go over her testimony once again. He also arranged for the technician from the FBI lab, Dr. Fred Cesarano, to be in his office the day before to prepare him for both his direct testimony, and the cross-examination he would face at the hearing.

When Michael left his office with Jeanette, Dr. Cesarano, Tony, and Dina Mitchell, they were ready for battle.

"Mr. Gioca, I've read your papers and I've read the defendant's response. I'm ready to hear your argument and if necessary, I'm prepared to hear from your witnesses," Judge Cooper said when she took the bench.

For the next thirty minutes Michael argued to have the grand jury testimony of Eva Snow read to the jury at the retrial of Jackson Chase.

Under New York law, if a material witness to a crime is somehow made unavailable to testify for the prosecution, by the defendant, or someone on the defendant's behalf, with his knowledge, or at his instruction, the court has the discretion to permit prior sworn testimony, material to the issues of a trial, to be read to the jury.

The jury may then put whatever weight they deem appropriate on the testimony. In other words they can reject it or they can accept it as they would if the witness were testifying live in the courtroom before them.

To permit Michael to have the testimony read, the judge needed to find: that Eva Snow was unavailable to testify because she was dead; that her testimony was material to the issues at trial; and, the defendant himself engaged in, or acquiesced in, wrongdoing that was intended to, and did cause the unavailability of the witness. To make those findings Judge Cooper ordered that Dr. Cesarano and Jeanette Longo testify.

Jeanette was first. She testified to everything she told Michael in his office. She was particularly adamant when she told the court that the photo she picked out of the array that Michael showed her was the "Scary guy I saw outside Dr. Aronowitz' office."

Try as he did during cross-examination, Combes could not shake Jeanette from her testimony. In fact she became more insistent as he hammered at her that she was mistaken. Getting nowhere with Jeanette after keeping her on the witness stand for one hour, he finally announced that he had no further questions.

Next Michael called Dina Mitchell who told the judge about her surveillance of Rev. LePage and how many times she witnessed the reverend in the company of "A guy named Jiz, the person in the photo I took, that Jeanette Longo picked out of the array my partner and me put together."

Instead of leaving well enough alone, Combes made the mistake of asking Dina a question he did not know the answer to. "Ms. Mitchell, you say you saw Rev. LePage in the company of that man whose photo you took, correct?"

Dina answered, "Yes."

"But you never saw them together other than walking on the street in close proximity to one another, right?"

"Wrong, counselor," Dina answered. "I saw them together going into the reverend's apartment building, which is right above his church, and where he lives with several of his followers. I also saw them eating lunch together in a diner near the church, many times. I saw them both greeting and speaking to the reverend's parishioners outside the church on Sunday mornings, and it looked like Jiz had a lot to say. And, every day of Chase's trial I saw them leave the reverend's apartment building together, get into the reverend's car, and be driven together to this courthouse. I even followed Jiz up to this courtroom a few times and saw that he sat in the last row of the spectator section when the trial was ongoing."

Combes asked nothing else of Dina. He finally realized he had done enough damage to his case.

Michael finished up with Dr. Cesarano. He was magnificent. He told the court in minute detail about his procedures and what he found in the throat of Eva Snow.

He concluded with, "Your Honor, my conclusion to a reasonable degree of medical and scientific certainty is that Eva Snow died of asphyxiation caused by a man with curly red hair having forced an object deep into her throat, an object that left cuts and bruising in the area where I found several red curly hairs, which DNA analysis proved came from a male."

Combes' lame cross-examination was an attempt to pit his findings against the lack of those findings by the New York City medical examiner. When Dr. Cesarano finished explaining the equipment at his disposal that the local medical examiner did not have, and how that equipment allowed him to conduct an examination of Eva that was impossible for the ME in Brooklyn to conduct, Combes knew he was defeated.

After Michael rested his case, Judge Cooper asked Combes if he had a defense case to put before her. When he hesitated before answering, Judge Cooper jumped in and asked, "Where is Mr. Jiz? Are you calling him to rebut all this?"

Combes didn't answer right away. After shuffling a few papers on his table he finally looked up and told the judge that he was not calling Jiz, "Because I'm unable to. Neither I, nor Rev. LePage has seen him since the mistrial ruling. He has not gone to see Mr. Chase, he has not been back to the reverend's church, and Rev. LePage never had a way to contact him. Jiz would seem to always just 'be there' when the reverend wanted to, or needed to, see him. So, Your Honor, I have no witnesses to call. I rest on the record."

"Very well, I'll hear your summations now, gentlemen," Judge Cooper told the attorneys.

Michael spoke first. In addition to highlighting the evidence he presented in support of his motion, he made sure to point out that Jiz was in the back of this courtroom "Every day of the trial," and that during his direct testimony and on cross-examination, Rev. LePage told us all how "close Jiz, he, and the defendant are."

"Your honor, based on the record of this hearing and what you saw and heard during the trial, I ask you to grant my motion, and allow Eva Snow's grand jury testimony to be put in evidence and read to the jury in the retrial."

Combes was next.

After his summation which consisted of a terse denial that Chase had anything to do with Eva Snow's death, Judge Cooper said she was ready with her decision.

"Mr. Gioca, I find you have established all that's necessary for me to allow you to have the sworn grand jury testimony of Eva Snow read to the jury at the retrial of the defendant. I hereby rule that you will be permitted to do so."

Michael now had a puncher's chance of convicting Chase and defeating the EVIL ONE. And he didn't waste it.

CHAPTER
TWENTY-SIX

Mid-morning on Saturday, the second day of jury deliberations, Michael was sitting in his office with Denny James, Tony Martino, and Paul Sira, when he received the call.

After three weeks of trial, and a day and a half of deliberation, the jury had reached a verdict.

They immediately put on their jackets and left for the courthouse.

The cops insisted on being with Michael for support, and he was grateful for their company. They had gone through the first jury's deliberations together, and having seen how devastated Michael was when the mistrial was declared, they wanted to be there for him in the event of a similar, or worse, result. If it was a happy ending, they wanted to be with him to celebrate.

When the four men got to the door of Judge Cooper's courtroom, Michael glanced over at Paul Sira and noticed a large bulge under the light jacket he was wearing.

He knew that Denny James and Tony were unarmed because they told him they were when they got to his office. He also knew that neither liked to carry while off-duty. Sira, however, arrived just before the call about the verdict, and in the rush to get to the courthouse he didn't tell Michael that he was armed.

Although it was the weekend and the courthouse was officially closed for business, there was a working metal detector set up in the lobby, manned by court officers. However, when Michael and the cops all produced their law enforcement credentials, they were allowed to bypass the detector.

On a regular court day, a police officer attending a trial as a spectator or witness was permitted to be armed. But out of courtesy to the court officers who are assigned to protect the judge and keep order in the courtroom, it was customary for the cop to alert them that he or she was carrying. If that didn't sit well with the court officers, the cop would be asked to bring the gun to the chief court clerk's office where it would be locked in a safe until the police officer was done in the courtroom.

Before he opened the courtroom door Michael asked, "Paulie are you armed?"

Sira didn't hesitate. He answered, "Yup. I got my Glock."

Before Michael could say anything, a concerned Tony and Denny James grabbed Sira and took him away from the door.

"Mike, you go in and we'll be there in a minute," Tony said.

A few moments later the three cops entered the courtroom and sat in the first row behind the prosecution table. Tony whispered to Michael that it was "All okay. We took the Glock off him. I got it in my belt."

The jury found Jackson Chase guilty.

Michael turned to Tony, Denny, and Paul and gave them a thumbs up. Each had a big smile and were congratulating one another until the judge told them to quiet down. Judge Cooper discharged the jury, and after the last juror left the courtroom the three cops started celebrating.

Denny and Sira embraced and grabbed Tony in a bear hug. Sira, the most exuberant of the three, reached over the rail separating the spectators from the well of the courtroom, grabbed the now standing

Michael, kissed him on both cheeks, and whispered , "Mr. Gioca, thanks. I'll take it from here." Michael couldn't hear everything after, "Thanks," except the words, "...From here."

Believing Sira said "Where does he go from here?" Michael answered "There'll be a sentencing, then he's going back to prison."

Sira didn't react to Michael's answer. He simply looked at him and smiled.

Judge Cooper asked for order, and told everyone but Chase and Combes, to be seated.

Neither Tony nor Denny James noticed that Sira moved and sat right behind the defense table.

Judge Cooper addressed the defense attorney. "Mr. Combes, please check your calendar and give me a convenient date six weeks from now for the sentencing of your client."

Combes said, "Yes Your Honor, give me a moment," as he reached into the inside breast pocket of his suit jacket. At the same time Sira slid his hand down to his right ankle and retrieved a small .38 caliber snub nose revolver from a holster.

Before Sira could fire, Combes' hand came out of his pocket with a small gun and shot Jax Chase in the side of his head, killing him.

The courtroom erupted into chaos. The court officer assigned to Judge Cooper whisked her off the bench to safety, as two others grabbed Combes to restrain him. Yet another tended to Chase, who had collapsed right behind the defense table.

Michael's immediate reaction was to leave the well of the courtroom and retreat to the empty spectator section where he was surrounded by Tony, Denny James, and Paul Sira, who was able to slip the .38 back into his ankle holster during the bedlam that erupted after the shooting.

After a minute or two, Combes was taken out of the courtroom in handcuffs, as emergency medical personnel rushed in to work on Chase.

Michael and the cops stayed in the courtroom curious about Chase's condition. After a few minutes they learned that Chase couldn't be saved. One EMT told Tony, "He was dead before he hit the courtroom floor."

With nothing more to do Michael and his group left the courtroom and walked to the elevator. Shocked at what he just witnessed, Michael exited the elevator in the courthouse lobby and didn't notice right away that several of the jurors from the trial were standing around. They were waiting for him.

He walked in their direction and stopped when the foreperson asked if they could talk to him. Michael was anxious to hear what they had to say.

However, if they had somehow learned about the courtroom shooting and wanted to ask him about it, he would have to tell them that he couldn't discuss it. The murder may become his next case, especially if, as he suspected, the EVIL ONE was behind it.

He was relieved when they wanted to talk about the trial and Eva Snow.

After hearing what the jurors had to say it was clear that Eva's grand jury testimony made all the difference. As he knew it would be, what Eva told the grand jury provided the 'additional eyewitness' that the jurors in the first trial said Michael needed to convict.

They said that Eva's testimony about what she witnessed at the scene of the shooting, and her later identification of Chase, "Neutralized the erroneous description of the second shooter that Gabriel Angelos put out over the NYPD radio."

What they told him next made Michael's day, despite the fact that a few moments before a murder was committed just a few feet away from him.

"Mr. Gioca, you gave us real witnesses, while the defense gave us that phony reverend. We never wavered. From the first day of deliberations it was clear that all of us thought that Chase deserved to go to prison for the rest of his life."

'Where he's going,' Michael thought, *'Will make Attica look like Paradise Island.'*

Michael thanked the jurors for their service and their comments and left the courthouse.

Later, when they were back in Michael's office toasting the verdict, aware of only the Glock that Sira had, he asked Tony about 'The gun.' Tony's response shocked him.

"Mike, I swear I had no idea about the .38 that he had on his ankle."

"Tony, what the fuck are you talking about?"

"While you were talking to the jurors, Paulie was fidgeting with the right cuff of his khaki's. I had a bad feeling, so I asked him if he had an ankle holster. He said he did. Mike, the Glock was a ruse to distract us. He made sure you noticed that he had it, knowing you would make sure he was disarmed so the Glock wouldn't make it into the courtroom. He figured once we took it from him we wouldn't look for another gun, which he had stashed in an ankle holster."

"Holy shit Tony, he was going to shoot Chase?"

"Mike I ain't gonna' say that, but you can draw your own conclusion."

"Paulie is very emotional," Tony continued. "He said he vividly remembers putting Massey in his car and driving to the hospital while Denny tried to save him. He told me all that will be with him until he dies. He said he didn't think he could be in that courtroom and hear about another hung jury, or worse, an acquittal, of the guy 'who did that to my brothers and do nothing.'"

"Wow!" Was all Michael could say. However, by the look on Tony's face he knew the detective didn't tell him everything.

"Tony there's more, isn't there?"

Tony nodded. "Paulie said that even if Chase was convicted he wouldn't sit by and let him be sentenced, because he knew that Chase had escaped from prison once, 'And that fucker could escape again,' were his exact words."

"Strange as this sounds Mike, when Combes killed Chase, he saved Sira's ass."

"Yeah," Michael said, "The last thing we needed was for you and Denny to collar Sira for shooting the defendant in that courtroom."

"Mike, you got that right."

That evening Michael and Kathy celebrated his win at his favorite Italian restaurant. *Vite* in Astoria, Queens was owned by two of his friends.

Pino, a native of Sardinia, and Carmelo, who was born and raised in Sicily, stood by Michael during the dark days after his divorce. They always made him feel at home whether he was alone, or with his sons, who loved going to *Vite*.

If they were there for dinner, Michael Jr. and Kevin usually ordered *Vite's* pizza to start, followed by their favorite, pasta Bolognese. And when they were there for brunch, the *panettone* French toast always made them smile.

It had been a while since Michael was at *Vite* with a woman, so when he walked in with Kathy, Pino who was working that night, gave him a hug and a kiss on each cheek, before asking, "*Michele*, it's good to see you, but who is this beautiful woman?"

After he introduced Kathy, Pino seated them and had a waiter bring three glasses of *prosecco*. Pino in his typical flamboyant manner said, "It is good to see you smiling my friend." He then raised his glass to toast "The happy couple," he said.

The night couldn't have gone better. The food was spectacular, the wine, a fine vintage, and Kathy never stopped smiling. To top it off, when Michael asked for the check, Pino told him, "The night is on me. Congratulations on your big win today."

Michael had no idea how Pino could have possibly known about the verdict and when he turned to Kathy with a puzzled look on his face, she couldn't help but laugh.

"That was me," she said. "When you went to the bathroom, Pino came over and told me he never saw you so happy. He even thanked me for putting you in such a great frame of mind. That's when I told him about your big win. You're not angry I did that, are you?"

Michael nodded vigorously in the negative.

He was relieved that he didn't let the Massey and Tenuta families down, and he was ecstatic that he had a person in his life who appreciated the work he did and understood when that work took him away from her.

He smiled and thought '*I really love her.*'

Kathy noticed the smile and knew exactly what it meant. She had fallen in love with him as well.

On the drive to Michael's apartment, where Kathy was staying the night, Michael's cell phone rang. He answered it using the Bluetooth hook up he had in his official car.

"Mr. Gioca, it's Bob Lataweick," the caller said. Lataweick was a detective investigator on the Brooklyn DA's staff who worked nights on the office's 24 hour front desk taking calls when police officers and civilians needed help from an assistant district attorney. Michael knew Bob for as many years as he worked for the DA's office.

"Bob what's up?" Michael asked. "Mike I'm sorry to bother you but I just got a call from a prisoner in the Brooklyn House of Detention. He says he has information you'll want to hear related to the case you just tried. He said it's urgent and he needs to speak to you as soon as possible but he won't talk on the phone. He doesn't want you to visit him either. He wants you to bring him into the office to talk. He's worried that if someone sees you with him he's gonna' get 'shived.'"

"Bob, what's his name?"

"He said his name is Frankie LePage, the son of Rev. Vernon LePage."

PART TWO

CHAPTER TWENTY-SEVEN

When Michael got to his office on Monday morning he immediately asked to see Tim and Dina. He told them about the call from Frankie LePage and asked them to prepare an *Order to Produce*, which required the Brooklyn House of Detention to transport Frankie to Brooklyn Supreme Court.

From there they could take custody and bring him to Michael.

Because he was so intent on getting all that done, Michael didn't notice the envelope with his name on the floor under his desk chair, until he settled in after the two investigators left the office.

The envelope had clearly been there for some time. It was dirtied with marks like it had been stepped on.

'What the hell is this?', Michael asked himself.

He opened the envelope and saw that it contained a note from one of the DA's investigators who Michael recalled was manning the security desk on Saturday morning, the day of the verdict.

The note was dated that Saturday, and the time the message was received was just after he was called to the courthouse for the verdict.

The note read: "Mr. Gioca, just after you left for court, Jax Chase called the desk and left this message for you- '*No matter what happens I want... no, I need, to talk to you.*' I'm going off-duty, which is why I left this on your office chair." It was signed by the investigator.

"Shit, shit, shit," Michael said to no one.

After reading Chase's message, the events in the courtroom on Saturday now made sense to him.

'That's why Combes killed him,' Michael thought to himself. *'The EVIL ONE found out that Chase contacted the office, and HE needed to stop him from talking. And, I'm sure the call from the reverend's son is not a coincidence.'*

Michael called Monsignor Romano to fill him in.

"*Michele,* long time no hear, my friend," the monsignor said when he answered Michael's call.

Other than leaving a voicemail message on Romano's phone to tell him about the verdict, Michael hadn't spoken to the cleric all weekend. Instead, he decided to make the most of his Sunday with Kathy and remain radio silent.

"Sal, I apologize, I should have spoken to you directly about the victory, but honestly, I was with Kathy Saturday night, and all day Sunday. It would have been difficult to talk without raising her up as to who I was talking to. I hate to lie to her. I figured that the important news was the conviction."

Romano couldn't even pretend to be annoyed or angry. He was happy and proud of his friend for securing another win in the war against Satan.

"Mike, it's okay. I was just breaking chops. However, I would have liked to congratulate you," Romano replied.

"Caldwell and I are very proud and extremely grateful for all your hard work. Now what's up? I have the feeling you called to either tell me of a development, ask me for something, or both."

Michael told him about Frankie LePage's call and the note.

"Sal, I think both are connected somehow. I'm having Frankie brought in this afternoon to chat. I'll call you when I'm done. Who knows if we may be going to battle again."

At 3:30 that afternoon Frankie LePage was seated in a rackets division conference room nervously shaking his right leg. When Michael came in he introduced himself and to calm Frankie down, asked him if he was hungry.

"Do you want something to eat and drink before we get started?"

"Mr. Gioca, that's a big yes! I'm starving. Lemme' get a burger, fries, and a coke. I'm hungry all the time. The food in the Brooklyn House is shit."

Michael laughed to himself when Frankie mentioned the jailhouse food. Several years before he was assigned to debrief a mafia hitman who was born and raised in Sicily. On the first day of their debriefing sessions, Michael asked the hitman the same question he asked Frankie, and the hitman's answer was almost identical. The only difference, the hitman said the food in the Brooklyn House was *merde,* the Italian word for 'shit.'

When the food arrived, Frankie ate it like it was his last meal. Michael added chocolate cupcakes to the order, and they were a hit. When he was finished, the reverend's son said he was ready to talk.

"Mr. G my father, and that prick Jiz, are bad people. They hate the police and you all. I got lots to tell you, but I need your help."

"I'm listening," Michael said.

"I'm sure you know that I got convicted a couple of years back on a fraud rap."

When Michael nodded indicating that he did, Frankie said, "That was all my father. It was his con that I was working. I was sent to Attica, where I got to know Jax Chase. Jax was good people. He helped me out of a bad situation in the joint and saved my ass."

"I'm down here now because my father promised to have Combes handle my appeal, which is supposed to be in court very soon. But things have changed. My scumbag father ain't helping me no more. That's why I need your help. I ain't lookin' for no freebee.

You help me, and I help you. And trust me, you ain't gonna' be sorry you did."

Frankie stopped and took a deep breath before continuing. "As I said, my father has always been a con man. But now, since that fuck Jiz come around, he a murderer. Shit, they both murderers, and they belong in hell."

Michael said, "Frankie I'm not saying 'no' to helping you, but before I commit to anything, I need some understanding of what you can give me."

"Okay," Frankie said. "I'll give you something for free. Then you tell me what you gonna' do for me. If I like it, I'll tell you everything about my father, and what he and Jiz have done in his so-called church, in the name of religion."

"Here's a taste: fraud, rape, and murder."

Frankie had Michael's attention.

"Okay, give me my freebee," Michael said. "Then I'll listen to what you want before we go any further."

Frankie nodded, "Mr. G, my father, and that fucking piece of shit Jiz, had my friend Jax killed. Combes shot him on their orders."

"How do you know that?" Michael asked.

"Because they told me they was gonna' kill him. They was afraid Jax was gonna' rat. They asked me to get an inmate in the Brooklyn House to shiv him. They was offering ten grand. I told them to go fuck themselves. Jax was my friend and saved my life."

"This is the story. My father and Jax had a beef over the rev takin' care of Jax' appeal if he got convicted in your case."

"My father said no he wasn't gonna' help."

"He told Jax near the end of the trial that if he got convicted, he'd be on his own. He told him that he first got involved with Jax because of Jiz, then much more because of me."

"Daddy told Jax that he done spent a lot of money for Combes and wasn't gonna' spend no more. He say that he done enough for Jax."

"If you ask me, that there was Jiz' doing, probably because he had no more use for the guy. My father knew how much Jax done for me, so there ain't no way that he would cut him loose unless someone whispered in his ear. You feelin' me?"

Frankie continued, "Chase got pissed, and he threatened my daddy."

"He say that my father *better* make sure he had a lawyer to handle the appeal, or else."

"The Rev didn't want to hear that shit, so he told Jax if he knew what's good for him, he better keep his mouth shut."

Frankie said that his father told Jiz about the conversation with Jax, and Jiz' response was that Jax couldn't be trusted.

"He say, 'Convicted or not, 'Jax got to go.' That's when they came to me about the shiv, and I told them no."

"A few days later, my father came to visit me. He said that he and Jiz would get someone close to Jax to do it. And then he tells me that as punishment for me refusing him, he was pullin' Combes from my appeal." He said, "Combes probably ain't gonna' be around to do no appeal, anyway. Time for you to grow up, son."

"I was so pissed that I wanted to reach out to you right then. I also wanted to alert Jax to what they was cooking up. But then I thought if they wanted Jax killed so he wouldn't rat, if they found out I went to you, and I tipped Jax off, I'd be a dead man."

"I was a pussy. But now that they murdered my man, fuck 'em, and here I am."

Frankie asked for a bathroom break before they went any further. That gave Gioca time to think.

'The EVIL ONE made sure Chase wasn't around to talk. But what HE didn't anticipate was Frankie LePage.'

'There is no doubt', Michael said to himself, '*The next battle with the EVIL ONE is about to begin.*

CHAPTER

TWENTY-EIGHT

When Tim returned to the conference room with Frankie, Michael excused himself and went to his office to call Monsignor Romano.

Earlier he promised the monsignor that he would let him know why Frankie LePage wanted to talk to him. Now that he knew, he called to ask Romano to convince Caldwell to agree to make Frankie a confidential informant.

Michael knew that he couldn't bring Satan to justice, but he could saddle *HIM* with another defeat by putting the reverend behind bars. That's why he wanted... no needed, Frankie LePage.

However, before agreeing to take Frankie on as a CI, Michael knew that Caldwell and his people needed to know why he was so important.

His strategy was to first convince Romano that Frankie was essential to defeat the EVIL ONE again.

Then Michael needed to assure the monsignor that what Frankie was demanding was a price worth paying.

The government would have to engage an attorney to represent Frankie on his appeal *OR* speak to Brooklyn DA Price and persuade him to agree to either a sentence reduction, or an outright dismissal of Frankie's case.

And having Frankie as a CI would require that he be taken out of the Brooklyn House of Detention for his safety and housed in a secure federal facility.

In Michael's experience none of this was impossible. It had been done before.

As Chief of Rackets he arranged for witnesses and confidential informants who were under indictment or doing prison time, to be represented by lawyers who were not their original attorneys.

He also arranged for them to be housed in secure locations where they were protected by the district attorney's detective investigators, and NYPD detectives.

And when appropriate, he favorably disposed of their cases. All the law required was that he inform the court and a defendant's attorney of what he did.

Therefore, Michael felt that with the power and might of the federal government at his disposal, Caldwell would readily agree.

Michael prepared for the call to Romano by outlining Frankie's information, and what he was asking for. He also outlined the reasons for agreeing to what Frankie wanted and why he was so important.

He did all of that on a legal pad, much like he did when he prepared for a closing argument at the end of a trial.

When he was ready, he dialed the monsignor.

He opened the conversation with, "Sal, Frankie LePage told me why Jackson Chase was murdered, and that Jiz instigated it." For the next thirty minutes Michael delivered his summation.

When he was done Romano told him he wanted a little time to think about it before he reached out to Caldwell.

"Mike, Caldwell may disagree, but I'm inclined to recommend that he give you what you want."

Michael was encouraged and settled in to wait for the verdict.

While he waited he asked Tim and Dina to order pizza. When it arrived, Frankie again showed them what he thought of the food in the Brooklyn House. He practically inhaled four slices and washed them down with three cokes.

It was 9 p.m. when Michael's phone rang. It was Romano.

"Michael, Caldwell said yes! You have his approval for it all. He even called DA Price who looked at Frankie's case. Once you're done with him, Price has agreed to recommend to a judge that his sentence be reduced to time served."

"As for housing, you'll have to cover tonight. But starting tomorrow Frankie will be escorted by federal agents to a nearby secure location where he'll be guarded 24 hours a day and you'll have complete and total access to him."

"Sal, cover tonight? How am I going to do that? Frankie is here only on a temporary *Take Out Order*. I have to get him back to the Brooklyn House tonight."

"Michael, it's been taken care of. After Caldwell spoke to DA Price, the district attorney called both the New York State Corrections Commissioner, and the warden of the Brooklyn House of Detention. When he told them why he was calling, he dropped the words, 'national security matter,' and used John Caldwell's name. That did the trick. They agreed to release LePage into your custody."

"Thank you Sal. You've come through for me yet again. Please thank Caldwell and let him know that my gut is telling me he won't regret this decision.... The one who will, is the EVIL ONE."

When Michael went back to the conference room, he put his hand out to shake with Frankie, and said, "Welcome aboard. I'm going to help you, because you're going to help me."

Frankie spent the night with Tim Clark and Dina Mitchell in a $400 per night suite in the Brooklyn Marriott Hotel.

The next day he was whisked away to the Fort Hamilton Army Base by Caldwell's agents, who identified themselves to Frankie, Tim, and Dina as detectives from the NYPD Intelligence Division.

Fort Hamilton is located in the Bay Ridge section of Brooklyn, on the borough's southern coast. It sits adjacent to the Verrazano

Bridge, which connects Brooklyn and Staten Island, and fronts a section of the Atlantic Ocean known as the Narrows. In both feel and location, it's as far away from the mean streets of Brooklyn as one can get without falling into the ocean. In the summer it's an oasis from the concrete jungle with plenty of trees and expansive lawns. In winter, with a cold wind coming off the Atlantic, it can feel like Siberia.

Years before in his capacity as Chief of Rackets, Michael handled a corruption investigation with Brooklyn Supreme Court judges and Brooklyn politicians as the targets.

Two of the defendants in those cases, who Michael identified as possible cooperators, were brought to Fort Hamilton following their arrests, to see if they were interested in helping the district attorney in return for leniency.

It was winter, and on the days they were brought to the fort the conditions were particularly harsh. Snow covered the ground, and the 20 degree temperature felt much colder because of the fierce wind off the Atlantic that pummeled the army base.

Both arrestees later told Michael that the environment played a large role in their decision to become witnesses for the district attorney. And because of the conditions, the judge specially appointed to hear the cases, referred to the fort where the interviews were conducted, as 'the gulag.'

The building where those witnesses were spoken to was the office of the US Army Criminal Investigation Division (CID). With Caldwell's help, it would be Frankie's home for the foreseeable future, and where Michael would debrief and interview him.

Michael wanted Frankie to settle in and get accustomed to his living quarters before he began, what he knew from experience, would be many days and nights of interviews.

He let a few days go by before he traveled out to the fort to begin the debriefing.

It was right after breakfast when Michael walked into a conference room in the CID headquarters for the first of many sessions with his new confidential informant. Frankie was sitting at a large table chatting with a couple of the agents who seemed entertained by whatever story the younger LePage was telling them.

When Frankie spotted Michael, he got up and surprised Gioca by embracing him in a bear hug. “Mr. G, I can’t thank you enough,” he said. “My room here is aright, and the food ain’t bad. These guys, pointing to the agents, are good company. They like my stories and jokes. Shit, this is better than home.”

Michael smiled, told Frankie he was pleased that he was happy, then said, “But now it’s time to work. Are you ready?”

“You bet your ass I’m ready,” Frankie answered.

“Okay. Let’s start as far back as you can remember,” Michael told him.

“It was before I was born, but I can tell you how my father got started, because me and my brothers heard the stories from him and his crew while we was growing up.”

Michael was surprised to hear that Frankie wasn’t an only child. “You have brothers?” he asked.

“Yup, I got three. But only two was in the game,” he said.

Michael asked, “The Game?”

“Yeah. Mr. G. I told you my father is a con man, and he taught us how to run all sorts of cons. That’s how I got my ass arrested. But I’m getting ahead of myself. Let me start at what I was told at the beginning.”

For the next five days Frankie LePage told Michael everything he knew about the sordid history of his father and his ‘so-called’ church, his followers, or as Frankie called them “His cult,” his wives, and what happened to it all when, “That motherfucker Jiz came into my father’s life.”

CHAPTER TWENTY-NINE

Vernon "The Rev." LePage was born in 1950 in Beaufort, South Carolina to poor migrant workers who picked tobacco, cotton, fruits, and vegetables in their home state and others, throughout the American south.

When Vernon was 12 years old, his father died. Because his mother Becky couldn't afford to raise and feed her son, she sent him to New York City to live with her brother Teddy, a motorman on the city's subway system, and his wife. They had no children and were happy to have their nephew live with them.

Vernon was enrolled in the city's public education system, but he hated school. He was a chronic truant who spent most days hanging with local teenage hoodlums, drinking cheap wine, and learning how to shoplift.

By his eighteenth birthday, Vernon accumulated an extensive juvenile record of crimes far more serious than petty theft. Grand larceny, weapons charges, and even rape, highlighted the future phony reverend's rap sheet. But he spent no time in jail because the Family Court judges before whom Vernon appeared were more interested in reform than punishment.

In his early twenties, Vernon prowled the streets of Manhattan dressed like his cinematic idol, the lead character in the 1972 movie *Super Fly*. His flamboyant mode of dress and manner caught the attention of a Manhattan scam artist and hustler, known only as 'Momma Trudeau.'

She liked Vernon and hired him to be her chauffeur and apprentice. Working for Momma provided Vernon with his elementary school education in the art of scamming the public. His secondary and collegiate education came later when Vernon hooked up with a fake preacher, Donald E. Dawes.

The phony cleric provided Vernon with the blueprint for what became his depraved and perverted enterprise in Brooklyn. An operation that turned murderous, "When Jiz hooked up with my father," Frankie told Michael.

In 1970, Dawes established a phony church in Manhattan. *The New World Order Church of God.* It became the epicenter of a scam that netted him millions of dollars per year.

Dawes first noticed the up and coming con man who Momma had working for her, when a member of his 'flock' was scammed out of several thousand dollars by the sweet talking Vernon LePage. Rather than being angry, Dawes was impressed and recruited Vernon to his organization a year later after Momma Trudeau died.

Dawes recognized that the suave, sweet talking, good looking LePage was the perfect choice to run Dawes' new scam.

Vernon's role was to procure women who Dawes dressed as Catholic nuns and sent out across the streets of Manhattan to solicit 'donations' to his church.

To get them to work for his boss, Vernon sold the women on the notion that Dawes had a mission in Africa that provided meals and clothes to small children whose parents were too poor, and politically oppressed, to care for them. As an additional incentive, he promised to pay them a percentage of whatever they collected.

The silver tongued LePage quickly assembled a stable of twenty, mostly young, women. The group included his cousin Sarah, and her best friend Helen, who would later marry Vernon and give birth to Frankie.

The clerical habits the women dressed in were similar to those worn by the Catholic Order of the Sisters of St. Joseph. The 'nuns' spread out across Manhattan, hitting up suckers in places such as Macy's Department Store, the New York subway, and the teeming streets of New York's Times Square.

The scam was a success. Dawes and Vernon knew that few would turn down a nun asking for money to feed hungry kids. However, it was not without its problems. One sunny summer afternoon in Times Square, Sarah, Helen, and Vernon were arrested by the NYPD Vice Squad.

The three were working the tourists on what is known as 'The Crossroads of the World,' when they were spotted by a tourist they scammed several months before.

After gladly donating to the phony cause, that tourist called the Sisters of St. Joseph's main convent to praise the work the nuns were doing with Reverend Dawes for the African poor. When she was told there was no such charity, and the sisters of their order do not openly solicit donations on the streets, the victim reported the scam to the police.

The vice squad opened an investigation and alerted the patrol officers assigned to Times Square to be on the lookout for the trio. When the victimized tourist saw the scammers, she pointed them out to a uniformed cop who made the arrest.

Sarah, Helen, and Vernon pled not guilty and went to trial. The women were convicted, while Vernon, who testified on his own behalf, was acquitted. His silver tongue worked its magic again.

Sarah and Helen were given non-jail sentences, and after paying a fine, were back out in the streets preying on unsuspecting tourists and gullible New Yorkers.

Over the next several years, Vernon and his crew of 'nuns,' made so much money for Dawes, that Helen, who was now Mrs. Vernon

LePage, convinced him to become 'Reverend LePage' and open his own phony church in the Borough of Churches, Brooklyn.

The church, later described by Michael in his summation at the reverend's criminal trial, as a 'House of Horrors,' was located on Nostrand Avenue in the Midwood section of the borough.

The Nostrand Evangelical Church of Hope was situated in the store front of a four story, ramshackle building Vernon bought with the money LePage and Helen made while working for David Dawes.

Vernon and Helen lived on the second floor above the church in one of two apartments. The other housed their four sons, Frankie, the oldest, twins Zeke and Isaiah, and Noah the youngest. The apartments on the third and fourth floors of the building were where the young women Vernon lured to his 'service' lived.

Unlike the Dawes' 'nuns', who all went home after their day on the streets, LePage wanted his 'nuns' to be close to him when they weren't working. His reasons: maintain control and have them handy when he wanted sex.

To make himself known in his new neighborhood LePage hung a large sign on the front door of the church announcing himself as a 'Doctor of Metaphysics and Theology.'

The sign also contained a menu of sorts. It listed what the reverend and the *Church of Hope* offered to the public: weddings, funerals, and a regular Sunday service where he 'preached the gospel of the Lord and healed the sick.'

The con man did it again. Word spread quickly throughout Midwood and adjacent neighborhoods that Reverend LePage was performing miracles on Nostrand Avenue. Soon his Sunday service was standing room only. Followers, among whom were some of Brooklyn's most prominent citizens, flocked to the *Church of Hope* to hear the reverend and watch him perform.

None of his services were free.

When he performed a 'healing', it was always on someone from outside the neighborhood who LePage paid to pretend he needed God's help. When the phony 'sick or injured' one announced to the congregation that he was 'cured,' donations flowed like holy water into the church's Sunday collection baskets.

In addition to the 'healing scam,' the reverend ran his version of the fake nun racket.

To acquire the women he needed, LePage, dressed like his favorite character, Super Fly, and prowled the streets of the city in a sleek, chauffeur driven Cadillac, hunting for women he would eventually drug, rape, imprison, and put on the streets to solicit 'donations.'

He looked for the young and vulnerable, and lured them to his lair with the promise of a rent free home, food, money, and a place in heaven. But the reverend had no intention of saving their souls. To him they were chattel.

Once reeled in, he seduced them using alcohol and serious drugs. And when they were hooked, the women were sexually abused and raped by LePage, and imprisoned in those third and fourth floor apartments above the church. They were only let out to roam the streets dressed as nuns soliciting alms for the poor.

Frankie told Michael that each day he and his brothers drove the women to different locations across the city to panhandle.

"When they got back each night, they was locked into their rooms except when my daddy took one of 'em to his 'special' room to have sex. By the time I went away to prison, my daddy fathered about 26 kids with them women. By now it could be even more."

"And if them kids acted up, my father would have us put 'em in cages with no food. Sometimes he even beat them to teach them a lesson."

"What about your mother? Where was she in all this?" Michael asked.

"Mr. G, I ain't seen my mother since my baby brother Noah was three years old. From when I was old enough to know what was going on, my daddy treated my ma like shit. In addition to fucking women right under her nose, he would beat her when she complained."

"One day she musta' had enough, because when I got up and went to eat breakfast and my mother weren't there in the kitchen, Zeke and Isaiah told me that she took Noah and left during the night when daddy was passed out from drinking. None of us seen her since."

"Did you and your brothers speak to your father about it?"

"Yeah we did. And what we got was him sayin' 'Fuck your mother. She ain't been good for us and the church for a couple of years.' He said, 'She somehow found the real God and didn't want no part of us anymore. Forget her, you got me and that's all you need.' You believe he said that about his wife, our mother?"

"How did you and your brothers react?"

Frankie dropped his head and said, "We ain't done nothin.' If we went against him he woulda' beat the shit outta' us. And we had no money to leave. The only money we had was what he gave us. Thank God my ma had money stashed away so she could leave and be okay."

Michael just shook his head in disbelief.

"Frankie, I'm sorry to hear that. Your father deserves everything I hope to dump on him. What a piece of shit."

"Let's get back to talking about the women," Michael said.

"You mentioned your father mistreated them. When they were out on the street begging, did any of them ever go to the police to report what he was doing to them?"

"From what I saw, when I was growing up, and before I went to Attica, the women who was recruited early on were like zombies. They did whatever they was told. Daddy had them hooked on drugs and he was their supplier. They wouldn't dare rat him out, or else they'd get a beating in front of everyone and no drugs when they needed a fix."

"But my brothers tell me that some of the recent ones got balls. I ain't seen it personally because I been away, but apparently they don't give a shit. They talk back to daddy, and a few even threatened to go to the cops if he didn't free them. That was a big mistake. Zeke and Isaiah say that with Jiz around, suddenly some be disappearing."

Frankie said that his brother Zeke told him that one day shortly after he dropped off one of the women in Coney Island to beg, he was grabbed by the cops and arrested for rape and larceny.

"But Zeke was released because the DA said the cops ain't have enough evidence."

"That night when he got home Zeke told daddy. Daddy went upstairs and grabbed the woman, Natasha was her name, smacked her around, and accused her of ratting out Zeke. She denied it, but daddy didn't believe her. Zeke said daddy talked to Jiz and the next thing he knew she ain't around no more."

Frankie said that Zeke also told him that a week or two later, his brother Isaiah dropped off two 'nuns', Sammi and Alexa, in Times Square. "He say that they was tight with Natasha. None of 'em had any kids, so they be together all the time in the apartments."

"When Isaiah went to pick them up at the end of the day, they was not at the pickup spot. Isaiah waited and a good hour later he saw the two come out of the subway."

"Zeke say that Isaiah told daddy, who confronted them."

Vernon accused them of going to Brooklyn and ratting him out to the DA's office because they were convinced that he murdered their friend Natasha.

The two women vehemently denied the accusation and begged that he not punish them. The reverend calmed them and assured them that he believed their denial.

"Mr. G, Isaiah and Zeke told me that the next morning them two women were nowhere to be found. They disappeared."

"That's Jiz for ya'."

Pretending not to know what Frankie was saying, Michael asked, "What does that mean?"

"From what my brothers be tellin' me, Jiz be whispering into daddy's ear and suddenly all three of them women disappeared. I know they dead, and Jiz and my daddy killed them."

"That's all good intel Frankie, but it's not direct evidence I can use in court. You may be right but I don't have any bodies. All I have is your brothers telling you that three women disappeared after your father accused them of going to the police to inform on him."

Frankie began to smile.

"What's so funny?" Michael asked. "You ain't getting' the deal you want unless I get a case to try."

"Mr. G, who said I was finished with what I got to say? I got exactly what you need. I got a confession from my father."

"Way to bury the headline Frankie," Michael said.

"When my daddy came up to Attica to visit just before I was transferred to Brooklyn, I asked him about what Zeke and Isaiah was sayin' about them women. I asked him, 'Did you kill them 'cause they ratted on you?' Now whispering he say, 'Yeah. You ain't got to worry. Me and Jiz took care of 'em. They not gonna' hurt us no more.'"

Now it was Michael who was smiling.

Frankie saw his reaction and added, "And that ain't all. I got the name of someone who used to be tight with my father, but he in jail now. I seen him in the Brooklyn House a couple of times before you guys pulled me out. Trust me when I tell you he knows where the bodies are buried, and probably a whole lot more."

"From what I been told by my brothers, he pissed at my daddy because the Rev. cut him out when Jiz came on the scene. And he believes that Jiz set him up to be arrested so my daddy would kick him outta' the whole operation. I'm sure he'll help you as long as you help him. You know what I'm sayin'."

CHAPTER THIRTY

Winsell Myles was in the Brooklyn House of Detention awaiting his next court date after being indicted for a crime he didn't commit.

One day after lunch he was in his cell reading when a corrections officer told him to get his jacket, "You're going to the DA's office."

Winsell had no idea what was happening and he told the officer that he was not interested.

"You ain't got no choice. Two DA investigators got a *Take Out Order* for you. Now get your jacket and don't give me a hard time."

"This ain't right," Winsell said. "I want my lawyer."

"The investigators told me to tell you that your lawyer will be there. Now stop with the bullshit and get your fucking jacket."

Winsell put his jacket on and turned to be handcuffed behind his back. When he got to the jail's reception area, Tim Clark and Dina Mitchell were waiting for him. They introduced themselves and told Winsell not to worry, "Nothing is going to happen unless you and your lawyer agree to it."

When Frankie LePage told Michael that Winsell Myles was someone who might be interested in cooperating, he asked Dina to find out what Myles was charged with, and who represented him. The charges were two counts of gun possession, and his attorney was Thomas Rand, who Michael was familiar with.

Rand was a veteran of the Brooklyn criminal defense bar, and although he was experienced and competent, he was not considered to be among the upper echelon of Brooklyn defense attorneys.

In his early days in the DA's office Michael would often face Rand in the arraignment courtroom of Brooklyn Criminal Court. It was a place where inexperienced ADA's like Gioca learned the moving parts of the criminal justice system, and how to handle the pressure of appearing before a judge.

On most days it was a legal circus. Lots of cases, lots of defendants and their lawyers, and lots of police officers and victims to listen to.

On his first day there, he represented the prosecution in over a hundred new arrest cases. After court, an exhausted Michael walked back to the DA's office and thought '*they didn't teach any of that in law school.*'

Rand was a regular figure in arraignments. As a member of a panel of private attorneys that accepted assignments from the court, he represented indigent defendants who could not afford to hire a lawyer. He would sit in the courtroom most of the day waiting for the presiding judge to tap him to represent what would be his next client. It was a way for a private attorney who didn't have a thriving law practice to pick up work and pay the bills.

Rand was assigned to represent Winsell Myles when he was brought before the court to be arraigned on charges of weapons possession. According to the criminal complaint, two guns were found in his car.

At their first meeting in the cell behind the arraignment courtroom, Myles told Rand that the weapons were not his, and he had no idea how the two very powerful handguns got into his car.

Rand made that argument to the court, but because of the type of guns, and Myles prior felony convictions, the judge set bail in an amount he could not afford. He was remanded to the Brooklyn House of Detention where Frankie LePage spotted him. On the next visit with his brothers, Frankie learned that Myles had a falling out with their father several weeks before he was arrested.

Five days after the arraignment, Myles was indicted and faced significant jail time if convicted of possessing guns he claimed he never laid eyes on.

Although Michael was circumspect about why he wanted to talk to Myles when he called Rand, the attorney readily agreed to meet. He saw it as a potential lifeline for his client.

Winsell Myles was escorted by Tim and Dina into Michael's office. Sitting in one of the office chairs was Thomas Rand.

"Good afternoon Mr. Myles, I'm assistant district attorney Michael Gioca. Sorry to spring this unexpected visit on you, but it's important for both of us that we talk. Mr. Rand has been fully briefed on why you're here and I'll leave you two alone so he can fill you in."

Twenty minutes later Rand and Myles were ready to hear what Gioca had to offer.

Michael began by explaining how he learned of Winsell Myles.

"Frankie LePage, who knows you pretty well, suggested we talk. He told me that for as long as he could remember, you and the reverend were, using his word, 'tight.' He now believes his father's new found friend, Jiz, came between you and his dad, and there was a falling out. I'm interested in hearing what *you* have to say about your relationship with the reverend. And what you know about the disappearance of three of the reverend's women, Natasha, Sammi, and Alexa."

"I know that you're under indictment," Michael told him, "But Mr. Rand said you're innocent. You believe you were set up. Is that right?"

Myles answered, "Yes. But it ain't my *belief*. I *know* the rev and his fucking friend Jiz done it."

"I'm proposing a deal," Michael said.

"If you have what I believe you have on the reverend and Jiz, and are willing to share it with me, and testify against them, I promise to help you. I'll look into your case and if you're right about it being a set-up, I'll find it. Once I do, your case will disappear... legally. And even if it wasn't a set-up, I promise that your cooperation will go a long way toward minimizing any punishment you face."

"Now, I'm going to get a cup of coffee so you can think about it and discuss it with Mr. Rand. But before I do, I want you to know that this offer is only good for today. If you turn it down we'll take you back to the Brooklyn House and this meeting never happened."

Michael started to get up from his desk, when Myles said, "Mr. Gioca, I don't need no time to think on it. I'm in."

"Just one thing," he added, "When you get your coffee, get one for me too."

Michael returned with coffee for all, and with a selection of sweets from a coffee shop near the office. He knew that the desserts would go a long way toward making Myles happy and cooperative.

After spending weeks in the Brooklyn House eating the shit the jail passed off as food, Myles looked at the box of donuts, cookies, and muffins and couldn't help but smile. He then stood and hugged Michael.

For the remainder of that afternoon, and for the next three days, Winsell Myles told Michael a story that the most successful fiction writers couldn't conceive of. A tale that would make the most horrific, and graphic, Hollywood slasher movie seem like a Disney film. Fact truly was stranger, and after hearing Myles, more deadly, than fiction.

CHAPTER THIRTY-ONE

Winsell Myles was born and raised in the Bushwick section of Brooklyn, in recent times one of the borough's trendiest neighborhoods. But when Myles grew up there, not so much.

His mother was a home health aide and his father worked as a hospital orderly. Because Myles was an only child his mother and father doted on him. They sent him to a private high school in western Queens, only a short bus ride away from his home. After graduation Myles wanted to get a job and make his own money, but his parents encouraged him to register in a college program. He enrolled in a City University Of New York community college, but he wasn't happy.

When he completed the two year program he knew that he was done with school. It was time to get a job and find an apartment of his own.

His first job was as a salesman for an optical company. He traveled around New York City visiting optical stores selling eyeglass frames made in China, although each of the boxes containing the frames was marked 'Made in Italy.'

Myles was good looking, polite, and persuasive, which made him a successful salesman. But not successful enough to satisfy Myles. His salary was low and the percentage of each sale that was used to calculate his commission was not high enough to adequately supplement the low wages. He wasn't making enough to support a family which he hoped to start with a young woman he met while peddling his eyewear in a store where she worked. After a year, he told his boss that he was quitting.

Myles and his lady, Nika, got married six months later when he began working for The City of New York in the Brooklyn Medical Examiner's Office.

Myles applied for the position of morgue attendant when he saw an advertisement for the job in the civil service newspaper, *The Chief.*

After taking a civil service test, which he had no trouble passing, and impressing the medical examiner's hiring group in an interview, Myles was chosen. He now had the security and benefits of a civil service position, which covered his wife and their soon to be first child.

Being raised by parents who worked in health related positions and hearing their stories of difficult patients and hospital gore, Myles was not squeamish. He attended autopsies as part of his job at the morgue and was particularly interested in watching the ME cut out and dissect the organs of the deceased.

When an autopsy was completed it was Myles job to clean up and return the body to one of the refrigerated compartments where it was stored until a funeral home claimed it or transported to Potter's field for an anonymous burial.

Myles told Michael that he met Reverend LePage one night on Flatbush Avenue, not far from the medical examiner's office. The avenue is one of Brooklyn's busiest streets with stores, restaurants, and bars that attract plenty of pedestrian traffic.

Myles just left a bar where he often went for a drink after a harrowing day at work, when he saw a shiny red Cadillac pull to the curb. He watched as the driver lowered his window and engaged several young ladies in conversation. When Myles moved closer so he could hear, he told Michael that the driver was, "This dude dressed like Super Fly."

Myles said, "The guy must have had a good line of bullshit because the women seemed excited by what he was saying and two of them jumped into his car."

Before the Cadillac pulled away from the curb, Myles approached the driver and started a conversation of his own.

"When LePage introduced himself as a reverend I thought, '*What kind of reverend drives a big red Caddy trollin' for women.*' He must have read my mind because he told me he was recruiting the ladies to join his church, and to work in the charity he runs for poor and starving kids in Africa."

"Then outta' nowhere he asked me if I had a job."

"I told him where I worked, and what I did, and he smiled. I thought that reaction was weird and was about to tell him that, when he asked if I wanted to come work for him. I was shocked because I just met the guy, but I wanted to hear what he was offering. So I asked him."

LePage told Myles that he needed a chauffeur and a bodyguard because he was putting himself in danger recruiting women whose families could "Look to hurt him for 'stealing' their daughters."

"I ain't ever worked in security but I was in good shape and could always handle myself, so I asked him what it paid. When he gave me the number I said yes on the spot. Mr. G, it was three times what I was making at the morgue. And with the bonus he promised if things worked out between us, it was enough for me to buy my own health insurance for my family."

Myles said he resigned his job at the morgue the next day and began driving for LePage that night.

He told Michael that he soon learned why LePage was so successful in attracting women to his cause.

He asked lots of questions of the women, probing for weaknesses, gullibility, and things like unhappiness at home, if they had a home. He probed for signs of abuse, asking if their parents, caregivers, or whomever they were living with, were mean, always angry, and mistreated them.

He also looked for young women who were rebellious, and ready to do anything that pushed the envelope.

"When he got the answers he was looking for he went into his pitch. He had a way with words," Myles said, with a touch of admiration in his voice.

Michael nodded, having experienced that silver tongue at the Jackson Chase trial.

"Mr. G that man was the smoothest bullshit artist I ever heard!"

"When he got through with his rap of promising them a home, money, new clothes, food, and a place in heaven, they couldn't get into the car fast enough."

"Sometimes we didn't have enough room for everyone that wanted to join up. So he had me drive him and the first load of women to his church, and then go pick up the others."

It took some time before Myles learned what was really happening to the women once they were settled into the third and fourth floor apartments above Lepage's church.

In addition to driving the reverend around town looking for women and driving the reverend's wife wherever she wanted to go, Myles told Michael he drove the women, dressed as nuns, to locations where they would beg for money.

"Most of the time it was me driving with either Zeke or Frankie riding shotgun. Sometimes it was the sons alone who ferried the nuns, and other times it was just me."

"After I been working there for a good while, on one of the days when I was driving alone, one of them women got into the car and she looked terrible. A couple of blocks from the church she even vomited out the back window of the car. I pulled over to help her and

I seen that her eyes were all glassy and she didn't even know who I was."

Myles said that when he told her he was going to take her to a hospital, she freaked out and begged him not to. She was shaking and appeared very frightened. When he asked her what was wrong she told him, "It's just the pills and vodka the reverend gives us if we're good girls. I took too many and drank too much and was awake all night. But if he finds out I went to a hospital I'll be punished."

"So after I dropped her off at her spot, I went back to the church and saw Frankie and Zeke hanging outside. I asked them about the alcohol and drugs, and they told me, 'That's the way the rev controls them. First he hooks them on drugs and vodka. Then if they don't do what he wants them to do, he threatens to deny them that shit.' Both then started to laugh."

"When I asked what was so funny, Zeke says, 'That's how he gets them to fuck him. If they don't want to, or they don't feel like it, he don't give them the pills and vodka, and he beats them in front of all the others.'"

Michael knew from talking to Frankie that his mother no longer lived with the reverend, and he asked Myles about her.

"How did Helen deal with all that?"

Myles dropped his head and said, "I really liked Miss Helen. She was always good to me, asking about my family and such. It's sad, but she put up with that shit until the beatings and the fucking got way outta' hand. Every time one of them women got pregnant by the reverend, she told me, it was like him sticking a knife in her back."

"She and the reverend would have all sorts of arguments, and I knew it was a matter of time before she would do something."

He said that one night when everyone was asleep, Helen took her youngest son Noah and left. She didn't tell anyone what she intended to do and didn't leave a note for the reverend or for her other sons.

Myles said when he reported for work at the church that

morning Rev. LePage was 'going crazy.' He was ranting about how she took his boy, and how he had no clue where she was, or where she was going.

"But Mr. G, he didn't give a shit about Helen leaving and taking Noah. He told me he was worried about her going to the cops or to the DA because he said she knew all about his scams and how he treated the women."

"He was afraid that she would look to get back at him for all the fucking, and all the kids, he produced."

Myles said that it wasn't long after Helen left that LePage hooked up with another woman and married her.

"His new wife, Belinda, was exactly what he was looking for. Not because she was attractive, or nice, she was the opposite of those things. It was because she promised that as long as he paid her she'd do what he wanted, which was to keep them women in line."

"Why did he get married again?" Michael asked. "If all he wanted was someone to be a disciplinarian. She didn't have to be a wife."

"He done it for show," Myles answered. "He had all those people in his congregation fooled. He was supposed to be a man of God so he had to have a wife at his side to keep up appearances."

"He told them suckers one Sunday morning that Helen was a heathen and he had to cast her out. That's when he introduced Belinda as his new wife and partner. He said she was his angel, 'sent to me by the Almighty in my hour of need.'"

"Did Belinda keep the women in line as he expected?"

"Oh yeah! If she didn't there would be hell to pay from LePage. He'd smack her around. That's why when a woman talked back to her, or told her to 'go fuck herself,' when she asked them to do something, she tried to work it out. That usually resulted in Belinda getting cursed out and then going to the reverend and telling him."

"Once I seen what he did after Belinda ratted out one of the women. It was much worse than anything he done when Helen was around. And after it was over I could see that even Belinda thought it was too much."

"Tell me about it?" Michael asked.

"This is what happened. He called everybody who was in the house, including me, to the living room of his apartment. He then stripped the woman of her clothes and told her to get on the floor spread eagle. He said to her, but he meant it for all of us, that he was about to teach her a lesson for her own good."

"He told me and Zeke to hold her down as he took his belt off. He then whipped the shit outta' that lady. When he was done he went into the kitchen and came back with a bottle of vinegar. He told me and Zeke to hold her down again as he stood over the woman and poured the vinegar on her open wounds. Then he throws a towel to one of the others who was watching and says to clean her up and mop the floor."

Myles said that after the beating, the buzzer for the apartment sounded. He looked out the window and saw a cop car outside.

"The woman who was beaten was screaming so loud that someone must have called them," he told Michael.

He said LePage ordered him and Zeke to keep the woman quiet and he went down to speak to the police.

"What happened?" Michael asked.

"Not a goddam thing," Myles answered. "The rev came back upstairs, and with a big smile on his face he announced, 'It's good to have important friends.'"

"Any idea what he meant?"

"Yeah. Some in his congregation are big, important, people in Brooklyn. He mustta' dropped a name or two and the cops went away."

"Did a beating like that ever occur again?"

"Nah. He didn't stop the beatings, but he never used the vinegar again."

At that point Myles stopped talking and dropped his head. Michael got the sense that he had more to say but was reluctant, even ashamed, to do so.

"Winsell, there's more, isn't there?" Michael asked.

Myles, without picking his head up, just nodded.

"Listen If you want my help, you're going to have to give me everything," Michael said. "What are you not telling me?"

Myles looked at him and said, "Women started disappearing."

"How?" Michael asked.

Myles gave him a one word answer, "Jiz."

CHAPTER
THIRTY-TWO

It was late in the afternoon and Michael decided to call it as day.

Two and a half long, difficult, days into the debriefing Myles had reached a point in his narrative where Michael felt a meal and a good night's sleep would let him relax before he opened up about the disappearance of the women.

And, although he was anxious to hear about the role Jiz played, Michael knew he too needed a break. The most crucial aspects of Myles' story were coming up and he wanted to recharge and be ready for what would be an important third full day with Reverend LePage's former right hand man.

After their first day together, when Myles agreed to cooperate, Michael had arranged through Monsignor Romano and John Caldwell to keep Myles in a hotel under guard for at least the duration of his debriefing. After which, depending on what he said, and if a case could be made against the reverend, Myles would either remain under guard in a safe location, or be sent back to jail to stand trial.

Myles and his attorney were happy when Michael called it a day. Tim Clark and Dina were on duty that night to guard Myles at his hotel, and after he had a few private words with his lawyer, the two investigators escorted him out and drove to where he was being held.

When Michael got back to his apartment he called Monsignor Romano.

After he brought the monsignor up to date on how well Frankie LePage was handling life at Ft. Hamilton, and what he learned during the last two and a half days with Winsell Myles, Romano asked if Michael believed another battle with the EVIL ONE was on the horizon.

"Sal, from what Frankie told me his father could be indicted for larceny by fraud, rape, and possibly murder, right now. But I haven't yet gotten corroborating evidence of the EVIL ONE's role in any of it."

"However, if I was a betting man, I would stake all I have on *HIM* being the prime instigator with the reverend in the murder of Jax Chase."

"I believe that tomorrow Myles will give me evidence that several missing women from the reverend's cult were actually murder victims. He's already hinted that Jiz was responsible."

"I'll keep you posted," Michael said.

After he hung up with Romano, Michael called his father and his sons.

Although he was tied up first with the Chase trial, then with the Frankie and Myles debriefings, he regularly checked in, but it had been a while since he spoke to them at length.

The chat with his father lasted just a few minutes. However, it was long enough for Michael to hear that his dad was feeling good and keeping busy with his work at the Veterans of Foreign Wars post where he was the treasurer. Before they hung up Michael checked with him to schedule a Sunday dinner with his grandsons.

"Mike, for you and the boys, every Sunday is good for me," his father told him.

When he reached Michael Jr. and Kevin, both were involved with homework. But that didn't stop them from spending an hour talking with Michael.

They caught him up on their lives, in and outside of school. And even though they congratulated him after he won the Chase trial, they wanted to hear all the details of the case.

Michael told them what he could, and to get them back to their studies, made an excuse that he had work to do. Before signing off he asked about dates for a Sunday dinner with him and their grandpa.

Michael didn't think it would be difficult for the boys to come up with a good date, but he had a rude awakening. Both were involved with girls, and for the next few weekends they were busy. When they gave him a Sunday three weeks away, he booked it.

"I'll be in touch before then. Now get back to your homework. Stay safe. I love you."

'Wow! I'm getting old," Michael said out loud to his empty apartment after he hung up with his sons.

"They both have girlfriends! I remember when I was changing their diapers," he said and shook his head in disbelief.

Michael had one more call to make before he settled in for the night.

"It's me," he said when Kathy Baer answered her phone.

"Mike I know," Kathy said laughing. "You say that every time. I have you in my contacts so your name pops up when you call."

"Sorry, you're right. I'm a bit frazzled. It's been a long few days and I need sleep. I miss you. How are you?"

Michael and Kathy spent the next hour catching up. Michael talked a little about his investigation and Kathy told him all about a new case she was involved in. Always concerned about the EVIL ONE using Kathy to get to him, Michael pressed for details on her case. When Gioca was satisfied that *HE* was not involved, he changed the subject and asked Kathy out to dinner for Saturday night.

"Yes," she answered, adding, "And I'll make breakfast for us on Sunday morning."

"It's a date. Kathy, stay safe. I love you."

When his alarm went off early the next morning, a fully refreshed Michael jumped out of bed, put on his running gear, and went for a long, head clearing run through the deserted streets of Carroll Gardens and neighboring Red Hook.

At 8 Michael walked into his office to find Tim, Dina and Myles eating breakfast in the conference room.

Myles looked well rested. The two investigators, not so much. Both were somewhat disheveled and glassy eyed from no, or very little, sleep. Their appearance was evidence of a job well done. Winsell Myles was safe and sound and loving the omelet and fries his protectors bought for him.

Michael greeted Myles and asked if he slept well. When Winsell nodded that he had, Michael told him to enjoy his meal. "We'll get back to work when Mr. Rand gets here."

At 9:30 the lawyer arrived and Michael got right into the debriefing.

"Winsell, I want to pick up where we left off yesterday," he said. "You seemed to imply that this fellow Jiz was involved in the disappearance of a few of the reverend's women."

"Mr. G, I wasn't *implying* nothing. I *know* Jiz and the reverend killed Natasha, Sammi and Alexa!"

"How do you know?" asked Michael.

"Because I helped them get rid of the bodies."

Having learned from Frankie's debriefing that the reverend and Jiz killed them because LePage believed they were informing on him, Michael now wanted to hear if Myles told the same story. It was his way of testing the veracity of both informants.

"Let's start with Natasha," Michael said. "What did she do, or what were you told she did, that caused the reverend and Jiz to kill her?"

Myles began by telling Michael that Natasha was the woman who got sick in his car and vomited. "She's the one who didn't want me to take her to the hospital."

Myles said someone told the reverend about the incident, and although he was happy that she didn't go to a hospital, "I got the feeling that from then on the rev didn't trust her. He was afraid that she was weak and might do something that would put the police onto him."

"A few weeks later, Zeke drove Natasha to Coney Island and dropped her off at the Nathan's hot dog place to beg for money. I was told that ten minutes later, Zeke was sitting in his car talking on his phone when two cops came to the car and told him to get out. When he did, they arrested him. He was released by the DA early that night and when he got back to the church, he told the rev what happened."

"A couple of weeks later, I'm in the rev's office in the back of the church when I hear him call out for me. He tells me to come to the cellar, which was one floor below the church."

When he got down there Myles said he saw the reverend and Jiz standing over Natasha. Her throat was cut. He said that her body was on the floor next to an old bathtub.

He described the tub as having four short legs and raised off the floor by two bricks under each leg. "Under the center of the tub was one of those round wood burning outdoor firepits that some people have in their backyard. I knew someone who had one and we toasted marshmallows over it."

Myles said there were logs burning in the fire pit heating up what smelled like cooking oil which filled the tub.

"I asked the rev what happened, but Jiz answered. He told me, 'Shut the fuck up and do what the rev tells you to do.'"

"I looks over at LePage and he says that since I worked in the morgue, I seen lots of bodies being cut up. He tells me, 'cut this bitch into small pieces, and put them into the oil when it starts to boil.'"

"I told them to go fuck themselves."

"I says I ain't getting' involved with no murder, and I start to leave. That's when Jiz grabs my arm and gives me a look that was pure evil."

"Mr. G, I almost shit my pants."

"He tells me if I don't do what they want, he's gonna' go to my house, he even knew the address, kill my son Dustin, and rape 'that beautiful wife of yours who you met in that optical store, until she begs me to stop or can't walk no more.' I wanted to strangle that fuck and I went after him, but the rev stepped between us."

"Did you know Jiz well enough to tell him such details about your family?" Michael asked.

"I ain't never told him nothin' about my family. Even the rev didn't know those things. I have no Idea how that motherfucker found all that out."

Michael knew but of course he couldn't tell Myles.

"So after Jiz threatened your family, what did you do?"

"What you think I did?I ain't have no choice."

"With those two fucks standing about ten feet away, I starts to cut up Natasha's body with a power saw that the rev handed to me. And I tossed each piece of her into the boiling oil."

"Mr. G, it looked like I was fryin' chicken."

CHAPTER THIRTY-THREE

Myles said that a few weeks after they killed Natasha, Jiz and the reverend did the same thing to Sammi and Alexa.

"The three women were friends and lived together in one of the apartments on the fourth floor of the church building. None of them had kids, so they was together all the time. From what I could see, they were very close."

"When Natasha disappeared Sammi and Alexa be askin' the Rev and Belinda where she went. Of course they got no answer."

He told Michael the story of Isaiah dropping the two off in Times Square one day, and when he returned later to pick them up, they were nowhere in sight.

"Isaiah said he waited for about thirty minutes, then he saw them coming out of the subway. When he asked where they been, they said in downtown Brooklyn where there was department stores and lots of shoppers who they was begging from."

"Isaiah told his father all that and a few days later is when I seen both women with their throats cut, just like Natasha, laying in the cellar next to that tub."

Myles said the reverend told him that he and Jiz killed Sammi and Alexa because he believed they was "rattin' him out to the DA's office about Natasha bein' missing."

When Myles told Michael that he cut up their bodies and boiled the parts as he did to Natasha, he asked, "What happened to the burnt remains of the bodies?"

"I drove upstate to a spot deep in the woods where the rev has some bullshit camp, and dumped what was left of Natasha into a lake on the grounds. Then when they killed Sammi and Alexa, I did the same thing with their remains."

Myles' answer surprised Michael.

That was the first he heard that the reverend owned property outside of Brooklyn.

Armed with that information Michael began to formulate a plan for the trial of LePage. A trial he now knew was inevitable.

It was lunch time and when the food Tim and Dina ordered for Myles and Rand arrived, Michael took a break.

While they ate Tim stayed in the conference room and Dina accompanied Michael to his office.

"You need to find that camp," he said to Dina.

"I have an idea, but I won't be able to do anything unless you find that piece of property."

"I won't need both you and Tim sitting in with me this afternoon. I want you to go property hunting. Speak to Myles before I start up again. I'm sure he can point you in the right direction."

Dina spent thirty minutes with Myles going through the route he took to LePage's property. When she was satisfied she had enough information to work with, Dina left, and Michael resumed the debriefing.

"Let's talk about your arrest. How did that happen?"

Myles told him that when he returned to the church after dumping the remains of Sammi and Alexa, Belinda, the reverend's wife called him into her room.

"Belinda was always good to me and she liked Natasha, Sammi, and Alexa. She warned me about Jiz and told me to be careful. She said that Jiz told the rev that I needed to go because I knew too much and was a risk. The fuck wanted to kill me!"

Belinda told Myles that the rev liked him too much to kill him, and he had something else in mind to get him out of the way.

The reverend knew that Myles had a criminal record for drunk driving when he was in college. On one of those occasions, Myles hit a parked car which the owner's insurance company determined was a total loss. Myles pled guilty to a felony and received probation because of his age.

A year later, Myles was driving drunk again, and hit a pedestrian who was severely injured. This time his conviction carried a sentence of one year in jail, making Myles what the law calls, 'a second felony offender,' which meant that a future felony conviction would carry a significant prison sentence.

"I'm sure that the rev told Jiz all about my record. And since he didn't want to kill me he told the prick to set me up. Another felony arrest and conviction would mean I'd do a lot of jail time, maybe life, and I'd be outta' their way. And that's what he did."

Myles said Jiz knew that the reverend was going to ask him to run an errand for which he had to use his car. So, he planted two guns in Myles' car and broke one of its taillights.

When Myles was several blocks from the church he was pulled over by an NYPD radio car.

"I asked the cop who came to my window why he stopped me. He said that I had a broken taillight. My first reaction was 'that's bullshit', but when I got out the car and looked, I seen that he was right. Then I hear the other cop, who was lookin' into my car, say 'grab him. He's got guns.'"

"Right then I knew that this was what Belinda was talking about when she told me that the rev 'had something else in mind' to get me outta' the way. When I drove to work that morning my taillight wasn't broken, and sure as shit those guns wasn't mine. The rev and Jiz set me up good."

When Michael was finished with his debriefing of Myles, it was clear that LePage, with the EVIL ONE being the instigator, murdered the three women. Coupled with what Frankie told him, he had enough evidence to indict Vernon LePage.

However he wasn't satisfied he had enough to convict him at trial.

What was missing was irrefutable evidence that Natasha, Sammi, and Alexa were dead. He needed their bodies, or what was left of them.

With Frankie LePage safe in Ft. Hamilton, and Winsell Myles under guard in a secure location that Caldwell convinced the FBI to allow him to use, Michael concentrated on finding the LePage property where the remains he needed were dumped.

Dina Mitchell was making progress in her search but it was not moving quickly enough for Michael. Although he convinced the two main witnesses against Reverend LePage to testify, based on his experience, witnesses like Frankie and Myles could easily change their minds. He had to get them into the grand jury, and under oath, to solidify their cooperation.

Two weeks had passed since Michael gave Dina the task of finding the property and he was running out of patience. He decided to call Monsignor Romano hoping the cleric could convince Caldwell to use his federal law enforcement connections to assist Dina. However as he was about to dial the monsignor, Dina walked into his office. The big smile on her face told him she hit paydirt.

"I found *LePage Acres,*" she announced.

"*LePage Acres*, what the fuck is that?"

Laughing, Dina told him it was the name of the reverend's camp.

"It's located in the Catskill Mountain region, deep in the woods just outside of Bethel, New York. He named the camp after the old TV show *Green Acres*."

"Great work Dina. How did you find it? And how do you know he named it after the TV show?"

Dina surprised him with her answer. "I had some unexpected help."

"I spoke to Frankie thinking he would know where the camp was. He told me he had been there as a kid but had no idea of the location. But he said his mother Helen might know."

"He knew how to reach her and was able to get in touch."

"Frankie told her what I was looking for and she agreed to talk to me. She told me, '*LePage Acres,* is the name of the camp. That fool named it after a TV show he liked. It's near Bethel, New York, up in them Catskill Mountains.'"

Dina said after talking to Helen she contacted the Bethel police.

"They confirmed what LePage's wife told me. I asked if the camp had a lake on the grounds and they said that it did."

"Michael, what do you want to do?"

He knew, but he had to first discuss it with Romano and Caldwell.

"Dina, again, great work. I have some ideas but I want to think about my next move. I'll let you know when I'm ready."

That night Michael met Romano at *Emilio's*.

Over lasagna and a bottle of *Chianti Classico* Michael filled in the monsignor on everything he had gotten from Frankie and Myles and then told him about Dina's finding.

"Sal, I want to dredge the lake. I need to find whatever is left of those bodies. And if that's not doable, I need divers to go in there to search. If they do find body parts or remnants of body parts, I want to send them to the FBI lab for analysis. Any DNA the lab can pull out of whatever is found I want to try to match to Natasha, Sammi, and Alexa. Please ask Caldwell to see what he can arrange."

Roman listened carefully to everything Michael told him and when he was finished, all the monsignor could do was shake his head.

"This guy claims to be a reverend? What a disgrace! He's nothing more than a criminal who the EVIL ONE found and used. Whatever you need Mike I'll make sure Caldwell gets it for you. I'll reach out to him tonight."

It was midnight when Michael's phone rang.

It was Romano.

"Mike, make a list. Caldwell will make sure you get it all."

CHAPTER THIRTY-FOUR

Two weeks later, on a cold early spring afternoon, FBI scuba diver, Agent Kelly Pistone, searched the bottom of the lake on *LePage Acres* and hit a macabre jackpot. The human remains, and the remnants of gold and silver colored jewelry she found, filled a small bucket.

Michael's original idea of dredging the lake couldn't be done. The Army Corps of Engineers determined that it was too dangerous. They feared the ground around the small body of water would collapse, taking their equipment and anyone working it into the lake.

Dina and Tim, who were lakeside, took custody of the bucket and turned it over to the city medical examiner's office as Michael directed.

Curious as to how he managed to get the Army to take a look, and FBI to help him out, they asked Michael when they got back to his office.

He didn't give them a complete answer, however he didn't lie either.

"I called in a favor from a longtime friend. He made it happen. Let's hope it was all worth it.

Under the law of New York State, to obtain an indictment for murder, and later a conviction, Michael needed to prove that the three murdered women were once alive. In the usual murder case the body of the murder victim is identified by someone who knew the victim in life. Usually a family member or friend's ID satisfied the law. Here with only bits and pieces of the bodies, Michael needed all the help he could get to establish what the law required.

The statements of Frankie and Myles were certainly on point, but he didn't feel confident that their statements alone would convince a jury and establish that necessary element of the law.

They both had serious criminal records and a defense attorney would use that to argue that their testimony was not worthy of belief, beyond a reasonable doubt. He couldn't take that risk. He needed hard evidence. The remains of Natasha, Sammi, and Alexa, along with testimony from someone who knew them, would do the trick.

Therefore he arranged for the city medical examiner to pack up what was recovered from the lake and send it to Dr. Fred Cesarano at the FBI lab where he would try to extract DNA from the remains. He knew from his experience with the Chase case, that the FBI's equipment was far superior and more sophisticated than any the city ME had at his disposal.

If the doctor was successful with step one, extracting DNA, his next challenge was to prove that it belonged to one or more of the murdered women. To do that he needed known DNA specimens from the three to make comparisons.

To acquire specimens, it was first necessary to identify the three women beyond their first names. While Dina was working to locate *LePage Acres*, Michael gave that task to Tim.

He started by talking to Frankie LePage and Winsell Myles. They were no help. All they knew about the women were their first names.

Helen LePage was no help either. She told Tim that she never wanted to know the family names of any of the women the reverend recruited. And furthermore, she didn't even recall anyone named Nastasha, Sammi, or Alexa.

Frustrated, Tim told Michael he was stumped. He didn't know where to turn in order to get what Michael and Dr. Cesarano needed.

Learning their identities and in turn finding their families was essential. That would allow Cesarano to extract DNA from relatives and compare it to any DNA he could get from the remains recovered from the lake. A match or matches would give Michael irrefutable evidence that LePage was guilty of murder, and another defeat for the EVIL ONE.

'*How am I going to get what I need?*', Michael thought to himself after talking to Tim.

That's when the advice of his friend the monsignor came to mind. "You have an ally. Don't be hesitant to call on Him for help," Romano told him early in the war.

Michael checked his watch and saw that if he hurried he could make it to the 12:30 mass at St. Charles Borromeo, the church a few blocks from his office.

Before mass began, Michael knelt and prayed. He ended with, "I need your help. I can't let *HIM* win."

When the service was over, Michael was leaving the church when a priest came out of nowhere and approached him.

"You seem troubled," the cleric said.

Michael was startled, and surprised by the comment because he didn't think he was exhibiting any outward signs of concern.

"Father, we've never met. And you don't know anything about me. But you're right. I am troubled and came to mass to ask for God's help.

"I know," the priest said.

"Michael, have faith. Your prayers will be answered."

With that the priest turned away and seemed to disappear into the darkness of the church.

When he got back to his office, Dina and Tim were waiting for him.

"You have a visitor," Dina said.

When Michael asked who it was, Tim answered. "It's Belinda LePage, the reverend's wife."

"What does she want?" Michael asked.

"We don't know," Dina answered. "She'll only talk to you."

Michael asked Dina to bring Belinda into the conference room. When she walked in he could see from the look on her face that she was determined to talk.

He also saw fear.

After introducing himself, he told Belinda that if she wanted to speak to him, Dina and Tim would have to be present. Belinda nodded and said, "Okay."

Michael asked her if she wanted something to drink. She declined and got right into what she had to say.

"Mr. Gioca, I can't spend another day around my depraved husband, and his vile, brutal sidekick Brother Jiz, as he calls him. I've had enough of their killing and their mistreatment of women. I want to end them."

"I came to you because I seen how you handled the Chase trial; I know you're the man who can do it. I will tell you everything I know if you agree to open an investigation into those two bastards."

'*She has no idea that we're well into that investigation,*' Michael thought.

Belinda continued. "The information I have will disgust and shock you. Those two are animals. I need you to promise to protect me from them."

Michael felt like he did as a kid on Christmas morning. The anticipation of what Belinda had to say, and the excitement of 'ending' LePage and Jiz brought back memories of how he felt when he got out of bed and saw the gifts under the Christmas tree, and the excitement when he opened them.

"Mrs. LePage..." was as far as Michael got when she interrupted him. "Please don't call me that. I don't want to hear the words, 'Mrs.

LePage' ever again. My family name is Shaw. Please just call me Belinda."

Michael began again.

"Belinda you have our interest, " he said pointing to Dina and Tim. "But before I can give you the protection you're asking for I need to hear what you have to say. I need something to tell my boss if I'm going to ask him for the authorization to house and protect you."

Without hesitation Belinda said, "I understand."

"I'll start by telling you how I met Vernon, and what motivated me to come to you today. If you're satisfied, and we cut a deal, I'll tell you about the murder of four women who worked for us."

"I'm listening," Michael said.

Belinda told him that she met LePage at a political function for one of the reverend's "Big shot" friends. She said, "He was charming, polite, and very charismatic. I took a liking to him and we began dating. He told me he was a bachelor."

The reverend moved quickly. After two months he asked Belinda to marry him. "It was one of those whirlwind courtships."

"I'm no spring chicken, and he swept me off my feet. He was kind and attentive, and when he talked with that silver tongue of his, it was impossible to say no."

She said they were married by Jiz, which nearly caused Michael to fall out of his chair. Seeing his reaction, Belinda told him that she understood his shock.

"When I saw that freak with the red dreads, I almost walked out on the wedding right then and there."

"Vernon took me aside and calmed me down. He said that Jiz was a good man, a fully recognized minister in New York State, and his assistant pastor. He gave me a hug and a kiss and persuaded me to let it all be."

"Only after the ceremony did Vernon tell me he had been married. He said his wife Helen was a heathen who left him, after which they was divorced. But I later learned from Helen herself that they was never divorced. She also told me that ever since she left, Vernon was looking for a new wife, but only to impress his congregation."

"When I found that out, it was the beginning of the end for me."

"Okay that's all interesting, but let's get back on track. Tell us what brought you here today?" Michael asked.

Belinda told Michael about a young woman she recruited to be one of the reverend's nuns.

"Once I married Vernon, he told me all about his scam of sending women out into the streets of the city to solicit donations for an African charity which didn't exist. I'm not gonna' sit here and tell you that it offended me. I was right there with him in this con."

"And, because I was, he gave me the responsibility of helping him recruit women and to keep watch over them in the field, and when they was home. I was like their den mother. I looked after them. But if any gave me a problem, Vernon told me to let him know. He then did what he thought was best to see to it that the woman never disobeyed me again. And yes, that included corporal punishment, as Vernon liked to call it."

"Do you know anything about drugs? And raping the women? Were you aware that he would sexually abuse them?" Michael asked.

Before she answered Belinda dropped her head and began to weep. "Yes," she answered.

"I ain't proud of turning a blind eye to what Vernon was doing. And I ain't saying what I'm about to say as an excuse, but what he did was always behind a closed and locked door. I had no way of seeing for myself what went on."

"He didn't do it to all the women," she said. "He only fucked the ones he thought was sexy and hot. They, of course, never said nothing to me. I would find out from the others, the ones he wouldn't fuck, and wouldn't give drugs to."

"They felt he took care of the ones he bedded better than them. They was jealous. When they came to me to complain, I would say that I'll deal with it."

"Finally, after I got lots of complaints, I went to speak with Vernon."

"What happened when you confronted him?" Dina asked.

"He started to laugh and denied it."

"He say, 'Pay them no mind. We gots lots of women around here and you know how females like to gossip. I don't pay attention to any of them. That's your job.'"

"I shoulda' seen through his bullshit denial, and demanded he stop. But I didn't 'cause I was afraid. I seen what he did when he punished the disobedient ones."

"And Mr. Gioca, when that scary, mean, SOB Jiz got involved, women started to disappear."

"Belinda, I distracted you with my question about the drugs and the rapes," Michael said. "Tell me about the young woman you recently recruited. Does she have something to do with why you're here?"

Belinda nodded and said, "Her name is Riley."

She told Michael that she met the young woman in Manhattan not that long ago. Riley was in line ahead of Belinda in Starbucks, and when her order was ready she began to look through her purse for money to pay for it.

After a minute or so, Riley told the counterman that she didn't have the money to pay because, "I must have left my wallet at home."

Belinda said, "When the server was about to take the food and coffee away, Riley began to cry."

"She told the counterman that she only lived a block away and that her mother was sick, and the order was for her."

"Riley told the guy, 'My mom loves the muffins and coffee from here, and it'll make her feel so good if I bring her this stuff. Please let me take it to her before the coffee gets cold, and I'll be right back with the money.'"

"Mr. Gioca, she seemed so sweet, but I knew right away that she was scamming the guy. She had such an angelic face, and a nice polite way about her, that the counterman couldn't say no. He told her to take the coffee and food, adding, 'I hope your mom feels better', as she left the store."

Belinda said she followed Riley out and walked behind her. When she got about two blocks from the coffee shop, Riley stopped and sat down on a bench. Belinda told Michael that when she got to where Riley was sitting the young woman was eating the muffin and drinking the coffee.

"I had to have her for the church. With that face and her sweet way, I knew no one would turn her down when she asked for money, especially dressed in that nun's outfit."

"It took me about fifteen minutes to get her to agree to join us."

"Riley Caine was my prized recruit. And as I got to know her, I grew very fond of her."

Belinda continued. "Riley quickly settled into one of the apartments and was even better at the work than I thought she'd be. Very few people refused to give her a 'donation.' She also got along well with the others and seemed happy with us."

"Then about a week ago, I was checking on the women as I did nearly every night. When I got to Riley's room she was crying and very upset. When I asked her what was wrong, at first she wouldn't tell me. But when I finally got her to talk she said that earlier that night Jiz came to her room and raped her. She said she tried to fight him off but he was too strong, and he threatened to cut her throat if she didn't fuck him. When he was done he told her that now she was his girlfriend."

"Riley told me that when Jiz left, she was upset and frightened. She looked for me, but I was busy. She said she then went to Vernon and told him what Jiz did."

At this point in her story Belinda got up from her seat. Clearly upset and angry, she started to pace up and down in the conference room. No one said a word. When she got back to her chair she grabbed it and said, "That motherfucker laughed, and asked her, 'Was it good?'"

Belinda then slammed her hand on the conference table, sat back down in her chair and began to mutter to herself.

"It's time for a break," Michael said.

CHAPTER THIRTY-FIVE

Twenty minutes later, a now calm Belinda resumed her story.

"After Riley told me what happened, I knew she couldn't stay there and needed my help to get out. She wanted to leave right then, but there were too many people awake in the house for her to get away undetected. I told her that we'd have to wait for the right time so she could get out and be as far away as possible before anyone found out that she was gone."

But, she and Riley had a plan. They would pretend that all was normal for a few days. Then when Belinda felt the time was right, she'd alert Riley to be ready to leave that night.

"Two nights ago when everyone was asleep, I went to Riley's room but she wasn't there. At first I was worried, but when I didn't see her things, I figured Riley didn't want to wait and just took off."

Belinda said that when Riley didn't come down for breakfast as all the women did before they hit the streets, she went to the reverend and pretended to be upset that Riley was missing.

"I told him that Riley is not at breakfast. I said that I went to her room to look for her and it looked like she left."

"Did he say anything to you?" Michael asked.

"He said, 'You ain't got to be concerned with Riley no more.'"

"That scared the hell outta' me. I knew what that meant. Riley was dead!"

"Vernon and Jiz musta' found out that she wanted out. They couldn't let that happen after Jiz raped her. She was a threat to them, just like those other women who disappeared."

"And knowing them two, since I was so close to Riley, it was just a matter of time before they blamed me. I know what they was capable of and what they done to the others. I didn't want to die. That's why I'm here."

Michael thought to himself, *'For your sake and mine, I'm happy you made that choice.'*

"Belinda I understand completely. You did the right thing."

"Now tell me what you know about the other women who disappeared."

Belinda nodded and said, "That was Natasha, and the sisters, Sammi and Alexa. They was murdered!"

"And I know they was, because Vernon told me that he and Jiz killed them."

"Here's the story. In my job I got to know all the women who worked for us. And as I told you, I checked on them almost every night. A while back, well before I brought Riley into the house, for a few nights I ain't seen Natasha in her room. All her things was there but not her."

"Then it was Sammi and Alexa. Them sisters was close. And like with Natasha, their stuff was in their room, but not them."

"So I go to Vernon to find out what was going on. I found him down in his office behind the church, with Jiz."

Belinda said that when she walked in she confronted LePage about the missing women.

"I first asked him if he knows why Natasha wasn't around, and then I asked about Sammi and Alexa."

"He looked at me and said, 'Yeah, I know. They was a problem and we eliminated them.'"

"When he said 'we,' I looked over at Jiz and that red headed motherfucker was laughing."

Michael asked Belinda how well she knew the three murdered women.

"I knew their names and what they was willing to tell me about themselves, which wasn't a lot."

She told him that Sammi and Alexa Rivera were sisters that were abused by their father, but their mother refused to leave him. And Natasha Popov never knew her father. She was raised by her mother, who died a couple of years before. All she had was an aunt, her mother's sister.

"With those backgrounds it was easy for Vernon to recruit them," Belinda added. Close to tears once again, she said, "Mr. Gioca, I liked them three very much. They was good girls who never gave me a problem. They didn't deserve what them two animals did to 'em."

Michael asked if their bedrooms remained unoccupied after they went missing.

Belinda nodded. "Yeah. After they disappeared, Vernon left the rooms as they were. He wouldn't touch nothing or put anyone in them because he said he wanted the others to think that the three would be back."

"Does that mean their belongings are still in the rooms?"

Belinda nodded.

"What about Riley's room?" Michael asked.

He didn't have her body or her remains, but he wanted to be prepared in the event either turned up.

"Just like the others Vernon ain't touched it."

"That's good."

Belinda didn't know why Michael asked about the rooms and the belongings, but he seemed very pleased by her answers. So she seized on the moment and asked, "Do we have a deal? Did I tell you enough for you to get them sons of bitches and put them in a cage forever?"

Michael smiled and told Belinda that they had a deal. However, he needed her to do something that was crucial to making a case that would result in convictions.

"I want you to go back to the church apartments. Collect any hair brushes and combs belonging to the women, along with their toothbrushes and night clothes."

"And Belinda, it's very important that you keep what you find separated so you can tell me to whom each item belonged."

"No problem. If I go now I can do it without anyone knowing. The women are all out begging, and the reverend and Jiz ain't there. Vernon told me this morning that they was gonna' go around checking on the nuns out in the streets."

"But there's one problem," she said. "The last time I went into Riley's room I told you that I didn't see any of her stuff around."

Then as if the proverbial light bulb went off in her head, Belinda began to smile.

"Why the smile?"

"I just remembered something," she answered.

"The night before she disappeared, Riley stayed with me in my room. She had a small bag with her toothbrush, a hair brush, a night gown, and clothes she wore the next day. In the morning she used my bathroom to brush her teeth, fix her hair, and take a shower. She dried off using one of my towels. That stuff is still in my bathroom."

"Great, bring all of that back," Michael said.

"And when you're there," he added, "Pack up what you need for yourself. You're never going back to that hell house. We'll protect you until after you testify, and then I'll find you a permanent home far away from Brooklyn. How does that sound?"

Belinda didn't answer right away. She stood, approached Michael, who was now standing, engulfed him in a hug, and said, "That sounds like heaven."

"One other thing. When LePage gets back home and you're not there he's going to wonder where you are. Do you have family who live outside the city?"

"Yes, I have an aunt who raised me when my mother passed away. She lives in North Carolina. Why?"

"I don't want LePage to know you're with us. So I want you to text him when you're on your way back here with Tim and Dina. If you write that there's been an emergency with your aunt and you had to leave immediately for North Carolina, will he buy that?"

"Yeah I think so. He knows I was raised by my Aunt Sophie, and I was telling him not that long ago that I hadn't seen her for a long while and was thinking of going home to visit. So this shouldn't come as too much of a surprise. I'll write that I'll call or text him as soon as I can, and I'll be back when my aunt is okay."

"Great," Michael said.

Dina and Tim drove Belinda to the church building and parked down the street so they could watch the entrance to the apartments while she collected what Michael asked for.

The investigators had her cell phone number and would call her if they saw anyone entering the building.

About thirty minutes later, Belinda came out with a suitcase that contained her clothes and toiletries, and four plastic bags, one each for the items belonging to Natasha, Sammi, Alexa, and Riley.

While Dina and Tim were with Belinda, Michael called Monsignor Romano.

He filled in the cleric on everything Belinda told him, and on the cooperation agreement they reached. He also told the monsignor that she was out collecting items belonging to the women that were murdered for DNA analysis and for comparison to the remains from the lake. And if found, to the body or remains of Riley Caine.

"Sal, I'll explain in more detail the next time we're together, but Belinda is a home run. This is LePage's wife! She knows all the secrets and is anxious to help us put him away."

"Of course she wants Jiz behind bars as well, so I'll have to come up with something to tell her when we don't bring *HIM* in."

"Mike, that all sounds great, but how can a wife testify against her husband? Isn't there a privilege?"

"There would be if they were actually married," he answered. "But they're not."

"His wife Helen told us that she walked out on him and they were never divorced. He bullshitted Belinda to get her to marry him."

"To be absolutely certain, I had Dina check that out. She found their marriage license on record in New York City, but there is no record of any divorce for Vernon and Helen LePage. And there is no marriage license on file for Belinda and him."

Michael asked for permission to put Belinda up for the night, under guard, and then into protective custody until after a trial.

Romano told him he would check with Caldwell, but he was sure there would be no problem.

Ten minutes later Romano called him back and gave him the okay.

"Wow! That was fast, for a guy your age," Michael said with a laugh.

Not in a laughing mood, Romano said he recognized the importance of his request to a case against LePage, and he didn't want it on his conscience if anything happened to Belinda.

Then he added, "And let me remind you, wiseass, we're the same age!"

Thoroughly chastised, Michael said, "'Thanks is what I should have said, instead of making a stupid joke. How about we have dinner and we share a bottle of red so I can apologize properly?"

The monsignor agreed and three hours later the two old friends were at their table in *Emilio's,* sharing a bottle of *Nero d'Avola*. They clinked glasses and Michael told the monsignor that he was sorry for the wise crack he made earlier that day.

"Apology partly accepted," Romano said. "It won't be completely accepted until after we finish the dinner you promised, and you leave the tip." They both laughed and the monsignor asked Michael for an update.

"Dina and Tim are back with Belinda and will be staying with her in the Marriott tonight. I'll make other arrangements in the morning," Michael said.

"How did it go at the church apartments?" Romano asked.

Michael told him Belinda scored.

"She was able to get hairbrushes from all four of the women, but no combs. She also brought back toothbrushes, and night clothes belonging to all of them. Sal, with the equipment the FBI lab uses in these situations, I'll be very, very surprised if we don't get DNA matches for the remains that came out of the lake, and if we ever find Riley. Before I left the office, I called Dr. Cesarano to tell him what Belinda recovered, and he agreed."

Just then their pasta arrived and the two dug in.

While waiting for the main course, Romano asked Michael a question that seemed to come out of nowhere and shook him to his core.

"Mike, after Winsell Myles told you about the lake, and the remains, knowing you as I do, you were frustrated at not having the means, or the evidence, to identify what was found. Am I right?"

Michael nodded.

"So I'm curious, did you think it was dumb luck when, out of the blue, Belinda LePage showed up at your door? Or did you believe something or someone else was responsible?"

Michael put down his glass of wine, shook his head and asked, "You know I went to mass and prayed for help. Don't you? *AND*, you know about that priest in St. Charles and what he told me."

With a slight nod, the monsignor smiled.

"Thank you."

CHAPTER THIRTY-SIX

The next day Michael wasted no time. He had Dina and Tim transport the items Belinda recovered to the FBI lab. Dr. Cesarano assured him that he would begin his analysis as soon as he received them but cautioned that it was going to take some time to arrive at a conclusion, if at all.

Confident that the results would be positive, Michael began to prepare Frankie LePage, Winsell Myles, and Belinda for their testimony in the grand jury.

Although he was sure that the reverend had no idea that he was under investigation, Michael knew never to underestimate the EVIL ONE. He took no chances. He had several of Caldwell's agents follow the reverend and watch his church on a twenty four hour basis. If they thought LePage was running or preparing to run, they were under orders to arrest him.

The witness prep went well. His three star witnesses were ready to testify. All Michael needed to proceed was word from Dr. Cesarano that he had positive results.

In the middle of his third week of work, Cesarano called a very anxious Michael. "I haven't finished my analysis. This is going to take longer than I thought. As soon as I have results I'll call you."

Michael now had a decision to make.

He wanted to secure an indictment against LePage quickly so he could be arrested and behind bars where he couldn't hurt or kill another disobedient 'nun.' But without positive results from Dr. Cesarano, an indictment based in large part on LePage's confessions to Frankie, Myles, and Belinda, was susceptible to being dismissed for insufficient evidence.

After saying a silent prayer for guidance, Michael made his decision. He would go to the grand jury without results from Cesarano and if the jury indicted, he would vigorously defend any defense motion to dismiss.

The grand jury presentation went smoothly.

Michael called Romano to tell him that the grand jury deliberated for less than two minutes and returned an indictment against Vernon LePage, and an unnamed co-conspirator, for the murders of Natasha Popov, and Sammi and Alexa Rivera.

"Sal, the jurors told me that LePage confessing to three different people was the clincher."

As soon as Michael filed the paperwork with the court, a warrant was issued for Vernon LePage. The agents who were watching him made the arrest outside the church as he walked to his car.

Jiz was nowhere in sight.

The next day LePage was arraigned on the indictment in Brooklyn Supreme Court.

Because he was unable to arrange for an attorney of his choosing, LePage was represented by a member of the Legal Aid Society. When the legal aid lawyer told him he was being charged with the murders of Natasha, Sammi, and Alexa, the very overconfident defendant just smiled.

Thinking that his reaction was strange, the attorney asked about the smile.

Before LePage answered he wanted to know if their conversation was privileged. When the lawyer told him it was, LePage said, "I ain't worried, counselor. They got to have bodies to prove I murdered someone. And they ain't got no bodies."

The arraignment judge remanded LePage to jail with no bail. He was told by the court to hire his own lawyer for his next court date in two weeks.

The case was assigned to Supreme Court Judge Tomas Dades for trial. He was a hard nosed, no nonsense jurist who would not be affected or influenced by Reverend LePage's notoriety or his popularity among Brooklyn's elite.

Before he left the arraignment courtroom, Michael approached the judge and had her sign a search warrant for the reverend's entire building and his car.

Early the next morning, led by Dina and Tim, a squad of Caldwell's agents, who Michael told his investigators were police officers from the NYPD organized crime task force, descended on LePage's building, and seized his car which was towed to NYPD auto pound.

They began their search of the building in the basement and immediately hit pay dirt.

The old bathtub, talked about by Winsell Myles, was still sitting atop the wood burning apparatus.

Inside the tub, lining the bottom, was charred material that still carried the faint odor of burnt flesh. It was carefully collected by a crime scene expert and packaged for delivery to Dr. Cesarano for processing.

When Dina called Michael to tell him about the discovery in the bathtub, he thought, '*maybe we found Riley Caine.*'

Also recovered and sent to Cesarano for analysis were several men's belts with stains that appeared to be blood, and every set of nun's clothing from closets in the rooms occupied by the women who prowled the streets soliciting money for the reverend.

When the search was complete Dina called Michael to tell him.

For cover, knowing full well what the answer would be, Michael asked Dina if they found anything connecting Jiz to the murders, to the basement, the church, or to any of the apartments above.

Dina's answer was no. But she added, "Maybe there's something on the belts to connect him to all this."

Knowing there wouldn't be anything, but once again as cover, Michael simply said, "Yeah, maybe."

It was close to midnight when Dina and Tim returned to the rackets division. They were surprised to see a light on in Michael's office. When they went in they saw he was fixated on his computer screen and was typing away.

"Mike, it's late. What are you doing?" Dina asked.

He didn't respond. Instead he held up his right index finger indicating that he would be right with them.

When he stopped typing he spun around in his chair and said, "Guys, I'm preparing for a superseding indictment against the reverend. I believe what you found in that bathtub are the remains of Riley Caine."

"It's going to be a while before we get results from Dr. Cesarano, but I'm going to bet that I'm right, and bring back Belinda to testify to the circumstances surrounding Riley's disappearance. Then I'm going to ask the grand jury to hang another charge on LePage, the murder of Riley Caine."

CHAPTER THIRTY-SEVEN

Two weeks after the reverend's arraignment on the first indictment, Michael walked into Judge Dades' courtroom armed with a new one. It contained the charges from the first one, and an additional one against LePage for Riley's murder.

When the judge took the bench and told his clerk to "Bring him in," Michael expected Reverend LePage to be escorted into the courtroom. Instead Elton Combes, dressed in a business suit carrying a file folder, walked in, flanked by two court officers.

Combes looked at Michael, nodded and sat at the defense table. Shortly thereafter the defendant was brought in. The reverend greeted Combes and was told to sit by the judge.

Michael had no idea what was going on and when he stood to find out, Judge Dades told him to be seated. "Mr. Gioca, I know what you're thinking. I'll explain. But first put your appearance on the record."

"Michael Gioca, representing the people, your honor."

The judge then pointed to Combes.

"Elton Combes representing the defendant Reverend Vernon LePage, your honor."

'What the fuck is going on,' Michael thought, just as Judge Dades began to explain.

The judge said that a week before, a letter from LePage was hand delivered to his chambers. In it the reverend informed the judge that he wanted Elton Combes to be his trial attorney.

LePage wrote that while he was locked up, several prominent members of his congregation visited him and asked how they could help. He told them he wanted the approval of the administrative judge for the Supreme Court in Brooklyn to allow Elton Combes to be his attorney for this murder trial and he asked for their help to get that approval.

LePage's argument, which his congregants agreed with and made to the administrative judge, was that Combes was an excellent attorney, and thoroughly familiar with him and the workings of his church. Subjects, he claimed, were at the heart of this case. And although Combes was under indictment himself, he was innocent until proven guilty, and therefore still an attorney in good standing in New York State.

After the judge revealed the contents of LePage's letter, he asked "Does the prosecution want to weigh in on the defendant's request?"

Michael, certain that the EVIL ONE was behind this unorthodox move, was too sharp to object and give the defense a point for appeal: that the defendant was unfairly deprived of his right to the attorney of his choice.

And he wasn't worried about Combes pulling something during the trial that he couldn't handle. He had crossed swords with him in the Jax Chase case and knew how Combes operated in a courtroom.

Michael told the judge he had no objection to LePage's request, and the judge made his ruling.

"After due consideration, and with the approval of the administrative judge, I will allow Mr. Combes to represent Vernon LePage in the trial of this indictment."

The remainder of the court appearance was taken up by LePage's arraignment on the new indictment.

Michael handed the document to the judge's clerk and to Combes. He told the judge what it was and asked that LePage be arraigned on the new indictment which superseded the original one.

Combes read it and immediately objected.

"Your honor this new indictment contains a count for the murder of someone named Riley Caine. I have no clue who that is and I ask the court to postpone any arraignment until I confer with my client. I may want to address this charge before he's arraigned on it."

The judge told Combes that this wasn't the time for objections.

"Mr. Combes, all we're going to do is arraign your client on this new indictment. I assume he'll plead not guilty. I'll give you time to confer and prepare any motion papers you deem appropriate."

LePage was arraigned. After which the judge ordered Michael to turn over to the defense, no later than a week from that date, discovery material it was entitled to, including the witness testimony from the grand jury presentation.

He then set another court date in a month, for pre-trial motions. "Plenty of time for you to get your papers together," the judge said to Combes.

"Gentlemen, my thinking right now is that we'll begin jury selection for our trial three months from today. That should give you both all the time you need to be ready."

"Is there anything further before we adjourn?" the judge asked.

"There is your honor," Combes said. "Because both my client and I are incarcerated in the Brooklyn House of Detention, I ask the court to order that I have unfettered access to him. Also that defense witnesses be permitted to visit and consult with me so I can prepare a defense and be ready for trial on the date the court sets."

Judge Dades was prepared to rule on the request. However before he announced his decision, he wanted to hear what Michael had to say.

"Mr. Gioca, do you have any objection to what Mr. Combes is asking for?"

As with the issue of Combes' representation, Michael was not going to fall into a trap.

If he objected, which he was sure the EVIL ONE was counting on, and the judge denied the request, on appeal if the defendant was convicted, the defense would have another strong argument that the defendant was unable to prepare his defense, thus denied full and fair representation by counsel.

That was an assertion that an appellate court could find was a violation of LePage's constitutional rights under the sixth amendment of the US Constitution. The court could reverse the conviction and order a new trial, or worse, reverse and dismiss the indictment.

Michael wasn't going to play *HIS* game.

"Your honor, the people have no objection to Mr. Combes' request."

"Very well. There being no objection, I grant Mr. Combes' request and order the Department of Correction, specifically the warden of the Brooklyn House of Detention, to comply with that request. If, however, a problem arises in the implementation, I order that all parties come before me so I may resolve the issue."

"If there is nothing further, I'll see you gentlemen in one month for pre-trial motions."

Michael complied with the judge's direction and turned over all discovery material to Elton Combes earlier than was required. And prepared an answer to a detailed and lengthy motion filed by Combes to dismiss the indictment due to 'improper and insufficient evidence.'

Combes' arguments were, first: the prosecution cannot prove that the 'so-called' victims were actually victims. Therefore there is insufficient evidence to prove murder. Combes wrote, 'the People have no bodies; therefore they cannot prove these women were murdered. For all we know they could just as easily be runaways who chose to live where they cannot be found. That's not murder, your honor.'

And second: that the defendant's wife, Belinda, was called to testify against him, in violation of the confidentiality privilege that exists between a husband and his wife.

Michael had no trouble answering the arguments.

On the day of the hearing on the pre-trial motions, Judge Dades first listened to Combes who explained in detail his two arguments for why the indictment, "Must be dismissed."

After hearing him, the judge asked Michael to respond. "However," he said, "There is no need for you to address his insufficiency of evidence argument. I believe that is a jury question."

"So restrict your response to why I shouldn't dismiss the count in the indictment charging LePage with the murder of Riley Caine? It's clear from the grand jury presentation that it relies entirely on the testimony of Belinda Shaw, who Mr. Combes argued is the wife of the defendant. Why isn't her testimony protected by the spousal privilege?"

Michael wasn't certain that Dr. Cesarano would be able to determine that what was recovered from the bathtub were Riley's remains.

If they weren't, he wouldn't be able to proceed and would dismiss the count himself.

However, if they were her remains, he didn't want to reveal so early in the case, the evidence he would introduce to prove LePage murdered her.

"Judge, as to that count, I'd ask the court to reserve decision on dismissing it. When and if I decide to present evidence as to the murder of Riley Caine, we can revisit Mr. Combes' motion to dismiss the count."

"Very well," the judge said. "I'll reserve decision until I have to make one."

Judge Dades then set a date in two months for the trial to begin.

Combes and LePage weren't very upset by the judge's ruling.

Michael heard LePage in a very low voice use the word, "Lake."

Then in a voice meant for Michael to hear, LePage said, "Gioca can't show that jury nothing. No bodies, no crime. And don't worry about Belinda. She's a dumb bitch and don't know no better. They musta lied to her or threatened her to get her to the grand jury. But she loves me too much to testify here."

He and Combes started to laugh as they were led out of the courtroom.

Michael's calm demeanor belied the excitement he was feeling.

As he packed up his briefcase he thought: *'I know Dr. Cesarano is gonna' come through. And LePage has no idea how much Belinda hates him. In two months, they're not going to be laughing.'*

CHAPTER THIRTY-EIGHT

For the next two months Michael worked harder than he ever had preparing for a trial. It was him against Combes, LePage, the reverend's influential followers, and of course, the EVIL ONE.

***'Gioca Doesn't Have a Body or Bodies**,'* was the theme in the city newspapers, on local radio shows, and TV, when they ran stories about the case.

The reverend's congregants and followers worked overtime, talking to any reporter, commentator, blogger, and podcaster that expressed interest in the case.

Their message, 'No body, No crime.'

Knowing that when the trial started he wouldn't have much free time, Michael took a break from his preparation to attend his niece Michelle's third birthday party with Kathy.

Surrounded by his family and friends, Michael had a great time. The food was terrific and the wine even better.

In the car driving home after the party, he turned to Kathy and said, "Spending the last five hours with the people I care about most, and not having to think about LePage, was exactly what I needed. I didn't realize how much the grind I've been subjecting myself to over the last couple of months has worn me down. Today recharged my battery."

Kathy just smiled. She was thankful for what the party did for Michael because she was worried about him.

The few times she and Michael managed to get together while he prepared the case, Kathy saw signs of him wearing down. Michael always totally immersed himself in a case. So exhibiting signs of wear and tear was not unusual. But never to this extent.

The usual pressure that comes with handling an important case was compounded by the extraordinary press attention, and personal attacks from prominent political and business figures who LePage counted among his friends and followers.

As the start of the trial grew near, the attacks appeared in the media more frequently. It was taking a toll on Michael. Unlike in prior cases, he seemed to be having difficulty ignoring it, and shaking it off, which is why Kathy considered the party a Godsend.

On Monday morning, one week after the birthday party, Michael walked into Judge Dades' courtroom ready for trial. However getting to the courthouse was not easy.

He had to navigate a sea of protestors outside the building.

Many held signs bearing a photo of LePage standing at the pulpit of his church dressed in clerical vestments, with the word 'INNOCENT' emblazoned above his head.

All were chanting, "No body, No crime."

The chants were led by someone who Michael couldn't locate in the crowd. If he had, he would have seen that it was a woman with red dreadlocks wearing a black covid mask.

Other protestors were circulating on the plaza in front of the courthouse, and on the paths from the street leading to it, handing out flyers with a different photo of LePage.

He was pictured standing in front of a rustic cabin bearing the sign "*LePage Acres*," surrounded by smiling children. Under the photo was a paragraph detailing all the supposed work LePage did for his community and its children.

As Michael started up the courthouse steps one of the protestors handed him a flyer. He stopped and read it.

When he was done, he said to the young woman, "You forgot some things. Why doesn't it mention the fake nuns LePage uses to collect money for his bogus charity; or that reverend con man rapes them when they get back to his church after begging all day?"

The protestor's response was, "Fuck you, pig."

Michael laughed, crumpled up the flyer, and tossed it into the first wastebasket he saw when he entered the courthouse.

At exactly 9:30 a.m. Judge Dades took the bench, closely followed by court officers who escorted LePage and his attorney into the courtroom. At the defense table their handcuffs were removed, after which the judge asked Combes if the defense was ready for trial.

He answered that it was.

When asked, Michael answered that the prosecution was also ready to proceed.

Dades told his clerk to call for a jury panel.

Twenty minutes later fifty citizens of Brooklyn, from all walks of life, were seated in the courtroom's spectator gallery to await the call of their name.

The first fourteen called filed into the jury box to be questioned about their fitness to sit as a juror in the case of *The People of the State of New York v. Vernon LePage.*

The jury selection process took all day. And by 5:15 p.m. twelve jurors and four alternates were sworn in.

They were a cross-section of Brooklyn's melting pot population. Seven men and nine women; black, white, Hispanic, and Asian; blue and white collar workers; all members of various religions.

During his questioning it was clear that Combes wanted jurors who practiced a religion, regardless of faith.

His reasoning: they would have a difficult time believing that 'a man of the cloth,' as he called LePage, could be a murderer, and therefore would be more likely to acquit him than non-believers would, especially in the absence of any bodies.

Michael found it ironic that a defendant under the influence of Satan, the epitome of anti-religious thought and practice, was searching for jurors for whom religion played a significant role in their lives.

However, he anticipated that Combes would employ that strategy, and in the days leading up to jury selection thought about how *he* should proceed.

Michael decided that practicing a religion, absent other reasons, was not, in his mind, a disqualifying factor for a seat on this jury. In fact it was just the opposite. He felt strongly that it was a reason to keep the juror.

He believed that such individuals would be appalled when he proved to them that Vernon LePage was nothing more than a con man posing as a cleric, in order to fleece unsuspecting citizens. And when they heard about the murder and dismemberment of four young women, and his rape of others who lived in his church building, Michael was sure they would be horrified and disgusted.

Therefore, much to Combes' satisfaction, and more importantly to Michael's delight, all twelve regular jurors and three of the four alternates professed to being practicing Jews, Catholics, and members of several Protestant denominations.

After opening statements by the attorneys, in which Michael methodically laid out the case he intended to prove, and Combes simply said repeatedly, "No body, No crime," as he paced in front of the jury, Gioca called his first series of witnesses, family members of Natasha, Sammi, Alexa, and Riley.

Michael asked each how they were related to the four women, then showed each a photo and asked if they knew the person depicted. When they answered "Yes," he asked for their names.

Michael then moved each photo into evidence.

He ended the questioning of each witness with, "When was the last time you or heard from ...?" using the name of each woman.

To a person their answer was, "Not for months."

Combes did not cross-examine any of the family members.

Frankie LePage was next. And his testimony was devastating.

He began with the history of his father becoming a very convincing con man and bogus preacher, to recruiting women who he dressed as nuns to scam people, to his raping the ones he was attracted to, and ending with Vernon's confession that he killed Natasha, Sammi, and Alexa.

"He told me he killed them because he believed they went to the cops and the DA to inform on him."

On cross-examination, hard as he tried, Combes couldn't shake him.

Michael's work with Frankie paid off.

He told him to be honest about all the wrong he was involved in, and to be candid when he was asked about his conviction and sentence for fraud and larceny.

When Combes pressed him on the conviction, Frankie simply said, "Yeah, I did all that. Being con men was me and my brothers' way of life because of him," he said pointing to his father.

"In fact that time I got caught, the one you was just asking me about, that was a con my daddy taught me. He called it 'his specialty.'"

With that answer, Combes decided to end his cross before he got himself and his client in so deep they'd drown.

Winsell Myles followed Frankie.

When Michael announced him as his next witness, he heard LePage say something under his breath but he couldn't make out the words.

When he looked over to the defense table, he saw LePage shaking his head from side to side. The reverend was clearly not happy. He knew that Myles was prepared to tell the jury about the house of horrors that was *The Nostrand Evangelical Church of Hope.*

Winsell Myles didn't disappoint.

He laid out every sordid detail of the reverend's illegal business. The fake nuns, the horror LePage put them through if any one of them disobeyed him or his wife Belinda, and the rapes he perpetrated on the 'nuns' he found "hot and sexy."

When he got to the murders, Myles hesitated and choked up as he told the jury that LePage told him to "Chop up the dead girl's bodies and burn them in hot oil."

He testified that initially he refused but when his son and wife were threatened, "I had no choice."

Before he continued with Myles, Michael glanced over at the jury. He saw all the women and several of the men with tears in their eyes.

Then he showed Myles the evidence photos of the four women and asked if he recognized them.

Myles answered that he knew three of them.

He identified Natasha, Sammi, and Alexa by name, adding, "They were the dead women I seen in the church basement that LePage said he killed, and told me to cut up and burn."

As for the photo of Riley, Myles said he didn't know her. "She musta' came to the house after I was arrested," he said.

"Let's talk about the arrest you just mentioned. Tell the jury what happened." Myles laid it all out for them and ended by pointing to LePage saying "He set me up."

Michael ended his examination at that point.

He didn't ask Myles about dumping the body parts into the lake because he still hadn't heard from Dr. Cesarano.

True to his name, Gioca was gambling.

He was certain the defense would be 'No body, No crime.' And he had faith that the doctor would come through for him.

When he did, Michael planned to recall Myles in rebuttal, when his testimony about dumping the body parts would have the most impact.

On cross Combes spent his entire examination on Myles' criminal record, and that he cut a deal with the prosecution to save himself from a lengthy prison sentence.

"Mr. Myles, you're under arrest right now for a felony crime, isn't that right?" Combes asked.

After Myles said he was, Combes continued. "And you have two felony convictions already on your record, isn't that right?"

Again Myles answered that Combes was correct.

"So, if you're convicted of the felony you are now under arrest for, you'd be what the law calls a 'persistent felony offender', meaning you're gonna' go to jail for a very long time because that's the law. Am I right?"

Myles said he was.

"But when the DA steps in and helps you, because you cut a deal with him in return for your lying testimony against Reverend LaPage, you're gonna' save yourself that long prison sentence. Isn't that right?"

Michael prepared Myles for this line of questioning so he was ready.

"No Mr. Combes, that ain't right," Myles answered.

"First of all I ain't lyin' about the reverend. I seen each of them women with their throats cut, lying on the floor of his basement. He told me he killed them, and because he knew that I once worked in the city morgue and watched lots of autopsies, he asked me to cut them up and burn their bodies."

Myles wasn't finished. When Combes began to say something, Myles held up his hand and said, "Don't interrupt. I'm not done with my answer."

"Right now I got no guaranteed deal with the DA," he said. The DA told me that I have to tell the truth up here, and if I do, then he'd talk to my lawyer about a deal. Whether I gets that deal is in Mr. Gioca's hands."

Combes sat down after that answer. The deal question was a mistake, and Combes was smart enough to cut his losses.

After Myles was dismissed from the witness stand, Michael asked the judge for a conference outside the presence of the jury.

With the courtroom cleared, Michael told the judge his next witness was Belinda Shaw.

CHAPTER THIRTY-NINE

"During pre-trial motion practice, I…." Michael never finished his sentence because LePage exploded.

"What kind of fucking game are you playing Gioca?" LePage screamed.

"Belinda Shaw is my wife! She can't testify against me. You may have tricked her to go into the grand jury and because of that your case will suffer."

Not finished with his rant, LePage took a breath and said, "If you put her on the witness stand, I promise, you're gonna' be sorry." LePage threatened.

Combes tried to calm him down but it was to no avail.

Realizing that his client was digging himself a hole bigger than the one he was already in, Combes told LePage to sit down and shut up.

"I'll handle this," he said.

Turning to the judge he said, "Your honor, I object and renew my motion to dismiss the count in the indictment related to the death of Riley Caine, and to dismiss the entire indictment."

"I apologize for his outburst, but my client is correct. In New

York, a spouse cannot be compelled to testify against her husband. The spousal privilege prohibits such testimony."

"As your honor knows, the count in the indictment charging my client with the murder of Riley Caine, is wholly dependent on the testimony of Belinda. At a minimum it must be dismissed. However, because Mr. Gioca called Belinda to testify in the grand jury, in violation of the spousal privilege, the presentation was tainted, and therefore the entire indictment must be dismissed."

The judge looked at Michael and asked him what he had to say.

"Judge as I was saying a few moments ago, before I was interrupted, I do intend to call Belinda Shaw to testify on the people's case. When we were arguing the pre-trial motion to dismiss the indictment, I told the court that I was not sure at that time if I would call her. I am now. I'm prepared to argue why New York's marital privilege law does not apply here."

"Mr. Gioca is Belinda Shaw the defendant's wife?" the judge asked.

"No your honor she isn't."

That prompted LePage to get out of his seat and lunge for Michael, saying "You son of a bitch." In doing so, he knocked over Combes before four court officers grabbed and restrained him.

When order was restored Michael said, "There is no spousal privilege between Belinda and the defendant."

"As the court is aware, under New York law for the privilege to apply the parties must be *actually and legally* married. In addition, there is no privilege for *bigamous marriage*."

"When the defendant supposedly married Belinda Shaw, he was legally married to his wife Helen LePage. The defendant and Helen never divorced."

"Investigator Dina Mitchell from my office, researched this and is prepared to testify that she found a duly recorded marriage license for the defendant and Helen, which I have here, but no record of a divorce."

"She will also testify that there is no marriage license on file for Belinda Shaw and Vernon LePage."

"The so-called marriage between Belinda and the defendant is not a marriage at all. And even if there had been one, it would be bigamous. In either case, the spousal privilege is not available to this defendant."

When the judge asked Combes for a response, the attorney looked like he wanted to crawl under the defense table. He leaned over and spoke to LePage before asking the court to give him until the morning to respond.

"Your honor, I want to do some research of my own and I'll be prepared to address this matter when we reconvene in the morning."

Dades gave him the evening, saying, "Mr. Combes unless you have irrefutable evidence that Mr. Gioca is wrong, I suggest you spend the evening preparing for cross-examination."

Back at the jail, Combes and LePage sat in a room set aside for inmates to confer with their attorney. Combes had his work cut out for him. He never thought he'd be in this position because he was certain, based on what LePage told him, that Belinda Shaw was the wife...the lawful wife of his client.

He expected, at the very least, the judge would dismiss the count of the indictment dealing with Riley's murder, because Belinda was the sole witness who testified about it in the grand jury. And he hoped, but was less confident, that the judge would dismiss the entire indictment because of a taint, as he argued.

Now, it didn't seem likely that either would occur.

He had to prepare to cross-examine Belinda Shaw.

"Reverend with all due respect, I believe you haven't been totally candid with me. If you want me to help you get out from under these charges, I need to know everything," Combes said.

"Are you two legally married? And what can she tell the jury if the judge rules that she can testify?"

LePage hesitated before answering, "We're married in the eyes of God. And she knows nothing."

When he heard that answer, Combes thought, *'He's fucked! The judge is going to allow her testimony, and she's probably going to bury him.'*

The next day in court, Combes' worst fears came true. Belinda was permitted to testify, and she did just what Combes thought she'd do.

She began by telling the jury how LePage lied when he told her that he was an ordained minister.

"He also lied when he told me that the guy who married us, Brother Jiz, as he called him, was also an ordained minister and could legally perform the ceremony. I know now that Jiz was not a minister. He was just one of Vernon's flunkies."

"Our so-called marriage is a sham."

She told the jury all about LePage's charity scam.

"Vernon was running with women who he sweet talked, lied to, and plied with drugs and alcohol in order to get them into his church, into his bed, and keep them there."

"Once they were hooked, he dressed them as nuns and sent them out into the streets of the city collecting for a charity that doesn't exist. That money went right into his pocket."

"Why did you go along with this?" Michael asked.

"Mr. Gioca, I learned very quickly that to get along, I had to go along. If I didn't, Lord knows what would have happened to me. I wasn't gonna' test him. Until it got too much."

"We'll get to that in a few moments."

"Let's talk about the camp for poor kids that he claims to run. Is that legitimate?"

Belinda laughed before answering, "That piece of land with the pond he liked to call a lake, is in the middle of nowhere and isn't a camp at all. "*LePage Acres* is part of his scam."

Belinda told the jury about the photos LePage had of him with kids, standing in front of a sign that read, *LePage Acres.*

Michael showed her one of the flyers that was being passed out in front of the courthouse.

"Yeah that's one of those fake pictures," Belinda said.

Michael moved it into evidence.

"The pictures are phony," Belinda continued. "They were photoshopped by one of the women in the church who had computer skills. She didn't want to do it, but Vernon ordered her to. And if she refused and disobeyed him, there would be hell to pay."

"Ms. Shaw, what, if anything, does the defendant do with photos like the one in evidence."

"He shows them to suckers to get them to contribute."

"A few moments ago you told the jury that if the woman who created the photos refused Vernon's order, 'There would be hell to pay.'"

She answered, "That's right."

"What did you mean by that?"

"He would punish her, as he did to anyone who disobeyed him or did something he didn't like."

"Tell us about this punishment. Did you ever witness it?"

"Yes, more times than I care to remember."

Michael watched the jury as Belinda graphically described the punishment LePage meted out. Some buried their heads in their hands, others had tears in their eyes, but all had a look of horror on their faces.

"Now you know why I did what I was told. I didn't want that to happen to me."

"Let's talk about Riley Caine. Did you know her?" Michael asked.

"Yes I did."

Belinda told the jury how she and Riley met, and how she recruited her for the church. She testified that Riley was very successful in getting people to part with their money.

"I knew she'd be good at collecting and I figured that would please LePage and he'd leave me alone. And I was right."

"During her time in the church, me and Riley became very close. She was like the daughter I never had. That's why when she was sexually assaulted I was so angry."

Belinda told the jurors about Jiz raping Riley.

"She came to me one night all upset and distraught and told me that Jiz raped her. And if that wasn't bad enough, he told her that she was now his girlfriend, letting her know he was gonna' rape Riley whenever he wanted to."

Belinda began to weep.

"What, if anything, did you do, when she told you that?"

"As I said, I was angry as hell, so I went to the reverend and told him what his boy did."

"Did he say anything?"

"Yeah. That piece of shit asked me, 'Was it good?'"

"What was your reaction?"

"I decided to leave him and that church."

"My plan was to escape with Riley the very next night after everyone was asleep. But it didn't work because he..." pointing to LePage, "Murdered her before I could get her away from him and Jiz."

Belinda was now crying uncontrollably. The judge asked if she wanted a break. Belinda just shook her head. "I'll be okay, your honor. I want to continue," she said.

"LePage told me that he killed her because he was afraid that she would go to the police and report the rape. He said he couldn't let Brother Jiz be arrested."

Michael followed with questions about Natasha, Sammi, and Alexa.

Belinda testified that she knew all three and was fond of them.

"Do you know where they are today?"

"LePage told me that he killed them."

"He said they were a problem. So he eliminated them. When I asked him what the problem was, he said he suspected that they were ratting him out to the police and district attorney."

"One last thing Belinda. Were you asked to collect items from the rooms that Natasha, Sammi, Alexa, and Riley lived in at the church?"

Belinda answered that she was and told the jury that she recovered items that belonged to the four women, from each of the rooms.

She testified that she was instructed to bag the items according to whose room she took them from, which is what she did.

Michael asked what happened to the four bags. "I gave them to Dina Mitchell from your office."

Michael finished his direct of Belinda and turned her over to Combes for cross-examination.

He surprised everyone in the courtroom by asking only a few questions, all designed to throw blame onto Jiz for everything. Then he sat down.

LePage was not happy.

Michael rested his direct case.

At this point in the trial, the defense, under New York State law, had the right to ask for a dismissal of the indictment if the prosecution did not establish a *prima facie,* i.e. obvious, case of murder against the defendant.

Combes made a vociferous argument for dismissal, citing the 'No body, No crime,' mantra he employed during his opening statement.

Michael held his breath and prayed that his response, pointing out that a case consisting of LePage's confessions to three different people, and the disappearance of the four women he confessed to murdering was *prima facie,* would be compelling enough for the court to deny the motion and allow the trial to proceed.

That would give Dr. Cesarano more time to analyze the remains from the lake and the bathtub. And positive results, would give Michael grounds to rebut what he expected the defense to be, 'No body, No crime.'

Winsell Myles testified to dumping the body parts into the lake, testimony by the FBI diver and Dina Mitchell about recovery of remains in the lake and bathtub, topped off by Dr. Cesarano, would make it very difficult for a jury to send Vernon LePage home.

If the judge agreed with Combes and dismissed the case, Michael would never forgive himself for taking the chance and proceeding to trial before Cesarano finished his work.

Gioca the gambler won again. Judge Dades respectfully disagreed with Combes and denied the motion.

Michael said a silent 'thank you' prayer.

After the judge's ruling Combes asked to begin the defense in the morning.

The judge dismissed the jury and Combes and LePage were brought to the cell behind the courtroom to await transport back to the Brooklyn House of Detention.

As Michael was packing his briefcase a court officer approached him and whispered that the defense team had a very loud and animated discussion while in the cell.

"It seems that the reverend ain't very happy with his lawyer's performance," the officer said. "In fact I heard him say that if Combes didn't start doing his job a 'whole fucking lot better', he better watch his ass when they get back to the Brooklyn House. Keep up the good work Mr. G. You got them runnin' scared."

CHAPTER FORTY

That evening after dinner in the jail's mess hall, Combes was told by one of the correction officers that he had a visitor. Thinking it was strange for the jail to allow a visit at that hour, he was about to ask who it was, when the officer told him, "It's your lawyer. The warden gave him permission to see you because you're on trial with LePage and weren't here during regular visiting hours."

When he walked into the visitors room, he saw Jiz sitting at a table. Combes recognized him immediately even though he cut his red dreadlocks and was wearing a black covid mask which covered the mole on his left cheek.

The last time Combes and Jiz were together was at LePage's church when Jiz told him he had to shoot Jackson Chase.

"That fuck Chase is gonna' rat on the rev and me when he gets convicted tomorrow," Jiz told him back then. "You got to make sure that don't happen."

"That lawyer's court ID card of yours gets you into the courthouse without a search," Jiz had told him when he handed him a small pistol.

"Put this in the inside pocket of your suit jacket and when he's convicted shoot him."

When Combes balked and said he wouldn't do it, Jiz showed him a photo of his wife and three young kids. He said, "I'll cut them up and fry them in oil while you watch if you don't kill Chase. And if you think LePage is gonna' stop me, he'll be right next to me with a saw in his hand. Oh! And that's after he fucks your wife on the church basement floor."

The next day he shot Jax Chase in the head.

Combes sat down at the visitors table across from Jiz knowing full well what *HE* and LePage were capable of doing. "What the fuck do you want?" Combes asked him.

Jiz smirked and said, "I got some trial advice for you."

As Combes got up to leave the table, Jiz said, "I still got that picture of your wife and kids." Combes sat back down.

Jiz said that *HE's* been keeping tabs on the trial and "It ain't lookin' so good for that fuckin' Gioca. He don't have enough. Frankie, Myles, and that bitch Belinda ain't gonna' do it. No body, No crime, right?"

Jiz continued, "The way I see it, the only chance Gioca's got is if LePage testifies for himself. Gioca will cut him to pieces on cross, and he'll be convicted very quickly. So you got to make sure LePage don't get on that witness stand."

"The rev is important to me," Jiz continued. "I need him free and out there doing what he does... and what I want him to do."

Jiz then laughed and said, "The rev thinks I'm one of his people. But he's got it wrong, he's one of mine."

On the subject of LePage testifying, Combes and Jiz agreed.

"I'm with you on that. The reverend cannot testify if he wants an acquittal."

"Besides, I don't need his testimony to win. I'm going to establish his defense and win this case using the reverend's important, and influential friends who are prepared to say everything I've been telling them to say."

"First, they'll tell the jury what a great guy he is. And that he's incapable of doing what he's been charged with."

"And second, they'll say that the women he's charged with killing aren't dead at all! They simply left the church."

Combes continued, "When I ask how they know that, their answer will be that they've recently seen women walking around the neighborhood begging for money."

"With the witnesses' impressive political and social status, the jurors are not gonna' have any problem believing their bullshit."

"And with a jury made up of people who told me they were members of one religion or another, they won't ever convict a preacher."

Hearing that, Jiz was convinced that Combes would do what he said. But to make sure, *HE* wanted to remind Combes what was at stake if he had second thoughts or changed his strategy.

"You got a case of your own coming up. I can help you win it...if you keep him off the stand. If you don't, accidents to prisoners awaiting trial like yourself, are known to happen. You don't want to have a shiv stuck in your belly by some psycho inmate, do you? Who'll take care of that hot wife and those cute kids of yours if you ain't around?"

Combes got the message.

When Jiz left, Combes went back to his cell to prepare the direct examinations for the witnesses he intended to call to testify in the morning. He would hold off discussing Jiz' 'trial advice' with LePage until after they testified.

Over the next two days, seven character witnesses, who Michael thought were unconvincing liars, testified for the defense. Each followed the script that Combes laid out for Jiz during his jail visit the day before.

However, because it would seem odd for all seven to have recently seen the women LePage was charged with killing, Combes asked only the three with the most impressive credentials and backgrounds about the sightings.

On cross-examination, Michael established that all the defense witnesses were ardent followers of the reverend, and his preaching. And since they only socialized with him at church sponsored events, they had no idea what LePage did in his private time.

Michael also confirmed that they knew the reverend used 'nuns' to raise money for the church and his charity. But were unaware that the 'nuns' weren't actually ordained religious. That the women were recruited by the reverend off the street, in bars, and clubs, was a surprise to them.

And as for the witnesses who testified to recently seeing the women who the prosecution claimed the reverend killed, Michael asked if the sightings were after the defendant was arrested and charged with their murders.

When each said it was, he followed with, "Did you report those sightings to the authorities?"

When all three witnesses told him that they did not, Michael pressed them.

"You told this jury that Reverend LePage was your pastor, your minister, your friend, yet you didn't go to the police, or to the DA's office, or to the media, to report that your reverend is being wrongfully charged with murder because you saw the women he supposedly killed, out walking the streets of Brooklyn?"

Once again, all three witnesses answered that they did not.

With the last of those answers Michael announced that he had no further questions.

It was lunchtime and Judge Dades released the jury for an hour. However, before he adjourned he asked Combes if he had any additional witnesses.

The attorney hesitated before telling the judge that he needed the lunch hour to talk to his client before he could answer.

When he heard what Combes said LePage exploded.

"What the fuck do you mean, 'you need to talk' to me before you answer? I'm gonna' testify. They ain't got no bodies. I didn't kill those women and I got to tell that to the jury, myself."

When Combes tried to calm LePage and tell him that they'd talk about it during the break, the reverend got more agitated.

Judge Dades stepped in. He told the court officers to take the defendant and Combes back to the holding cell, "So they can confer in private."

Combes thanked the judge, and LePage said, "Your Honor, I'll see you in an hour... when I take the witness stand."

When they got into the cell, they found their lunch, a bologna sandwich and coffee, waiting for them. They agreed to quickly eat before talking again.

Once they were finished, Combes spoke first.

"Vernon, they don't have the bodies of those women. All they have is the testimony of your convict son, and that predicate felon Myles, and that woman Belinda who you yourself told me was a moron. If you get on the stand Gioca will cross you. He's good. You might think you can handle him, but if you slip up just once, your ass will be his. Let's leave well enough alone."

LePage listened but said nothing.

Combes continued with what he thought would be the clinching argument. "Reverend, Jiz came to see me in jail last night. He agrees with me. He doesn't want you to testify. His exact words, 'Gioca could trip him up.'"

LePage still said nothing, and Combes thought to himself, *'maybe I got through to him.'*

But then the reverend slowly stood up and approached Combes. When LePage was an inch from his face he said, "Fuck you. And fuck that dreadlock wearing motherfucker too."

"I don't give a shit what you two assholes think. I know what needs to be done. Remember, you and him work for me, and neither of you tells me what to do. I'm getting on that witness stand to tell those jurors that Reverend Vernon LePage didn't kill those women.... No body, No crime, Mr. Combes."

When the trial resumed, Elton Combes announced, "The defense calls Reverend Vernon LePage to the stand."

In the last row of the spectator section, which was filled with LePage supporters, a strange looking guy wearing a black covid mask covering the large mole on his left cheek, vowed to himself, *'someone will pay.'*

CHAPTER FORTY-ONE

Having lost the battle to keep LePage off the witness stand, Combes decided that his direct examination of the reverend would be short and to the point.

He established that LePage was the founder and pastor of *The Nostrand Evangelical Church of Hope*, and that he ran a charity for children, supported by donations to his church.

LePage told the jury that the donations came from, "my congregation, my many followers, and from the solicitation of alms from the good citizens of New York City."

"Who collects those donations from New Yorkers?" Combes asked.

"The sisters of my church," was LePage's answer.

Combes asked LePage to tell the jury how those 'sisters' are brought into the fold.

"I have a great and loyal following. I appear on radio, TV, and podcasts here in New York to talk about my wonderful charity. And when I do, my phone rings off the hook with women who want to help me in my mission. Now, I don't take all who want to help. I choose only those who I believe are sincere in their desire to sacrifice themselves and their time to help others."

'And who you want to get into your bed' Michael thought when he heard that answer.

"Where do the sisters live?"

LePage told the jury that he houses them in apartments on the floors above the church. He added, "I also feed the sisters, and provide for all their needs.'

"How long does a sister stay with you and the church?"

"Some have been with me for years. Others stay for shorter periods of time and leave when they want, or they must. If there are emergencies at home with their families, and a sister must leave to tend to it, she goes with my blessing.".

"Now, there are some instances when a sister or sisters will leave without me knowing," LePage continued. "However, when that happens, I usually find out the next day when my wife Belinda, who looks out for the women, tells me."

Combes asked, "Have women left and not returned?"

"Mr. Combes, I don't run a prison. The sisters are free to leave whenever they choose. Some return and others do not. I'm their pastor, not their jailer."

Combes wound up his examination when he showed LePage the photos of Natasha, Sammi, Alexa, and Riley and asked if they were sisters of the church.

"Yes they were. But they chose to leave and have not returned."

"Do you know where they are?"

When LePage answered that he didn't, Combes ended with, "Did you, or anyone under your orders, or at your direction, kill those women, then chop up and burn their bodies?"

Before he answered LePage turned to the jury and in as sincere a voice as the phony cleric could muster, said, "Mr. Combes, the Bible says, 'Thou shalt not kill.' I'm a man of God, and I do not disobey His commandments or break His law. I save souls. I don't destroy and desecrate bodies."

After a pause for effect Lepage said, "I did not kill those women."

Following a fifteen minute break, Michael began his cross-examination.

As he rose from his seat, he looked back to the last row of the spectator section of the courtroom, the EVIL ONE was not there. Michael later was told by a court officer that, "The guy with the mask," left the courtroom at the conclusion of LePage's testimony on direct.

'I guess HE didn't want to stay for the massacre,' Michael thought, as he prepared to take apart LePage and his story.

"Reverend LePage, at what school did you study to become a Christian minister?" was Michael's first question on cross-examination.

"I didn't study at no school. I studied under the Right Reverend David Dawes, in his church over in Manhattan."

"Is that the Reverend Dawes who ran a charity scam, using women dressed as nuns to solicit and beg for money in places like Times Square, Macy's department store, and the New York subway, for a non-existent charity?"

Keeping his cool, LePage answered, "I have no idea what you're talking about Mr. Gioca."

"Sure you do Reverend. Didn't you, and your wife Helen, work with Dawes and recruit women to run his scam?"

"Me and my wife worked for Rev. Dawes but our solicitation of alms for the poor was all on the up and up."

"So I guess that when you, Helen and Sarah were arrested in Manhattan many years back, for scamming a tourist, that was all a mistake?"

"Mr. Gioca, I was found not guilty."

"But Helen and Sarah were convicted after trial, right?"

"Yes"

"And you were with them when they did the crime that they were convicted for, right?"

"Yes I was but it was all a mistake. No one should have been arrested and convicted. Reverend Dawes ran a legitimate charity."

"So how do you explain Dawes being arrested, and charged, with larceny by fraud just coincidentally when you and Helen took off for Brooklyn?"

"We left to start our own church."

"You left because you were worried that you'd be caught up in Dawes' mess, and perhaps be arrested yourselves? Isn't that right?"

"As I just told you, we left to start our own church."

Michael wouldn't let up.

"A church where you employ the same method of collecting alms, as you call them, from unsuspecting citizens who believe they are contributing to a cause that helps children in need."

LePage remained silent.

"You recruited women, just as you did for Rev. Dawes, dressed them as religious nuns, and sent them out onto the streets of New York City to solicit money for your so-called charity. Right?"

"Mr. Gioca, my charity is real. And the sisters who collect for it are members of my church, ordained by me to be messengers of God."

"If your charity is real, as you say, what is its name?

"It's named after my church, 'The Church of Hope Charity.'"

"If it is 'real,' as you say, why isn't it registered with the State of New York, or with any governmental body charged with overseeing such charities to ensure that they are not fraudulent?"

"My charity is registered with God," LePage answered.

When he gave that answer Michael heard a noise coming from the defense table. He glanced over and saw Combes fidgeting in his seat. Clearly he was not happy with the reverend's response.

Michael then asked for the photos of Natasha, Sammi, and Alexa, that were in evidence, and handed them to LePage. When he asked if the reverend recognized the women in the photos, LePage said, "As I told Mr. Combes, I do recognize them."

"They were all 'sisters' of your church, who collected for your charity, weren't they?"

"Yes. Natasha, Sammi, and Alexa. Wonderful women who I am very fond of."

"Where are they now, reverend?"

"I don't know. They left my house and I haven't seen them since. I hope they are all doing well."

"You know they're not well, because you murdered Natasha, then Sammi and Alexa, didn't you?"

"No!"

"You killed them because you believed they were ratting you out to the police for all the crimes you were committing with your so-called charity, and for raping several of the 'sisters' who were collecting for you?"

"No!"

"Natasha was first, then Sammi and Alexa, right?"

"No!"

"Reverend, who is Winsell Myles?"

"He's a young man that I hired to be the custodian of my church."

"And when you hired him you knew that he was previously employed at the office of the city medical examiner, and worked in the morgue, correct?

"Yes!"

"And you also knew before you gave him the job in your church, that among his duties at the medical examiner's office was to witness and clean up after the body was dissected during an autopsy, correct?

"Yes. Winsell told me all about seeing that horror."

"And because of his experience at the city morgue, you knew Myles had the knowledge to cut up bodies, right?"

"No!"

"Which is why you told him to chop up the bodies of those

women, and burn them in a bathtub in your basement that you filled with hot oil, right?"

"No!"

Michael had a photo marked for identification.

"Reverend, look at this photo. That's the bathtub in the basement of your church, isn't it?"

"Yes, we use it to clean the statues, and other items from the church sanctuary. They're large so we use the tub to do a good job," LePage answered.

"Isn't that the tub in which you had Winsell Myles burn the bodies of Natasha, Sammi, and Alexa?, after you ordered him to cut them into little pieces?"

"No!"

"And then had him take their remains and dump what was left of those three women in the lake on the property you own in upstate New York, which you call *LePage Acres?*

"Mr. Gioca, I do own *LePage Acres*, but I'm a man of God. You heard all those witnesses tell that to the jury. I would never... no, I *COULD* never do any of that."

Michael asked the court clerk for the photo of Riley Caine. He handed it to LePage and asked if he recognized the person in the photo.

"Yes, that's Riley. She is my wife Belinda's favorite. She was a very devout sister and collected a good deal of money for our charity before she too left the church."

"Do you know where Riley is today?"

"Mr. Gioca, if you would let me ask my wife Belinda, I'm sure she would know and I can then answer your question. Better yet, if you want to know where Riley is why don't you ask Belinda yourself? You seem to have brainwashed her."

Michael ignored the brainwashing crack and asked his next question.

"Reverend LePage you killed Riley because after she was raped by one of your followers, Brother Jiz I believe you call him, you were concerned that she would report him to the police. Isn't that right?"

"No!"

"After killing her, you and Jiz dismembered her body, you must have been paying attention to how Myles did it, and burnt it in that same bathtub where the others were burnt, right?"

"No!"

"But you didn't have time to clean Riley's remains out of the tub because you were arrested. Isn't that right?"

"Just as I said when you so cruelly accused me of killing the others, I didn't kill Riley." LePage turned to the jury and continued his answer, "If I had even suggested she be punished or disciplined, Belinda would have my ass, and I'd be sleeping alone," he answered with a laugh. "Ask her if you think I'm lying."

"Reverend, maybe I will," Michael shot back at him.

That remark prompted another nervous reaction from Combes and a very loud, "Objection, your honor."

Judge Dades sustained the objection and told Michael to move on.

"I'm almost done," he said, before asking, "You told us that you didn't kill the women in the first three photos I showed you. Is that right?"

"That's correct."

"And you didn't have their bodies chopped up, and burnt, correct?

"Once again correct, Mr. Gioca."

"And you deny having the remains of Natasha, Sammi, and Alexa dumped in the lake at *LePage Acres,* right?"

"Yes, right."

"Also, there couldn't be any remains of Riley in your tub because you never killed, chopped, and burnt her, am I correct?"

"Yes, yes, yes, you are correct. I killed no one. I didn't kill, chop or burn any one, let alone the sisters of my church who work so hard for me and the poor children," an indignant LePage answered.

Michael now played his trump card.

During the lunch break, he had heard from Dr. Cesarano.

"I have the evidence you need to prove the murders," the doctor told him. The DNA in the remains from the lake matched the DNA of Natasha, Sammi and Alexa. And the DNA from what was recovered in the bathtub was a perfect match for Riley Caine.

"So if I were to tell you," Michael said to LePage, "That we found the charred body parts of Natasha, Sammi, and Alexa, in *your* lake on *LePage Acres*, and Riley's burnt remains in the bathtub in the basement of *your* church, what would you say, reverend?"

Before he gave his response, LePage turned to the jury and said, "Please excuse my language."

He turned back to Michael with his answer, "I'd say you were full of shit! If you got body parts, where are they?"

In response, Michael turned to the jury and said, "Stay tuned."

CHAPTER FORTY-TWO

Combes objected to the theatrics and moved for a mistrial.

Judge Dades overruled the objection, but admonished Gioca.

"Call your next witness, Mr. Combes."

"The defense rests, your honor. And renews its motion to dismiss the indictment."

The judge quickly denied the motion and asked Michael if he had any evidence in rebuttal.

"Yes your honor, we do. But given the late hour I'm asking the court to allow me to begin tomorrow morning.

"Very well," Dades replied. He dismissed the jury, telling them to be back at 9:30 a.m.

When the jurors were out of the courtroom, Combes was the first to speak.

"Judge, if there is to be a rebuttal case I want to know who Mr. Gioca intends to call so I can prepare for my cross."

The judge asked Michael if he had a list of witnesses, and if so he should turn it over to Combes.

Michael answered, "Now that I've heard the entire defense,

including the defendant's testimony, if the court gives me a few moments, Mr. Combes will have a witness list right now."

Winsell Myles topped the list, which also contained the names of Dina Mitchell, Special Agent Kelly Pistone, the FBI scuba diver who recovered the remains from the lake at *LePage Acres,* and Dr. Cesarano.

Combes showed the list to LePage, who read it silently.

Instead of quietly consulting with Combes, LePage exploded again, this time directing his vitriol at his lawyer.

"This is just a re-hash of the lies he put before the jury earlier in the case. You can't let him do that. You got to stop him, Combes. What the fuck am I paying you for?" he asked, then answered his own question.

"It ain't to roll over and let that son of a bitch steamroll me into a conviction."

"Do something you pussy!"

Combes, thoroughly embarrassed, addressed the court.

"Your Honor, I again apologize for the outburst. As you can imagine, my client feels his freedom is slowly being taken from him and I understand his anger and frustration. I hope the court does as well."

"Having said that, I strenuously object to this rebuttal. Like my client, I too believe it is merely a repeat of the direct case, which is not permitted under our law."

Judge Dades, who up to that moment had been very patient with LePage and his outbursts, ignored Combes, and addressed him.

"Your attorney has apologized for you, which isn't good enough for me. You disrespected this court, not once but twice, and if you don't apologize right now, I will hold you in contempt. And since you're already in jail, I'll assess a fine that you won't be happy with."

The judge ended with, "Remember, if you're convicted I'm the one who will sentence you."

Combes leaned over and spoke to LePage. The defendant then asked the judge for permission to speak. Dades nodded and LePage, in a voice dripping with phony sincerity, said he was sorry.

"It won't happen again, your honor."

Dades nodded, and said, "Very well.... Now Mr. Combes take the evening to prepare for the rebuttal case. Your objection is overruled. I'll see you gentlemen back here at 9:30 a.m. "

The next day, Michael's first rebuttal witness was Winsell Myles.

After taking him through the dismembering of the three women, and the burning of their bodies once again, Michael had Myles to tell the jury what he did with their remains.

"The reverend told me to clean out the tub of what was left of them women and take it up to his camp and dump the remains in the lake."

"How many times did you travel to the camp with remains?" Michael asked.

"Two times. The first time was to dump what was left of Natasha, and then I brought the remains of Sammi and Alexa."

Michael handed Myles the evidence photo of Riley Caine, and asked, "When you testified on direct examination I showed you this photo, and you told the jury that you didn't know who she was. Is that right?"

"Yes."

"Did you dismember her body and burn it in the reverend's tub?"

"No. I ain't ever seen her before you showed me her picture."

"So if her remains were found in that tub, you weren't responsible for them being there. Is that correct?"

"Yes."

When Michael was finished with Myles, Combes once again asked some questions about his criminal record, his potential predicate felony status, and his 'deal with the DA,' as he called it.

Myles' answers were exactly the same as when he was questioned about the same subjects during Combes initial cross-examination.

"Yes. I have a criminal record."

"Yes. I face becoming a persistent predicate felon."

"I have no deal with Mr. Gioca."

After Myles' last answer, Combes sat down. He had no additional questions for him.

Michael was shocked, and somewhat worried by Combes' tactics.

'Is he trying to set up an ineffective assistance of counsel point for LePage's appeal if he's convicted?' he asked himself.

He would learn much later that Combes was doing no such thing.

Myles was followed to the witness stand by FBI agent Kelly Pistone. She told the jury that she was part of the official FBI evidence gathering team and a skilled scuba diver.

Agent Pistone recounted the events of the day she searched the small lake on the LePage property near Bethel, New York.

"I was asked to search the bottom of the lake for anything that looked like human body parts. I recovered items that I believed fit the description, put them into a bucket I had with me, and later bagged the items so they could be analyzed in the FBI lab."

Michael established the chain of custody for what Agent Pistone recovered, ending with her testimony that she turned the bag containing the material over to Dina Mitchell for transport to the FBI lab.

Michael showed Pistone a plastic bag, which she identified as the one she packed with the material she recovered at the bottom of the *LePage Acres'* lake. He then introduced it into evidence.

On cross, Combes only asked about the chain of custody of the material Pistone recovered and bagged.

Michael's next witness was Dina Mitchell.

Dina testified to being present in the basement of the reverend's church when material from the bottom of an old bathtub was collected and bagged.

She added that she brought that material, and material that Agent Pistone recovered in the lake, to the FBI lab and handed it to Dr. Fred Cesarano.

Michael showed Dina the bag that contained the material from the bathtub. She identified it and Michael moved it into evidence.

On cross, as with Agent Pistone, Combes centered his questions on the chain of custody of the bag that contained the material from the bathtub in LePage's basement. And when he made no headway with Dina, he told the court that he had no additional questions.

Dr. Cesarano was the prosecution's next witness.

After testifying about his credentials as a forensic pathologist, the doctor told the jury that he was the recipient of two plastic bags containing material he was asked to analyze and identify, if possible.

His initial findings were that the material recovered at the bottom of the lake and from the bathtub, was human remains.

He then analyzed the remains in an attempt to extract DNA.

"Were you successful?" Michael asked.

"Yes. I found DNA in the material from the lake. It belonged to three different females."

"What did you do next?"

"I analyzed the material I was told came from the bottom of a bathtub and extracted DNA. It belonged to a female as well. However, it was from someone other than one of the three women from the lake."

Dr. Cesarano told the jury that investigators working for the prosecution gave him four bags, each marked with a different name: Natasha Popov, Sammi Rivera, Alexa Rivera, and Riley Caine.

He told the jury what those bags contained, and that the items belonged to the individual whose name was written on each bag.

"I analyzed what I was given and was able to extract DNA from items in each bag. I then compared that DNA to the DNA samples I recovered from the material found at the bottom of the lake, and from the bathtub."

"What did you find, doctor?"

"My conclusion is that the DNA from the remains found at the bottom of the lake matched the DNA I found on the items from bags marked Natasha Popov, Sammi Rivera, and Alexa Rivera."

"And the DNA from the material found at the bottom of the bathtub, matched DNA I extracted from items in the bag marked Riley Caine."

"Therefore I can say with a reasonable degree of medical and scientific certainty, that the body parts found in that lake are those of Natasha Popov, Sammi Rivera, and Alexa Rivera. And the material recovered from the bathtub are the remains of Riley Caine."

When the doctor finished his answer, Michael looked at the jury. In the many years he had been trying cases, this was the first time he saw all twelve regular jurors and the alternates, nodding. It told him that Dr. Cesarano was a hit!

'*LePage is fucked!*' he said to himself as he sat down.

Combes' cross-examination was pathetic. He stayed away from any questions regarding the remains found in LePage's bathtub hoping the jury would forget what they heard. Instead he chose to concentrate on the remains from the lake.

However, he obviously did no homework on DNA and had no clue as to what to ask. He floundered around the issue of chain of custody, and then made the mistake of challenging Agent Pistone's ethics and competence, which the doctor had no trouble handling.

"Agent Pistone and I have worked many cases together," Cesarano began, "and I know her to be an extremely competent, ethical, careful, and very precise law enforcement officer. So I have no doubt that what she said came from the bottom of that lake is precisely what she found there."

"Doctor, if, as you say, Agent Pistone's dive into the lake resulted in her finding, what you call 'human remains,' where are they? Did you conveniently use them all up in your analysis?"

"No," Cesarano answered.

"Well then, I'll repeat my question, where are they?', Combes asked, now in a very loud voice."

Before answering, the doctor turned to the judge and asked, "May I go into my satchel, your honor?" When the judge said that he could, Cesarano reached into his bag and produced a plastic container similar to a piece of Tupperware. He opened the top and took something out and placed it on the witness stand in front of him.

The doctor then turned and addressed Combes, "You asked where the remains were... here they are Mr. Combes." The doctor then held up a wire ring of human fingers, toes, and several assorted bones that Michael asked him to construct, for a situation like this.

After that answer Michael said to himself, '*I was wrong, LePage is VERY fucked*!"

Combes slunk back to his seat and announced, "I have no additional questions for this witness."

Dr. Cesarano was Michael's last witness. However before he dismissed him he had a few questions on re-direct.

"Doctor the body parts on that ring, how did you get them?

"They were brought to my lab by your investigators."

"Were they what you used to determine that the remains in the lake belonged to the women you named during your direct examination?"

"Yes. And also included on this ring is a finger bone from the items recovered from the bathtub. It belonged to Riley Caine."

Michael offered the ring into evidence and said, "I have no further questions."

Judge Dades asked Combes if he objected to the ring being admitted into evidence.

"Of course I do your honor."

"Overruled," said Judge Dades. "Mr. Combes, if not for *your* interrogation of Dr. Cesarano, this item wouldn't be in this case. The ring is now in evidence."

"Mr. Combes, do you have any surrebuttal?"

"The defense rests," was his curt reply.

Michael glanced over at the defense table. The look on LePage's face and his demeanor reminded him of cartoon characters from his childhood, who when angry were pictured with smoke shooting out of their ears.

The reverend was ready to explode.

CHAPTER FORTY-THREE

With the evidence portion of the trial complete, Judge Dades told the jurors that the closing arguments by the attorneys was the next order of business. However, because it was Friday afternoon, he dismissed them until Monday morning.

"Please be in your jury room at 9:30 sharp," he said.

When the jury was out of the courtroom, Combes moved, yet again, for a dismissal.

The motion was denied.

The judge asked the lawyers if there was any further business before they adjourned.

Michael said no.

When the judge looked over at the defense table he saw LePage and Combes deep in discussion.

After waiting a few minutes Dades interrupted and asked, "Mr. Combes, is there anything further that we need to address before we adjourn?"

Combes slowly rose from his seat and said, "No your honor, not at this time. My client and I have a lot to talk about, and we'll do that back at the Brooklyn House."

"Well gentlemen, I'll see you all bright and early on Monday morning."

Michael's intention was to spend the weekend working on his closing argument after having dinner with Kathy on Friday night. But he had a few phone calls to make before he picked her up.

His first call was to Monsignor Romano to give him an update. Romano was pleased with Michael's report and told him he'd be praying for him.

"I'll dedicate my Sunday mass to you and your success Michael. The Lord has a way of listening to us priests when we talk to him at mass."

His next call was to his father to check in and to let him know that all was well.

He also called his sons who told him about their weekend plans. "Guys, that sounds terrific. Have a great time, just be careful. I'll call you when the trial's over and we'll set up dinner with grandpa. I love you."

Kevin said, "Good luck with the trial Dad." Michael Jr. added, "We love you too."

Dinner with Kathy at his favorite restaurant, *Vite,* in Astoria, was just what Michael needed before he spent the weekend deep in thought and preparation.

They didn't talk about his case but spent the entire three hours discussing what Kathy was working on and planning their next vacation.

As much as he wanted to, Michael didn't spend the night at Kathy's apartment. He dropped her off and promised to call her when he finished writing his closing.

"I'll call you sometime on Sunday so you can wish me good luck," before he kissed her good night.

"Michael, good luck comes to those who make it. Knowing you, you're gonna' be fine."

After spending all day Saturday working on his closing, that evening Michael took a walk to *Vinny's of Carroll Gardens* to stretch his legs and get dinner. *Vinny's* was a popular local take-out restaurant known for the veal parmigiana and *broccoli rabe,* which Michael once told Monsignor Romano, were close to his mom's and grandma's.

"Having eaten both your mom's and grandma Rachele's cooking, that's very high praise Mike," the cleric told him.

Back in his apartment and half-way through his meal, Michael's phone rang. He didn't recognize the number but he answered. It was a correction officer who worked in the Brooklyn House of Detention.

CO Nick Sementelli was Michael's neighbor. He lived directly across from him on Sackett Street. When Michael moved into the apartment a few years before, Sementelli recognized him from the TV news reports of one of the high profile cases Michael handled for the DA and welcomed him to the neighborhood. They became quick buddy's and often spent time chatting while sitting on the front stoop of one of their buildings.

"Mike, it's Nick Sementelli."

"Hey Nick, I didn't recognize the number. What's up? Is everything okay?"

"I'm working. And I'm calling to alert you to something. I know you're on trial with the phony reverend's case. He and his inmate lawyer had a visitor just before visiting hours ended this afternoon. Mike, the three got into some kind of disagreement and were shouting at each other for a good twenty minutes."

"They were in a room reserved only for clients and lawyers, but somehow this weird looking guy got the warden's permission to join them. Apparently he told the warden that he was working with the lawyer on the reverend's case."

Without hearing another thing about him, Michael had a good idea who the third guy was. To be sure he asked, "Nick what did the third guy look like?"

When Nick told him and mentioned the "Fucking ugly mole on his left cheek," Michael wondered, '*What could the EVIL ONE be cooking up?*'

"Nick, did you hear anything that was said?"

"Mike we're not supposed to listen in on attorneys and their clients, and I didn't. But they were shouting so loud I could hear some stuff. It seemed as if the reverend wanted to do something that the lawyer and the third guy were against. All I could hear clearly were the words, 'closing argument.'"

"Thanks for the heads up Nick. Are you working tomorrow?"

When Nick told him that he was, Michael asked him to keep an eye out, and if there was a repeat of that screaming match, "Please let me know."

"You got it Mike," Nick said before he hung up.

"What the fuck was that all about?" Michael said out loud to his empty apartment. "Whatever it is, can't let it distract me."

True to his vow, Michael didn't let Nick Sementelli's call distract him from putting together a closing argument that he was proud of. By the time he called Kathy on Sunday night, Michael was certain that it would put the finishing touches on a conviction for Vernon LePage.

Bright and early Monday morning Michael finished his run through Red Hook, ate breakfast, showered, shaved, and was in his seat at the prosecution table in Judge Dades' courtroom at 9:30 a.m.

The judge took the bench and asked his clerk where the defense team was.

A court officer answered.

"Your honor, the defendant and his lawyer are in the holding cell. They're having a disagreement, so we didn't want to bring them out until you were apprised of the situation."

Judge Dades told him to bring them into the courtroom, "Now."

After their handcuffs were removed, Combes told the judge that LePage wanted to speak to him before they proceeded to summations.

When Michael heard that, he thought that the disagreement must have something to do with the EVIL ONE's visit with them in jail on Saturday.

He would soon find out that he was right.

"Rev. LePage, what do you want to say to me?" the judge asked.

"Judge, this is my life here," he began, "And I don't want anyone but me talkin' to this jury about my case. So after consultation with the Lord, I decided that I'm going to sum up myself."

"Mr. Combes disagrees, as does a trusted ally and advisor of mine, but I want the jury to hear from my mouth that I didn't do these horrendous things."

Judge Dades addressed Combes, "Before I decide, I'd like to hear from you."

"The reverend told me that on Friday night the Lord appeared to him in a dream and told him that he needed to address the jury himself," Combes said.

"Your honor, I have done all I can to dissuade him from what I believe is a fool's errand. But the reverend said God has spoken and he trusts in Him. Judge, there is nothing more for me to say."

Michael listened and thought it all through.

'The EVIL ONE was trying to change LePage's mind about delivering the summation himself. That's what the disagreement in the Brooklyn House was all about. HE wants to win! HE wants to beat me, Romano, and Caldwell. LePage summing up doesn't give HIM the best shot at doing that, especially after his dreadful performance on cross-examination.'

'If the judge lets the reverend sum up and he's convicted, Satan loses again...and someone will pay.'

The Judge gave LePage what he asked for, and for the next two hours the reverend lectured, chastised, and admonished the jury.

Michael later told Romano, "If the EVIL ONE was there to hear LePage's performance, *HE* would have struck him down where he stood."

"Sal, I expected he would deliver a calm, well thought out, sermon, ending with LePage humbling himself, and asking the jury to send him back to his church to continue the work of saving souls for the Lord. Instead, it was more akin to the lecture from a stern and angry parent to a misbehaving child."

"He talked...no, he preached, *AT* the jury, not *TO* the jury."

"He asked them, in a soft voice, filled with fake sincerity, 'How can people such as yourselves, people who profess to practice a religion of one kind or another, ever doubt a minister, a preacher, a man of God, when he tells you that he did not kill anyone?'"

"Then in a voice so loud that he could be heard in the hallway outside the courtroom, LePage bellowed, 'The simple answer is you *CANNOT,* and you *WILL NOT.'*"

LePage ended by telling the jury of a divine reward if they voted to free him and warned of divine punishment, "Like God driving the fallen angel from Heaven," if they voted against him.

"'Good people,' LePage said, 'Finding me not guilty will be your stairway to heaven...but finding me guilty will be your elevator to hell.'"

"Then he raised his arms, looked up as if to speak to the Almighty, and shouted, 'Hallelujah, hallelujah, praise the Lord!" He wiped the sweat from his brow and sat down.

"Wow! That sounds like quite a performance," Romano remarked.

Michael's summation was markedly different from the roller coaster that was LePage's closing.

For the first forty minutes he detailed all the evidence amassed against the reverend. He reminded the jury of how the witnesses corroborated each other and were supported by the physical evidence.

Then he tugged at their heartstrings.

He pointed to the first row of the spectator section of the courtroom where the families of the four victims were sitting and admonished the jury to never forget their heartbreaking testimony, and the profound loss they suffered.

"Young women who were first conned into leaving home to work for a phony preacher. Then plied with drugs to the point that they became addicts, and thus dependent on, and obedient to, their supplier and their rapist, lest he cut off for their steady supply of drugs."

"Four daughters and sisters who their families will never see again because they were brutally murdered by LePage."

"Three of them butchered, burnt, and dumped into their final resting place, an anonymous lake in a remote part of upstate New York. And one in an old bathtub in the basement of his so-called church."

He paused for effect before saying, "And, all they have left of their loved ones, are the pieces on that wire ring put together by Dr. Cesarano."

Michael ended by walking over to the defense table, pointed to LePage and said, "Don't be fooled by the title he uses, and how others refer to him. Or that his name is on a storefront in Midwood, that he calls a church."

"This is not a reverend, or a man of God. He's a fraud, a con man, a scam artist. And today in this courtroom, when he stood before you and told you to believe him, that was his latest and most desperate scam."

"Vernon LePage doesn't practice religion, he mocks it. That clerical collar he wears, and the nun habits he dresses those victimized women in, are nothing more than costumes. On Halloween kids put on costumes and then go out to entice folks into giving them candy. LePage's trick or treating is designed to fool unsuspecting people like you and me into giving money to a charity that doesn't exist anywhere but in his evil mind."

"Would a true man of God, cajole and con young women into his home, get them hooked on drugs so they'd be compliant, and then rape them whenever he felt the urge, as his son Frankie told you he did?"

"Would a true man of God, kill, dismember, and burn Natasha, Sammi, and Alexa as Winsell Myles and Belinda Shaw told you he did... and confessed to?"

"Would a true man of God, tolerate the rape of Riley Caine? Then kill, dismember, and burn her body, as Belinda Shaw said he did... and confessed to?"

"The answer to all those questions is a resounding NO!"

"Ladies and gentlemen don't allow the slick words of this con man to trick you into a decision. Let the law and the evidence be your guides to a just and fair verdict."

Michael paused before ending with, "He put those four young women on that stairway to heaven well before their time, and in doing so, when his time comes, he reserved himself a spot on that elevator to hell."

"Do what's right. Do what justice demands. Convict Vernon LePage."

CHAPTER FORTY-FOUR

Michael was surprised that it took three days for the jury to convict LePage.

When he spoke to several of the jurors after the verdict, he understood why Combes worked so hard in jury selection to ensure he had a jury dominated by people who practiced a religion.

The foreperson, who voted to convict from the first day of deliberations, told Michael that three jurors who were more devout in their religious beliefs than they let on during jury selection, couldn't bring themselves to believe that LePage was a fraud. Thus they had difficulty accepting the fact that a minister would be involved in the horrific and brutal acts he was charged with and could not vote to convict him.

"So, those of us who were with you, used Belinda's testimony to change their minds. We pointed out that, until she left him, Belinda was closer to LePage than anyone. She was his trusted companion. Which is why he felt confident that he could tell her what he had done, without concern that she would go to the police."

"Then we compared what Belinda told us to what Frankie LePage and Winsell Myles said, and pointed out that their testimony corroborated everything she swore to."

"But what ultimately convinced the three to see it our way, was the testimony about the remains of the four women."

"We asked them if they thought it was a coincidence that remains belonging to the four missing women were discovered in a lake on LePage's property and in a bathtub located in the basement of his church."

"And as for that bathtub, we asked the three to give us a logical explanation of why such a thing was sitting on a fire pit in a building in the Midwood section of Brooklyn, if it was not used for what Winsell Myles said it was. They couldn't, and finally came around."

"I'm sorry it took so long to get there, Mr. Gioca, but the end result is that we did. Personally, I hope that phony, brutal, bastard goes to prison for the rest of his life."

Michael thanked the juror, and when he left the courthouse he said a silent prayer to his ally above.

In his office when he got back were Dina, Tim, and a bottle of champagne. Tim did the honors of pouring three glasses after which he and Dina toasted Michael.

It was now his turn. He held up his glass and told the investigators that the victory was theirs as well.

"I know it's a cliché, but I could not have done it without you."

He told them what the juror said about the importance of Belinda's testimony in securing the conviction. "She was as good as she was on the witness stand because of you two. She trusted you and opened up to me because of the relationship she had with you. And you kept her safe. Thank you."

Michael begged off a dinner invite saying he was very tired. But the actual reason was the invitation Romano sent in a text while they were sipping their champagne, asking him to meet the monsignor and Caldwell at *Emilio's*.

Michael hated lying to Dina and Tim, but the oath of secrecy he took trumped those feelings.

They agreed to postpone the dinner until the following week, finished their champagne and left. Michael packed up his briefcase and headed out to meet his bosses.

After congratulatory cocktails, and a cold antipasto that Emilio brought, 'on the house,' the three settled in for a discussion while they waited for their pasta course.

It was unusual for Caldwell to join him and the monsignor at *Emilio's* so Michael braced himself for what he expected would be a new assignment or bad news.

What it was, stunned him.

"Michael, we have a sensitive matter to discuss. It involves Elton Combes," Caldwell began.

"While the jury was deliberating the lawyer who's representing him in the case where he's charged with murdering Jax Chase, contacted DA Price and asked for a meeting. At the meeting the lawyer told Price that Combes wants to speak to you."

"The attorney led Price to believe that his client has information you'll be interested in, and that he's willing to plead guilty in the murder case."

"That's curious. Did the lawyer tell Price what Combes wants in return?" Michael asked.

"No. He said Combes will only discuss that with you."

"Okay. His case is on in two weeks. I'll contact the lawyer and arrange for a meeting in my office as soon as possible."

Several days later Michael was sitting in his office with Combes' attorney Paul Franks, when his client was brought in from the Brooklyn House by Tim and Dina.

"Before we start, would you like to talk to Mr. Franks alone?" Michael asked Combes.

"No. In fact I would like Mr. Franks to leave. I want to speak to *you* alone."

Franks balked, and leaned in to speak to Combes so Michael couldn't hear what he wanted to say, but Combes backed away and told Franks, "Please leave. You can wait outside and when I'm done we'll call you back in."

Franks looked at Michael, who shrugged and asked Tim to bring him to the conference room. "Mr. Franks, would you like a cup of coffee while you wait?" Tim asked.

Franks said yes and was escorted to Michael's conference room.

With Franks out of his office, Michael asked Combes what he had to tell him.

"Mr. Gioca, you may find what I'm about to say strange, but I assure you it all took place as I will describe."

"The day before summations LePage and I were conferring, when that asshole Jiz was escorted into the attorney-client visiting room. Both my client and I were surprised and I asked how *HE* got in. *HE* said someone made a call to the warden and told him that I asked for Jiz to be there because *HE* was my paralegal and I needed *HIM* with me when I spoke to LePage."

"Of course it was all bullshit. Jiz was there to, as *HE* claimed, 'Help me get LePage to see the light and back off his desire to sum up himself.'"

"*HE* did take my side but as you know we were unsuccessful in changing LePage's mind."

Combes told Michael that after LePage was brought back to his cell, Jiz asked the correction officer, who was to escort him back to his cell, "To give us a few minutes so we can talk."

Jiz told Combes that *HE* knew that LePage was a hopeless case and would get himself convicted. "*HE* told me that *HE* wasn't concerned because *HE* had a plan to get LePage out of jail."

"*HIS* exact words were, 'Chaos will reign, and LePage will be free.'"

"Then *HE* warned me." 'Do nothing to upset my plan, or you will pay dearly.'"

"Mr. Gioca I just listened and nodded, because that's all I could do. I had no ability to say anything other than 'okay.' It was like *HE* had taken control of my body, my mind, and my spirit."

Combes continued, "Well you know what happened to LePage, who, strangely, handled the conviction very well. After the verdict we were back in the cell behind the courtroom and LePage was all smiles. He saw the depressed look on my face and told me not to worry. 'Jiz and me got this all worked out.'"

"Now, what I'm about to tell you is why I needed to talk alone."

"Last night Jiz came to visit me in the Brooklyn House. Somehow *HE* knew that I was coming to see you today. How the fuck did *HE* find that out?" a frightened and shaken Combes asked.

Michael ignored the question and told Combes to go on.

"Jiz said, 'When you go to see Gioca, tell him that he didn't win.'"

"*HE* said, you, Caldwell, and Monsignor Romano may think it was a victory, but it's not. *HIS* exact words were, 'It's just the beginning of a new phase,' whatever the hell that means, 'that will shake Brooklyn and the city to its core.'"

"And just like the night in the attorney-client visiting room before summations, I could do nothing other than nod and agree."

Combes was not finished. He began to wring his hands and started to sweat.

"Elton, I know there's something else. What is it?" Michael asked.

"Mr. Gioca, I don't know for sure what's going on, but I know it's not good. Please don't think I'm crazy when I tell you that I believe I've been possessed by a demon."

"I can't say 'no' when I need to, as I've just told you, and, I felt I was under a power I couldn't resist when I was given that gun and shot Jackson Chase."

"I've been doing some research in the jail's library and I found similar cases involving inmates in upstate prisons."

"According to the warden of the prison where a couple of those inmates were housed, they believed that they were possessed by a demonic force that took control of them and caused them to commit the horrific crimes that landed them there."

"The warden wrote that it was so bad that he called in a priest who performed the Catholic rite of exorcism on the inmates. And after the rite was performed the inmates felt that they were back to their old selves."

"You were the prosecutor in those cases, and a Monsignor Romano, was the exorcist! And unless it's a major coincidence, I'm sure he's the same Monsignor Romano mentioned by Jiz, along with you and someone named Caldwell."

Michael heard all he needed to hear. He asked Combes, "Just what do you want from me?"

"Mr. Gioca, I will plead guilty to the murder of Jackson Chase. In return I want you to arrange for the monsignor to perform an exorcism on me!"

"As I said before, I don't know what's going on with you, Jiz, and the others, and I don't want to know. What I do know is I can't live like this. I need to get my free will back!"

"Please help me."

PART THREE

CHAPTER FORTY-FIVE

Two weeks after the trial ended, Michael and Kathy left for the vacation they planned during the LePage case. In the ten glorious days they spent at the Club Med, Punta Cana resort in the Dominican Republic, the words "Vernon LePage" were never spoken. Sun and fun were the only things on their docket.

However, the day Michael returned to work, he was back in Judge Dades' courtroom for the sentencing of LePage.

The courtroom was packed with the friends and families of the murdered women. Some were there to deliver to the judge a 'victim impact statement' on behalf of Natasha, Sammi, Alexa, and Riley. The others were in attendance to witness a monster being sentenced to life in a cage.

Before he left for the Dominican Republic, Michael submitted a recommendation to the court in which he asked for a sentence of twenty five years to life in prison for each murder. All four were to run consecutively. He wanted to ensure that LePage never took another breath of free air. If New York State had a death penalty, he would have asked the judge to impose it.

Because of Elton Combes' deal with Michael, he could no longer represent LePage. The day after the deal was reached, Michael notified the court, and Judge Dades convened a session in which he told LePage to find another lawyer. When LePage told the judge he couldn't afford one, Dades appointed an attorney to represent him for the sentencing and to handle LePage's appeal.

Ennis Whatley, one of Brooklyn's finest appellate attorneys, agreed to take the case and was seated at the defense table when LePage was brought into the courtroom. They shared a few words before Judge Dades asked if the defense was ready to begin.

Whatley said that he was, and Michael indicated that the prosecution was also ready.

After four heartbreaking victim impact statements were delivered, it was Michael's turn to speak. When he was done there was not a dry eye among those in the spectator section, with one exception.

It was the bald guy with the large mole on his left cheek sitting in the last row staring menacingly at Gioca. The EVIL ONE was not happy.

When it was the defendant's turn, as he did with the closing argument, LePage spoke for himself. Judge Dades had heard it all when LePage testified for himself and was not moved by anything the phony reverend said.

Now it was the judge's turn to speak.

"Mr. LePage, you are an ignominious thug. In all my years on the bench I've never encountered anyone as contemptible. You are a person who's lived a life of perversion, lies, and violence. But that stops today. For your barbarism and the utterly inhuman conduct toward the young victims who had their whole lives ahead of them, I hereby sentence you to four consecutive sentences of twenty five years to life in state prison."

"And if by some miracle you are considered for parole, I hereby order the parole authorities to notify me so I can personally appear as a witness at your hearing. It will be my pleasure to tell the parole board that you don't deserve to be free. You deserve a place on that elevator to hell you threatened our jury with."

The judge then turned to the court clerk and said, "Please take this human garbage out of my courtroom."

With that everyone in the spectator section stood and applauded Judge Dades...again, with one exception.

On his way out of the courtroom LePage turned to the spectators, and with a smirk on his face shouted, "This is not over."

Only the guy with the mole in the last row nodded in agreement.

That night Michael had dinner with the monsignor.

The two waited for Emilio to pour the *Brunello di Montalcino*, then toasted another victory over the EVIL ONE.

Michael filled in Romano as to what was scheduled for the trial witnesses, and for Elton Combes.

"Combes will be the last one we deal with. Once he's sentenced he'll be sent to Green Haven where the warden is prepared for you to perform the exorcism Combes requested. When the time is right, Warden Daniels will let me know."

Over the next several weeks, as Michael promised, Frankie LePage was sentenced to time served and released from custody. Frankie reunited with his brothers Zeke, Isaiah, Noah and their mother.

Winsell Myles' trumped up gun possession case was dismissed. In return for his cooperation, he was allowed to plead guilty to Attempted Concealment of a Human Corpse, a misdemeanor. Like Frankie, he was sentenced to time served, and returned home to his family in Midwood.

As a bonus, Michael and DA Price spoke to the city medical examiner's office and convinced him to re-hire Myles.

As for Belinda Shaw, on the afternoon following LePage's sentencing, she was driven to LaGuardia Airport by Dina and Tim. She was bound for Raleigh, North Carolina, where Caldwell's people rented a beautiful two bedroom apartment for her in a gated community.

Once settled into her new home, she began a new job as the receptionist in the local office of the FBI.

Caldwell was so grateful for her cooperation that he made sure she'd never have to worry about where her next paycheck would come from.

Before she boarded the plane she embraced Dina and Tim, and through tears she thanked them for saving her life. "I'll never forget you," she said.

And as she handed her boarding pass to the airline rep at the gate, she turned to the investigators and said, "Please tell Michael to take care of himself, and to always watch his back. Let him know that I'll be praying for him."

With the witnesses settled, it was time for Combes to plead guilty, be sentenced, and sent to Green Haven.

One month after LePage was sentenced, on a bright, clear day that mirrored his mood, Elton Combes, with his lawyer Paul Franks at his side, stood before presiding judge Frances Mercurio in Brooklyn Supreme Court.

Combes was upbeat because he knew that when the court session was over, he'd be one step closer to being free of the demon that possessed him.

Pursuant to his deal with Michael, Combes pled guilty to the lesser homicide charge of Manslaughter in the First Degree for killing Jackson Chase. And based on Gioca's recommendation, the judge promised Combes a sentence that would allow him to one day be back with his family.

Two weeks later, with his wife Margo and their three children, Keisha, Kyle, and Kevin, in the courtroom, Combes was sentenced by Judge Mercurio to seven to twenty one years in prison.

Before being taken away to await his transfer to Green Haven, the judge allowed Combes to hug his family and say goodbye. Then they were escorted out to the courthouse corridor where their sobbing could be heard throughout the courtroom.

With tears in his own eyes, Combes asked the court if he could have a word with Michael. Paul Franks gave his okay and Judge Mercurio told him, "You have two minutes."

"Michael," Combes began in a whisper, "I want to thank you for everything you've done for me. When I get to Green Haven I can't wait to meet Monsignor Romano and be free of the dark force that has controlled me for so long."

When Michael wished him good luck, Combes said one final thing, "Be careful."

CHAPTER
FORTY-SIX

In late spring the two hour drive from Brooklyn to Stormville, NY, in Dutchess County, home of Green Haven Correctional Facility, was a pleasant trip. The trees lining both sides of the Taconic Parkway were in full bloom and their beauty posed a mild distraction to Monsignor Romano, as he navigated the winding highway.

According to his GPS, the cleric would arrive at Green Haven at 10 a.m., when he was to meet with Warden Daniels to discuss the details of the Rite of Exorcism he was to perform on Elton Combes. However, slowing down to take in the beauty of the foliage was going to make him a bit late.

"This beauty is too spectacular to ignore," he said to himself, knowing that what was ahead for him with Elton Comes could become very ugly.

'I know the warden has been through this before, so I'm sure his assessment that Combes is ready is correct,' Romano reflected as he pulled up to the security booth at the main gate of the prison at 10:20 a.m.

Twenty five minutes after he was checked in at the gate where he and his car were searched, Romano made his way to the staff parking lot where the warden reserved a spot. After a short walk to Daniel's office the monsignor was welcomed by the warden and the two sat to discuss Elton Combes and the exorcism.

Because there was no way of knowing how long he'd be in Stormville, Romano reserved a room in a motel close to the prison where he would stay until he freed Combes from Satan's hold.

That evening Combes and the monsignor had their first of what would be many sessions together.

While Romano was in Stormville, Michael resumed his duties as Chief of Rackets, ever vigilant about making sure that his cover remained secure.

In his private life, he took advantage of the lull in the war against Satan and had several dinners with his father and his sons. He also spent many nights with Kathy when her job, with its long hours, permitted.

Michael also did something that was out of the ordinary, he had dinner with Caldwell at *Emilio's.* He wanted to discuss what Combes told him Jiz said just before LePage was convicted: "Chaos will reign and LePage will be free."

"John, knowing the EVIL ONE as I do, *HE* communicated those threats to Combes knowing they'd get back to me. As for the first one about reigning chaos, there's nothing we can do to prevent it since we can't predict the future. We don't know what's coming, or when it's coming, nor do we know what form this upheaval will take. However, if something does happen, we'll deal with it then. On the other hand, the threat that 'LePage will be free', is something we can take steps to prevent."

"Michael, I agree with you about the chaos. We'll cross that bridge when we have to. Now tell me what you have in mind about *HIS* other comment, regarding LePage?"

Michael began by reminding Caldwell that the EVIL ONE had successfully orchestrated the escape of Sabar and Jax Chase from Attica.

"Therefore we know *HE's* capable of pulling off a LePage escape, especially if he remains in the Brooklyn House, where security isn't what it should be. So, we need to contact the state prison authorities to find out what prison he's going to and have them move him as soon as possible."

"When we know where he'll be housed, we can tell the warden that LePage is an escape threat and advise him to take steps to ensure that the EVIL ONE's prediction never becomes a reality."

Caldwell agreed. "Mike, I'll get on it tomorrow. By the way, have you heard from the monsignor?"

Michael told Caldwell that he hadn't.

"I'll only hear from him when he's done."

At the end of three long and difficult days, Romano visited the prison chapel where he prayed to thank the Lord for giving him the strength to exorcize the demon from Elton Combes.

After his prayer, Romano, accompanied by a correction officer, made his way to the warden's office to give him the news.

In the corridor outside the office, an inmate approached Romano. The monsignor hadn't noticed him until the correction officer ordered the inmate to stop. When Romano saw who it was he smiled and said to the officer, "It's alright. Please let him come so I can talk to him."

"Monsignor, it is good to see you," Patrick Patron said, as he embraced the cleric. "I guess you're here to help another one of us who came under the demon's power. I hope you helped him as you did me."

Romano hadn't seen Patrick since the exorcism that Patron requested after he was sentenced to life in prison for the murder of Firefighter Louis Amato.

A couple of years before, while under the control of the EVIL ONE, Patrick set fire to the garage and storage facility of a Catholic church in Brooklyn. When firefighters responded, Patron, doing the devil's bidding, lied and told them there was a person trapped inside the burning structure. However, the building was empty.

Firefighter Amato rushed in to save the non-existent person and was killed when the building's roof collapsed on him.

Michael convicted Patron of murder, and he was sentenced to twenty five years to life in prison. Shortly after he arrived at Green Haven, where he was to be housed for the duration of his sentence, Patron exhibited behavior that the warden recognized as demonic possession.

The warden reached out for help; a call that was answered by Monsignor Romano.

"Patrick, it's good to see you," Romano said. "Considering where you are, I hope all is well."

"Monsignor, I'm as well as I can be. I owe my life to you and to God. I have a job here and I stay away from trouble. I'll do my time and hope for an early release when I'm eligible for parole. Please pray for me."

"Patrick I certainly will. And when you're eligible for parole I want you or your counselor to call me. I'd like to testify on your behalf before the parole board. I believe my opinion will carry great weight with them. Now go with God."

Patrick was so overwhelmed by the monsignor's offer that he dropped his head so no one would see the tears.

"God bless you Monsignor," he said.

Romano's meeting with Warden Daniels lasted just over an hour, after which the cleric left the prison and headed to his motel to pack. It was early evening, but he was worn out from the exorcism rite. He decided to get a good night's sleep and return to Brooklyn in the morning.

Before he turned in for the night, Romano called Margo Combes to make an appointment to see her when he got back to Brooklyn. He promised Elton that when the exorcism was done, he would personally bring his wife the good news.

In the days and weeks leading up to Combes talking to Michael, she had long discussions when she visited him in the Brooklyn House about his belief that he was possessed. She was skeptical at first, but ultimately came around to agreeing with him.

Elton Combes was close to Vernon LePage, who took care of him for many years, even helping him with his law school tuition. He was aware of LePage's charity scam, but turned a blind eye because LePage was so good to him.

When he was asked by the reverend, and his new assistant pastor, Brother Jiz, to defend Jackson Chase, Combes happily agreed.

The lawyer devoted all his time and energy to the defense because the reverend told him that Chase's acquittal was very important to him. Unfortunately despite his hard work, Chase was convicted. Combes tried the case to the best of his ability and made all defense decisions in consultation with his client, without interference.

Combes told his wife that it wasn't until he was told by LePage and Jiz that he had to shoot Chase to protect them, that he began to feel that he was not in control of himself.

"Margo, I wanted to, but I couldn't say no. And on the day I did it, I was unable to stop myself from pulling the trigger."

Then came the reverend's trial.

He told Margo that he didn't believe it was in his, or LePage's, best interest for him, a prisoner, to act as LePage's defense attorney. But when he voiced that opinion in a jail house meeting with Jiz and LePage, it was as if they had not heard a word he said. "Brother Jiz made it very clear that it was me, and only me, who would represent the reverend."

"Again, I was unable to say no. The words just would not come out of my mouth. All I could do was nod in agreement. Then there were times when Jiz would take part in meetings I had with the reverend, and I felt that *HE* was in control, not me, the person trying the case."

Recognizing that he needed help, the couple made a joint decision which brought him to Michael.

Margo Combes was happy to hear from Romano. They made an appointment to meet at her home in two days. An appointment that would set off a series of events, about which Caldwell would later remark, “Michael, it’s time to cross that bridge. The chaos has arrived.”

CHAPTER FORTY-SEVEN

They sat in the living room of the Combes' home on Avenue K in the heart of Midwood. Over coffee Romano told Margo that her husband was free of the demon. She was overjoyed.

"Monsignor, how was he emotionally, when you left?" she asked as she refilled his coffee cup.

"Mrs. Combes, Elton told me that he literally felt a weight had been lifted from his shoulders."

Margo began to cry. When Romano moved to comfort her she said, "No need monsignor. These are tears of joy. I can't wait to tell the kids when they get home."

"There's something else we need to talk about," Romano told her.

"Elton didn't want to speak about this on the phone, and because he doesn't know when you'll be able to visit him, he asked me to tell you about a decision he's made about his future."

Margo wiped her tears and anxiously asked, "What is it?"

"He wants to become a Catholic."

"Before I left," Romano continued, "we spoke to the prison chaplain, a priest from a nearby Catholic church, who has agreed to provide instruction to Elton so he can be baptized in the Church."

Margo was surprised but not upset.

"After all he's been through with that phony reverend, he needs to do what will make him happy and bring him comfort. When I speak to him I'll be sure to tell him I support his decision and, who knows, maybe me and the kids will follow him to the baptismal font."

Romano smiled and told her, "If that's what you decide to do, call me. I'll help make it happen."

The cleric finished his coffee, wished her good luck, and told her he would pray that she, Elton, and their kids would finally find peace. He said goodbye and left.

It was afternoon and the late spring sun was still bright when the monsignor got into his car which was parked in the Combes' driveway.

The radio came on when he started the car and he began to back out.

He didn't hear the electric motor scooter flying down the sidewalk in front of the Combes' house ridden by a man with a large mole on his left cheek. Nor did he see it momentarily stop, then take off.

What he did hear, just as he was about to leave the driveway and back into the street, was a black woman with long red dreadlocks, screaming, "The priest hit the kid. I think she's dead."

Romano jammed on the brakes and got out. Laying at the curb, near the rear fender on the passenger side of his car, was a young girl bleeding from a head wound. Next to her was a badly damaged bicycle.

As Romano knelt to help her, he looked around for someone to assist him. The only person on the street was the woman, now screaming even louder. He managed to call 911 and comforted the young girl, who was alive, while they waited for an ambulance.

The woman's wailing caused people in the private homes and

apartment houses on the block to look out their windows, while others came out onto the street. A crowd began to gather around the monsignor and the young girl. He asked them to back up so when the ambulance got there the paramedics would have room to tend to her.

His request was ignored as the crowd closed in tighter. To make matters worse, the woman with the dreadlocks, who started it all, was now revving up the crowd, yelling, “Where are the cops? They need to get here and arrest this fucking priest before his people get him outta’ here. You know how them idol worshippers stick together.”

Two ambulances arrived three minutes apart. The paramedics in the first one, which belonged to a private neighborhood emergency response group, immediately began to tend to Romano.

That outraged some in the crowd who began to shout, “Why are you helping the fuck who did this. It’s the little girl who needs you.”

Later, when interviewed, those paramedics told the police, “When we jumped out of the bus, the first person we saw was the priest who had blood all over him. We thought he was hurt, which is why we went right to him.”

They said they didn’t see the young girl until Romano, who was holding her, told them it was her that needed help.

When paramedics from the second ambulance, belonging to the FDNY, moved in to tend to the girl, they told Romano to go with the first paramedics so they could examine him to be certain that he wasn’t injured.

As the monsignor walked with them, the paramedics commented that the gathering crowd was becoming angry and hostile. For the first time Romano saw the entire scene and it frightened him. He heard angry comments accusing the paramedics of ignoring the young girl and trying to get him out of there.

“Where you goin’ with that drunken priest?” someone in the crowd asked. “You better not be tryin’ to sneak him outta’ here.”

Another said, “He needs to be in cuffs.”

The crowd surrounded both ambulances and continued to grow, spreading to the sidewalk on both sides of the street. Heard above all the street noise was the woman with the dreads, joined by others, demanding that the police, who were now on the scene, arrest the "fucking priest. That bible thumping motherfucker ain't gonna' get away with this."

While Romano was being examined by the paramedics, Margo Combes came rushing toward him.

"Are you okay monsignor?, she asked.

"I'm fine Margo. It's that young girl who needs help."

When Romano mentioned a young girl, Margo covered her mouth and looked worried.

"Margo, what's wrong?"

"What does she look like?" she asked.

He told her as best he could, adding a description of the bike lying next to her. Margo gasped and rushed off toward the paramedics who were still tending to her. When she got to the ambulance and saw the girl, Margo let out a scream.

It was her daughter Keisha.

The crowd had grown exponentially and the police officers on the scene fearing trouble, called for assistance. When back-up arrived a sergeant said to the paramedics who were with Romano, "We got to get him outta' here."

"Sergeant, I want you to know that I didn't hit that young girl," Romano told him.

"Father, I believe you," the sergeant said. "I don't see any damage on your car, and I see red paint on the girl's bike. Your car is black."

"Thank you," Romano said.

"Now what about my car?" Romano asked, pointing to it still partly in the Combes' driveway.

"Father, the Accident Investigation Squad (AIS) is on the way. Give me your car keys and I'll make sure the car gets to the 70th Precinct parking lot when AIS is finished processing it. But you have to get out of here."

The sergeant asked the paramedics if Romano was injured. When they told him he wasn't he called over a uniform cop and asked for the breathalyzer kit NYPD patrol officers carry in their radio cars.

"Sorry Father, we need to do this so no one will second guess us later."

Romano told him he understood and the cop administered the test under the sergeant's supervision.

When it was determined that Romano was not intoxicated, the sergeant told the officer, "Take the priest into the stationhouse. Bring him up to the detective area. I'll call the desk officer to let him know you're coming and I'll tell him to alert the detective squad commander."

Turning to Romano he said, "Father, the test confirmed that you aren't drunk. Not that I ever thought you were. So some advice, between you and me, when you get to the stationhouse say nothing, and call someone. A lawyer, your bishop, anyone who can help. This crowd is lookin' to hang you. And from their mood and what their sayin', I think we're in for a long bad night."

When Romano was escorted, unhandcuffed, to a police radio car and got in, the red dreads woman saw him and went nuts on the cop with him.

"You fucking pig," she yelled. "Why you ain't arresting him? Did he tell you he'd do something for you, like forgive you for diddling young girls? Which you probably do. Or for fucking around on your wife? Like all you cops do. Or for taking money from drug dealers to let them go? Which you pigs do all the time."

The woman wasn't done. She climbed onto a nearby parked car and began to preach to a crowd that gathered around her.

"We need to stop them pigs," she implored. "They threw our dear Reverend LePage in jail, and he ain't done nothin'. I seen that fuck hit the girl with his car and they gonna' let him go. Why? 'Cause he's a priest and he's white? We can't let that happen."

With that more than twenty young men surrounded the radio car. They began pounding on the windows, on the front hood, and the trunk. Encouraged by the red dreads woman, a few climbed onto the car's roof, grabbed the bar containing the car's emergency red and blue lights, and began to shake it, trying to break it off.

Only when a dozen cops ran to the car to push the men away, did those on the roof jump off.

Finally, the driver was able to move the radio car.

As he drove away he looked into his rearview mirror and saw that people in the crowd were now jumping onto cars parked up and down the street, breaking windows, and smashing headlights. Some even surrounded a small compact car and began to violently shake it. Later when riot police arrived, the car was completely turned over.

And just as the radio car with Romano turned off the block, the first Molotov cocktail exploded onto the street, bringing cheers from a crowd that now numbered in the hundreds

A full scale riot had broken out.

CHAPTER FORTY-EIGHT

When Romano got to the 70th precinct detective squad room, he was met by the commanding officer who brought him into his office.

"Father, I'm Captain Teo Galetta. Please have a seat. I need to ask you a few questions about what happened this afternoon. You're not under arrest so I'm not going to read the Miranda warnings. Before we start/ is there anyone you want to call?"

Remembering the advice the sergeant gave him, the monsignor said there was and asked for a place with some privacy to make the call.

The Captain left the office, and Romano called Michael.

When Michael answered he jokingly asked, "Hey Sal, are you calling to tell me you're stuck in traffic out near Combes' house. I hear there was some kind of car accident, and the neighborhood is going nuts."

When Romano told him what happened and where he was, Michael quickly left his office and headed to the station house.

On the way he called Caldwell to fill him in on the limited info he'd gotten from the monsignor and promised to keep him informed.

At the station house Michael showed his credentials to the desk officer and asked for "The priest who was brought in this afternoon."

The desk officer told him to go up to the squad room. When he walked in he saw a detective he knew and asked for "the priest."

The detective pointed to the commander's office where he saw Romano sitting and chatting with Captain Galetta.

"Hey there Cap," Michael said when he entered the room. "Long time no see."

Michael and Galetta knew each other from a case they worked on when Galetta was a detective.

A woman who was visiting a patient in Kings County Hospital, stepped onto the elevator in the lobby. Before she was fully into the car, and before the elevator door closed, it began it's ascent, trapping her leg between the floor of the elevator car and the wall of the elevator shaft. When her screams were heard by hospital personnel, an orderly ran to the elevator room where a technician was working. He shut down the power to the entire system and the fire department was ultimately able to extricate the woman.

Initially the incident was thought to be an unfortunate accident, but when the city buildings department began to investigate they found evidence of negligence.

The matter was referred to the NYPD, and 70th precinct Detective Galetta was assigned. Because of the unusual nature of the incident, Galetta asked the Brooklyn DA's Rackets Division for assistance with the investigation.

Michael assigned the case to himself. He and Galetta conducted an extensive investigation, after which Michael charged the elevator technician with negligent assault on the woman. He was only hired because he lied about his qualifications, training, and experience, and neglected to take necessary safety precautions before he began his work.

He failed to close off the elevator to passengers on every floor of the building; he failed to post warning signs outside the elevator doors on each floor; and he didn't turn off the power to the bank of elevators that he was working on.

The repair company, and its owner, were also charged with negligent assault for failing to properly vet the technician's background in elevator repair.

Michael tried and convicted the technician and took guilty pleas from the repair company and its owner. The technician was sentenced to four years in prison. As part of the plea agreement with the company and its owner, ten million dollars was paid to the victim, and the company was stripped of its license to do business in New York State.

"Mike it's good to see you again," Galetta said as they shook hands.

Not knowing that it was Gioca who Romano called, Galetta asked, "What are you doing here? Things may be heating up on Avenue K, but what does that have to do with rackets?"

"Nothing yet. But you don't yet know who's behind that mess out there. Could be gangs, which falls under my purview. However, I'm here because the monsignor called me. We're old friends and he knows where I work."

Galetta was surprised. "Mike, I just have a few questions for the prie...sorry, the monsignor. He's not under arrest and is free to leave any time."

"Teo, please, for old times sake, tell me what you want to know before the monsignor answers. If I think he should get a lawyer you can stop right there and he'll come back with an attorney."

"Mike, no problem." When Michael began to ask Romano to leave, he was stopped by Galetta.

"The monsignor can stay. He should hear what I have to say. If he wants a lawyer I won't go any further."

Galetta said, "Right from the outset the sergeant who first responded to the accident never thought that the monsignor hit the young girl with his car."

"While I was waiting for whomever the monsignor called to get here, I heard from the Accident Investigation Squad that his car has been definitively ruled out as the vehicle that hit the victim."

Galetta continued, "And the young woman, Keisha Combes, although badly hurt, is awake in the hospital. She suffered a concussion, a leg broken in two places, and a broken ankle. But she was anxious to talk."

"One of my detectives interviewed her, and she told him that the monsignor did not hit her."

"Keisha said she was on the sidewalk with her bike in front of her house waiting for the monsignor to pull out of her driveway. As he started to back out, an electric motor scooter, driving on the sidewalk at full speed, plowed into her and knocked her to the ground. Her left leg was still in the peddle stirrup of her bike when she was hit. She landed on that leg and immediately felt a great deal of pain."

"She told the detective that the motor scooter rider stopped momentarily then continued past the monsignor's car and rode away."

Michael asked Galetta if the young woman got a look at the rider.

"Mike when he stopped for that moment she said he looked down at her and laughed before riding away. She only saw the left side of his face. But she did tell my guy that he had this ugly mole on his cheek."

Romano was stunned when he heard that. Michael too was stunned, but not surprised.

When Galetta was finished, without even consulting with Romano, Gioca told him to ask the monsignor anything he wanted.

For the next forty minutes the captain questioned the cleric. Satisfied that he covered everything he told Michael that he could take Romano home.

After hearing the description of the rider, there was no doubt in Michael's mind that the EVIL ONE was behind the street chaos and violence that followed the scooter incident. Therefore, since any prosecution that came out of it all would be his, he asked Galetta to keep him informed on the progress of the investigation.

"Since the monsignor is only a witness, I have no problem keeping this case. And with what's going on in the streets around Avenue K I have a feeling you're going to need my help."

"Mike, I'm happy to have you," Galetta said.

Just then a uniformed cop walked into the captain's office and whispered something to him. Galetta went to a window that faced the street in front of the station house and was surprised by what he saw.

Seeing the look on the captain's face Michael asked, "Teo is there something wrong?"

"Mike, there's a crowd of about a hundred people out there. I can't hear what they're saying, but one of the cops assigned to building security just told me that they're rowdy and calling for the priest to be locked up."

Galetta called down to the front desk and told the sergeant on duty to send a few cops up to his office. He said, "I have a witness and an ADA that needs to be escorted to the ADA's car which is parked in our lot."

When Michael and Romano walked out of the station house with a police escort, the woman with the red dreadlocks saw that the cleric was not handcuffed. She climbed onto the roof of a parked car and began to rile up the crowd. "They ain't even handcuffed that rosary rubbing motherfucker. He's with the prick DA that convicted our reverend. They gonna' let him walk. We can't let 'em get away with it.... No justice. No peace."

As the crowd began to surge toward Michael and the monsignor, the cops escorting them stepped in.

Someone in the crowd threw a punch at one of the cops, and when he retaliated, a mele broke out.

Thankfully. Michael was able to get to his car and drove out of the station house parking lot without further incident. He headed for Red Hook.

"Sal, please call Caldwell and tell him to meet us at his office," Michael said.

"The motor scooter rider with the mole, and the woman with the red dreads inciting the crowd both here and at the scene of the accident... it's the EVIL ONE."

"And we need to talk."

CHAPTER FORTY-NINE

It was close to midnight when Romano and Michael walked into Caldwell's office on the second floor of the innocuous looking building that served as his headquarters.

Because neither Michael nor the monsignor had eaten anything since lunch, on the way to meet Caldwell, they stopped at *Vinny's of Carroll Gardens*, a popular Italian takeout restaurant on Smith Street near Gioca's apartment.

When they walked into Caldwell's office, each had a veal parmigiana hero and a beer. And so Caldwell wouldn't feel left out, Romano brought him a large cappuccino and a cannoli.

As the three ate and drank, Michael and Romano filled Caldwell in on the day's events beginning with the monsignor's visit to Elton Combes' wife and ending with their narrow escape from the 70th precinct station house and parking lot.

When they were done, Gioca asked for and received Caldwell's assurance that he'd speak to DA Price and arrange for him to handle any prosecution that came out of the incident with Keisha Combes and the rioting that followed.

"John," Michael said, "There's no doubt that *HE's* behind it all.

The injury to Combes' daughter Keisha, is punishment for him coming to me and for the exorcism."

"The monsignor being accused of a crime, and having to go through all that he did today, is just blatant revenge for our war against *HIM.*"

"And *HE's* behind the street unrest too. But I think *HIS* motive for inciting the riots on Avenue K and in front of the 70 stationhouse is more insidious than just disrupting life in Brooklyn."

"John, remember when we had dinner at Emilio's, I told you what *HE* said to Combes near the end of LePage's trial: 'Chaos will reign and LePage will be free.' The chaos is here, and I believe *HE's* going to somehow use it to break out LePage from the Brooklyn House."

Michael told Caldwell that coincidentally he had checked with the warden at the Brooklyn House on LePage's status, before he heard from Romano. "He told me that LePage still hasn't been moved to an upstate prison. When he called to ask about the delay, someone in the State Department of Corrections named Emily Worthen, told him that they were waiting for paperwork from him before they could arrange for LePage's transfer."

"John, the warden said he sent that paperwork weeks ago! This is *HIM* again."

"Mike, I'll call Ms. Worthen in the morning and straighten it out," Caldwell said.

"Great. In the meantime, I'll make sure the warden at the Brooklyn House tightens the security around the reverend until he's taken upstate."

Just as Michael finished talking, Caldwell's phone rang. As he listened his face told a story that Michael knew was not a happy one.

"Guys, there are massive riots all over Midwood. Property damage, cops and civilians hurt, and hundreds of arrests."

"Mike, that bridge I said we'd cross when we got to it... we're there."

CHAPTER FIFTY

For the next four days, Midwood and the surrounding neighborhoods were engulfed in violence.

The disturbances on Avenue K, and in front of the precinct station house, that began with angry words, devolved into two-and-a-half hours of bottle and rock throwing.

By 11:00 p.m. the rioting had spread. Roving bands of youths wandered through the neighborhood stoning homes and assaulting people, none of whom had anything to do with Keisha Combes' injury or the decision not to arrest Romano. It was simply violence for violence sake.

The police response was met with resistance by the mobs, resulting in dozens of arrests and scores of police officers being taken to Kings County Hospital for treatment for injuries ranging from cuts and bruises, to broken bones.

Overnight the violence increased and cars up and down the streets of Midwood were damaged, set on fire, and in some instances overturned.

On the second day, the Mayor ordered schools in the area closed, and houses of worship shut.

Catholic churches in the area suffered extensive damage. Stained glass windows were broken. Any statues that adorned the churches' exterior were toppled and shattered. A large crucifix in front of the Church of St. Michael was torn down, and the statue of Christ on the cross was covered by a cardboard cutout of Satan.

Before the mayor's order to shut down the churches, rioters had gotten into the Church of Our Lady of the Rosary and pulled the religious artwork the church was noted for, off the walls, knocked over statues, and overturned the racks holding lighted devotion candles which resulted in small fires breaking out all around the church.

A young seminarian living in the church's rectory while under the tutelage of the pastor, Fr. William Dempsey, heard the racket caused by the vandals, and saw flames in several parts of the sanctuary. He grabbed a fire extinguisher from the rectory basement and rushed into the church to extinguish the fires, and to persuade whoever was there to leave.

The morning of the third day of rioting, Fr. Dempsey reported the seminarian missing. It would be days before his fate was known.

That afternoon, the governor called in the New York State National Guard to help the NYPD quell the violence. The sight of armed troops riding through Midwood and patrolling the surrounding neighborhoods did the trick. Although dozens of arrests were made, adding to the hundreds that were locked up the two previous days, the mobs slowly began to retreat. By the morning of the fourth day, there was only sporadic violence, which was quickly dealt with.

At the end of the four days, property damage to homes, businesses, and cars was estimated to be in the tens of millions. Hundreds of rioters and innocent citizens were injured, many hospitalized. Businesses that were locked down, and citizens who were unable to travel to work, suffered losses in the millions.

But it was the large number of arrests by the NYPD and the National Guard that Michael later determined to be key to the EVIL ONE instigating the mass rioting. They presented problems in the stationhouses across the borough, in Brooklyn Criminal Court, and in the Brooklyn House of Detention.

It was just as *HE* counted on.

Arrestees were jammed into precinct holding cells before they were transported to the criminal court for arraignment. The administrative judge for the court ordered that the arraignment courtrooms operate around the clock to alleviate the overcrowding. Judges were called in from home to relieve exhausted colleagues and keep the line moving.

The prisoners held on bail and not released were quickly moved to the Brooklyn House of Detention to make room in the courthouse holding cells for new arrestees awaiting arraignment.

As a result of the sudden and vast increase in the number of prisoners at the Brooklyn House, the jail was in chaos. Security was stretched thin as the number of lawyers and family members demanding to visit their clients and loved ones had increased exponentially.

Because of the increased number of correction officers needed on the jail's upper floors where prisoners were housed, the visitors' intake desk inside the front entrance to the jail was manned by civilian clerical employees, instead of uniformed personnel.

On the afternoon of the third day of rioting, the line of prisoner's family members wanting to know the whereabouts of their loved ones stretched around the block. Attorneys who needed to meet with unlucky clients held on bail, and those who needed to confer with prisoners not caught up in the rioting, but in the Brooklyn House waiting for trial, or transfer to an upstate prison, were forced to wait hours.

Just after 2 p.m. an older man dressed in a business suit and wearing a straw fedora, approached the young clerk manning the visitors' intake desk. He identified himself as Ennis Whatley and presented an official New York State Office of Court Administration attorney identification card to the intake clerk.

"I'm here to see my client Vernon LePage," he told the clerk. "He's due to be transferred upstate and I need to confer with him before he's moved."

Pressed for time because of the line of people waiting to speak to her, the clerk gave a quick look at the ID card and the photo affixed to it. Satisfied that the person standing in front of her matched the photo, she quickly consulted her computer for the name of the attorney of record for Vernon LePage and found that it was Whatley.

She also checked to see if LePage was waiting to be moved to an upstate prison. After confirming that he was, she called the command post on the floor of the jail where LePage's cell was located and told the officer who answered, "LePage's attorney is here to see him. Please have him brought down to the first floor attorney-client meeting room."

She told Whatley to place his briefcase on the table next to her and open it. The clerk saw there were no weapons in the case and directed the attorney to go through the metal detector at the entrance to the corridor that led to the attorney-client meeting room.

After doing so without incident, the attorney walked to a security gate ten feet from the room and was buzzed through it by the intake clerk. The attorney entered the room, which had no windows, and sat to wait for his client.

Ten minutes later a handcuffed Vernon LePage was escorted in by a correction officer. His handcuffs were removed, and he sat across from the attorney at the small table in the center of the room.

Before he left them alone, the officer told the attorney, "When you're done, pick that up," pointing to a wall phone, "and let whoever answers know that. They'll buzz you out." Turning to LePage he said, "You sit and wait until one of us comes to get you. It's busy so it may take a while."

An hour later their meeting was over. The attorney did as he was instructed. He walked out of the room, leaving his client sitting at the table.

He put his hat on and was buzzed through the gate outside the meeting room. He walked past the intake desk, tipped his hat to the clerk, whose attention was on a loud family member of an inmate demanding to see him, and left the jail. Outside he was picked up by a waiting car and driven away,

Thirty minutes passed before a correction officer opened the attorney-client meeting room door to retrieve the prisoner.

The room was empty. Vernon LePage was gone.

CHAPTER FIFTY-ONE

Michael was in his office when he heard from the warden of the Brooklyn House that LePage had escaped.

He called Dina and Tim and told them to get their car. "I'll meet you in front of the building. LePage has escaped. We're going to the Brooklyn House."

When they arrived at the jail, they parked in the rear of the building in a spot reserved for correction personnel. With the warden's permission, they entered the building through the prison personnel entrance and made their way to his office.

Warden Kirby Robertson was a twenty-five year veteran of the city Department of Corrections. He had been in charge of the Brooklyn House for the past ten years. Until that day he never had any prisoner successfully escape from his jail.

He told Michael, "We've had prisoners attempt to make their way out of here, but we always managed to prevent it. Guys have tied bed sheets together to lower themselves down from the gym on the top floor, others have hidden in delivery trucks, and a couple have even tried to pry the steel guards off the windows in out of the way areas, but what LePage pulled off...is a first for me."

"How did he do it?" Michael asked, knowing in his gut that the EVIL ONE had made good on both of *HIS* boasts to Elton Combes. Chaos did reign, and LePage was free.

The warden told Michael everything.

"Dina please call Ennis Whatley. Tell him it's urgent and he's needed in Warden Robertson's office immediately. If he asks what it's about, tell him it concerns his client Vernon LePage."

"Warden while we wait for Mr. Whatley, I'd like to talk to the intake desk clerk, the CO who brought LePage to the interview room, and the one who went to retrieve him after the attorney visit."

"Let's start with the clerk."

When Wanda Holden walked into the warden's office Michael could see that she was terrified. '*I'm sure she believes she's going to be fired,*' Michael thought. So, if he was going to get anything useful out of her he had to calm her down.

"Ms. Holden I can see you're very upset. But you're not in any trouble. You were duped by a very successful con man and his accomplice. The escape was not your fault."

The clerk told Michael everything that occurred at the intake desk with 'attorney Ennis Whatley.'

While she was telling her story, the real Ennis Whatley was escorted into the warden's office. Wanda looked at him as he sat down and had no reaction.

Michael asked him. Whatley's reaction was that he had no idea about any escape and had nothing to do with it.

Michael assured him that he was not under suspicion and asked him to go along with what he was going to do with Wanda when they went back inside.

When the two returned to the office, Wanda finished her story. After which Michael pointed to Whatley, asked, "Do you recognize this man?"

"Never seen him before in my life. Who is he?"

Whatley reached over and offered his hand to Wanda and said, "I'm Ennis Whatley, Vernon LePage's attorney. It's nice to meet you."

Taken aback, Wanda said, "You're not the man who identified himself to me as LePage's attorney. And it wasn't your photo on the attorney ID card that he showed me. You're a big strapping guy, with a full head of hair. The one who came to me was thin built, had some gray in his longer, thinning hair, and was older. And, you don't have an ugly ass mole on your left cheek like he did."

It was clear that the EVIL ONE took advantage of the turmoil in the visitors' intake room caused by the rioting *HE* started.

HE used Whatley's name and created a counterfeit attorney's ID card, to which *HE* affixed *HIS* photo, to get *HIM* passed security and into that windowless attorney-client meeting room.

It wasn't until Michael spoke to the two correction officers that transported LePage to the attorney meeting, and who went to retrieve him after the meeting, that he would have a full picture of how *HE* was able to free LePage.

Matt Judge, the CO who brought LePage to the room, told Michael that when he arrived with LePage, the attorney was already inside the room.

"Did you get a good look at him?" Michael asked.

"Yes, of course."

Pointing to Whatley, Michael asked, "Officer Judge, is this the attorney?"

"No it ain't. The guy I saw was thin built, with graying hair."

"Did you notice anything else about him?"

"Yeah, he had this weird looking mole on his left cheek. I thought the guy may have had cancer."

Before he interviewed the next correction officer, Michael wanted to let Whatley get back to his office.

"Ennis thanks for meeting me on such short notice. I'll keep you informed on the search for your missing client. But if you hear from LePage, which I doubt, please let me know. I'd love to help you talk him in. I can guarantee a peaceful surrender."

Whatley thanked him and told Michael that within the bounds of his ethical obligations he would call him if he heard from LePage.

"Hopefully we can make him understand that for his safety, turning himself in is his best course of action."

The two attorneys shook hands and Whatley left.

CO Roman Rios was the officer assigned to bring LePage back to his cell.

He said that when he entered the attorney-client room he expected LePage to be waiting. However, the room was empty.

"I thought maybe they gave me the wrong meeting room because there's six of 'em on the first floor. So I called central to ask. As I'm doing that I look down and see an orange jumpsuit that the prisoners wear, under the table. I immediately call an alert over the radio that a prisoner is missing and ask for the warden to report immediately to the meeting room."

"Did you ask any of the jail personnel working near the meeting room if they saw anything?"

"I did. A couple of people said they saw 'the attorney in the straw hat' leave the room and head for the visitors exit. They said they didn't see anything else until I started asking questions."

Rios began to shake his head.

"What's bothering you officer," Michael asked.

"Mr. G, we know LePage got out because he switched clothes with the lawyer. What I can't figure out is where did that fake lawyer go? There was no way for him to get out. I checked that room for any weakness in the concrete floor and I found none. And the walls are all solid. What did he do? Vanish into thin air?"

'That's exactly what HE did', Michael muttered under his breath.

He couldn't tell Roman the truth so as he did in past situations like this one, he lied.

"Roman this is not on you. The investigation has just started. We have a lot of good people working on it. I'm confident we'll find the fake lawyer."

"Before I let you go, one last question," Michael said. "Was there anything else about the room or the jumpsuit that you haven't mentioned?"

Rios answered, “Yes. There was something in the jumpsuit.”

Not expecting that answer Michael was surprised. He looked over to Warden Robertson as if to ask if he knew what Rios was about to tell them, but the warden seemed equally shocked.

“Officer Rios, what was it?”

“When I picked up the jumpsuit I noticed a piece of paper with writing on it sticking halfway out of a pocket. When I turned it over to the crime scene people I told them that I touched it. I apologize. But I was so shook by what happened that I had to see if there was anything on the note that might tell us where the prisoner went or where the fake lawyer got to.”

“What was written on the paper, Officer Rios?” Michael asked.

“Chaos will reign, and LePage will be free.”

CHAPTER FIFTY-TWO

Before he left the jail, Michael asked the warden to package and send him anything belonging to LePage that was found during the search of his cell which was in progress.

"I'll have the crime lab go over whatever you find. Who knows. Maybe he got sloppy and left a clue behind."

Knowing who orchestrated the escape, Michael didn't expect they'd find anything of investigative value. But knowing LePage and his massive ego, he could have defied the EVIL ONE and not fully followed *HIS* instructions. Michael was certain that LePage still believed that he was in charge, when in reality *HE* was in charge.

Back at his office Gioca called Romano to let him know of the escape, and to fill him in on the details.

"Sal, because of the hundreds of arrests from the riots, the Brooklyn House is packed with prisoners. As a result the warden was forced to assign an inexperienced civilian clerk to the visitor intake desk because he needed all his uniformed personnel on the upper floors of the jail where the cells were filled to capacity."

"The EVIL ONE took advantage of that chaotic situation and

pretended to be LePage's attorney, Ennis Whatley, there for an attorney-client visit."

"*HE* transformed himself into a LePage look alike, dressed in a business suit and wore a straw fedora. When *HE* and LePage met in that windowless room, the EVIL ONE gave *HIS* suit and hat to LePage."

"After an hour-long 'attorney-client' meeting, LePage, looking like the fake Ennis Whatley, walked past the unsuspecting clerk and out of the jail. The EVIL ONE then vanished."

"It worked like a charm."

"And to rub our noses in it, *HE* left a note in the pocket of the prisoner jumpsuit LePage discarded when he dressed in the business suit."

When Michael told the monsignor what the note said, the cleric dropped his head and said to himself, *'figlio di puttana.'*

Over the next few hours Michael conferred with the NYPD crime scene unit, after it completed the search of LePage's cell and found several items that could possibly help in finding LePage: note pads; books with writing and strange markings in the border of some of the pages; and an unauthorized burner cell phone that somehow was slipped into the jail by a LePage visitor.

Michael made sure that the items were delivered to the police lab whose commanding officer promised an expeditious and thorough examination of them.

The crime scene investigators also confirmed what CO Rios told Michael about the attorney-client meeting room. The concrete floor was totally intact, as were the walls. One investigator joked that whoever got out of that room had to be supernatural. He had no idea how close he was to the answer.

Warden Robertson called to report that a complete and thorough search of the entire jail building did not turn up "that phony lawyer."

He told Michael that he wasn't giving up.

"I've enlisted the Sanitation Department, the Department of Buildings, and the city plumbers, to do a search of all the pipes in this building and below ground. If the fuck slipped into a pipe or a storm drain or a sewer, they'll find him."

Michael knew it was hopeless, but commended the warden for his efforts, nonetheless.

Then he reached out to Caldwell. After filling him in on the escape, and all that was being done to track down LePage, he asked him to enlist the federal law enforcement community to help in the search.

"John, since the EVIL ONE is behind this LePage could turn up anywhere in the country and even outside of it. With the tentacles the feds have here and around the world, putting them on alert can't hurt, and it may very well help. It won't blow our cover because they'll be looking for LePage, a living breathing human, not an evil spirit."

Caldwell agreed. "I'll put the word out immediately. Send me LePage's photo and whatever info you have on him."

"Also send me the info on where his family is now living. I know where Belinda Shaw is, and I'll alert that FBI office. It's Helen and his sons that I'm concerned about. That prick may be looking for revenge. When I get that info I'll take the necessary precautions."

"And speaking of revenge," Caldwell continued, "you take care of alerting the NYPD to pay special attention to Winsell Myles and his wife and son and call Green Haven to alert the warden to tighten security on Elton Combes until we find this mutt."

Michael was thrilled with Caldwell's attention to this, but he couldn't help feeling that despite all their efforts, LePage would never be found.

By afternoon on the fourth day since the rioting began, quiet returned to Midwood. National Guard troops and NYPD riot squad officers had restored order.

Brooklyn's businesses, home owners, those whose cars were destroyed, and its houses of worship, began the clean up and recovery from their four days in hell. Long time residents of the borough quoted in city newspapers called them 'The worst days in the history of the borough.'

The next day schools in Midwood reopened, citizens who were trapped in their homes and apartments during the unrest, were out and about buying food and other necessities that ran low during their unwelcomed lock down.

The bars and restaurants that suffered no damage, reopened for business. Those less fortunate were also open, but only to begin the long process of repair and restoration.

Worshipers, from every religion practiced in Midwood, flocked to their temples, mosques, and churches to give thanks to their God for bringing peace back into their lives.

Most were fortunate that their houses of worship were either untouched or suffered only slight damage. Roman Catholic churches were not so lucky. All suffered significant damage to their interiors and to statuary on the outside of the buildings, but it all paled in comparison to the devastation inflicted on The Church of Our Lady of the Rosary.

Small fires that began when rioters overturned racks of lit worship candles, spread throughout the sanctuary and caused irreparable damage. Every flammable item in the fire's path ignited causing the flames to spread to the wooden paneling that covered the walls. Drapes that surrounded the stained glass windows caught fire and soon the wooden rafters that supported the century old church's ceiling were engulfed in flames. Although the fire department did its best to extinguish the fire, it wasn't enough to prevent the rafters from collapsing, followed by the entire ceiling.

The firefighters were fortunate to escape unharmed. However after the fire was extinguished and the cleanup began, the FDNY made a gruesome discovery.

Richard Rattigan, the young seminarian from Ireland studying under the pastor of Our Lady of the Rosary, was found buried in the debris of the collapsed ceiling.

At first glance the firefighters who found him thought he had been crushed to death. But on closer inspection they discovered a much different cause of death.

PART FOUR

CHAPTER FIFTY-THREE

Michael was in his office going over copies of what was found in the search of LePage's cell, looking for any clue that might lead to his capture, when his cell phone rang. It was Kathy Baer.

"Hey this is a nice surprise," he said. "Are you calling to invite me to dinner tonight...at your place?"

When he received no response, he realized that Kathy was calling with bad news, new business, or both.

If he bet on it being 'both', he would be a winner.

"Michael, I'm sorry. This is business, bad business. FDNY found the body of a seminarian in a church out in Midwood, Our Lady of the Rosary. When they first saw him they believed he was crushed to death when the church ceiling collapsed from a fire started by rioters. However, when they removed the debris that covered him, they found that he had a bullet wound to his chest, right through his heart. I'm calling you because I know you've been working the riot cases and I thought you'd be interested in this one."

"Kathy, where are you now?" Michael asked.

"I'm at the church. I think you should get over here."

When Michael arrived the morgue wagon was parked outside the church. *'Good, the body's still here',* Michael said to himself as he made his way through the police line and entered the church vestibule. Kathy spotted him and called him over to where the seminarian's body was found.

Michael lifted the sheet that covered the young man and saw that miraculously his face had not been destroyed by the falling debris. Michael said a silent prayer thanking God for sparing the seminarian's family the trauma of seeing him that way and having to wake him in a closed coffin.

"Kathy, any idea what happened, and why was he here?"

"Mike we've got bits and pieces of information and the best we can surmise is that he somehow made his way into the church to put out the fires that were started by rioters who knocked over the racks of devotion candles."

"How can you say what his intention was? Did someone see him or did he tell someone where he was going?"

"No. But we found *that* lying next to him."

Kathy pointed out a fire extinguisher on the floor next to the body. "The pastor told me that the extinguisher was kept in the rectory basement. So again, we believe he grabbed it and came in here to put out the fires."

Kathy continued, "When the first firefighters got here small fires were smoldering all over the sanctuary. And I believe that they ignited those curtains and other flammable material, then spread to the walls. And like the fire that killed Louis Amato, the pillars holding up the ceiling were compromised and it came down."

"The shock, however, was that Richard, the seminarian, most likely didn't die from the ceiling collapse. The ME believes he was already dead from a gunshot to his heart when the debris fell on him. He'll know for sure after he does the autopsy."

"Have your investigators canvassed the area for witnesses?"

"We just started but we may have gotten lucky. A few people who wouldn't give their names, told one of my guys that they saw gangbangers pile into the church before the fire started. They also heard them chanting 'burn it down.' I'm having my guys check with the 70th precinct to see if there were arrests inside the church, or anywhere around it. Maybe we'll get lucky."

Michael thanked Kathy for the info and told her he was definitely going to assign himself the seminarian's murder case, "So please keep me posted on any developments. And Kathy, if you can do it, I still want to have dinner with you tonight. We can go to *Queen* on Court Street near my office."

All Kathy could say was, "We'll see. I might be here well into the night."

Michael headed back to his office and on the way he called Romano to fill him in.

"Sal, it's hard to say right now if *HE's* involved any more deeply than just starting the riot. But Kathy is the lead investigator and to be safe I told her I'd assign the case to myself. When I know more I'll let you know. Please notify Caldwell so he can clear whatever he has to with the DA."

It was near 6:00 p.m. when Michael heard from Kathy.

"Great, you're done. When can you get down here? It's a short walk to *Queen,*" Michael said when he answered the phone.

"Michael, that dinner will have to wait. We found a witness," Kathy told him. "Checking with the 70 for arrests around the church paid off. Meet me at the stationhouse."

Kathy was sitting in Captain Galetta's office when Michael walked in.

"Hey Mike. Long time no see," Galetta joked. "I was just telling Fire Marshal Baer about an arrest we made that may help with the seminarian's murder. I can't be sure what day it was because it's all been a blur. I've had about 10 hours sleep over four days, but I know the arrest was after the church fire."

"One of our patrol officers arrested a guy for breaking into cars on the block behind Our Lady of the Rosary. He's a gang member and when he was put into the cells downstairs he was confronted by several members of a rival gang. They threatened to 'fuck him up', his words, when they all got to the Brooklyn House after they were arraigned."

"For several hours this guy, Felice Delgado, street name, 'Filly,' tried to get the attention of one of the cops near the cells to alert him to the threat. But the cop wouldn't pay him no mind."

"Finally, when he was getting his bologna sandwich this morning, he whispered to the cop who brought him the food, that he had been threatened, and more importantly, that he had info 'about the shooting of the priest.'"

"When I was told what Delgado said, I knew this guy was someone we needed to talk to. No one except the fire marshals and a few detectives knew that the seminarian had been shot."

"Teo, have you or your guys spoken to him about the shooting?"

"We did very briefly and then we called the fire marshal's office because I knew they were assigned to the case. An hour later Fire Marshal Baer walked in and here we are."

"Delgado is in the interview room with one of my guys. He's all yours."

When Michael and Kathy walked into the room, the gangbanger was shaking like a leaf. He was holding a cup of water and had a half-eaten *McDonald's Big Mac* on the small table in front of him. He put the water down and looked apprehensively at Gioca and Baer.

After Galetta's detective left the room, Michael introduced himself and Kathy to the prisoner.

"Mr. Delgado. I'm told you have some information about the death of the seminarian in Our Lady of the Rosary. Is that right?"

Delgado looked at Gioca and said, "Seminia... what the fuck you talkin' about?"

Michael corrected himself. "Sorry, I mean the priest who you say was shot."

Delgado nodded and said, 'Yeah, I got info but you gotta' help me out before I tell you what I know."

"What kind of help are you looking for?" asked Kathy.

"Listen, after I got busted for breakin' into that car, they put me in a holding cell and some dudes from the '25Killers' seen me. Me and my boys be beefin' with them for a long time and they hate my ass. They threatened to beat the shit outta' me when we all get to the Brooklyn House. But if they find out what I know about that priest that got shot, I won't just get my ass kicked, they gonna' kill me."

Michael told Delgado to explain.

"Mr. G, I'm sure it was one of the '25Killers' who shot that priest!"

"I was in the church to see what I could steal. I seen three guys knocking over them candles and fires be startin'. The priest comes in with a fire extinguisher and confronts them. One of them, all I seen of him was the mole on his left cheek, says to his buddy, 'There's one of them priests, fuck him, shoot his ass.' The guy then shoots the priest."

"How do you know they were '25Killers'?" Michael asked.

"When they ran out after the shooting I seen they was wearing '25Killers' colors. They got this big red '25' on their jackets."

"What about the shooter? Did you see his face?" Michael asked.

Delgado hesitated before answering, "No."

"Mr. Delgado, that's good info but it won't help us catch them. You didn't see their faces. A mole on one guy's cheek is not gonna' help us," Kathy said.

'It'll help me', Michael thought when she said it.

"Wait, I got more," Delgado said. "I was duckin' down so they won't see me, but just before they shot the priest I seen this homeless guy walk into the church. After the shooting the three ran and they banged into the homeless guy and knocked him down. He definitely saw the shooting."

"How do you know that?" Kathy asked.

"Because before I ran out of the church I stopped to help the guy get up. He says to me 'I seen what they done to the priest. They surely going to hell.'"

CHAPTER FIFTY-FOUR

"It's a starting point," Michael said to Kathy when they stepped out of the interview room.

"Delgado says he didn't see the shooter's face but I'm not buying that. His hesitation before answering tells me he knows the guy but is too frightened to ID him. We'll keep working on him."

Kathy agreed.

Michael continued, "Even if he ultimately can't or won't identify the shooter or the accomplices, looking ahead to a trial, he's an important witness, nonetheless. He'll set the stage for the jury. We have to make sure nothing happens to him."

"Michael I don't think the FDNY is gonna' want to foot the bill to keep him safe until we solve this," Kathy said.

"I figured that, but don't worry. I'll speak to my people and we'll work it out. I need to get Delgado out of here and put him somewhere safe."

After Teo Galetta agreed to release Delgado into Michael's custody, he and Kathy explained to him what was going to happen.

The gangbanger was more than appreciative. With tears in his eyes, he hugged Michael and thanked Kathy.

"Youse saved my life," he said.

When Tim Clark and Dina Mitchell showed up to take him to the DA's office Delgado couldn't get out of the stationhouse fast enough.

Earlier, Michael talked to both Romano and Caldwell, and both agreed that the EVIL ONE was behind the murder of the seminarian. Because Delgado was a necessary witness, if *HE* was to be defeated once again, they agreed to what Michael proposed to keep him safe.

Once he had their approval, Gioca explained to Delgado that he would become a confidential informant and would remain in custody, under guard, in a secure facility until he was no longer needed as a witness.

Frankie LePage's former living quarters at the Fort Hamilton Army base would become Delgado's temporary new home.

They also promised that if he cooperated fully, even if the authorities were unable to identify and arrest the seminarian's killer, the charges against him would be dropped and he would be moved out of Brooklyn to a place where he wouldn't have to look over his shoulder for '25Killers' gunning for him.

With Delgado secure, the fire marshals, and the 70th precinct detective squad, under Michael's supervision, began the search for the homeless man Delgado spoke about.

With Galetta's permission, Michael stationed himself at one of the detective squad room's desks. He wanted to be ready to interview the guy when he was found. However, after three days the identity of homeless man was still a mystery.

Four days into the search, on the way to his desk in the 70 squad room, Michael ran into PO Gabriel Angelos who was headed out on patrol.

"Mike, it's good to see you. Some of the guys said you were working out of the squad room but I never heard on what. I wanted to come up to say hello and to offer my help if you needed me. But because I worked every day of the riots, with very little sleep, when things settled down, the bosses told me to take a few days off. Today is my first day back."

"Gabe, no need to apologize. I know how crazy you guys have been. The streets were a disaster. I'm just happy you're in one piece. I know lots of your brother and sister cops weren't so lucky."

"Thanks, Mike. I appreciate that. Now, if you can tell me, what are you working on?" And can I help?"

Michael told Angelos he was there on the church shooting and told him about Delgado and the homeless man.

"Gabe, the homeless guy is important to making a case, but we haven't been able to locate him or anyone who might know who he is."

Angelos smiled and said, "I'm sorry we didn't talk sooner. I think I can help you. I not only saw the guy your looking for but I seen three guys run out of Our Lady of the Rosary the day of the fire."

Angelos told Michael that he was on patrol a half block away, when a call came over his radio that the church was on fire and there may be people inside. He ran to the church and when he got to the cobble stone path leading to the front steps, he saw three guys run out. All were wearing '25Killers' colors.

Gabriel said, one guy, who he got a good look at, was stuffing something into his waistband. Another was wearing a covid mask, "but it didn't cover the large growth on his left cheek. As for the third guy, I never saw his face."

"Because there may have been people in the church who needed to be rescued, I didn't chase them. Instead I stepped inside to the front vestibule and saw this homeless guy staggering around. He looked shaken up. The fire was spreading fast, so I grabbed the guy and took him outside to the street. When I asked him if there was anyone inside, he said 'everyone ran out.'"

"At the time I had no idea what he was talking about but after hearing what you just told me, I can see why he's a key witness."

"Gabe, did you get the guy's name?" Michael asked.

"I asked him and he told me his name was John. Which was probably bullshit. But that's my post, I'll ask around. If I come up with the guy, what do you want me to do?"

"Take him into the station house. He's a material witness. I'll get an order from the court so we can hold him if he doesn't want to stay with us voluntarily."

Michael thanked Angelos and wished him good luck.

Another week passed and the homeless man remained unidentified. Michael didn't know how much longer he could stay at the desk in the 7-0 squad room without his rackets staff becoming suspicious. Worried that his cover could be blown he decided that he would leave the station house that day.

As he packed up his briefcase, his cell phone rang. It was Dina Mitchell.

"Dina what's up? Is everything okay with Delgado?"

"Mike, it's more than okay. He told Tim and me something I know you'll want to hear. Are you still at the 7-0?"

"Yes but I'm leaving. Bring Delgado to my office and I'll meet you there in an hour."

Michael said a quick goodbye to Captain Galetta, thanked him for the use of the desk and asked to be notified, "No matter the time," if the homeless man is located.

"Don't worry Mike. After me you'll be the first to know."

An hour later Michael was sitting at his desk in rackets when Dina and Tim walked in with Delgado.

The first thing Michael noticed about him was how much healthier he looked from the last time he saw him. The track suit he was wearing was brand new, as were his snow white Adidas running shoes, and he was carrying a cup of Starbucks coffee.

When he sat down, he smiled and said, "Hey Mr. G, how are you?"

"Well, obviously not as good as you," Michael jokingly answered. "The government is sure taking good care of Filly Delgado."

Dina then said, "Mike, it seems the way he's being cared for, has caused Filly to have a 'come to Jesus' moment. He told Tim and me this morning that last night he remembered something that he didn't tell us when we first spoke."

Now looking at Delgado, Dina said, "Tell Mr. Gioca what you told us."

"Mr. G first I gotta' thank you for puttin' me up in that Army building. The cops and Dina and Tim been great to me. I ain't ever been treated that good in my life. And I got to say, it's relaxed me. I ain't got to think about the streets and if I'm gonna' get shot or stomped on. And I know when my next meal is comin'."

Michael looked at his watch and said, "Filly, what do you have to tell me? I got things to do, so get to it."

Delgado said, "I remember now who shot that priest."

"Wait, you told us that you didn't see his face, now you 'remember' something you didn't see? You expect me to buy that shit?"

"Mr. G, I'm sorry I didn't tell you everything back when we first spoke. I was scared. I didn't know what would happen to me if I told you who it was. I ain't ever trusted the cops and I know you work with them, so I couldn't trust you. But now that I see you're a standup guy, and will protect me, I gots to tell you everything."

Michael was annoyed, but strangely he could understand why Delgado was reticent about identifying the killer. In his experience guys like Filly grew up to distrust 'the man,' and getting them to come around always required him to work overtime. It seemed that giving Delgado the semblance of a normal life, with three meals a day and security around to keep him safe, did the trick.

"Okay Filly, I hear ya'. Now tell me, who's the guy that shot the priest?"

"It ain't a guy. The shooter's a girl. The '25Killers' call her Rosie."

CHAPTER FIFTY-FIVE

"Her full name is Rosemary Woodhouse," Tim told Michael. "I checked with an NYPD buddy of mine in the Brooklyn Gang Squad and Rosie is well known to them. She's the queen of the '25Killers'. She's older than most of them but they all look up to her because her now dead 'old man,' was the founder of the gang back in the day."

"Mike I'm told that she's a mean motherfucker and as tough as they come. She takes no shit from anyone and gives it out pretty good. My buddy told me that she's been suspected of doing several homicides but neither they, nor the homicide squad, could ever get anyone to give her up."

"Well that explains Delgado's reluctance to ID her," Dina added.

"I'll call Galetta and let him know who we're looking for," Michael said. "You two get Delgado back to the fort. Your security relief should be there. Then come back here. We've got work to do."

"No problem Mike," Dina said. Then she added, "Something is bothering me. Tim's guy said Rosie is a tough nut, and the queen. Why is she taking orders from the guy with the mole? He told her to shoot the seminarian, and she did it. That doesn't make sense."

Of course, it made perfect sense to Michael. But he couldn't tell her that. Instead he simply said, "Dina, you've got a point. Hopefully we'll straighten it out when we get her."

Days turned into weeks and neither Rosie, nor the homeless guy, were found.

One night over dinner at *Emilio's* Michael remarked to Romano that the EVIL ONE is "Really working overtime to keep Rosie under wraps. And If I were a betting man, my money would be on us finding the homeless guy dead. *HE* can't risk the guy walking into the 70th precinct one day looking for help and a sandwich."

"Michael, sadly, I think you're right. But we must keep looking. Caldwell told me today that fifty agents from our group are going to help in the search. They're reporting to Capt. Galetta tomorrow."

"Wow! That's great. But what's their cover story?" Michael asked.

"The agent in charge has already spoken to Galetta. He told him that when the Attorney General, who's a staunch Catholic, heard about the seminarian's murder and the church fire, and learned that the NYPD was having difficulty locating the shooter and the homeless witness, he put together a group of agents to help."

"Galetta was so grateful for the assistance. He's getting lots of heat from City Hall to solve the murder. He didn't question anything. All he said was, thank you."

Unfortunately flooding the streets of Midwood with an army of federal agents to search for Rosie and the homeless guy didn't produce the results everyone hoped for.

As spring turned into summer, the Church of Our Lady of the Rosary was surrounded by scaffolding and cranes. Construction workers swarmed all over, as repairs to the roof, ceiling, and walls were underway.

The work, while well received by the church's parishioners, made it impossible for the priests of the parish to hold daily and Sunday masses. Most of the congregation made their way to neighboring churches to worship, but as the summer heat became more intense, elderly parishioners and those who were disabled, found it impossible to make the trek.

To discuss a solution to the problem, the parish council of Our Lady of the Rosary convened an emergency meeting one evening on the front lawn of the church. Many ideas were discussed. The one that carried the day was suggested by several of the parish's successful business people.

They would contribute to the purchase of a large tent that would be erected on the church's expansive front lawn. The tent would be large enough to sit fifty or so parishioners for mass, with enough space left over for standing room.

The council also voted to enlist several carpenters that were members of the church's congregation, to build an altar and pulpit for use at the services held in the makeshift church.

The last items the council needed were chairs for the congregants.

The day after the council meeting word spread throughout Midwood, and by late afternoon two of the areas large catering establishments committed to donating one hundred folding chairs, more than actually needed, for use in the tent when it was ready to hold services.

The parish council's ideas and proposals were presented to Brooklyn's Bishop James Wiley, who agreed to support them with prayers and money.

Two weeks after the bishop gave his blessing, the tent, altar, and pulpit were ready for the inaugural mass which was to be held at 12 noon on the third Sunday in June. And although all of the folding chairs were set up, there was still enough room for standees who didn't mind worshiping while on their feet.

Bishop Wiley said yes to the parish council's request that he officiate at the mass and asked his good friend Monsignor Salvatore Romano to assist.

Invitations to the service were extended to the commanding

officer of the 70th precinct, to Detective Captain Galetta, Fire Marshal Kathy Baer, and her supervisor.

Michael was also invited but unfortunately the mass conflicted with a prior engagement he was committed to. Michael Jr. was graduating from St. Francis Prep High School that Sunday, and he would not miss it for anything in the world.

Michael sent his thanks and regrets to the parish council president, who fully understood.

That Sunday morning Kathy dressed for the mass, while Michael, who had spent the night with her, dressed for the graduation. What had become their usual Sunday morning routine was interrupted by events they both considered extremely important.

"Kathy, please give my regrets once again to the parish council and tell them that if not for Michael Jr.'s big day, I would have been there."

"Mike I'm sure they know that, but I'll tell them anyway. Now, it's getting late and I have to drive to Midwood and you out to Queens. So let's go. I'll see you later. And remember you promised to make up tonight, what we didn't have time for this morning," Kathy said, smiling.

Michael grabbed her, kissed her hard on the lips and said, "Sealed with a kiss."

The tent looked beautiful when Kathy walked in and sat down at the end of the second row of seats. Local florists had donated large displays that were placed around the altar, while the muted sunlight coming through the white tent's roof added a mystical glow to the interior. Candles at the foot of the altar also created a spiritual atmosphere that Kathy thought could never be replicated.

Mass was wonderful. The bishop's homily carried the message of hope and rebirth, which all those who attended prayed would be the case for the actual church structure of Our Lady of the Rosary.

After communion had been distributed, Kathy was approached by the parish council president.

"Fire Marshal Baer, I know this may be inappropriate, but it's extremely important. Please come with me."

Kathy did as she was asked and walked with him to the rear of the tent. "What's wrong?" she asked. "You look like you've seen a ghost."

The council president told her that he knew she was the investigating fire marshal assigned to the church fire because the pastor told him when they were putting together the list of invitees for the mass.

"He also shared with me, in strictest confidence, the name and photo of the person you are looking for who shot the seminarian and started the fire."

Now shaking he said, "I stepped outside the tent a few moments ago to retrieve the collection baskets, and I saw a group of people dressed in those gang colors. They're all standing at the curb in front of the church. They look like trouble. That Rosie woman is out there with them."

"Are you sure?" Kathy asked.

"Yes. Ever since the pastor showed me her picture I've been on the lookout for her as I move around the neighborhood. But what is she doing here?"

'She's taunting us, and showing off to her gangbangers,' Kathy thought but didn't say. *'Because we've never released info that we're looking for her, she believes she's gotten away with murder and arson. She has no idea that she's walked right into the lion's den.'*

Kathy told the council president, "You stay right here, while I go get some help."

She walked to where Capt. Galetta was sitting and whispered that she needed to talk to him.

Kathy repeated what the council president had said and told the captain that she was going to step outside the tent to confirm the sighting. "If she's out there I'll give you the thumbs up, and you'll need to call the precinct for back up."

It took her less than five seconds to confirm that it was Rosie. The gang moll was sitting on an electric motor bike pointing to the tent's front opening. It appeared to Kathy that the group was there to cause trouble.

Rosie was directing some of the gang to go down the block and others to move up. Kathy figured they were getting prepared to harass the congregants when they came out of the tent and began to walk home.

The mass was ending when Galetta told Kathy, "An unmarked squad car should be pulling up any second now. Let's casually walk out to the sidewalk and be ready if Rosie tries to make a run for it when my detectives go to grab her."

As they walked past the fence surrounding the church lawn, three detectives got out of their car and grabbed Rosie without incident.

"What the fuck are you doin?" she screamed as the congregants leaving the tent stopped to gawk.

After she was handcuffed, Kathy walked up to Rosie and told her, "You're under arrest for the murder of Richard Rattigan, and..." pointing to the ruins of Our Lady of the Rosary, "for destroying God's house."

Rosie looked at the ruins, said, "A fire extinguisher?" and started to laugh.

CHAPTER FIFTY-SIX

After the graduation, Michael and his family celebrated Michael Jr.'s achievements with a great lunch at *Cara Mia*, a restaurant they had been going to since he and his sister were kids.

Jr. was valedictorian, scored nearly straight A's, and was accepted into the prestigious School of Pharmacy at St. John's University. When he toasted his son, Michael became emotional. After the toast everyone sat, except Michael. He remained standing, turned to his ex-wife Kathy, lifted his glass again and said, "Thank you, I celebrate you as well today."

Michael drove his father home. Before getting out of the car his dad hugged him.

"What's that for?"

"That's for being a good man, and the best father you could be to Michael. What that kid has done is something for which you, and as you pointed out, his mom, can be proud of. Bravo! Michele. I love you."

He watched his father get in the house, wiped a tear or two from his eyes and headed back to Brooklyn.

Just as he was getting onto the Long Island Expressway, his cell phone rang. It was Romano.

"Monsignor, I hope you didn't make any mistakes assisting your boss at mass this morning," Michael joked. Just then he heard what sounded like a siren and many muffled voices in the background.

"Sal, where are you?"

"Michael I'm at the 70th precinct station house. Kathy and Captain Galetta arrested Rosie Woodhouse outside the tent following the mass. I think you need to get over here as quickly as possible."

Michael turned on his car's siren, put the red bubble light he carried on the dashboard, and sped to the 70.

An hour later Gioca walked into Galetta's office and saw Kathy and the monsignor in conversation. To protect his cover, he walked up to the pair, greeted Kathy, and pretended not to know Romano.

"Michael," Kathy said, surprised to see him. "What are you doing here? More importantly, who told you?"

Michael lied. "Teo Galetta called me as I was driving home from the graduation," he answered. "Congratulations on the arrest."

Then turning to Romano, Michael offered his hand and said, "Father, I'm Assistant District Attorney Michael Gioca. Nice to meet you."

"Oh, forgive me," Kathy said. "This is Monsignor Salvatore Romano, a friend of Bishop Wiley. We asked him to come in because we questioned everyone involved with setting up the mass."

"I was just finishing up with the monsignor, who told me he has no connection to Our Lady of the Rosary. He was here today because he was invited by the bishop to assist with the mass."

"It's very good to meet you *monsignor*. And I apologize for demoting you when I introduced myself." Michael hated lying, and it was killing him to pretend to not know Romano, but keeping his cover intact was paramount.

Romano shook off the demotion remark and joked, "No worries, Mr. Gioca, we clergymen tend to look alike."

After a bit of chit chat Romano congratulated Kathy and asked if he could leave.

"Yes, monsignor, we're done with the questions. Enjoy the rest of your Sunday."

Michael shook the monsignor's hand, and said it was nice to meet him.

When Romano left the squad room, Michael breathed a sigh of relief. *'It's a good thing that Teo Galetta didn't come in while Sal was still here,'* he thought. *'Our charade of not knowing each other would have been blown to bits.'*

For the next thirty minutes Kathy filled Michael in on the events at the tent, including the comment about the fire extinguisher. "Mike, she wants a lawyer now, but that statement she made to me at the scene was spontaneous. I never asked her a question," Kathy told him.

"At first blush it sounds like an incriminating statement, especially with her laughing," Michael said. "The obvious conclusion is that Rosie was mocking the seminarian who tried to put out the fire with only a fire extinguisher. And, that she knew he did because she was there and saw it."

"I can make that argument to a jury. Coupled with Delgado's testimony of seeing her shoot Rattigan it's good evidence. What will make it *great* evidence is if the fire extinguisher was never mentioned in any news stories about the fire or in any TV or radio reports. Then I can argue that the only way she could have known about the extinguisher was if she was there and saw it."

"Before I'm comfortable using the statement at trial we'll need to check all the news stories and media reports about the fire."

"Okay. What do you want to do now?" Kathy asked.

"I want to conduct a line up."

Just then Galetta walked in. "Teo can you have your guys round up five women who resemble Rosie so we can do a line-up?"

"Sure. I'll send a few over to the shelter on Nostrand Avenue, and have them look for stand-ins. The women there are happy to cooperate because they like the twenty bucks we pay."

"Tell them to call from the shelter when they have the women. Then I'll call Fort Hamilton and have the people with Delgado bring him here. And Teo, can you reach out to Gabe Angelos and ask him to come in? I want to see if he can ID Rosie."

"Mike, no problem. When I got back here after the mass I saw Gabe downstairs at the desk. He's working today. When we're ready for him I'll have the desk officer call him on the radio."

It was 5 p.m. by the time the line-up was set, and Delgado and Angelos were ready to view it.

Delgado was first. He was nervous when he was brought into the viewing room. The first thing he said when he saw the viewing window was "Mr. G., don't shit me. You're sure no one can see me?"

"Filly, this is a one-way glass. The other side is a mirror. The people in the line-up can only see their reflection, and they can't hear anything said in this room."

"Now when I lift the shade you'll see six women each holding a number. Take a good look. If you recognize any of them, tell me what number she's holding."

Michael raised the shade and without hesitation Delgado said, "It's number 4."

"Who's number 4?" Michael asked.

"That's Rosie. She's the one I seen shoot that priest."

Next was Gabriel Angelos.

Michael had the women switch up their numbers before he would show them to Gabe.

"It's number 6," Angelos said. When Michael asked from where he recognized her, Angelos told him that she was the person he saw running out of the church stuffing something into her waistband, the day of the fire.

"I seen her for sure. No mistake. But that day I thought it was a guy because she was dressed like a guy."

Because the Fire Marshals office was the lead investigating

authority on the case, Kathy booked Rosie and charged her with the murder of Richard Rattigan and the arson that destroyed Our Lady of the Rosary.

That evening she met Michael at the DA's office after Rosie was lodged in the Brooklyn House of Detention to await arraignment the next day. Kathy was needed to provide information that Michael included in the criminal court complaint, a document necessary for the court to arraign Rosie.

When he completed the paperwork it was 9.p.m., and both he and Kathy were starving.

"Since we both have to be in court in the morning, stay at my place tonight. It's closer to the courthouse," Michael said.

Kathy agreed but told him that she had to go to her apartment to get what she needed for the morning.

Since she took her car to the mass, Michael followed her in his car. Kathy quickly packed what she needed. They then drove to an all-night diner in Michael's neighborhood and feasted on pancakes, eggs, bacon, toast and decaf coffee.

When they finally dragged themselves into his apartment Michael said, "I know we have some unfinished business from this morning, but since we're both wiped out, how about we give each other a rain check for the next time we're together."

"Counselor, you took the words right out of my mouth. Let's go to sleep."

At 10 a.m. the next morning Kathy was standing in the arraignment court at the prosecution table next to Michael. Her prisoner Rosie Woodhouse stood at the defense table with a legal aid lawyer, who pled her client not guilty. Michael outlined the evidence against her, including Rosie's statement to Kathy, and asked the court to remand her without bail.

When Rosie's attorney objected to Michael's request and asked the court to release her client in her own recognizance, the judge stifled a laugh.

"She's charged with the murder of a seminarian inside a Catholic church that she is charged with burning down, and you want me to release her? Counsel, she has more motive to flee than any defendant who has ever come before me," the judge said before he remanded Rosie to the women's jail on Rikers Island, without bail.

After the gangbanger was escorted out of the courtroom, Kathy smiled, turned to Michael and shook his hand. In the very back of the courtroom the young guy with a covid mask covering his face, smirked and said under his breath, "Smile now, because it won't be long before you're crying."

Exhausted from the previous day's events and her fitful sleep, Kathy declined Michael's invitation to dinner.

"Mike, I'm going home. I can finish my paperwork from there. You have the grand jury tomorrow so don't stay in the office too long. Go home and get some rest."

Michael understood and although he hated to give in to his fatigue, he agreed.

"Kathy I haven't made a decision yet about using Rosie's statement in the grand jury, or to save it for trial. Can you be in my office tomorrow afternoon? If I decide to use it in the grand jury, I can prep you before you testify."

Kathy said she'd be there.

"Great. Get a good night's sleep."

The two parted ways in front of the courthouse. Michael headed to his office, and Kathy, unbeknownst to her, with someone following, made her way to the "L" train, the subway line that served her Williamsburg, Brooklyn neighborhood.

The room where the grand jury sits is located on the first floor of the Brooklyn Supreme Court building. On the morning of the grand jury presentation, Michael met Delgado and Angelos in the courthouse to prep them for their testimony, rather than his office.

He'd had several bad experiences with witnesses in cases

involving the EVIL ONE and Michael didn't want to put Delgado and Angelos at risk by walking them from the DA's office building to the courthouse and exposing them to *HIM* or *HIS* minions.

Although concerned with the safety of both men, Michael knew that Gabe Angelos was more at risk. Being a patrol officer who worked the streets, he was far more vulnerable than Delgado, who was under guard. Michael hoped his decision to use the courthouse for prep would give Gabriel enough cover to keep him safe.

Although Delgado and Angelos testified well, Michael detected a problem with the grand jurors.

After a witness in the grand jury is questioned by the prosecutor, the rules permit the jurors to request that the ADA pose additional questions. Filly was a gangbanger and Michael sensed, after hearing the questions the grand jurors wanted him to ask Delgado, that his credibility was questionable in the minds of some jurors.

When added to Angelos' testimony that he did not see a gun in Rosie's hand when she went to her waistband, Michael knew the case needed a boost if he was to secure an indictment.

Even though he was uncertain about using Rosie's statement to Kathy at trial, to bolster his case here in the grand jury, he decided to put it in evidence. His thinking was that there wouldn't be a trial if there was no indictment.

However, before he called Kathy to the witness stand, Michael needed to have one other witness testify.

When he returned to his office after spending the morning in the grand jury, he reached out to the fire company that responded to the church and asked that the firefighter who found the seminarian's body come down to the grand jury.

He was Michael's first witness during the afternoon session.

The firefighter told the jurors that he and his company responded to the fire at Our Lady of the Rosary. After it was put out he and his colleagues began to clear the rubble from the ceiling collapse and discovered the body of the seminarian.

"Next to the body we found a fire extinguisher," he told the jury.

Kathy was next. Michael prepped her in his office, after which they walked to the grand jury.

Unlike Delgado and Angelos, Michael didn't think it was necessary to keep Kathy under wraps as a witness. She was at Rosie's arraignment with him when he asked the court to deny bail. He used Rosie's incriminating statement to her as a reason for doing so.

Also, because Kathy was a veteran Fire Marshal, who carried a gun, and was part of a large squad of law enforcement officials, Michael believed the EVIL ONE would never attempt to harm her.

He would soon learn how wrong he was!

In the grand jury Kathy testified that she saw the seminarian's body lying on the floor of the church surrounded by the ceiling rubble. And like the firefighter, saw a fire extinguisher next to his body.

Michael then took her through the arrest at the church tent and asked her to tell the jurors what Rosie said just after she was put in handcuffs.

Kathy did so, and the one-two punch of the firefighter and Kathy did the trick.

After less than five minutes of deliberation, Rosie was indicted for murder and arson.

Two days later a violent explosion rocked Kathy's apartment and nearly cost Kathy her life.

CHAPTER FIFTY-SEVEN

On the day of Rosie's arraignment, when Michael and Kathy parted ways outside the courthouse, the person who went down into the subway behind her, was a member of the '25Killers', sent by the EVIL ONE to follow her.

When she got off the subway, the gangbanger trailed her to the apartment building where she lived.

After she went inside, he looked for her name on the building's intercom directory and found her apartment number.

The next day, after Kathy left for work, the gangbanger, and one of his fellow '25Killers', snuck into her building using a basement door, whose lock he tampered with the night before.

The two made their way to Kathy's fourth floor apartment, picked the lock on the door, and went in. First, they ransacked the apartment, stealing anything they thought they could sell. Then they drank her beer and ate the cold cuts and cheese she had in her fridge.

Finally, late that afternoon they did what they went there to do. They disconnected the gas line from her stove so her apartment would fill with fumes.

The two left the building, assumed watch across the street, and waited for their target to come home.

At dusk, the two gangbangers saw Kathy enter the building and waited for a light to come on in her apartment. When it did, one of them called her landline telephone and watched as the apartment exploded.

That was their cue to run.

Fortunately, Kathy was neither killed nor hurt.

When she approached her apartment door she smelled gas. Her experience and training kicked in and she didn't go inside. She walked across the hall to the building superintendent's apartment, knocked on his door and told him she smelled gas.

She cautioned him not to go into the apartment, but he ignored her. When he entered he turned on a light. From the hallway Kathy heard her landline telephone ring, after which the apartment exploded into flames.

The super was not severely injured because Kathy was able to get him out of the apartment before the fast spreading fire reached him.

She quickly called 911, identified herself to the operator, reported the explosion and fire, and asked for an ambulance to respond.

The heat from the fire triggered the sprinkler system in her apartment, and in the common hallway on her floor. It also set off the smoke alarms in every apartment on the floors below.

The sprinklers, however, did nothing to prevent Kathy's apartment and everything in it from being totally destroyed.

Thankfully the smoke alarms alerted the tenants who were home, and other than the superintendent, no one was injured.

It took several fire companies to get the blaze under control, and to limit the fire damage to the two fourth floor apartments. Smoke damage, however, was pervasive throughout the entire building. The hallways and apartments on every floor below Kathy were affected.

Shortly after the firefighters arrived on the scene, announcements were made over loudspeakers affixed to FDNY cars and trucks for those who lived in the buildings on either side of Kathy's to evacuate.

In addition to the residents from those neighboring buildings, people from all over the neighborhood joined them on the street to watch the spectacle.

In the days that followed, fire marshals and detectives conducting their investigation spoke to people who were in that crowd of onlookers. Many of them mentioned seeing an individual in the crowd who caught their attention.

They described him as middle aged, thin build, with long black hair, and a large ugly mole on his left cheek. When asked why he caught their attention, they all said, "He looked weird and he was laughing as he watched the flames spread."

One of the onlookers, a woman who said her name was CiCi, told the fire marshals that a friend of hers confronted the "weirdo" and angrily asked him what was so funny.

CiCi said, "The guy leaned into my friend and said something that I couldn't hear. But whatever he said caused her to go white! She ran off screaming."

When the investigators asked for the friend's name and where they could find her, CiCi told them, "Her name is Mona Blanco." She paused and added, "But I haven't seen her since she ran from that fuckin' weirdo the night of the fire."

The fire marshals were quickly able to locate an address for Mona Blanco. However, when they went to her apartment to speak to her, a neighbor told them, "Mona never came back to her apartment after she went to watch the fire a few nights ago."

CHAPTER FIFTY-EIGHT

Michael had just finished preparing the paperwork to file the indictment against Rosie with the clerk's office in Brooklyn Supreme Court the next day and was packing his briefcase to head home.

It had been a busy few days so he was looking forward to spending a quiet night checking in with his father and his sons, and chatting with Kathy before he went to bed.

His office phone rang. He didn't recognize the number but knew from the exchange that it was from someone in the NYPD.

"Is this Assistant District Attorney Gioca?" the caller asked.

When Michael said it was, the caller identified himself as Captain George Dietrick, the commanding officer of the 94th precinct.

Immediately Michael tensed up. He knew that Kathy's apartment in Williamsburg was in the 94.

"Captain, what can I do for you?"

Dietrick told Michael about the explosion and fire.

"Fire Marshal Baer was not hurt," he said. "Her neighbor, the super, however, was injured, but thanks to Baer's quick thinking and heroism, not seriously. She saved him by pulling him out of the apartment, as flames threatened to burn him alive."

"Baer is here in the stationhouse and told me to tell you that you need to get down here right away. Apparently there is a strong connection between this fire and one that your office, the 70th precinct detectives, and the fire marshals are investigating."

Michael told Dietrick that he would be there in thirty minutes.

When he walked into the captain's office at the 94, Kathy was deep in conversation with her boss, Chief Fire Marshal Lopez. Michael politely interrupted and Kathy engulfed him in a hug.

"Was that a 'Baer hug'?" Lopez' joked, breaking the tension in the room, as Kathy let go of Michael.

Michael introduced himself and sat with Kathy and Lopez as she filled him in on what had occurred. Lopez then brought him up to speed on their investigation which was in the preliminary stages.

"What I can tell you," Lopez said, "is that there is no question that someone tampered with the gas stove connection in Kathy's apartment. We also found that the lock on the back door to the building was tampered with, which is how we believe the perp or perps got in. And the lock on her apartment door was jimmied."

"What I was discussing with Kathy when you got here," Lopez continued, "was the connection between this fire and the one at Our Lady of the Rosary."

"One of my investigators spoke to a gentleman who lives two buildings down from Kathy's. He said that just after the explosion, he saw two guys who had been standing across the street from her building, run away. He followed them, but lost sight of 'em when they went down into the subway at the corner."

"Why is that strange?" Michael asked. "How does that connect the fire to Our Lady of the Rosary? Maybe they were frightened by the explosion and got out of there to avoid getting hurt?"

"Mr. Gioca, that would be a logical explanation, but that's not all the witness told my investigator. When he was asked for a description of the two, he said that he wasn't able to say what they looked like, but he was able to tell the investigator what they were wearing. Both were dressed in denim jackets which had ‘25Killers’ stitched across the back.”

Michael immediately thought to himself, *‘It’s HIM.’*

When they were done at the 94 Michael drove Kathy to his apartment.

“Stay the night and we’ll figure out what’s next in the morning,” he told her. He added, “And, you’re welcome to stay for as long as you need to.”

She was grateful but made it clear that staying with him was not a permanent solution.

“Thank you. I appreciate your offer. I’ll stay until I find a new apartment.”

“Michael, keeping separate apartments has worked out very well. I don’t want to jeopardize the good thing we have. Chief Lopez told me not to worry about rushing back to work, so I’ll start looking tomorrow.”

Although disappointed, Michael knew that Kathy was right. *‘One day it’ll be different,’* he thought.

Kathy asked him to drive her to a 24 hour drug/convenience store on Court Street near his apartment. “I need a few things,” she said.

“No problem. And on the way back we can stop at *Vinny’s.* I’m starving, and I assume you are as well.”

“Counselor, you took the words right out of my mouth.”

Over the next week, while Kathy searched for a new home, the investigation into the explosion and fire continued in earnest. The fire marshals were particularly intent on arresting those responsible as quickly as possible. One of their own had barely escaped with her life and lost everything she had.

Although her boss had given her whatever time she needed to find a new home, Kathy was anxious to get back to work. She used every contact she could think of to find an apartment, and it paid off.

A week after the fire, one of Kathy’s neighbors, the owner of a building down the street from her burnt out apartment, called the fire marshal's office looking for her.

When she reached Kathy she told her that one of the tenants in her building was leaving New York for a new job out west. If Kathy was interested, the apartment would be available in two weeks.

That night Kathy went to look at the apartment and immediately signed a lease.

On a Saturday, two weeks later, as her new furniture was being delivered, Kathy, with Michael's help, carried several suitcases containing a new wardrobe into her new home.

After a visit to a Costco in Long Island City, not far from the apartment, Kathy's kitchen and bathroom were stocked.

As much as she wanted Michael to stay the night, Kathy asked him for a rain check, which he understood.

"Mike, I want to spend the rest of the weekend putting the apartment in order. I promise that next Saturday I'll cook you dinner, and maybe we can try out the new bed," she said with a smile.

On his drive home Michael called Romano to set up dinner for Sunday night.

Since the time they spoke about putting Delgado into protective custody, a lot had happened. As hard as he tried, Michael was unable to keep the monsignor fully informed on every detail and development in what were now two investigations involving the EVIL ONE. He was simply too busy to give a blow by blow account as things happened.

"Sal, I know I've been remiss in keeping you up to date on the investigations. I have a lot to tell you. Let's meet for dinner at *Emilio's* tomorrow night and I'll bring you up to speed."

At 6 p.m. on Sunday evening when the monsignor walked into the restaurant, Michael was sitting at their table with two glasses of wine already poured.

Romano sat, checked the label on the wine bottle, and commented, "*Chianti Classico,* I'm impressed. You must be feeling pretty guilty."

In response, Michael picked up his glass and said, "I'm sorry."

For the next three hours, the two old friends ate a spectacular dinner, and drank a second bottle of wine, as Michael filled in the monsignor on every aspect of his case against Rosie, and the investigation of the fire that nearly killed the woman he loved.

"Michael the murder at Our Lady of the Rosary seems to be a strong case. But if I'm reading you correctly you feel there may be problems with it. Am I right?"

Michael explained that the case depended on the testimony of a gangbanger, a cop who only saw the defendant putting 'something into her waistband,' and a statement that a defense attorney would ask a jury to disregard because of its vagueness.

"If I had the homeless guy who saw everything, he would give me a third person who saw the defendant running out of the church and someone in addition to Delgado who saw her shoot the seminarian. With all of that I like my odds."

"Are your people still looking for him?" Romano asked.

"Yes. Caldwell's agents went back to DC, but the fire marshals, the NYPD, and my investigators are searching for him." Michael then paused before adding, "A few prayers from a monsignor would certainly help."

"You got it," Romano answered.

When the monsignor asked about the fire in Kathy's apartment, Michael didn't respond.

"Mike, what's wrong?" the monsignor asked.

He took a long drink from his wine glass before answering.

"Sal, I blame myself for what happened to her."

Puzzled, Romano asked him to explain.

"I exposed her," he said

"When Rosie was arraigned after her arrest, because I wanted to make sure that she wasn't released on bail, I told the judge that she made an incriminating statement to Kathy."

"Sal, from past experience, I'm sure *HE* was in the courtroom and heard that."

"Because I was worried that the grand jury might not indict with only Delgado and Gabe Angelos' testimony, I decided that I needed Kathy to testify."

"So I prepped her and then we walked to the grand jury. I'm sure *HE* was watching."

"Based on the evidence we've been able to uncover, I can say with certainty that *HE* had *HIS* minions from the '25Killers' blow up her apartment to kill her so she wouldn't be able to testify to that statement at trial.... And as a bonus, to punish me."

"Michael, it's understandable to blame yourself," Romano told him. "But it's not logical. Kathy is a law enforcement professional who knows the risks of the job, as do you. It was part of her job to relay the statement to you, and your job to ensure an indictment. Just be thankful that *HE* didn't achieve *HIS* goal."

"Now, about the fire in Kathy's place, how the hell did it start?"

After Michael told the monsignor the details, the cleric was puzzled.

"What has the landline phone got to do with the explosion, and why did she even have a landline?"

Michael explained that the FDNY mandates all fire marshal investigators have a landline. "It's to ensure that they can be reached in an emergency, if cell phone towers are destroyed or rendered inoperable."

As for the role the landline played in the fire, Michael said that he learned from a former mafia hitman informant, that he used the gas fume/landline phone method to send a message to someone who owed money to one of his mob bosses.

"After business hours the hitman broke into the target's place of business, a pizzeria, and disconnected the gas lines to the ovens and a stove. He left the store and sat in his car, a block away. He waited for an hour, then called the telephone landline in the store and watched as the business exploded into flames."

Romano still had a puzzled look on his face.

"What happens," Michael explained, "when the landline rings a spark occurs in the device which ignites the gas fumes that filled the place, causing an explosion and fire."

"Based upon a physical examination of the gas lines in Kathy's apartment we know they were tampered with. And her hearing the landline ring just before the explosion, along with witness accounts of seeing two men in gang colors run from the scene, the conclusion is that the mafia method to cause an explosion and burn someone out, was used here. The only difference is that the mob used the technique to send a message, whereas *HE* used it to kill a potential witness!"

CHAPTER FIFTY-NINE

The morning after his dinner with Romano, Michael was notified by the court that Rosie's arraignment on the indictment was scheduled for the next day.

He was told to report to courtroom #42 on the fourth floor of the Supreme Court building. 'Part 42', as it's referred to by the court personnel, was a place that Michael was thoroughly familiar with. It was Judge Frances Mercurio's regular courtroom where Michael had tried cases for well over a decade.

What was totally unfamiliar to him was the person who took the bench when Rosie's case was called. Instead of Judge Mercurio, Supreme Court Judge Regan Towers, took the bench.

Judge Towers, a judge from Orange County in upstate New York, explained that she was assigned to Brooklyn for the summer months to fill in for regular Brooklyn judges on vacation.

She told those assembled in the courtroom that she gladly accepted the assignment because she had never been to New York City, "Even though I'm 69 years old and have lived in New York State for all of them. When my husband was alive we talked a lot about visiting to see a Broadway show, but it never happened. Now, being offered an assignment to a hip and happening place like Brooklyn, that was something I couldn't turn down."

During the years that Michael worked as a prosecutor in Brooklyn, replacement judges presiding over cases during the summer months was a common occurrence. Therefore, he had no reason to be concerned...until he did!

It didn't take long for him to find out that who he, at first blush, expected to be a pleasant, polite, experienced, and fair judge, was anything but.

When Rosie's case was called she was represented by Julia Nicholas, the same legal aid attorney who handled her first arraignment in the lower criminal court.

The court session began with the clerk asking Nicholas if the defendant waived the reading of the indictment. This was a *pro forma* question, and the usual answer was 'yes.'

However, before Rosie's attorney could give an answer, Judge Towers interrupted and said, "In my courtroom I don't allow any defendant to waive the reading."

Luckily the indictment contained just two charges, so the reading took less than five minutes. In Michael's rackets cases the indictments were considerably longer and a reading of it could take thirty to forty minutes.

"Thank God, this was a short one," Michael thought to himself after the indictment was read."

The clerk then asked Nicholas how the defendant pled to the indictment. As she began to answer, the judge interrupted again.

"The defendant pleads not guilty," Towers answered.

Nicholas was surprised by the interruption. But Michael was troubled.

"A judge this involved, could be a problem," he thought.

He had no idea how right he was.

Judge Towers then addressed Michael.

"What have you got to say on the question of bail?"

He began by telling her that in the lower court the defendant was remanded. However, before he could ask that remand continue and give his reasons for the request, Towers banged her hand on the judge's bench and said, "I'm a Supreme Court judge, a lower court's ruling means nothing to me."

When Michael said that he wasn't finished with his argument, Towers stood, pointed at him and said, "If you address me disrespectfully one more time, you'll be spending the night in the Brooklyn House of Detention with a contempt citation. Do I make myself clear?"

"Yes," Michael answered. He then simply asked that Rosie be held on remand.

Towers turned to Julia Nicholas and asked, "What's the defendant's position on bail?"

Sensing an opening that favored her client, Nicholas took full advantage and asked that the defendant be released on her own recognizance.

"Your honor, as you know bail is designed to ensure that a defendant return to court to answer the charges against her. Ms. Woodhouse is a lifelong Brooklynite with deep roots in her community. She obviously doesn't have the means to run, evidenced by her inability to hire private counsel. And she has no place to run to. She has pled not guilty and is adamant about proving her innocence."

Being released without bail was unheard of in a case where the defendant was charged with murder. And although he had every reason to believe the judge would deny the defense request, Michael objected for the record.

However, before he could make an argument to support the objection, Towers overruled it, and released Rosie.

The judge set a schedule for legal motions to be argued in three weeks, with the trial to begin one week later.

Michael was not happy with the compressed schedule but he didn't dare say a word. Sitting in a jail cell was not how he wanted to spend his night.

When court was adjourned Michael could only shake his head in disbelief at what had occurred. He hung back before leaving the courtroom not wanting to run into Rosie, and the members of the '25Killers' who were there to support her.

It was abundantly clear to him that the 'Judge Towers experience' he was about to embark on was going to be a rough ride.

Indeed, as it would turn out the ride was considerably bumpier than Michael envisioned. Judge Towers would become his worst nightmare.

Back in his office Michael set up a meeting with Kathy, Dina, Tim, and Teo Galetta, for that afternoon. After what he witnessed in the courtroom, it was imperative that he tell them about Judge Towers and what he was up against, and to impress upon them to turn up the heat on the search for the homeless man.

Over the next three weeks Michael prepared motion papers, alerting the court and the defense that he was prepared to offer Rosie's statement to Kathy in evidence as part of the prosecution's case. And she would be in court on the day motions were to be argued to testify at a 'Huntley' hearing, where she laid out for the court the circumstances under which the statement was made.

He prepared a folder of all the investigative reports from the NYPD, the FDNY, and the fire marshals. It also contained the medical examiner's autopsy file, and a copy of the grand jury witnesses' testimony.

Michael had Tim Clark hand deliver the folder to Julia Nicholas, and to the court before the date he was required to. He didn't want to give Judge Towers a reason to disallow any of his evidence.

As the date to argue the motions approached, the identity of the homeless man was still a mystery. If Michael didn't have him by then, he knew that Towers would not allow him to testify even if Michael located him before the prosecution rested its case at trial.

The investigators re-doubled their efforts but it was to no avail.

When Michael walked into Judge Towers' courtroom to argue the motions, and for the Huntley hearing, he had no clue as to the whereabouts of his missing potential witness.

The court session was largely uneventful until the non-ruling that Towers made.

After Kathy testified to the circumstances surrounding Rosie's statement to her, the judge didn't rule immediately on the admissibility of the statement at trial. She reserved decision.

She told the attorneys that she would decide whether or not to allow the trial jury to hear the statement, when and if, the prosecution wishes to introduce it in evidence.

"Furthermore," she said, "Mr. Gioca, I order you to make no reference to the statement either in jury selection or during your opening statement."

Julia Nicholas was thrilled with the judge's decision. Michael was livid.

Respectfully, he asked the judge for additional time to argue, or, in the alternative, time to prepare a legal brief in which he would show that the judge's ruling was against legal precedent.

Towers denied both requests.

But it was her comment that Michael should have done a better job arguing his point, that caused him to lose his cool, and give the defense attorney an idea that altered the course of the trial when the judge ultimately agreed to implement it.

Michael couldn't contain himself. He slammed the prosecution table with a legal reference book as he was packing his briefcase, and said under his breath, "I just want a fair trial here, Judge."

Towers was about to leave the courtroom but stopped because of Michael's behavior. She re-took the bench and immediately held him in contempt of court.

She told him, "I warned you Mr. Gioca. Now you'd better call your office and get someone over here to argue why I shouldn't send you to the Brooklyn House for the night. While we wait you can sit in the cell behind the courtroom."

"Officers," she said to her court personnel, "let Mr. Gioca make his phone call and then take him into custody."

While all this was going on, Julia Nicholas took Rosie into a room, off the courthouse corridor, reserved for attorney-client matters. There she made a convincing argument as to how they should proceed at trial after hearing the judge's ruling on the admissibility of the statement to Kathy Baer.

Rosie agreed and a decision was made.

When she shared the decision, and the reasoning behind it, with her followers, they were pleased.

But none more so than the guy who wore the covid mask to hide the large mole on the left side of his face.

CHAPTER
SIXTY

At 4 p.m. Michael and his old friend Assistant District Attorney Barry Stein, walked out of Judge Towers courtroom. After spending three hours in the cell, Towers agreed to release Gioca after Stein promised that he would apologize to her on the court record, in addition to filing a written letter of apology with the Supreme Court clerk.

The *mea culpa* session took a few moments, after which Towers added, “Mr. Gioca, the next time we meet in this courtroom I want that apology repeated, on the record, in front of whoever is in here with us.”

“Holy shit,” Stein said as he and Michael walked back to the DA’s office. “I can see why you lost it with her. What a fucking bitch. She wasn’t satisfied that you apologized in an empty courtroom, so she’s gonna’ make you do it again to humiliate you in front of a courtroom full of people.... What a fucking bitch!”

Michael had a week to get his case in order, which he did, and to think about what kind of jurors he wanted.

For the entire weekend before jury selection, Michael worked hard on his preparation of questions for the potential jurors. The difficulty was in not knowing if Rosie's incriminating statement would be part of his case.

If the statement was in, Michael would ask questions to test how jurors felt about what he would argue was a confession.

If it was out, he would concentrate his questions on the jurors' feelings about evidence coming primarily from a gangbanger, and two members of law enforcement, which in some areas of Brooklyn was considered the enemy.

After a restless sleep, Michael awoke on Monday morning and went for a run through his neighborhood to think. As he passed St. Michael's, a small Catholic church in Carroll Gardens, he prayed to his patron saint for the strength to get through the day, and to deal with Judge Towers for the duration of the trial. *'She's going to be a handful,'* he thought.

At 9:30 a.m. Michael walked into Part 42 to find defense attorney Nicholas talking to the judge's clerk. Rosie sat in the gallery surrounded by her fellow '25Killers', all wearing gang colors.

'Something's up,' Michael thought to himself. *'We're picking a jury this morning. Why would Nicholas allow her client to wear that gang jacket? And why wouldn't she have told Rosie's people to tone it down and dress appropriately?'*

Then it hit him. *'Nicholas is going to waive a trial by jury. She believes that because the rulings have been favorable to the defense, Towers is sending a signal that Rosie should let her, and her alone, decide the case."*

At 9:45, Judge Towers took the bench and after the clerk called the case into the court record, Nicholas stood and announced, "After careful consideration and consultation with my client, the defendant waives her right to trial by jury and wishes the court alone to decide the matter."

Michael watched the judge as Nicholas was speaking, and when she was done he noticed the judge smile ever so slightly.

"The fix is in," he said to himself.

"But is she pleased or relieved?" It was difficult for Michael to tell.

When the trial was over, Michael would have his answer.

Because he didn't expect to begin the prosecution's case that soon, Michael had no witnesses there to testify. He asked for, and without objection, was granted an adjournment until the next morning.

"Be ready to call your first witness at 10:00 a.m.," Towers said.

He quickly packed his briefcase and made his way out of the courtroom passing through a mob of smiling gangbangers.

Back in his office he met with Tim and Dina.

After telling them what happened in court, he gave them a list of things he needed done right away.

They were to notify the guards with Delgado to bring him to the office immediately for a final prep.

Michael also told them to notify Gabriel Angelos that he was needed for trial prep, and to get to the DA's office as soon as he could.

And last, he asked them to retrieve the fire extinguisher found next to the seminarian's body from the police property clerk and secure it in the DA's office safe until he needed it in court.

Michael called the medical examiner's office himself. He notified the ME who performed the autopsy on the seminarian to be in his office at 8:00 a.m. the next morning. The ME would be Michael's second witness.

His first witness was to be Fr. William Dempsey, the pastor of Our Lady of the Rosary. He had identified Rattigan's body at the ME's office.

Michael called to notify him. Fr. Dempsey was fully prepped to testify by Michael weeks earlier, so the call didn't come as a surprise.

"Father, the trial's starting tomorrow morning and you'll be my first witness. Please be in my office at 9:00 a.m."

"I'll see you in the morning Michael," the pastor said, "and tonight I'll be sure to pray for you."

Michael's final call was to Kathy.

"The defendant waived a jury," he told her. "Judge Towers will be making the final decision."

Kathy could hear the concern and disappointment in Michael's voice. She knew all about the contempt citation and his three hour jail stay, and tried her best to remain upbeat after hearing the news.

"Mike, you have a very good case, and you're the best," she said. "The judge will see that and go your way."

"How can I help?" she asked.

Michael asked her to notify the firefighter who testified in the grand jury about seeing the fire extinguisher, to be on alert, "I might need him to testify as soon as tomorrow afternoon."

He also asked if she could come to his office that evening around 5:00 p.m. to do a final prep of her testimony.

"If Towers allows Rosie's statement in evidence, there's an outside chance we'll get to you tomorrow afternoon. I want to do a final prep before you testify. And after we're done, dinner at *Queen* is on me."

"I'll see you at 5," Kathy said. Before she hung up she added, "Don't let the bastards get you down.... And Michael, I love you."

Michael's day of witness prep went smoothly. He savored his first sip of the *Nero d' Avola* at *Queen*, and thanked Kathy for her help and, "More importantly, for putting up with my chaotic life."

Kathy nodded, toasted Michael, and wished him good luck tomorrow.

After dinner, Michael offered to drive Kathy home, but she declined. "Dinner was wonderful, and you needed the respite. Now you need to go home and get a good night's sleep. And besides, when you went to the men's room before we left, I ordered an *UBER*, and here it is."

Kathy kissed Michael and got into the car. Before the car drove away she lowered her window and said "I love you, and your chaotic life. Never forget that."

'The perfect ending to a really good day,' Michael thought, as he walked to his car. *'Let's hope that after tomorrow it'll be two in a row.'*

Much to his disappointment, it wasn't even close.

CHAPTER
SIXTY-ONE

By 5:00 p.m. the next day, the trial of *The People of the State of New York v. Rosemary Woodhouse,* was over. And for Michael and the prosecution, it couldn't have gone worse.

From his opening statement, through to his summation, Judge Towers did everything she could to ensure that Rosie would never see the inside of a prison cell.

The judge paid little attention to Michael's opening, which she told him to limit to three minutes. When it was the defendant's turn, she told Nicholas, "Counsel, I don't need to hear an opening statement from the defense."

As for the prosecution's case, she was indifferent, uninterested, and downright stoic with every witness, except for Fr. Dempsey. With him she was animated, disrespectful, and treated him with absolute contempt.

Her behavior towards the priest shocked Gioca.

Michael's last witness was to be Kathy.

However, when he announced that to the judge, Towers told him, "I've decided to suppress the defendant's statement to the fire marshal. The defendant was in handcuffs when she made it, and should have been advised of her Miranda rights, which she was not. I do not accept as truthful the fire marshal's testimony that the statement was spontaneous and not the product of questioning by her. Therefore I find that it was illegally obtained and cannot be used as evidence in the prosecution's case."

With no choice but to abide by the court's decision, Michael rested his case.

The defense didn't call a single witness.

After Michael's summation, which the judge interrupted numerous times by sustaining her own objections, Nicholas announced that the defense would rest on the record and waived presenting a closing statement.

Within a millisecond of Nicholas' announcement, Judge Towers found the defendant not guilty.

She stood and told Rosie that she was free to go.

Bedlam broke out in the courtroom, which was filled with gangbangers, all dressed in their gang colors. They cheered for Rosie, and then began to chant the judge's name.

Towers never left the bench. She watched the bedlam with an odd look on her face that Michael noticed immediately. He later told Romano, "It was like she was asking herself 'what have I done?"

Kathy, who had stayed for Michael's summation and was in the courtroom for the verdict and the bedlam that followed, walked with him back to his office and tried to cheer him up.

"It wasn't anything you did or didn't do," she said. "Clearly someone got to the judge."

She speculated that members of Rosie's gang may have threatened Towers unless she acquitted her.

"Remember Michael, Towers is 69 years old and comes from a part of the state where gangs and violence are very rare. If someone told her, for instance, that they'd burn down her home, or harm her family, if she didn't do what they wanted, and warned her against reporting the threat, it's perfectly understandable why she would give in to them. Losing her home or feeling responsible for someone in her family being hurt, or worse, is something that would be very difficult to recover from."

"When they burnt me out of the apartment I loved, I felt that my right to live a happy life had been taken from me. Fortunately I recovered quickly, but I had you, and I'm not 69."

Michael appreciated Kathy's words of support and encouragement, '*It's why I love her,*' he thought. But what she said about the fire in her apartment, and how it made her feel, struck a chord and rekindled in his mind an idea from the past.

When they arrived at his office Michael thanked her for the pep talk but turned her down when she invited him to dinner.

"Babe, I need to be alone tonight. I have some thinking to do. This case may not be over just yet."

Kathy had no idea what he meant. However, she learned from past experience with Michael that it's not over 'til it's over.

After Kathy left, Michael made a phone call to a former colleague, Jason Linares, who worked in the DA's appeals bureau before he left the office to enter private practice.

Several years before, Michael and Jason tried a high profile murder case. It was a particularly brutal and heinous crime, the murder of a seven year old boy, and the trial was covered in the news.

That was also an election year for the district attorney, and the pressure on Michael to convict was at a fever pitch.

The evidence was strong, the witnesses credible and reliable, but the jury did not convict. The 'not guilty' verdict sent shock waves through the city.

Then, like now, Michael refused to give up.

He remembered a lecture from a criminal law class he took. It gave him an idea. He spent days in the DA's law library doing research before calling his professor, the lecturer, to discuss his idea with him.

With the imprimatur from his teacher, Michael went to DA Price to propose a path to re-try the murderer.

The principle of double jeopardy prevented the defendant from being tried in state court on the same murder charge. However, he could be tried on a completely different charge using the same set of facts, in federal court.

Under federal law, murdering an individual is a violation of the federal civil rights laws because it deprives the victim of a civil right: the right to life.

Federal civil rights laws are not the same as state murder statutes. Therefore, a defendant acquitted of state murder charges, can be charged, tried, and convicted of a civil rights law violation and not claim a double jeopardy violation.

DA Price agreed and arranged to have Michael and Jason named as Special Assistant United States Attorneys which allowed them to prosecute the defendant in federal court.

The defendant was convicted of a civil rights violation and sentenced to federal prison.

However, while waiting in the federal Metropolitan Detention Center (MDC) in Brooklyn for the federal appellate court to decide his appeal, which was based on the principle of double jeopardy, the murderer was shivved in the shower. He died that night. Two days later his appeal was denied.

Because of his experience and the success he had with that case, Michael thought, '*It worked before, why not now?*'

His conversation with Linares lasted thirty minutes.

When he hung up, Michael said out loud in his empty office, "*Enjoy the win while you can, you son of a bitch. I'm comin' to get her.*"

The EVIL ONE wasn't there, but Michael was sure *HE* heard it.

That evening, at Romano's invitation, Gioca met him at *Emilio's*.

"Tough break Mike," Romano said. "I know how much work you put into that case, but with a judge who was clearly compromised... even you can't overcome that."

"Thanks Sal, your support is always welcome. And, you read my mind. I was going to call you. I have an idea, but I'm going to need

Caldwell's help to pull it off. With your help, I don't see how John can turn me down."

Romano didn't know what Michael was about to discuss with him, but he saw that his friend was animated and excited despite the bitter defeat he suffered earlier that day.

"I'm listening," he said.

For the next hour, in between courses, Michael explained what he wanted to do.

"I want to indict and try Rosie for federal civil rights violations," he said.

"Depriving the seminarian of his right to life by killing him, and depriving someone, in this case the entire congregation of Our Lady of the Rosary, of the right to freely practice their religion by burning down a church, are federal crimes. Therefore, the principle of double jeopardy is not a bar to the prosecution."

Romano understood. "But why do you need Caldwell and me?" he asked.

"Sal, to secure an indictment for the civil rights crimes, I need to be able to present the evidence to a federal grand jury. I can't do that as a state assistant district attorney. I'll need Caldwell to have me appointed as a Special Assistant United States Attorney, which will make me a federal prosecutor. That will allow me to bring this case into a federal grand jury."

"I'm confident the grand jury will indict, and I'll try Rosie in federal court. The penalty is ten years in federal prison for each violation. It's not the twenty five to life she would have gotten if convicted in state court, but twenty years is a long time for a woman of her age to spend in a cage."

"One last point, convicting Rosie in federal court, means *HE* loses again."

CHAPTER SIXTY-TWO

One week later, Michael was in Washington D.C., sitting in the US Attorney General's conference room with Caldwell and Romano. He was there to make his case to the AG for permission to indict Rosie Woodhouse for federal civil rights violations.

After listening to Michael's pitch, the AG had very few questions. Satisfied that Michael's idea was the right thing to do, he called his first deputy into the conference room and had Michael sworn in as a Special Assistant United States Attorney.

"Good luck. Get that bitch," the AG said while shaking Michael's hand.

Three weeks after the meeting, federal agents working for Caldwell's secret group, arrested Rosie as she sat on her Harley-Davidson outside the '25Killers' clubhouse preaching to her gangbangers.

Rosie was arraigned on the federal indictment and held with no bail by Justice Louis Francis of the US District Court for the Eastern District of New York. She was remanded to MDC to await trial.

When Michael got back to his office after the arraignment, he found a note from Dina Mitchell on his desk. It read, 'Judge Regan Towers called and wants to speak to you.'

It was late summer and Towers had not yet completed her assignment. Her temporary chambers were on the 10th floor in the Brooklyn Supreme Court building, which is where Michael called, but didn't reach her.

'She might be on the bench', he thought, and left her a voicemail message, in which he identified himself and told her that he was returning her call. He left his cell and office phone numbers and said he would be around all day. "If it's more convenient, I'll also be home tonight where you can reach me at any time," he added.

Michael never heard from the judge. At midnight, before he got into bed he checked his office voicemail just to be certain that he didn't miss a message from Towers. There was none.

At 5:00 a.m. Michael was in a deep sleep when his cell phone rang.

"Mike, sorry to wake you," Teo Galetta said.

"Teo what's up? Has something happened to my witnesses?"

"No Mike. I'm calling to tell you that Judge Towers was murdered."

"Her body was found on the steps of Our Lady of the Rosary. It's not a pretty sight. Her throat was slashed, and her tongue was cut out and pinned to the front of her blouse. Someone was sending a message."

Michael knew exactly who that 'someone' was, but he couldn't tell that to the captain.

"Teo, she called my office today asking to speak to me. I was at the arraignment in federal court and missed her call. When I called her back all I got was her voicemail. It seems that whoever killed her didn't want her speaking to me."

Although Michael knew that an arrest was unlikely, he told Galetta, "If you guys make a collar, it'll be my case. So call me if you need anything."

'I was right,' Michael said to himself when he hung up with Galetta. *'Towers WAS reached and likely threatened by the EVIL ONE. That's why she looked so troubled when she acquitted Rosie. She signed her*

death warrant when she called me, especially on the day Rosie was arraigned in federal court. The judge had something to tell me and HE couldn't let that happen.'

Cases move to trial quickly in federal court. And with the Attorney General and Caldwell interested in Rosie's case, it moved even faster.

Michael was delivering his opening statement at her trial a month after the arraignment.

To represent her, Rosie stayed with Julia Nicholas who had left the Legal Aid Society and opened her own law practice after her big win in the murder trial.

However, Justice Francis was not Judge Towers, so Nicholas did not waive a jury this time around.

Three days after the opening statements, the jury in the case of *The United States of America v. Rosemary Woodhouse,* returned a verdict of guilty on all counts.

When Michael spoke to the jurors after the verdict, they told him that Rosie's statement to Kathy was the clincher for them.

The NYPD never stopped looking for the homeless man. But as it turned out he wasn't needed. In the state trial, his testimony wouldn't have changed the outcome. And in federal court, not having him was of no consequence

With the federal trial over, Michael worked with Teo Galetta's detectives on their investigation into Judge Towers' murder. Although in his gut he knew who was responsible, he threw himself into the inquiry full time to keep up appearances and ensure that his cover remained intact.

As part of the investigation Michael drove to Orange County, NY and spoke to the judge's law secretary, Rosann Clark. While Towers was in Brooklyn, Clark remained in Orange County and worked from the judge's chambers in the county courthouse, located in Goshen, NY.

After his meeting with her, Michael was *certain* the EVIL ONE killed her boss.

Clark was visibly upset when she shook hands with Gioca and ushered him into Judge Towers' office to talk. After telling him how she met the judge, and how long they worked together, she could no longer hold back the tears.

Michael didn't immediately try to comfort her, because he felt that it was important for Clark to grieve.

After several minutes she calmed herself, and told Michael that shortly after the murder, a letter, addressed to Clark, arrived by courier.

"It was from Judge Towers," Clark said. "The courier told me that the letter was left with his service by the judge with instructions to deliver it to me if she died. He said that the judge's murder in Brooklyn was front page news and as a result his service was following her instructions."

"I read the letter. It's clear from what she wrote that the judge wanted you to have this," Clark said, and handed him the letter.

Michael read what Judge Towers wrote:

Dear Rosann,

I'm sorry to burden you with this, but I know you'll understand and do what I ask.

Shortly after I arrived in Brooklyn and was assigned the Rosemary Woodhouse murder case, I was approached one evening, by a man wearing a gang jacket and a covid mask, as I walked through the Brooklyn Museum. He addressed me by name, which surprised me. When I asked who he was, he said that it wasn't important.'

I would never be able to identify him because his full face wasn't visible. However, I couldn't miss his bloodshot eyes, and the ugly mole on his left cheek. He scared the hell out of me.

I asked him what he wanted, and he told me that I needed to make sure that the lawyer for the defendant in the Woodhouse case got the message that she should waive a trial by jury. And when she did, he said, "You need to find her client not guilty."

When I told him I would do no such thing, he came very close to me and threatened to kill my mother and my daughter if I didn't follow his instructions or went to the police.

To ensure that I knew he wasn't bluffing, he told me the name of the nursing home in Orange County where his mother is living, and the name of the facility for the disabled in Boston, where my daughter Laura, is a resident. And to make matters worse, he showed me photos of both of them.

I was frightened beyond belief, and never felt so alone. He left me no choice, I had to acquit in order to save my family.

After the verdict, I witnessed an outrageous celebration in my courtroom among the gangbangers and other followers of the defendant. Seeing it made me ill, because there was no doubt in my mind that the defendant murdered the young seminarian and burned his church down around him.

I'm ashamed of what I did, especially the way I treated Fr. Dempsey. But as with the 'not guilty' finding, I was just following orders. I want the people who know me, and who have supported me, to know that.

Before I sat down to write this letter, I reached out to Michael Gioca, the prosecutor. When he returns my call I will confess everything.

If I have to pay a price for what I did, so be it.

Because of the threat, I've taken steps to make sure that my mom and daughter are secure. I don't want my family to become victims because of my weakness.

Rosann, if you're reading this then somehow the man who threatened me found out that I called the prosecutor and killed me.

Make sure this letter gets to Mr. Gioca.

It was wonderful working with you.

Please pray for me and my family,

Regan Towers

Michael hated to lie or mislead Clark, but after reading the letter, and seeing the emotional state she was in, he couldn't leave without assuring her that he and the NYPD would continue to work to solve the judge's murder, even though that would never happen.

"I'm very sorry for your loss. I'll keep you informed of our progress, and if anything else develops up here that you think I should know about, please call me any time, day or night." He handed her his business card on which he wrote his personal cell phone number.

Before he left the office he put his hand out to say goodbye, however Clark ignored it. Instead she engulfed him in a hug and said, "May God bless you. I'll be praying for you."

On his drive back to Brooklyn, Michael was consumed by anger and frustration. Sure he convicted Rosie, but like others in the cases he fought and won against the EVIL ONE, Judge Towers paid the ultimate price.

CHAPTER SIXTY-THREE

Around midnight, two weeks after his trip to Orange County, Michael was sitting in the detective squad room of the 70th precinct interviewing Manny Colon, the homeless man the police were looking for since the death of the seminarian.

Earlier, Michael was dozing in front of the TV, when his cell phone rang.

Thinking it was Kathy, who promised to call after she finished with the paperwork in an investigation she was working on, he answered with a very risqué comment.

Michael was surprised and embarrassed when Teo Galetta said, "Michael, I'm flattered. I had no idea you felt that way about me," before bursting into laughter.

Gioca, now wide awake and embarrassed, couldn't help but laugh along with Galetta.

"Teo, I was expecting someone else to call, obviously. I'm sorry."

"No need to apologize Mike. I'll just have to remember this for my farewell speech at your retirement party. That is, if you ever retire!!"

After they both laughed again, Teo asked if he was sitting down.

When Michael told him that he was, Galetta said, “We have Manny Colon sitting in the squad room.”

“Teo, I know it’s late and I was half asleep, but I don’t know a Manny Colon. Who the fuck is that?”

“It’s the homeless man we’ve been looking for since the seminarian was murdered!”

“Holy shit,” Michael said. “He’s a little late. But did he confirm what Delgado told us he saw?”

“Yes he does, and more. He saw Judge Towers get murdered and gave us a description of the killer.”

“I’ll be there in half an hour. Keep him awake.”

When Michael arrived at the 70th precinct Gabriel Angelos met him at the front door.

“Gabe, it’s good to see you. What are you doing here?”

“Mike, I’m the guy who brought in Manny Colon. I had no idea he was the homeless guy we were looking for. I’ve known him for years. He’s a friend of my father. They worked sanitation together until Manny got fired a few years back for using drugs.”

“I was talking to my dad earlier tonight, and he mentioned running into Manny who he said was homeless. Then he tells me that Manny told him that he was laying low because he witnessed two murders in my precinct. He said one was a while back where a young priest was shot inside a church, and the other was more recent, a lady had her throat cut on the steps of the same church.”

“Gabe, how did you find him?”

“My father told me where Manny said he was staying. It’s a shelter in Bed-Stuy, miles from here. I went there around 8 o’clock and there he was just sitting in the shelter dining hall. I approached him and told him who I was. Mike, he remembered me from when I was a kid. We talked a little more and he finally agreed to come with me to the station house. He’s upstairs in the squad room.”

Although Colon was no longer needed in the seminarian’s murder case, the police were interested in hearing what he saw the night Judge Towers was murdered. Their hope was that he would give them what they needed to catch the killer.

Michael knew there would never be an arrest in that murder, but he couldn't tell that to the police. So while he pretended to be serious about interviewing Colon to help them apprehend the murderer, he had an ulterior motive. He wanted this eyewitness to confirm what he already knew about Towers' murder.

"Mr. Colon, I'm assistant district attorney Michael Gioca. Gabe Angelos told me you have some information about two murders that the police and me are interested in. Gabe also told me that because you know him and his dad that you're willing to share that information with us. Is that right?"

Colon answered that he was, but before he said anything he told Gioca that he was hungry and asked for something to eat and drink. Michael took a break while they waited for the food he ordered to be delivered.

After eating four slices of pizza and downing two cold Cokes, Manny Colon was ready to talk.

Michael began by asking Colon what he saw the day the seminarian, or 'priest' as Colon referred to him, was shot.

"It was a hot day, and I went inside the church to cool off and to try and get away from the rioting and shit that was happening. I never made it past the vestibule when I seen this priest come out of nowhere with a fire extinguisher in his hand. Them gangbangers in the church was knocking over candles and fires started all around. The priest tried to put out the fire when I heard one of the gangbangers, a guy, tell the lady gangbanger to shoot him. Then she shot the priest! I was so scared I could hardly move when this young Hispanic guy came to help me. I told him what I just seen and he got me out of the church."

"I took off and stayed away from that area until a few nights ago. I heard that the lady gangbanger I seen shoot the priest was locked up by the feds, so I wasn't afraid to come around here no more."

"It was late," Colon said, "and I was sitting on the church lawn under a tree. They be building the church back after it burned, when I see a big flashy red car, looked like a Cadillac, stop in front of the church."

"I watched as a guy got out of the front seat of the car, go to the door of the back seat, open it, and pull out a nicely dressed woman. She fought him a bit, but she was old like me and wasn't strong enough to break away."

"Can you describe the lady?" Michael asked

"Yeah, she was white, about my age, late 60's, and as I said she had on nice clothes."

Michael asked if he had ever seen the lady before. Colon answered that he had not.

"What about the guy who pulled her out of the car. Can you describe him?"

When Colon dropped his head and began to shake his right leg, Michael recognized that he was frightened, and said, "Manny I know you're afraid, but what you say here will stay here. No one will know what you tell us. And if it'll make you feel better, I'll make sure that you don't have to go back to the shelter and that you never have to come back to Midwood. We'll take you wherever you want to go."

Hearing that, Colon looked up and asked, "Will you get me to Atlanta? I have a sister and some family down there. I can live with her if she'll have me."

Michael assured him that would be no problem. "You call your sister when we're done, and I'll speak to her. I'm certain we can work it out."

Colon was ready to continue.

"We were at the point where I asked you to describe the man who pulled the lady out of the car. Can you do that?" Michael asked again.

This time Colon answered with no hesitation. "He's the gang-banger I saw in the church the day of the fire. He told the woman to shoot the priest. He had on a covid mask but I could see part of his face. He had a growth on his left cheek and he had these red like bloodshot eyes," Colon said with a shiver.

Galetta interrupted and asked, "Do you think you'd recognize him if you saw him again?"

"Yes. But I wouldn't be happy about it. Excuse my language, he scared the ever-lovin' shit outta' me."

Colon continued. "After he pulled the lady outta' the car he dragged her to the church steps and it looked like he cut her throat. It was dark but I seen a lot of blood. Then when she fell he leaned over her and I seen him doing something on or near her face. I couldn't see what, until I went over to her after he and that other guy left in the Caddy. I saw he cut her tongue out. It was somehow attached to her shirt. I grabbed my stuff and got outta' there. And I ain't told anyone about it until I seen Angelos' father."

Before Michael could ask another question, Colon volunteered, "I got the knife."

"What knife?" Michael asked.

"After I seen the lady all cut up, I was walkin' away and I seen the knife he musta' used, 'cause it was covered in blood, layin' on the grass next to the church steps. I picked it up and put it in with my stuff."

"In that stuff?" Michael asked, pointing to the plastic bags which Gabe said Colon was carrying when he brought him in.

"Yeah," Colon answered. He got up, reached into one of the bags and pulled out a large knife that still had remnants of what appeared to be blood on the blade.

Galetta called one of his detectives into the room and had him bag the knife as evidence.

"Manny, you've been very helpful. Before I make that call to your sister, is there anything else you want to tell me about the lady's murder."

Much to Michael's surprise, Colon said there was.

"The guy driving the Caddy," Colon said.

"What about him? Do you know him? Have you seen him before?" a curious and excited Michael asked.

"I know it can't be, since he's in jail, but the guy driving looked a lot like the reverend who used to have the soup kitchen at the *Nostrand Evangelical Church of Hope.*"

Both Michael and Galetta nearly fell out of their seats.

"How do you know that reverend?" Teo asked.

"I be goin' to that soup kitchen four or five times a week. Most times he wasn't there, he had these nuns workin' and servin' the food. But a few times he showed up, like Thanksgiving or Christmas wearin' an apron and dished out the turkey and stuff. When he did, there was always cameras around takin' his picture."

"After he went to jail, did you ever see him again around Midwood?" Michael asked.

"Nah, how could I? He's locked up."

When Michael was done with him, Manny called his sister. Michael spoke to her and after an hour of cajoling and negotiating, she agreed to let Manny stay with her until he found a place of his own.

Michael woke Romano, briefed him quickly on what Colon told him, and had him approve hotel accommodations for Manny for the night. The monsignor told Michael that in the morning he'd contact Caldwell and arrange for an airline ticket to Atlanta for Manny. The monsignor said he'd make sure to have agents meet Colon when he got off the plane and take him to his sister's home while more permanent accommodations were arranged.

Michael thanked the monsignor and apologized for the late call.

"No worries, because you're doing all the driving later this morning," Romano said.

A funeral mass for Judge Towers was scheduled for 11 a.m. at the Church of St. John the Evangelist in Goshen, NY. Rosann Clark invited Michael to attend. He thanked her and asked if a friend could accompany him.

Monsignor Romano was happy Michael asked him to attend the service.

During the drive to Orange County, Gioca talked in great detail about his interview of Manny Colon, including the sighting of Vernon LePage, who drove the EVIL ONE away from the scene of the judge's murder.

"LePage back in Midwood! Wow! As we used to say in the old neighborhood, the guy has balls," Romano remarked.

"But you know Mike, maybe them fleeing together in that car is an indication that the mayhem is over, and they've left Brooklyn. LePage, so he isn't captured, and the EVIL ONE because *HE's* satisfied with the turmoil *HE* created in the last year or so. Two dead cops, framing me for a serious assault on a young girl and inciting days of mass rioting, orchestrating the escape of a mass murderer posing as a Christian minister, killing a young man studying to be a priest, burning down a church, and finally murdering a judge."

Michael said, "Sal, I hear ya'. And I hope you're right."

"I certainly would welcome the EVIL ONE moving on. But LePage, I'm hoping that his arrogance leads him to believe that after laying low for a while, he can con his way back in, and resume the life he lost when I convicted him. I'd love to try him again for the escape charge, convict his ass, and send a message to the EVIL ONE that *HE* can't fuck with us, or beat us."

The mass was a beautiful tribute to Judge Towers. The homily delivered by the church pastor was a testament to the judge's strong faith, her love of family, and to the many works of charity she performed for the people of Goshen and Orange County.

At the conclusion of the service, the choir director asked those in attendance to join him in singing a closing hymn. He directed those who were unfamiliar with the words, to a particular page in the hymnal in their pew.

Romano didn't need the hymnal, but Michael did.

When he opened the book to the appropriate page, he noticed a folded piece of paper in the binding. Absent-mindedly he took the paper and put it into his jacket pocket before singing the closing hymn.

After the service, Michael stopped to chat with Rosann Clark, and to introduce Romano before heading to his car.

When he reached into his jacket pocket to get his keys, he found the folded piece of paper from the hymnal. Curious as to what it was, he turned it over before unfolding it, and saw his name.

When he opened it, he read what was written-

Why will man never understand
the Creator made me first
before Adam, of spit and dirt-
my rightful place, to reign on earth.
From Eden to the present day,
I am in all your work and play-
sin allows me to ALWAYS win.
You will ever pay, even if you pray.

"Michael, what is it?" Romano asked. He handed the paper to him and said, "Monsignor, our work isn't done."

ACKNOWLEDGMENTS

This is book 3 of a project that has been in the making for more than 30 years. The crimes described in the book, with a few variations, actually occurred in Brooklyn during my time as an assistant district attorney. They were investigated and prosecuted by me, along with the great detectives of the New York City Police Department, the dedicated fire marshals of the New York City Fire Department, and the extremely talented detective investigators and assistant district attorneys of the Brooklyn District Attorney's Office, led by DA Charles "Joe" Hynes.

I call the book a *"True Crime Fantasy,"* because the names of the characters, and some of the circumstances described in the investigation and trial of the cases, are fiction and were written to fit the overarching theme –the battle between Michael Gioca and Satan. Good versus evil.

I could not have written any of the *Fallen Angel* series without the support, constant encouragement, and artistic assistance of my brilliant, and talented wife, Lenor Romano, an accomplished designer and artist in her own right. Her contributions were invaluable.

Lenor, I will always love you.

I also have to acknowledge and thank my friend and editor Dr. Sheldon Shuch, Ph.D., who teaches teachers how to teach, readers how to read, and loves a good story well told. He watched over my narrative and grammar with the keen eye of a literature professor. Shelly thank you for your support, guidance, honesty and most of all, your friendship.

I want to express my gratitude to Dennis Hawkins, my good friend, who preceded me as Chief of the Rackets Division in the Brooklyn DA's Office, for his contribution to this book. An accomplished poet, his verse, the ominous message from Satan to Michael left in the hymnal at Judge Towers' funeral mass, provided the perfect conclusion to this story and to the book.

Lastly, I want to thank Stephanie Larkin, *la regina* of Red Penguin Books, who listened to my idea and had the interest, curiosity, and faith to give me the opportunity to write this trilogy. Without the hard work and dedication of her and her team, the story of *Fallen Angel* would not have been told.

Michael Vecchione

ABOUT THE AUTHOR

Michael Vecchione is the former First Deputy District Attorney in the Brooklyn District Attorney's Office. In over 30 years as a prosecutor, he served the people of the borough where he was born and raised, as Chief of the Homicide Bureau, Chief of Trials, and Chief of the Rackets Division. He retired in 2013, topping off a 40 year legal career. In 2007 he was awarded the Thomas E. Dewey Medal as prosecutor of the year.

He has co-authored four non-fiction true crime books, and three true crime short stories. The *Fallen Angel* trilogy is his first solo project and the books are works of fiction based on true events from his career as a prosecutor.

He is a frequent contributor to true crime productions and podcasts. He has served as an adjunct professor at St. John's University School of Professional Studies, and as an adjunct professor of law at St. John's University School of Law, Brooklyn Law School, and The Maurice A. Deane School of Law at Hofstra University.

He lives in Long Island City, New York, with his wife Lenor Romano.

Also by Michael Vecchione

Fallen Angel - A True Crime Fantasy

Fallen Angel - Book II

The War for the Soul of Brooklyn

Homicide Is My Business: Luigi the Zip—A Hitman's Quest for Honor

With Jerry Schmetterer

Crooked Brooklyn: Taking Down Corrupt Judges, Dirty Politicians, Killers, and Body Snatchers

With Jerry Schmetterer

Behind the Murder Curtain: Special Agent Bruce Sackman Hunts Doctors and Nurses Who Kill Our Veterans

With Bruce Sackman and Jerry Schmetterer

Friends of the Family: The Inside Story of the Mafia Cops Case

With Tommy Dades

True crime short stories:

"The Sculptress"

"Hand of the Killer- How a bloody palmprint and a baby's pacifier nailed a killer"

With Jerry Schmetterer

"Murder on the Bridge- From the files of Mike V."

With Jerry Schmetterer